All's Fair

All's Fair – Standard Edition

Copyright © 2026 by Natalie Marie

All rights reserved.

Paperback ISBN: 979-8-9948396-0-6

No part of this book may be duplicated, redistributed, shared, or made public in any size or quantity or by any electronic or mechanical means, without prior written permission from the author, except for the use of brief quotations in a book review. This includes but is not limited to piracy, resale, or revealing any major spoilers throughout the book before publication day in reviews and/or social media posts.

No generative artificial intelligence (AI) was used in the production of this work. The author expressly prohibits the use of this publication as training data for AI technologies or large language models (LLMs) for generative purposes. The author reserves all rights to license uses of this work for generative AI and the development of LLMs.

This is a work of fiction. Names, characters, places, & incidents are either products of the author's imagination or used fictitiously. Any resemblance to actual persons, living or dead, business establishments, events, or locales is entirely coincidental.

Editing: Jenny Ayers of *Swift Red Pen* | @swiftredpen

Cover Design & Proofreading: Alex of *Novel & Navy* | @novelandnavy

All's Fair

GAMBLE ON LOVE BOOK ONE

NATALIE MARIE

author's note

Thank you for picking up my debut novel *All's Fair*. This story has a heavy focus on the importance of mental health, specifically anxiety and panic attacks. I have mirrored most of this after my own experience with generalized anxiety disorder and history of panic attacks. Since anxiety can look different for everyone, please keep in mind Kane's anxiety is unique to himself. In order to keep in line with the plot, I took some creative liberties with the outcome of Kane's job at the end.

I hope you love Kane and Avery's story, but as always your mental health is the most important thing. If you have any questions regarding the contents of this novel before starting, please don't hesitate to reach out to me.

Trigger warnings include:

- Generalized anxiety disorder & panic attacks
- Mentions of childhood neglect
- Talk of child abuse (off-page)

- Gun violence (on-page)
- Parental abandonment
- Sexual content and explicit language
- Physical violence (on-page)

playlist

the 1 – Taylor Swift
loml – Taylor Swift
imgonnagetyouback – Taylor Swift
Out of My League – Aiden Bissett
Scared to Start – Michael Marcagi
Forget Me – Lewis Capaldi
Ghost – Justin Bieber
So High School – Taylor Swift
I miss you, I'm sorry – Gracie Abrams
Landslide – Fleetwood Mac
when was it over? – Sasha Alex Sloan (ft. Sam Hunt)
right where you left me – Taylor Swift
Tripping Over Air – Aiden Bissett
Caffeine – Max Drazen
Look After You – The Fray
Dancing With Your Ghost – Sasha Alex Sloan
WYD Now – Sadie Jean
Leaving – Zach Bryan
House With No Mirrors – Sasha Alex Sloan
Lie – Sasha Alex Sloan

Let You Down – NF
Exile – Taylor Swift (ft. Bon Iver)
Trauma – NF
Silver Spoon – Erin LeCount
If You Love Her – Forest Blakk
Don't Let Me Go – Cigarettes After Sex
Work Song – Hozier
Worst Way – Riley Green
If I Ever Saw Heaven – Roan Ash
So In Love – Icarus Account
Until I Found You – Stephen Sanchez
Novocaine – The Band CAMINO
Seventeen Going Under – Sam Fender
When Did You Stop Loving Me? – LANY
Prettiest Thing I've Ever Seen – LANY
Robbers – The 1975
Waiting Room – Phoebe Bridgers
Why – LANY
Iris – Goo Goo Dolls
Sound of Rain – LANY

To the forgotten children.
The ones who raised themselves, wondering why they were never enough. The ones who still battle that feeling to this day.
You are enough.

And to Mason, who showed me what true love looks like. Who is my safe space to land, always.

avery

ONE YEAR AGO

the 1 – Taylor Swift

"Kane, stop," I gasp as I jump off the couch, trying to flee. Big arms wrap around me from behind, pulling me back into a wide chest. The feeling of weightlessness hits me as I'm lifted off the ground, my eyes closing as I try to keep the tears of laughter at bay. He continues his invasion on my sides with one hand, holding me in place with the other.

"I'm sorry, I'm sorry. I know you're busy. But you looked too serious, pretty girl. I don't like when those little lines appear," he replies, turning me in his arms. He holds me flush against him, smoothing out the wrinkles between my brows with his thumb. His beautiful smile is stretched across his face while he stares at me with those warm, honey-brown eyes.

"You weren't even listening to the song I was playing, and that's when I know I've lost you. Talk to me," Kane pleads with me, switching our positions so I'm situated on his lap when he lowers us onto the couch. I straddle him, my body humming from the feel of his strong thighs under me.

Sitting on top of Kane is one of my favorite places. Usually, he towers over me, dwarfing me with his six-four frame, but in this position, we are finally eye to eye, allowing me to study his features. His striking brown eyes are trained on me, making me feel as if a meteor could hit, and all he'd care about is what I have to say. The look of complete adoration on his face stuns me almost speechless. Over three years together and it still feels as if we're those two teenagers, lost in each other, blind to the world around us.

Kane has the most beautiful face—I've always thought that. When he transferred into our senior year English class, I was struck dumb the second he turned that smirk on me. His hair was dark chocolate brown, almost black, his skin deeply tanned skin. He had strong Italian features—thick, dark eyebrows, a straight nose that seemed too perfect for his face and pink full lips that only quirked up more the longer I stared at him. He was sin personified, and I didn't stand a chance.

He still takes my breath away today, looking just as sinful as he did then, only with more prominent cheekbones and a jawline that could grace magazines, if only Kane cared enough. His soft stubble seems to grow the second he shaves it smooth. I love the feel of that short hair trailing along my body, sending goosebumps all over my skin in its wake.

I blow out a breath as I run my fingers through his silky, slightly curly hair, trying not to get distracted by his shirtless chest, littered with tattoos—most of which I've watched get inked on him over the years.

"I'm just worried. We graduate in a few months. I'm still waiting to figure out what I want to do next. College felt easy, as if we had so much time. But the real world starts soon, and what if I can't do it? I want to keep working at the animal rescue but what if there's something more out there I could be doing?" I say, refusing to make eye contact with him, twisting my too-thick brown hair—that escaped my bun long ago—in my hands.

He grabs my chin and forces my face up until his lips are a breath away from mine. His fingers are firm under my chin, making me stop fidgeting and place my hands gently on the back of his neck.

Graduating college together has been the dream over these past four years together, as high school sweethearts the odds have always been stacked against us—by parents and peers alike. Now that the future is on our horizon, Kane is months away from a Bachelors in Psychology to work at a local high school and me with my degree in business, hoping to apply all my gained knowledge to further our rescue's reach. On top of all of that, Kane still works part-time at a local bar that can take up most of his nights during the week.

"I don't know what's going to happen in the next few months, but I know with certainty that whatever you do, you will succeed. And I cannot wait to be in the wings watching you shine," he says assuredly, placing a soft kiss on my lips.

Heat sears through my body when he kisses me, and suddenly there's not a single worry in my brain. All I can think about is getting his sweatpants off.

I reach down, but he stops me and pulls back. I look up, finding his eyes dark with unmistakable lust and lips swollen.

"All I want to do is let you continue whatever slow torture you had in mind," he starts, and a smirk lines my face. "But I know how much you need to finish that paper, and I won't be the reason you fail the class this close to graduation." He plants one more gentle kiss against my lips.

I pout and he starts chuckling, running his thick fingers through my hair at my back—the strands finally escaping my bun completely—before smoothing it down my sides to my hips.

"Don't look at me like that, pretty girl. Or we will end up in my bedroom for the night, paper be damned."

I laugh as I pull back and start getting up.

"Okay, well if you're not going to feed me that way, then you better feed my stomach," I say, picking up my discarded textbook and paper that were abandoned when Kane started tickling me. I sit back down beside him as he picks up his Martin guitar and starts strumming, making me giggle and abandon my work once again to watch him. He plays the tune of "Truly Madly Deeply," knowing it will get a reaction out of me. It was the last song we danced to at our senior prom. I remember the world fading away as Kane and I swayed to the music, lost in each other. In that moment, I felt like I never wanted to be found.

I've always loved the sight of him with a guitar, fingers expertly working the strings, his soft but powerful tone. His voice is dark and gravely, hypnotizing me completely. My eyes wander over him with the guitar on his lap, up to his shirtless chest, over to the numerous tattoos scattered on his lean but impressive torso and arms. His biceps are thick from hours spent at the gym with Marcus, and I love how his forearms flex absently as he strums chords, switching to another one of my favorite songs.

I'm mesmerized by how beautiful he is, and watching his fingers strum the all-too-familiar tune sends shivers down my body, reminding me just how dexterous those fingers are.

He looks up at me with that soft look in his eyes he reserves only for me, and I swoon before he even utters the first words of the song. I lose myself in the soft lyrics of "Iris," remembering how this was one of the first songs Kane ever played for me, after he admitted he watched me play it on my phone countless times walking to and from class while pretending I didn't notice him behind me all those years ago. He said he instantly went home and started to memorize the chords so that when he needed to impress me, he had the perfect plan.

I could get lost in the sound of his voice. His deep, smoky tone has the ability to stop crowds, but Kane has never wanted to do anything with it. He always said he was gifted with that talent just for me. What a sap I was at seventeen, thinking it was the most romantic thing someone could ever say to me.

Now, the memory pulls an eye roll and a smile out of me, knowing he had this talent way before he met me. Kane has always loved music, and it was something we bonded over immediately when we met. We would spend hours together in his room, scrolling through songs to compare.

Every morning, I woke up to a good morning text and a song, either one to set the mood for the day or one that made him think of me.

He finishes the song and looks up at me. I can see everything in Kane's eyes—our future filled with marriage, babies and the laughter I know will follow us for years shines back at me, a mirror of what I'm sure he sees in mine.

Kane gets up and leans the guitar against the beige sofa that I convinced him to upgrade to—his old cracking leather couch had seen better days. He stretches as he turns to me, the muscles in his arms flexing and drawing my eyes to them, then down his body to his striking V-lines, like an arrow pointing to what I want most right now.

"Come on, pretty girl. Let me feed you before you jump me," Kane says as he grabs my hand and pulls me up. I wrap my arms around him and just bask in the feel of his warmth. I'm not sure how long we stand like that—moments seem to fly by with him. Since we don't have many nights like this anymore, it makes these moments even more special. No work or school distracting us, no future pressing in on us. Just these stolen moments away from the world in our little bubble I could live in forever.

Eventually, we break apart and head to the kitchen. I drop my textbook and notes on the counter before taking my place on my usual stool. I've claimed this particular one because it has the best view of shirtless Kane as he dances around the kitchen, somehow perfect at everything he does.

He turns to the fridge to grab what he needs for his famous pot pie. I always love watching Kane cook—the methodical way he chops vegetables, the silver knife glinting in the kitchen lights, the familiar rhythm almost enough to lull me to sleep. I'm competent enough to help, but he insists on taking care of everything himself so we can steal extra time talking together while he makes dinner.

While he works, he tells me about some of the drama that happened in his first couple of weeks shadowing a high school's counselor, whom he's taking over for next year. We already have the stress of being so close to graduation, and now Kane's taking on extra stress from the students he works with. He went to the most underfunded school in the county to work, but he knew those kids needed him more. While I love how big his heart is, I still miss him as he takes on extra hours and adds an hour commute to his day.

I'm pulled from my thoughts when I'm pelted with flying carrots, and I glance up to find Kane bent over laughing. He has a shit-eating grin stretched over his face, small lines that only show when he's really happy crinkling around his eyes. He clearly saw how lost in thought I was and wanted to distract me.

"Oh, so this is what we're doing, huh?" I ask as I pick up some carrots from the wooden cutting board, ready to throw them back at him.

"Oh come on, Avery, don't be a child and throw food. That's our dinner," he teases while backing up, throwing his hands up in an obvious surrender. I get down from my perch on the stool and slowly round the counter, hands full of ammo. He looks over at the cutting board, wondering how quickly he can get there and back before I begin my assault.

"Oh no, you don't get to do that. Don't dish it out if you can't take the consequences!" I shout as I start to throw the carrots at Kane. He dodges them dramatically, like they're actual missiles. The carrots ping off the refrigerator and upper white cabinets, scattering across the kitchen. Kane is doubled over, trying to protect his face and stomach from flying carrots as he grabs more and quickly throws them back at me.

We're both laughing so hard we can barely breathe by the time the last few carrots scatter across the kitchen floor. Kane shakes his head at the mess, still grinning as he finally saunters over to me. His hands drift down to my waist, lingering there as he walks me backward before lifting me up and setting me onto the counter.

I automatically wrap my legs around him and settle my arms on his shoulders. For a few seconds we just stare at each other, catching our breath, before Kane says, "I love you, pretty girl. And I can't imagine a time when that smile isn't the single greatest part of my day."

He leans in and presses a soft kiss to my lips. When he goes to pull away, I tighten my arms around him and deepen the kiss, fully lost in the feel of him and how I feel him harden against me. The world seems to melt away, and suddenly this is all that matters between us. His hands are firm around my waist as mine dive into his soft waves. His tongue strokes against mine, starting slowly before building the pace.

The kiss turns heated, all tongue and moans as we collide again and again. His hands are almost bruising my hips, and I feel the heat coil higher in my belly, painful with the need for him. All I want is to be closer.

"Your paper," he murmurs against my mouth, though his hands don't move from my body.

"What paper?" I moan back, pulling him to me as I deepen the kiss.

That's all it takes. Dinner is all but forgotten as Kane quickly shuts off the stove before whisking me away to his room.

We giggle between kisses as we stumble inside. He lays me down gently on his bed, hovering over me and staring at me like the world begins and ends in this moment. The soft comforter lies underneath me, and I feel overheated in all the clothes between us.

"I don't know what God I had to pray to deserve this life with you, but I know no matter what lifetime we find ourselves in, I will always find my way to you," he whispers, looking deep into my eyes. The moment around us stills, words falling away as he worships me as if I'm the one he prays to.

CHAPTER ONE

NOW

loml – Taylor Swift

The thing with first loves is they never truly leave you. They stitch themselves so deep in your very soul, that even when you've both moved on and the world barely remembers, you always will.

The first kiss, the first touch, the first heartbreak... They linger, marking you for life. The tears that were shed stain your soul. The music you consumed together late at night when the rest of the world was quiet becomes a ghost in your ears when those songs play in the grocery store, immediately taking you back in time to when you were young and in love. Those first loves created who you are and change you in ways you may never fully realize.

I met my first love back when I was naïve enough to think love was everything. Back when you could've told me anything would happen, except that I would lose Kane, and I could survive it. When our worlds were so consumed within each other, we barely saw much else. We found each other back when fairytales still felt possible and forever didn't feel like it was an unattainable construct staring back at us. From eighteen to twenty-three, my whole world revolved around one other being.

This isn't the first time the crushing weight of the phantom pain has threatened to drag me back under. The past month has been a blur of it, of getting myself up and moving because there's nothing else to do. The never-ending haze my mind has been stuck in rears with a vengeance.

The edges of my vision get blurry as my brain begs to drift back to the past and the comfort it offers me, wanting to cocoon me in its arms. Half of my heart is walking around, existing outside of my body, and I find myself wondering day after day if I will ever get that part of me back.

A soft hand on my arm pulls me back into focus. I wipe the lone tear that escaped while I was lost in my thoughts. I smile at Morgan, a silent apology for zoning out on her.

The lights of our local bar, The Grunge—named for the '90s grunge ambiance—are vibrant tonight, illuminating the bar top in a soft amber glow. Their locally famous Taco Tuesday has drawn in a bigger crowd lately, after word of their five-dollar margaritas and town-famous nachos got around, the place getting more crowded and boisterous as the night goes on. I've always found comfort in this place.

I stare at the half-empty strawberry margarita in front of me, its sugar rim thoroughly licked off and condensation dripping down the sides of the glass. The superior part of any good margarita is a sugar rim, salt nowhere to be seen with my sweet tooth. My *only* margarita of the night, since I need to be at the shelter first thing tomorrow.

"C'mon Ave, you can't really think pranking him is the

best idea right now," Morgan says, giving me an accusatory look over the rim of her third margarita.

Morgan Belle is my best friend, though she's so completely my opposite in every way. I look at her across from me at our four-person round table. Being complete opposites in looks and personality, you would never have thought we would be here today eight years later. Morgan has long blonde curls and dons a high-end designer wardrobe and perfectly applied makeup. She has an air of *don't fuck with me*, but even with that, you can't help but gravitate toward her. Her bubbly personality makes her shine in any room she's in, striking you dumb when she turns those rays onto you.

She's a stark contrast to me in my signature all-black ensemble—shiny Doc Martens and a miniskirt that's practically my second skin—along with the minimal makeup I decided to grace the world with still clinging to my skin after a full ten hours at the shelter.

"I know that wasn't the best scene, but there has to be an explanation. I mean, Kane and I have never actually had a conversation without you around about more than the shifting weather patterns, but I know Marcus would've told me. That fucker can't keep his mouth shut for more than five minutes," she finishes with a flourish, dipping her chip back in the queso.

The low beat of a song I plays in the background, and no matter how many sips of my drink I take, I can't seem to block out the words I know by heart—but from the low voice of the man who haunts me.

"Regardless of what Marcus tells you, Kane shouldn't be parading his newest conquest in front of me like the last four years meant nothing. It's been weeks! And he looks like that, with *that* and I just..." I stab my fiftieth chip into the almost completely cooled queso, unable to control the restricting feeling in my chest, my breathing shallow. I force myself to keep everything inside, so I don't lose it over a happy hour bowl of queso—and my ex's new blonde bombshell, apparently.

She rolls her eyes at the mention of Marcus, my other best friend who's practically been a brother to me since he moved in next door when I was five.

It's been forty-five minutes since I saw Kane enter the patio, and the feeling of the ever-present emptiness that's been invading my chest lately was replaced with a raging fire. He strode by looking like the devil himself, all black clothes and dangerous tattoos. From the endless silver rings that adorn his fingers to the untamed locks falling over his forehead, he's every woman's bad-boy dream.

My bad boy once upon a time.

I scoff and look over in the direction they went, but they're hidden from view by a pillar.

Thank you, universe, for that.

I turn and take in the bar around me. From the dingy and grunge dive bar appearance on the outside and the late '90s vibes of vintage music posters and colored vinyls lining the walls, down to the speckled floor I've walked across more than I have in my childhood home in the past five years, I've always found comfort in this place.

It's where I've found my stride the past four years, where I sat so many nights at the bar finishing my homework to steal just a few more minutes with Kane while he worked behind the bar. He kept me there with an endless supply of Coke and lemon as I waited for him to close up before we went to one of our places and ended the night together.

We were *that* couple. The couple that couldn't bear to

be apart, once upon a time. We lost each other long before the breakup happened. We would wait for each other after classes, find time to steal dates when others were struggling to even fit in their homework assignments.

I have helped Kane close this bar so many times. Wiping down the black resin counters and swaying to the low pop punk and indie folk playing in the background, only to feel Kane come up behind me and hold me to whatever song was playing, distracting us both from our tasks. We would always take longer to get things done, instead quizzing each other on music and trying to work on our perfectly curated playlist of our top-tier song selections. Each of us would add a new one to the surround system to see how quickly the other could guess it.

I hold the record of one chord progression, *thank you very much.*

My stomach twinges at the memory.

I snap myself back to the present for the second time tonight. The past seems to be haunting me more knowing that this is the closest we have been in weeks, and I blink back the tears that have built in the corners of my eyes.

Morgan stares at me, seeming to wait for an answer to a question I missed. She knows what the breakup has been like. I was held up in my room for the first week crying to my "sad girls cry" playlist, which I made after one particularly lonely night when I found Kane's notebook of lyrics tucked between the bed and the wall, after removing him from the music streaming account we shared. He deserves to suffer with bad music after breaking my heart.

This breakup shredded my soul, but I have been walking around as if I'm just fine. I mean, it was my idea to end it, right? He checked out and left me to make that decision all on my own.

I've kept myself from opening up completely to her about the breakup. Not for a lack of trying on her part. I think there was a moment when Morgan had me in a headlock threatening to delete our best friend's playlist after a particularly nasty crying session. I started to see why Marcus has called her Viper since the ninth grade. He still hasn't shared the actual reason but based on the smirk he wears and the blush that creeps across Morgan's face every time I ask, I figure it's probably best to mind my own business where they're concerned. We've all known each other since high school—the respective years, making us more family than friends.

It's not that I won't talk about it—it's that I *can't*. Because then it's real, and I have to decide what to do without him. As of right now, I've been surviving by dissociating from the present and pretending this isn't happening. My therapist, Susan, would tell me it's an unhealthy coping mechanism and that running from my problems will not, in fact, make them go away, so it's a good thing I've also made the mature decision to ghost her.

The way Morgan looks at me makes me think I've been spaced out for longer than I realize, but I'm too tipsy to care. Instead, I decide to make it my mission to finish our fourth refill of chips singlehandedly. Nothing heals more than a margarita and extra salty chips.

"I mean, I wouldn't hurt Kane, you know that. But I want him to hurt a little bit mentally. More psychological warfare than a physical one," I say, slurping the rest of my watery strawberry margarita. I'm ready to get out of here and back to my romance books where they always find a way back to each other.

Maybe this is what we need to find each other again, or maybe this will help me move on like Kane has. Pranks used to be something silly we'd do between houses, Morgan's and mine versus Kane and Marcus's, to keep the laughs going throughout our college years. Doing little things to annoy the others until we finally got each other back.

Morgan looks at me with a raised eyebrow, her glossy eyes reflecting her tipsiness. She slurps the last remnants of her usual prickly pear margarita. At this point, she just asks for "The Morgan," and the bartenders automatically know what she wants.

Unsure if she heard me the first time, I add, "Look, I'm doing this with or without you, but it would be more fun with help..." I leave my statement open with my eyebrows raised, waiting for her to respond. I'm guessing she's hoping that if she ignores me long enough, I'll change my mind.

"Fine! I thought maybe we matured since our college days," Morgan relents. "But if anyone finds out, I fought you a lot harder on this." She slams her empty glass down, bracelets clinking against the table.

"What first?" she asks with an almost manic glint in her eye. My regret about asking her to help just barely hits the surface before I knock it down and laugh at the ridiculousness of this day.

"I have the perfect idea," I say just as Marcus and Grayson sidle into the bar, laughing at some joke I'm sure only they will get. They make their way over to us, turning heads across the bar, and I roll my eyes with a giggle as I watch looks from women across the bar linger on them.

"Avery," Marcus says as he approaches our table, his effortless brown curls more wild than usual, a slight dent in them from his headphones. His pretty-boy looks are on full display tonight—his flannel open wider than most men would allow, and the deep tan of his skin visible. "And Viper," he adds, his gaze trained on Morgan.

"Bite me," she replies, giving him a look of disgust. She picks up her phone, pretending to be interested in anything but the smirk he gives her, even though I spot the redness creeping up her neck. A snort leaves my lips, earning me a death glare from her.

"I think that's supposed to be my line," Marcus retorts, winking at her. Grayson sends a dazzling smile my way and gives Morgan a quick hug before taking his seat. He sits there silently, ignoring the antics, his dirty blonde hair pushed back behind a ball cap and his team jersey still on, suggesting he came from batting practice. His first year on the B team is finally underway now that spring is here, and it's nice to see Grayson again since practice has taken up most of his time.

We abandon our previous conversation in favor of Marcus explaining his most recent run-in with his and Kane's upstairs landlord's newest fling of the week—someone who, at eighty-one, surprisingly gets more action than all of us put together—and I glance around, wondering if Kane is still here.

I look over at Marcus and Grayson and almost ask about Kane, but I'm not sure I'm ready to know the answer. Every song and sound of utensils clinking sends my already overwhelmed brain into a frenzy, and I realize I'm no longer in the headspace for being out. My mood has shifted, and I need the quiet darkness of my room to wrap around me like a warm blanket.

There are protests as I make my excuses, but I say my goodbyes, call an Uber and head outside to wait.

When I push through the front doors, a burst of cool air instantly sobers me up.

The weather has broken just enough this week to get us some relief from the relentless cold we've been having, announcing a change of the seasons is on its way in the south. I've lived in this small Tennessee town of Cherry Hill all my life—spring is always unpredictable, and with the sun setting below the horizon, a slight chill fills the air.

My new skirt and Doc Martens aren't helping matters, and it has me wishing I had added those new stockings that I picked up on Morgan's and my most recent shopping trip.

I check my phone to see where my Uber is, my finger hovering over the generic background I changed it to after the breakup, when a black SUV pulls up in front of me. The driver rolls down the window to confirm my name, and I quickly lock my phone and get inside.

I stare out the window as the lights blur past, lost in my head like I have been all night. Before I realize it, we're pulling up to my rented cottage and I get out with a quick, "Thanks," to the driver.

I don't bother to turn any lights on as I get ready for bed. Once I'm under the covers, I pull them up over my head and finally let out the tears I refused to let fall earlier.

CHAPTER TWO

avery

imgonnagetyouback – Taylor Swift

"Okay babe, I knew you were mentally unstable, but this has me ready to get your therapist's number ready to dial. What would Susan say, Avery?" Morgan asks, reaching for my phone.

I swipe it from its resting spot next to my laptop before she can grab it. I'm hunkered down at the kitchen table where I started my covert plan a few minutes ago. I'm googling numerous music stores around me—yes, plural, because once I'm committed to something, I will not do it half-assed—and find the numbers for the ones Kane is most likely to call. One good thing about spending the last couple of years with someone, you know how they think, even though I do wish I could forget sometimes.

"Oh please. If *this* is the biggest sign that I'm not mentally stable that's occurred in the past twenty-three years of my life, that's just sad. I need to step it up," I tease. "And Susan doesn't get my humor. I told three self-deprecating jokes last session, and she didn't even crack a smile." I hold the phone out of her reach while searching the store's website for their contact information.

Why do some businesses make that impossible?

"Well babe, I hate to break it to you, but I don't think your therapist is supposed to laugh at you," Morgan says, placing her hands on her hips. Her curly blonde hair is in a somehow chic messy bun even though she just rolled out of bed.

"I just can't have a therapist who doesn't get me. The vibes were off. Aha!" I shout when I finally find the right number to talk to a store associate. I'm so sick of having to yell at an automated machine just talk to a human.

I hold the phone up to my ear while it rings as I sit at our kitchen table in our dimly lit cottage. I was awake tossing and turning all night letting this idea simmer when the first prank struck me.

The morning sun is streaming through the front windows, another sunny day shining down on us. The spring is hitting us earlier than usual, a welcome reprieve from the seasonal depression that has clung to my skin. I realize that I probably could benefit from some vitamin D today and not lock myself in my room before I go to the shelter later.

"Thank you for calling Music and More, my name is Jess. How can I help you?" a chipper voice says from the other end of the line.

"Yes, hello, I need to purchase all your G strings for a Martin acoustic guitar," I say proudly while Morgan snickers behind me. I throw a middle finger up at her, staying in character.

Morgan continues laughing, now fully on board with my potential disastrous plan that came to me overnight.

"Uh sure, we have five on hand and two of the phosphor bronze strings coming in the next week."

I can hear the clicking of a keyboard in the background, along with a low male voice I can't quite make out.

"Perfect. I'll be by soon. Can you put it under, uh... Anne?"

When I hang up, I turn to Morgan with a huge, and slightly manic smile on my face.

"Oh, she's lost the plot for sure," Morgan whispers to herself as if I'm not sitting one foot from where she's washing the dishes, always taking care of me. My heart warms at that thought.

As someone who basically raised herself, with a mother who made time for everyone but me, it's nice to have someone around to help out with the small things. Someone who sees that you need help and just steps in because she knows I won't ask for it.

I grew up in an environment where love and care were not freely given, if given at all.

She finishes up our dishes and takes a seat next to me at our brown, well-worn table that has seen its fair share of game nights and tears—mostly from Marcus when he loses Pictionary.

I smile at the memory, then stand to get ready for part one of my mission.

"Look, I need you to call Marcus and convince him to let me in so I can grab it. Kane taught me how to replace them. I'll be in and out in minutes, but if I show up with just my key, he'll be suspicious. I told him last week it'll take another threat like the giant bee apocalypse of 2022 to get me back there."

I shudder at the memory of when not one, but two large beehives took up residence in our attic, slowly leading our little old cottage to a full-blown infestation. Morgan and I called Kane and Marcus with tears in our eyes, incoherently babbling to them, which then led to them showing up with bats, ready to jump into whatever was threatening us. After they finished going through the house, Kane took over calling an exterminator and going back inside for my things since I refused to step foot back in the cottage while those little demons were present. Three weeks later, we were finally able to move back in.

It's a day that will forever live in infamy.

"No," Marcus says before I even finish my sentence.

I stand outside the townhouse he and Kane have rented since freshman year. The pale blue exterior shines against the white door, the sun beating down on me. The sadness of being here after so much time away starts to cloud my thoughts.

I've seen many things here in the past few years—the parties that inevitably ended in disaster, Marcus's revolving door of girls, Kane and I growing through the years and the family get-togethers we used to have weekly when life started to get busier for everyone.

"Marcus, I need you. This is your time to shine. Your chance to run a covert mission like those video games you're always playing," I say sweetly, trying to butter up my oldest friend, now turned into my biggest obstacle. He's still blocking my entrance into phase one of my master plan I've dubbed *Make Kane Eat Shit*. It's a working title, but I think it has a nice ring to it.

"Or you could just talk to him. You know, communicate. We learned how to do that in Mrs. Meyers' first grade class." He shoots me a look that says I've lost my mind, his vivid green eyes imploring me to see reason as he places both hands on top of the doorframe, using all six-foot-three of his height to bodyguard the apartment.

"Please, you know the only thing we learned in Mrs. Meyers' class is that she's been cheating on her husband since 2002," I reply with sass, my hand going to my jutted hip, the irritation simmering that this plan isn't as foolproof as I'd hoped. "And pull your shirt down, Marcus Allen White. Those abs don't work on me," I add indignantly. Marcus has always been a ladies' man, complete with the stereotypical fear of commitment.

I quickly hit him in his lower abdomen, and his arms drop to block himself from other potential assaults. He stammers enough that I'm able to slip past him into their place for the first time in forty-six days.

Not that I'm counting.

I steel my spine and walk to the corner where Kane keeps his old guitar—next to his well-loved record player and the extensive vinyl collection he's been building for years. A shiny blue record I don't recognize is laying on the turntable, recently listened to.

What else have I missed?

I tear my attention from the vinyl, my eyes landing on the guitar that has played me every song I've ever shown an interest in since senior year of high school. It rests on its stand, the light brown wood still gleaming even after all these years.

The rest of the apartment looks exactly the same too. Looking from the kitchen to the living room, I expect to find things that have changed in my absence, but nothing has.

The dark green pillows we bought together still rest on the couch, and some of my romance books are stacked haphazardly on the bookshelves lining the sides of the TV. A mess of paper sits on the kitchen table, suggesting that Kane was working late and likely fell asleep before finishing, just like always.

I even spot the photo of us from the time I forced him to get on a ferris wheel down in California, tucked beside his "reading" glasses on the side table. He really needs them all the time, but he will never admit to being nearsighted.

I contemplate asking Marcus to remind him to wear them...but that's not my problem anymore. Tears start to well in my eyes. This place has always welcomed me and warmed me from the moment I've crossed this threshold, but I feel like an outsider now.

I am *an outsider now.*

I force my thoughts in another direction, reminding myself about Kane leading the blonde back to a private table at The Grunge and doing my best to ignore the lingering feeling of homesickness.

"Look, it's not that I'm not on your side—"

I whip my gaze to Marcus, my eyes narrowing at what might come out of his mouth next. He raises his hands in surrender where he's still perched near the door, as if I'm a live bomb ready to go off.

I just might, so I'm glad he's on alert.

"I'm just saying, is this really the best way to get his attention?" Marcus finishes, still standing away from me, like I might reach up and smack him at any moment.

"No, what I think is that he shouldn't be parading his new girlfriend around the bar he knows we all go to. He could have taken her anywhere, and he chose *our* bar,

Marcus!" I shout, reaching a volume that will probably have Mr. Wright calling in a noise complaint any minute.

The neighbor in the other half of the townhouse is known for being a little crazy. One minute he's throwing a raging party for the local retirement home, the next he's whining about noise in the middle of the afternoon on a Tuesday. How Marcus and Kane have lasted this long in this duplex when both could afford much nicer, I'll never know.

"Whoa, what do you—" Marcus starts, his brow furrowing and a slight frown forming across his olive skin.

"Enough," I demand, turning my back to him and resuming my mission. "Either help me, or forget that I was here, Marcus," I plead as I try to keep the tremble out of my voice. He catches it anyways, his eyes softening around the corners.

He lets out an overdramatic sigh but finally relents. "Fine. But if anyone asks, forget *I* was here. Kane won't be back until after six. His seminar is in the city this week."

I mentally calculate how far with traffic and know even if he was on his way, I still have time.

I'm tempted to ask how it's going, but I shake off the thought and return to my task.

I'm giggling to myself as I undo the first string to free it from the guitar with the pliers Kane keeps in his bedside drawer—Marcus could see how badly I could not face that today and took pity on me by going to grab them for me. I untie it from the tuning peg and wiggle it free. Kane taught me how to do this years ago, so he only has himself to blame.

I stuff the string into the bag and phase one of my plan slides into place.

"I also need you to intercept any packages he gets," I say, looking back at Marcus.

"Why?" he replies hesitantly, my behavior clearly scaring him.

"If he gets any packages, I need you to take them and call me."

"You're going to stop him from getting a new string?" he muses.

"Of course I am," I scoff. "He can get all the new girlfriends he wants, but they're not getting *my* music, that's for sure."

It no longer is *my* music, but I ignore that.

"Oh okay, so you just want me to casually commit a felony," Marcus gripes, leaning over the counter. His elbows rest on the granite countertops, messy locks falling over his forehead, his headphones perched on his head.

"It's not a felony," I say, rolling my eyes at him.

"Uh, yes it is. Tampering with someone's mail is punishable by a fine and even prison time. Prison! Do you know what they do to pretty boys like me in prison? I'll be someone's bitch, Avery." Marcus throws his hands up in the air to emphasize his point.

"You already are, Marcus. Would you rather be mine or some bald guy named Big Jim's?"

I chuckle, showing myself the door, knowing Marcus won't say no to me. Growing up as neighbors from the ripe age of five has made Marcus my oldest and closest friend—though I'll never say that in front of Morgan, because she wouldn't speak to me until I took it back. The competition between these two is never-ending.

As I walk out, I faintly hear Marcus say, "I'm jumping back on now, some random girl scout at my door wouldn't go away," into the headphone mouthpiece as he walks away.

I snort as I get into my car, the high of pulling off phase one already starting to fade. I wrap my hands around the steering wheel and drop my head against them for one breath. Then another. After a few seconds, I start the car, pull up Taylor Swift on my phone, and let the queen of heartbreak fill the cab as the streets blur in front of me.

CHAPTER THREE

kane

FOUR YEARS AGO, HIGH SCHOOL

Out of My League – Aiden Bissett

Another new town, another new fucking school because dear old Dad can't keep his dick in his pants. Another affair caused us to flee yet once again in an attempt to save a marriage that should've ended before my fifth birthday, yet here we are thirteen years later, still dealing with the same old bullshit. Why my mother hasn't left is beyond me. I tried reasoning with her for years, but she's always made excuses for him, so now I just block her out. She made her own bed, and now she gets to lie in it.

I'm pissed off at the world, hating every part of this place I've been dropped in, listening to this kid in front of me drone on and on—a student council member who was assigned as a tour guide to show me to my first class, as if I can't read the map they gave me.

Usually, I would be grateful for the help, maybe even strike up a conversation, but after a run-in with Dad and another lecture about taking school seriously in order to get into his alma mater—as if he couldn't buy the whole school to have me accepted—I'm not in the mood.

New places, new people, trying to make friends only to have to pack up and move again—I'm sick of it.

My all-black clothing coupled with my new hairstyle—shorter on the sides, longer on top—complete the whole fuck-the-world look I'm going for. Though, the lingering looks from girls in the hall tell me they don't seem to mind it.

Maybe this year won't be *all* bad. I can play ball, fuck some girls. One more year and I'll be gone. Off to college, preparing to join the family business I want absolutely nothing to do with. The D'Antonios started building their fortune when my great-granddad hit it big in oil and started his own investment firm. He started a legacy of D'Antonio men who know how to make money but have no fucking clue how to show up for their families.

I scoff to myself, and the kid showing me around looks in my direction. I send a small smile and thumbs up his way, and he turns back around.

I put my foot down when my father suggested a private school. I'm so sick of our inner circle, the fake as fuck smiles and even faker attitudes when they find out what your net worth is. As if money has bought any of them a clue.

This school is top-rated, though, with state-of-the-art gyms and practice fields and a long line of champion athletes. If I'm stuck here, at least I still have football. It's my last year to do something because I want it, not because my father decided it for me.

The school is laid out like a circle, with hallways branching off from the center. I missed the first period talking to the principal, so when we finally reach my second class, the kid showing me around turns to me and says,

"This is Mr. Adams, he's a really good teacher. He also coaches football as one of the assistants, so I'm sure you'll be seeing a lot of him. I have class on the other side, so I probably won't be here when you get out. Can you find your next class, okay?"

I nod, and he waves and takes off the way we came.

I take a small breath and steel myself as I push open the door. When I enter, everyone is still up and talking while the teacher is at the board writing something down. A large whiteboard takes up most of the front of the room, with a teacher's desk in the opposite corner from the door. Roughly four rows of five desks take up most of the room.

The teacher, Mr. Adams, looks up when he notices me at the door. He caps the marker and sets it down, a polite smile on his face. "You must be Kane," he says.

"Yes, sir," I answer, hands in my pockets, not yet looking at the other students, though the noise has quieted down a lot since I walked in.

Turning toward the class, Mr. Adams gestures to me, as if the whole class isn't already locked onto me at the front.

"Class, this is Kane D'Antonio, a new student. Please welcome him and take your seats. Let's get started."

The new student orientation never gets easier, even if being stared at doesn't bother me much. I care little about what people think of me, but there's always a hierarchy at schools, everyone falling into cliques made up of sports and social statuses. The haves and the have-nots. Whether society wants to believe they're a thing of the past or not, every school has one, and day one always begins with figuring out where you are going to fall into it.

After all the upheaval over the recent years, I'd just like a few chill friends to look forward to seeing, to try to enjoy my last year. Who knows, maybe I'll actually go to homecoming—though prom is a definite no.

It's never been hard to get girls, but my last name always sends some unwanted attention my way—people hoping to get in good with me to benefit from what that name offers. What they don't know is that I'd trade with any of them just to be free from the shackles of it.

I finally look out at the class, quickly glancing at each student until I get to the row closest to where I'm standing My gaze almost skips right over her at first. Then it whips right back to the most beautiful thing I've ever seen.

Her stunning blue eyes are locked on mine, her long brown hair falling over her shoulders. She has her full pink lips wrapped around a pen, as if she was mid-thought.

My tongue gets stuck in my mouth, and my palms instantly start sweating. I can't seem to tear my eyes from hers.

She sits forward in her seat, elbows braced on her desk, and the way her breasts are pushed up in a tight long-sleeve shirt, pulls my gaze there for a moment before I force it back to her eyes.

Cornflower blue.

I'm not sure I've ever been able to pick up a color that easily before, but the way they stare at me matches my mother's favorite flowers in her garden. Cornflower blue. Not as piercing and vibrant as a cerulean blue, more muted but no less stunning. My mother always built a new garden in any house we moved to. I used to work on it with her—that was our thing together.

My heart feels like it's palpitating, the beats feeling irregular in my chest.

Is this acid reflux?

Should I ask to see the nurse?

I've never experienced such a visceral reaction to another person before. The girl's eyes burn a hole right through me.

"Sit anywhere, Kane," Mr. Adams says, gesturing toward the seats and turning back to the board, effectively dismissing me.

I spot a seat behind the girl, so I urge my feet to move me closer to her. It's almost as if an invisible string is pulling me to her by some unknown force. My feet have no other choice but to be wherever she is.

The closer I get, the more stunning she is. Her features fit her face perfectly, light makeup dusting her face, the mascara enhancing her blue eyes. I don't think I've ever noticed such small details on a person's face before, but I cannot seem to stop myself from cataloging every detail, as if she might disappear at any moment. She tracks me with her eyes as I make my way toward my seat. Some people wave as I walk by, a few girls looking me up and down, but I ignore them.

As I pass by her, I get a whiff of something citrusy. I take the seat behind her and slide in, noticing her shoulders tense a bit. I drop my bag to the ground and lean back, legs spread slightly, unable to take my eyes off her.

Her long dark brown hair flows down her back, narrow shoulders followed by a slimmer waist. Her blue long sleeve shirt stands out against her pale skin. She reaches back and pulls all her hair off her neck, making that scent of hers drift toward me again.

Lemons. Fuck if I don't want to bottle that up and take it with me.

Never in my life have I cared to focus on a girl's scent before and fuck if I don't sound like some lovesick idiot, whimpering after her already.

Mr. Adams has started his lecture, yet I don't hear a word. Unable to wait a second longer to speak to her, I lean forward and tap her shoulder. She jumps in response before turning to me.

Fuck, do her eyes hold me hostage. They're even bluer up close, standing out against her dark hair and pale skin. I swear she's a fucking goddess sent to lure me to the underworld. A siren playing her music from her eyes only, snaring me in and never letting me go.

"Can I borrow a pencil?" I ask, a small smirk on my lips, deciding to pack on the charm. My hands are spread out on the desk, fighting the urge to touch her—because that would be fucking creepy, and the last thing I want to do is scare this girl off. I think I want her closer.

"Who the hell doesn't bring a pencil to their first day of school?" bursts out of her, shock on her face as if she hadn't meant to say that. Her cheeks turn pink under my gaze, and her teeth nibble her lower lip. I have to stop myself from reaching over and tugging it free. Her plump-as-fuck bottom lip reddens, sending a shock through me that goes straight to my dick.

Great, just what I need in the middle of class.

"I forgot," I admit with a cocky smile still on my face, shrugging. Fuck, I've never had trouble getting a girl's attention, but for some reason she seems immune to my charm. She furrows her brows as she bends forward and grabs a pencil out of her black backpack. She puts it on my desk, and just before she turns around, I add, "I'm Kane."

"I know," she says, a soft smile on her face. Embarrassment floods through me, remembering the teacher just introduced me. She goes to turn around again, but fuck, I'll do anything to keep her attention on me. Apparently, making a fool of myself is first on my list of things to try.

"What's your name?" I ask, needing to know with a sense of urgency I don't quite understand yet. All I know is that her answer might just be something I've been waiting for my whole life. She turns back to me, her face unreadable as she looks me up and down. What I wouldn't give to be inside her head right now.

She looks at me for a moment as if she's unsure whether or not she wants to answer. She reaches up and pushes a lock of her long brown hair behind her ear, giving me the most stunning, unobstructed view of her face, and I note a small diamond stud encased in black metal in her nose.

"Avery. My name is Avery," she says, her voice as sweet as honey, floating through my head again and again.

Five words, that's all it took for my entire life to change —somehow rearranging the very makeup of atoms, forever altering what made me before to make room for the girl sitting right in front of me.

She just doesn't know it yet.

CHAPTER FOUR

NOW

Scared to Start – Michael Marcagi

"You're just a big softy, aren't you?" I coo as Silver presses her too-thin body against me, covering my clothes in fur and slobber. The malnourished gray American pitbull terrier mix is a recent intake at Second Chances animal shelter, where I've been on staff for the past six years.

I started my junior year of high school as a volunteer, working my way up to a full-time position two years ago. I primarily work with the owner, Sharlene, on recent intakes, grooming, paperwork, adoptions and pretty much anything else you can think of. You name it, and I'm sure it's part of my job description.

Silver was found on the side of the road with her very pregnant belly on display. The visible outline of her ribs when she arrived made my heart ache with the hunger she must have been experiencing. Tears come to my eyes knowing she was most likely dumped, her old worn collared long cut off and trashed, her coat gleaming from her recent bath. She's very skittish around people, but after sitting with her for a while and letting her adjust to me, she's finally found her way into my lap.

Her soft but too skinny head rests on my leg as I stroke behind her ears, the day taking all the energy out of her. I find these slower moments here to be some of the best—gaining the trust of the animals who need it most and giving them another chance. From here on out, she gets warmth, food, rest and someone making sure her babies have the same.

I linger for a few more minutes before I get up to check on the volunteers and ensure Keith—another full-timer who occasionally takes overnights when our usual overnighter, Sam, isn't available—is updated on all our new intakes and animals that need medication.

I dust the piles of dog hair off my pants, constantly shocked when my black leggings are a multitude of colors by the end of the day. I lock up Silver's kennel and begin to make my way toward the front. Most of the dogs are asleep at this late hour, though a few wait by their gates, eager for any attention they can get. It makes my leaving take longer because, of course, I have to stop and give them all a proper rub and treat. Finally, I do one last check of the clipboards, ensuring all medications were administered for the night and signed off on.

My eyes snag on a familiar signature I can trace with my eyes closed.

Kane must have been here earlier. I know he still comes by and volunteers, though not as often as he used to—maybe four times in the past month, and never at the same time as me. I think Sharlene is secretly giving him my schedule. It stings to know he's been avoiding me, but my heart warms at the thought of him still coming by, seeing and loving on some of the lonelier residents.

As much as I wish all these dogs were adopted right away, that's not the reality for some shelter dogs. Senior dogs are often harder to place, especially when puppies are available.

My heart breaks thinking of all the dogs that still need homes, my mind stuck on Silver. She'll be one of the harder ones to get adopted. Her puppies will go first, while I'm sure mom will stay for a while longer.

I pull my phone from my pocket and bring up the shelter's profile online. I've been working so hard to keep it updated, filling it with adorable dog videos of our residents. I've somehow gained quite a following and it has really made a difference, with people traveling from towns away to adopt ones that we've showcased. The page has even had a few viral videos, helping with not only donations but also with getting the word out about how many shelter dogs are so desperately needing a home. People love seeing our "Dog of the Month" spotlight, which almost always guarantees an adopter or foster picking them up shortly after. My heart is floating with how great of a place the internet can be.

I upload a video of Silver from my phone, hoping it gains the traction I need to get her the rest and peace she so rightfully deserves.

I close out the tab before I'm tempted to look up a certain someone. He hasn't posted since we broke up, not that I'm checking. I still look from time to time to see if maybe he's uploaded a story, simply out of curiosity, but he's been radio silent.

Not that he posted that often when we were together. All his pictures are still up on his page, most of which are of him and me. There are a few of him, Marcus and Grayson and one from an open mic night I made him perform at, but even our prom photos are still there.

I sidle up to the front desk, also my makeshift office when I'm here. The front is decorated in lots of earthy tones with light beige walls and green accent chairs in the lobby. The place is immaculately tidy for an animal shelter. Sharlene is a stickler for cleanliness. Knowing most of these dogs have come from bad circumstances, she wants to set a precedent for how good these animals are taken care of going forward. The long wooden counter hides the desk behind it, paperwork covering all available spaces with applications, vet bills and all the other things it takes to keep this shelter running.

I huff out a sigh as I take a seat on the plush rolling chair that I picked out because the last one made my butt numb after only a few hours. Cracking my neck, which is stiff from sitting in the same position in the kennels, I log onto the computer and start to answer some emails.

"You're still here?" a voice calls from behind me, causing me to jump, hands flying up. A small chuckle follows as I turn toward the culprit, my heart still racing in my chest. Sharlene stands behind me with a knowing smile, one hip leaning against the desk. She's in her late sixties, with long black hair that's threaded with grays littering the front, but you'd never know her age at the rate she moves. Always on the go, from morning until night, keeping this place sparkling and running to perfection.

"Goodness, could you at least wear a bell or something before you go sneaking up on people?" I ask jokingly, my hand to my chest. I can't help the huge smile that fills my face as I stare at the one person who has always felt more like a mother to me than a boss.

"Now what fun would that be?" Sharlene teases with a

wink. "But really, what are you still doing here? I was just wrapping up with Keith and I saw you parked outside. Time to go home, get some sleep. Those bags under your eyes aren't getting any smaller." She grabs my hands and pulls me up off the chair, the exhaustion of the past couple days finally settling into my bones.

"Silver needed some extra love, so I was spending time with her. And checking some emails. Sometimes it's easier to be here and busy, you know?" I answer as Sharlene wraps me in a hug.

The sense of warmth and familiarity I didn't realize I desperately needed sinks into my weary bones as the smell of her Chanel No. 5 hits my nose. Her hug brings tears spring to my eyes as I soak in the warmth until we finally pull apart.

Standing a few inches taller than me, she grabs my cheeks with both hands and looks into my eyes. "How are you, honey?" she implores softly.

"I'm okay... It's been a rough few weeks," I say with a shrug, trying to keep the tears at bay.

Her eyes crinkle around the edges and soft smile lines around her mouth reflect just how much life she has lived. Sharlene opted to buy an animal shelter after she lost her husband, saying it gives her purpose in life. She came into my life when I needed it most, as a lost girl with parents who always seem to have better things to do. Sharlene saw something in me and decided to take me under her wing, and for that I will always be grateful.

"Have you two talked?" she asks, dropping her hands and grabbing a tissue from behind her, turning around and handing it to me.

"No," I reply, taking the tissue from her outstretched

hand. I wipe my eyes and blow my nose softly, trying to suppress the emotions threatening to assault me.

"Oh, honey..." she starts. "He asked about you today." She watches me, waiting for my reaction. My heart leaps at the idea, the tingles in my stomach taking flight, wanting to ask more, even knowing that maybe it's safer to keep it at that.

"How is he?" I ask, feeling safe to open up to her. Knowing she sees what I'm unable to say.

Her eyes soften before she speaks. Tucking a wayward lock of hair behind my ear that has fallen out of ponytail, she says, "He looks about as good as you do, honey."

The tears return with full force, all the emotions from the day hitting me at once. This is the first break I've given myself since I stepped through the door this morning into chaos. I pull in a breath and straighten my shirt, trying to shove my feelings back inside the little box I keep them tucked away in.

"Silver will probably give birth soon," I tell her, needing to change the subject. "The vet found six puppies on the ultrasound. She's in one of our quarantine rooms so we can monitor her closely and help her gain a little strength before those babies come."

Sharlene eyes me with concern for a moment before nodding, accepting that I'm still not ready to talk about it.

I'd much rather focus on the animals who rely on me. I've always been drawn to the hardest cases, fixing them up and caring for them until they're ready for adoption. Something inside me calls to their brokenness, almost as if healing them heals me in a way. A piece of my jagged heart fills every time I watch one go to their forever home.

Silver is just one in a long line of moms I've seen come

through here. When I started volunteering here in high school, I would mostly just walk and play with the dogs. The passion hit me as soon as I saw the first dog get adopted, and it felt so right to be along for the process. My degree in business was purely for my mother's sake, something she can brag to all her friends about without actually caring what I do with it.

Her lunches are filled with praise for her college graduate daughter, but my phone stays clear of anything from her.

After six months as a volunteer, I started pestering Sharlene for a full-time job, immediately falling under her wing and absorbing everything I could. How to care for the sick and more medically complex cases we have, assisting in deliveries if the vets are unavailable and watching some of the frail dogs turn to the healthiest, happiest dogs on their way to their homes. Somewhere along the way, this place stopped feeling like a job and started feeling like part of me.

Sharlene has cut back her hours lately, spending more time with her grandkids and taking care of the few more medically complex fosters that she takes home, while Keith and I handle the more day-to-day things that keep this place running. We have several part-timers and a few more full-time positions filled.

We run purely on donations, and a non-profit can be very hard. When Kane started volunteering with me in high school, a generous donation was suspiciously added to the shelter's account every month, like clockwork. He's never admitted that it's him, but the payments haven't stopped since, even now.

Luckily, we also have sponsors, fundraisers and community support to help keep us running and able to take as many dogs as necessary. No matter how tired I am when I get home from putting out fires all day, I'm thankful this is my job. Every day looks different, but when I look around at the end of the night, taking in the chaos, I know there's nowhere else I'd rather be.

After Sharlene takes off to check our new intake, I wrap up a few more emails. The never-ending inbox of emails marked urgent stares back at me as exhaustion finally seeps into my bones. Since the breakup, the only way I've been able to keep moving is by staying busy, knowing that if I give myself a break, the weight of my grief will pull me under again.

With a yawn, I push away from the desk. The animals have settled down for the night, leaving this place the quietest it has been all day. I adjust my hair and brush my shirt off as I stand up, grabbing my things and phone from the lockers in the back.

I ignore the texts waiting for me, knowing there's nothing I'm really hoping for in them. The air is brisk as I walk outside, the sun having set a couple hours ago. I forgo the coat I brought in this morning, letting the wind roll over my skin, goosebumps coating my arms as I walk to my car. I welcome the cold—the numbness of the weather washing over me, keeping me awake.

As I get into my car, I finally let my mind drift to Kane and what Sharlene said to me earlier—that he asked about me. As curious as I am to know exactly *what* he asked, I know he probably just feels guilty about moving on. Besides, if he really cared, he'd say whatever he needs to say directly to me.

I no longer have the strength to ignore the ache in my chest. As I drive home, the tears spill over, sobs racking my chest.

CHAPTER FIVE

kane

Forget Me – Lewis Capaldi

"What the fuck?" I mutter when I go to play my guitar and realize a fucking string is missing. I look up as Marcus enters the room during a rare break from the game he's been streaming on a platform he uses to make money while people watch him play his favorite games. Swinging his keys around, Marcus stops when he sees me tossing aside my guitar.

"What's up, man?" he asks, not looking at me as he grabs a drink from the fridge. I assume he restocked it today because this morning I was left with nothing but two butts of bread that I shoved in my mouth as I rushed out the door to get to school before it opened.

"My guitar," I say in disbelief. "It's missing a fucking string."

He looks visibly shocked as he stares at me with wide eyes before looking around the room as if he'll find the string or the culprit. "I was streaming all day, but I haven't noticed anything. I guess someone could have come over and I just didn't hear them with my headphones on, but I feel like I would have heard them. But I haven't noticed anything weird. I can't even play the guitar," he rambles. When he finally finishes speaking, he takes a big breath that he clearly didn't take during that entire monologue.

"Are you okay, dude? Did you take my string?"

Marcus spits out some liquid and wipes his chin, his entire shirt now covered in purple Gatorade. "What? I don't even know how to do that?" he says, more as a question than a statement. He caps his drink and places both hands on the counter before finally looking me in the eye for the first time tonight.

"Okay... Well, that's weird. I swear it was there last night. I was going to play after I got home from showing Lindsay some of the spots in town, but I was wiped so I guess I didn't look hard enough... Did I do it?" I wonder out loud, fisting my hair. Maybe the never-ending exhaustion from work at the bar and school has finally gotten to me. I look around the area as if maybe the string just jumped off the guitar itself and is waiting for me to find it. The ridiculous notion has me scoffing . These past few weeks have been hell. A haze of misery and self-loathing, and I must have finally cracked.

Unsure what else to do since it was Avery's night with our friends and I didn't want to face how empty the apartment would be, I decided to show my new coworker, Lindsay, around town. Morgan initiated a schedule on nights when the group gets time with one of us. All of us are just trying our best to navigate this new arrangement. But Lindsay's cool, and she talks enough so that I don't have to. When we met up with her girlfriend, I realized we had a lot in common, and it was nice to not feel the heavy weight of loneliness that's been a constant these past few weeks.

Neither of them missed the way I kept staring at Avery's contact all night, but they were kind enough not to say anything. I felt the need to call her all night, to tell her everything. From the stuff Lindsay said, to this new song I heard at the vintage shop we used to go to. I found myself wondering what would happen if I just sent one text.

Would she respond? Or would it push her further away?

"Yeah, dude, that's really weird. So, uh, I have to go, but I'll be back at 11. We're going to go see some new movie Morgan swears isn't a rom-com," he says, pulling me out of my thoughts. He grabs his keys and jacket because spring in Tennessee is always a gamble. You could be sweating one minute and bundled up the next.

I scratch the back of my neck, knowing that means Avery will be there. I hesitantly ask, "So, uh, how is she doing?"

It's the question I've only allowed myself to ask him every other day since the breakup, knowing I can't *not* know how she is, but also wanting to respect her and the breakup she wanted.

His eyes soften as he turns and gives me his full attention. I almost take my question back, knowing I won't be able to handle it if he tells me she's dating someone new. Rage burns through me at the thought.

He finally puts me out of my self-loathing misery. "She's okay. I mean, she's sad, we can all see that. But she won't talk about it, you know. She's working more at Second Chances, though, and that has helped," he answers hesitantly, like he's scared of my reaction.

What else could I want for her? I want her to be happy. I want nothing but the best for her. I know she'll flourish with whatever she does, I just wish I was still there to witness it. It's like going to see your favorite artist and no longer being in the front row, somehow getting pushed to the back, trying to see over everyone in front of you to catch even a glimpse.

Fuck if I haven't sat and mapped out every inch of her body the way I imagine one does in art, every inch and curve of her made to perfection.

I rub my chest, wondering if this tightening I feel every time I think of Avery is ever going to go away as Marcus leaves the apartment and shuts the door. I turn, wondering what to do now. With my guitar out of commission and my friends with the only person who's ever made me feel anything, I grab my water to go to my bedroom.

I call some stores around me to pick up a new string only to be told by every store in a fifty mile radius that their stock is sold out. I toss my phone away from me in frustration and decide to give myself the night to think of another solution.

What fucking luck.

I finish some notes I need to make about Trevor, a boy who has been coming into my office lately. We talk about mundane things mostly, like how his day is going, but I'm slowly trying to get him to open up. I'm hoping he starts trusting me more soon, because if I have to ignore one more odd-looking mark when he sits down, I might lose it. He's brushed everything off as an injury from work or simply being clumsy, but I wouldn't be doing my job if I wasn't exploring every path.

After that's finished, I scroll on Instagram, stopping when I reach Morgan's story and catch a glimpse of Avery in the back.

Her long dark hair that I've had sprawled across me—and woken up suffocated by—more times than I can count, the faint smell of lemons filling my nose. I spot a new dress I've never seen before and the boots I got her for Christmas. The ones I knew she wanted and saved a month's worth of tips for, because I knew she wanted the limited edition brown ones, and I refused to put it on my father's card and let it be another thing he could hold over my head.

I don't know how long I sit there and stare at this picture of her. I fixate on her smile that seems bright, her white teeth shining, but it doesn't quite reach her eyes. Those beautiful, brilliant blues look dim in comparison to when they used to fall on me.

I'm torturing myself with the idea that maybe this is all I'll get for the rest of my life, glimpses of her through a screen. I know it's not enough for me. I'm not sure I'll ever get enough of her. Which is a shame because I lost her, and I don't even know how.

I roll over and try to think of anything else. The sun will be up far too soon, and another day of counseling the young minds of South Hill High will keep my mind busy enough for me to get through the day without falling apart. It seems to be all I can do these days—just put my head down and get through.

An alert hits my phone and I jump up, getting tangled in the three layers Avery always insisted we needed, face-planting to the floor as I reach for my phone. I deflate when I see it's just my dad.

SPERM DONOR

You need to stop by in the morning to meet with one of my associates.

Yeah right, an *associate*. He means one of his golf buddies' daughters that he's been parading in front of me, like I'm looking for a wife's dowry to keep my family afloat.

He's just mad because I've been even more distant since the breakup. I have refused to use the credit cards he "gifts" me, keeping at least that much of his control out of my life.

Avery always told me I didn't need him or his validation. That somehow being me was enough. That his inability to love me did not have anything to do with me, but everything to do with him and how nothing will ever be good enough for him.

And I started to believe her.

But didn't Avery choose to leave just like everyone else? Didn't she take one last look at me and decide I wasn't enough for her too?

A familiar tightness starts to spread across my chest, the tingling starting in my fingers and my vision blurring at the edges. I grip my comforter and force myself to breathe before this turns into a full-blown panic attack. They've increased over the past month, that suffocating feeling waking me up more nights than not. I count and try to focus on each breath as the world spins around me.

Once my heart rate slows and the feeling has passed, I lock my phone and resume my self-deprecating inner monologue. I fall asleep to the thought that this is all temporary and that I *will* get her back. I'll give her the life she always pictured for us. Whatever she wants, she can have—I just need to figure out what went wrong.

And where did I put my fucking guitar string?

"Kane, I need you to meet with a student later today. They're new to the school, and they've been to four other schools in the past two years, so I just want you to check in.

Make sure everything is good at home, if you can," Principal Danner's secretary, Dawn, tells me as I walk in the front door. My bag is slung over my shoulder and my extra-hot latte burns my hands. My eyes are still heavy with sleep, and my hair refused to be tamed this morning, so I opted to leave it a mess of waves. I make a mental note to schedule a haircut as soon as possible.

"Sure thing, Dawn. Can you email any info to me so I can get a good understanding of their background?" I ask as I head toward my office, not bothering to wait for her response since I know Dawn will have everything to me within minutes. She is probably the most efficient person in this school, the glue that keeps this place running.

Being at one of the most underfunded schools in the district, it's hard to find good teachers and staff who are willing to work for pennies. The kids in this section are falling through the cracks, and the government is being less than helpful. That's the main reason I applied here—the forgotten kids. Whether forgotten by a messed-up system or by the people who were supposed to put them first but didn't.

Once I get into my office, I throw my bag on the desk and start up my computer. Taking a heavy pull from my drink, I let the warmth flood my system, giving me a boost to get myself together. I pull up my calendar and email, take in all the info Dawn has already sent me, and note that my calendar is full today. My weekly meeting with Trevor is at noon, and I'm hoping he shows up today. Sometimes he doesn't, but I always leave my door open anyway. I also made a note to follow up with another student after her two-week absence to see what we can do to get her caught up on her work and stay eligible for graduation.

I heave a sigh at how much there is to do, but a sense of

fulfillment hits me all the same. This is what I love, being helpful and giving some of these kids a voice they may not have otherwise.

My phone buzzes on the desk, already buried under all the files I've pulled for my morning sessions. I shuffle papers around, my sleeves already up to my elbows with the sweltering heat blasting from the vents. It buzzes again and I frantically look around for it, worried something has happened so early in the day.

SPERM DONOR

Answer your phone, Kane.

I raised you better than this.

As a scoff rises out of my throat, I put my phone on Do Not Disturb and hide it away. The looming shadow of my father clouds my mood as my first student of the day arrives.

CHAPTER SIX

kane

Ghost – Justin Bieber

My morning is full of back-to-back students, some with much to discuss and others I spent the whole meeting trying to pry any sort of information from. After dealing with everything— from students missing chunks of school and the resulting overload of missing assignments, to others wanting to work through the anxieties of the looming future—I'm thankful for a breather.

Looking at the last dregs of my second cup of coffee reminds me that I have yet to eat anything today. My lunch break is now, but I always block it off in case Trevor stops by. I've made it clear that my door is always open for him.

Staring at the unread group chat messages from Marcus and Grayson, I decide to reply after I've eaten something. But just as I stand up, a tuft of brown curls appears in my doorway.

I release a breath, some of the tension easing when I see Trevor. He looks tired, the ever-present dark under-eyes under this fifteen-year-old's eyes punching me right in the gut, like always. He should be playing a sport or getting in trouble with his friends, not working himself to exhaustion doing extra shifts at a mechanic shop in a not-so-great area of Cherry Hill—one of the few facts I've got out of him over the past two months. I make a mental note to talk to Marcus about giving him a job at his father's shop. Maybe a more stable and healthier environment would help this kid out a bit more, though it's on the other side of town which could be hard if he lacks the means to get there.

My heart clenches remembering how down he looked telling me, as if I would judge him for needing a job. Unfortunately, my last name is widely known in this town. From my father's never-ending real estate ventures to the construction company he owns, it's hard to go a few blocks without seeing "D'Antonio" plastered on something. It has made some kids wary of talking to me, knowing I may never understand their circumstances. But I have done my best to show them that despite what I came from, I am here for them, and no matter what, they matter to me.

I motion for Trevor to take a seat and close the door behind him. I opt not to say anything, letting Trevor start the conversation as I sit back down in my chair and straighten some papers, keeping my hands busy.

"Busy day, huh?" Trevor's small voice asks as he looks at the mountain of paperwork I'm behind on.

"Always busier than I want them to be, that's for sure," I reply, leaning back in my chair. I keep my eyes on him to let him know I am listening and engaged in this conversation.

He finally lifts his head up, and that's when I see it—a small bruise darkening his cheek. The deep purple can't be mistaken for anything else. My heart cracks open as I stare at it.

It's not the first time he's shown up here with a small

mark or unexplained cut. He always claims he tripped or got it at work, but after the fifth or sixth time, I couldn't deny that something worse could be happening to this kid. We're made aware of the signs early on, we go through rigorous training to spot when abuse could occur.

"Do you want to tell me?" I implore, leaving my tone with little room for argument.

"Fight at work, nothing to tell," he answers, his head down and fingers twisted in each other on his lap. I blow out a breath and let my heart rate settle before continuing.

"How are your classes? Is Algebra still giving you trouble?" I ask, changing the subject, hoping to get him to soften a bit today. Any information is good—it can tell me where his head is at.

Trevor shifts in his seat, holding eye contact with me finally, which I take as a sign that he isn't ready to bolt yet. I've gotten very good at reading body language from being here for the past eight months, knowing when to push some of these kids and when they just need me to listen. Sometimes, they just need somewhere to go and hide out without fear of being judged or ridiculed, hence my open-door policy. I want them to know they can come at any time for anything, even if it's just to sit. I try to avoid letting them ditch classes to do so, but many do, and I would rather them come here than go somewhere off campus and get into who knows what.

"Fine, it's easier now. Thank you for helping me find Katie," he says. Katie is an assistant for Algebra II and has taken on some students to tutor. She gets paid by the district to do so, and offers her time after hours. When I found out Trevor was struggling, I knew Katie was the best person to pair him with. She's easily the best tutor we have, willing to work harder to teach students like Trevor, who doesn't see much reason for even staying in school to learn things like algebra when he could be working instead. I'm grateful he's taking this opportunity to give it a try, and I'm relieved that he's feeling more comfortable in a class he was ready to fail out of.

"Of course. I'm proud of you for showing up. I know it's been a hard year, but going and trying is the best thing you can do and look at you. You're doing it," I acknowledge with a smile on my face. He ducks his head as the red in his cheeks deepens, the only recognition he heard me, which is all I want. To make sure he hears and knows that someone is proud of him.

"Yeah, I just wanted to come by and say thanks, I guess. I got a seventy-five on my last test. I know I can still do better, but hey, it's better than the twenty-nine on the last one," he jokes with a self-deprecating laugh. His boyish smile is long gone, and I watch him fiddle with his fingers in his lap, clearly uncomfortable talking about himself for too long.

Most of our sessions are short. A few sentences from him here and there, but it's a lot more than I used to get when we first started. Sometimes he would just sit in the room and not talk at all, scoffing anytime I tried to get him to open up. He used to hide behind "rich-boy" remarks he'd throw at me whenever the conversation got too close to anything real.

We finally broke that exterior when he realized I wasn't giving up on him. All I had to do was show Trevor that I'm not going anywhere—that I care, even if all I get from him is anger.

"Wow, a seventy-five. Trevor, that's great. Should I put down future goals to be a mathematician? Maybe we can look at colleges that have good math programs?" I ask with a laugh, getting a small chuckle out of him. His features have softened a bit, sitting a little bit more relaxed in the chair across from me.

"Yeah, I don't know, Mr. D. Let's not get too ahead of ourselves," he says with a laugh. "I just want to pass Algebra II so I can finally move on next year, finally."

Seeing him finally putting in the work and applying himself, I know he can do it. Even if he must add on an extra class to make it work, I'll be here to help him.

"You can do it. You *will* do it, Trevor. Just keep showing up. If you need a little extra help, you can come to me and we'll work it out, even if it means I have to figure out fractions again," I tease, hoping the familiar back and forth will help him to open up further. "How is work?" I ask, changing the subject again to keep him talking. I know I could be pushing my luck, but his tired eyes and the bruise haven't quite faded from my mind.

"Good. Sara was sick last week so I had to take a few days off, but she's feeling better now and back to school. Katie got my school work for me and even stopped by the garage to give it to me." He shakes his head in disbelief.

Sara is one of his two younger sisters. He hasn't explicitly told me their ages, just that they're in elementary school. It seems like the majority of their parenting falls on his shoulders, making sure they get to and from school. I noticed his absences last week, and I'm happy he's the one who brought it up. Anytime he's not in class, I have Dawn alert me so I can make note of it and watch for when he shows up next for a check in.

A lot of kids here skip or have more absences than the state allows, but I try to push as many as I can through on to the next year as long as they put in at least some effort. Some do have to repeat the year, and there's a long list of students with whom we've had to get child protective services (CPS) involved, but keeping Trevor off it has been a priority.

"That's good, Trev. Do you have any work you can catch up on now? I was going to go grab my lunch, but you can sit here and work before the bell rings," I suggest. He nods and turns to his backpack, taking out a few folders.

My stomach grumbles, reminding me I need to eat if I'm going to get through the rest of the day. Exhaustion is already creeping in as I think of everything that's left to do. Then again, without much to go home to, the dread I usually feel about having to work late isn't as strong. The walls at home feel darker and colder these past few weeks, every trace of Avery untouched since the breakup. Photos are still everywhere, following me around like ghosts from a past I can't let go of. Romance books still line my shelves, piles of them sitting on my bedroom floor. I still flip through them from time to time, just to remind myself of the times when Avery would sit with me on the bed doing the same. I was usually on my laptop working, with her little gasps when she hit an especially good part or the sound of a marker going across the page as she would underline something as my background noise.

Sometimes I would stop what I was doing to have her read to me the section that gave her that reaction. Sweet parts would bring a smile to her face as she read to me, while the spicy scenes would have her looking at me over the top of the book. We'd get lost in each other, work forgotten as I explored her body, memorizing every curve.

When I close my eyes, I still see her there, trapping me in the memories while the world outside moves on without me.

When I get back to my desk, Trevor sits in the same spot

reading from a textbook. I smile to myself at this small victory that he's here and working, then retake my seat and eat in silence.

The photos on my desk look back at me. One of Avery and me at graduation, caps on our heads and giant smiles on both our faces, the future seeming so bright and unexplored. The next one is all of us at The Grunge after one of my shifts, with those ridiculous pink, sparkly party hats Avery picked out since it was Morgan's birthday. There's a knowing gleam in her eye as she puts one on my head, knowing I would do anything she wanted me to, even wear a ridiculous hat around the bar. My arms are wrapped around the back of her—she fit so perfectly against my chest —with Morgan next to us smiling as Marcus made bunny ears behind her head and Grayson grinning broadly from the other side.

Both photos were gifted to me by Avery on my first day of work. I also added some posters on the wall to help make the place feel more vibrant. Green pillows and throw blankets sit on the couch against the back wall, all of which were also purchased by Avery.

She leaves her touch wherever she goes, and I have been unable to move a single thing since.

When the bell rings, Trevor packs his stuff up and turns to look at me. "Thanks, Mr. D," he says, shyness taking over his features.

"Anytime, Trevor. My door's always open, you know that," I return with a smile and wave as I throw my trash in the bin. He gives a half-hearted wave before he heads out, sauntering down the hallway toward the courtyard—and hopefully, his next class.

I let out a breath and get myself ready for my last appointments of the day.

CHAPTER SEVEN

avery

FOUR YEARS AGO, HIGH SCHOOL

So High School – Taylor Swift

"Hey guys, this is Kane. He's new, so I told him to come sit with us," Marcus says as he saunters up to our usual table in the cafeteria. I quickly look up from my food to see the gorgeous black-haired new kid from my English class staring straight at me, a soft smirk curling his lips. Stunned, I forget to chew my food and start to choke, quickly chugging my water to clear my throat.

"Fuck, are you okay?" Marcus asks, rounding the table to pat me on the back, but I'm stuck staring straight at Kane.

My cheeks heat with embarrassment as I finally clear my throat and mutter, "I'm fine."

Marcus and Kane sit down across from Morgan and me as Marcus says, "This is Avery, and the blonde bombshell on the right is Morgan." Shooting a wink her way, he adds, "Viper, you look good."

A "fuck you" look fills her face, but a blush works its way up her neck. Their teasing has been this way since we met Morgan freshman year, effectively making us a trio.

He's one of my closest friends, given his mother easily took on the role of mother to me when mine couldn't be bothered. He's been a constant in my life since.

Kane's gaze slides back to mine, and my stomach dips as I wait for him to say something. But Marcus, completely oblivious, leans forward and launches into a recap their most recent practice—because, *surprise*, Kane is also on the football team. Apparently, he's the new quarterback, easily replacing the old starting senior. He was recruited his first week here, as if his popularity wasn't already at the top of the charts from the moment he stepped foot in the school two weeks ago. He's dark and broody, with an air of confidence radiating from him. All the girls flocked to him, even more so because he's the first new student we've seen in our grade since sophomore year.

Kane sits with his food in front of him, eating his pizza while laughing at something Marcus said. I catch him stealing glances at me every now and again, forcing me to pretend like I haven't also been staring at him—even though he's caught me too.

I admire the way his tight black T-shirt hugs his upper arms, showcasing his obvious effort in the gym, and the slight curls in his messy black locks that give an effortless, just-rolled-out-of-bed look. It makes him way too hot for his own good.

Eventually, he meets my gaze and we hold eye contact.

"So, Avery," he says, "did you remember to bring me a pencil today?" A smile fills his face as I hit him with my best scowl.

"Wait, you know each other?" Marcus asks.

"Yes, we have English Lit together." Kane finishes off his pizza, and I watch his Adam's apple bob as he swallows.

"Yes, English. Where you need something to write with

every day, Kane," I say, looking at him while I stab my salad too forcefully with my fork. The way he gets under my skin like no one else is infuriating. Every time he drops into the seat behind me in class, chills cover my whole body at his proximity, paired with the unrelenting, pointless questions he tries to ask me until Mr. Adams finally asks us both to be quiet.

"Hey, I've only forgotten a couple times, and thank goodness I have such a great person in front of me to have my back." He winks at me and the butterflies in my stomach take flight, like they do every time he looks at me.

It's a strange and new reaction, given this boy frustrates me more than anyone else I've met. His cocky confidence annoys me as much as it interests me. He walks around as if nothing fazes him. He's not overly friendly, but I've seen him talk to more people this week than I have in three years going here. Not that I've tried that hard, preferring to keep to my small circle, but still.

I roll my eyes. "Or you could come prepared to class like the rest of us. I've lost three pencils so far, and those were my good ones," I snark, having no real comeback. I can never tell if he's flirting with me or trying to piss me off. Maybe both?

"I've never seen you need a pencil," Marcus says to Kane, his brow furrowed in confusion. "And we have three classes together."

A guilty look crosses Kane's face, and I gape at him incredulously. He's always finding little ways to bug me or distract me—always needing something and not listening to what the teacher is saying, forcing us to be partners.

I shake my head, ready to tell him off. But the bell rings, saving him from whatever accusation I was about to hurl at him. What, I'm not sure, and I don't let myself think about it as I sling my backpack—not a stylish choice, but my back thanks me for not lugging around a heavy tote bag all day—over my shoulder.

I'm reaching for my tray when two large hands steal it from me. I look up to find Kane dumping the contents along with his own before returning both trays. He looks back at me when he finishes, a smile tugging at his mouth.

Even more confused, I stalk off, but he quickly joins me, keeping stride beside me. I would normally put my white corded headphones on while I walk to class, preferring to be left alone rather than listen to the constant state of chaos around me, but I don't this time. Instead, Kane and I walk in silence.

I notice him fidgeting with his hands as we walk, something clearly on his mind, but I don't ask. When we get to my class, I turn, ready to ask Kane why he walked me all this way. I'm not sure what his schedule looks like, but I have yet to see him before or after this class. Not that I've checked *that* much—just a *few* times.

Except I don't get a chance to, because he suddenly grabs my arm, pulling me off to the side. He releases my wrist once we're out of the way, allowing students to pass us. Some shoot us a curious look, probably to gossip about later. Going to a smaller school doesn't mean less gossip, it means nothing stays a secret for long.

I stare up at him, a wrinkle between my brows as I wait for him to speak. My gaze drops down to his fingers, spotting four silver rings adorning them. A skull on his right pointer finger, and a silver band with words I can't read from this angle engraved on it on his other thumb.

"Go out with me," Kane finally says.

My eyes shoot up to him, and I stare at him for a couple seconds, an open and honest expression on his face. "What?" I stammer out, confused with the turn of events.

He drives his right hand through his hair, pushing those curls up and making it even messier.

"Go out with me," he repeats. "On a date." A smile graces his face. I hear the bell ringing around us, but neither of us moves, lost in our own little world in the corner of this hallway.

"You want to take me on a date?" I ask, still confused by what's happening. I loop my hands around the straps of my backpack. The heavy weight slowly makes my shoulders ache from carrying it around all day. Suddenly, I regret packing that extra romance book I didn't get around to finishing last night.

"I do. I was thinking maybe some food, or the movies. There's also this arcade I drove past the other day that could be cool Or maybe bowling—I'm not the best, but it could be fun. Or a picnic even, I'm not the biggest fan of the aviary, but I think if we pick a good spot, the geese might leave us alone." It all rushes out of him in one breath. His obvious nerves are evident, giving him a boyish quality popping along his usually severe features.

"I just, uh, would like to take you out. On a date. Get to know you," he adds when I haven't responded, still staring at him. I'm trying to grasp how a guy who looks like *him* wants to take *me* out.

I've always been told I'm too much. Too angry, too sad, too prickly, too in my head all the time. He could have anyone, and he's choosing *me*.

"Okay. Yes," I say, not fully processing the words as they come out. The answer shocks me but the look on his face keeps me from taking it back. My hands are gripping my straps for dear life, as if they can protect me.

The most dazzling smile takes over his whole face. His straight white teeth are on full display and, oh my god, *a dimple*. A perfect dimple on his right cheek, blaring at me, making heat flush up my neck and a small smile grace my lips.

"Really? Okay. Cool, yes," he says excitedly, like he wasn't expecting that answer. "Do you want to have dinner? I mean, we could make it a picnic dinner?" He takes a step closer to me. I'm unsure how long we've been out here, yet I'm in no rush to get to class, content in this space with him.

I release my straps and let my arms and shoulders relax from their tense position. "Yeah. A picnic would be fun." A smile stretches further across my face as the excitement in his shines back at me.

He steps closer, putting us toe-to-toe in the middle of the hallway. His fingers brush my cheek as he catches a stray lock of my hair and tucks it behind my ear, his hand lingering there for a beat.

I feel the ghost of his touch as his eyes track my face. Staring into his warm brown eyes, I can't help but think that this might be something life-changing standing in front of me.

"A picnic," he agrees, his hands dropping to his sides. The hand that pushed my hair back flexes, then he grabs my phone where I hold it between us. After sending a text to himself, he starts to back away from me. He keeps his gaze on me, as if he's physically incapable of turning away, and a shy smile takes over his face as he traces his bottom lip with his thumb. "I think you, pretty girl, might just be the greatest thing about moving here," he adds, scanning my body once more before finally turning and taking the hallway to the right.

I stay stuck staring after him long after he's gone.

CHAPTER EIGHT

NOW

I miss you, I'm sorry – Gracie Abrams

"Honestly whoever said this was a romcom, should really get the book thrown at them," Morgan moans as we walk out of the theater. She tosses her empty gummy straw wrappers and continues to munch on her extra-large popcorn that her and Grayson split.

Any mention of romance has my mind swirling with one thing only—a dark-haired man with eyes that stayed locked on mine.

Marcus let it slip he was at their place and explained his upheaval over the guitar string. It made me snicker to think of how frustrated he must be, but there's also something else layered under there.

Sadness. *Hurt.*

I've always been the first person Kane would tell everything to. Despite knowing I'm not anymore, I can't stop my traitorous heart from wanting to check my messages, hoping he's texted to tell me about it. We'd laugh about how absurd it is, and he'd wonder who could've taken it, knowing it was me.

I shake my head clear as we head home, Marcus and Grayson trailing after Morgan and me then setting themselves up in the living room. My heart pangs at the thought of one missing person that should be here but slowly the banter between Morgan and Marcus distracts me enough that my shoulders loosen a bit. I feel myself relaxing for the first time in a couple weeks.

The exhaustion of the last few weeks seems to be finally hitting me as my eyes start to droop. Laughter fills the room, and the TV blares from the seventh round of Mario Kart, when I decide it's time for me to look after myself. I can't keep going like this—the depression has been clinging to my skin, making every day feel ten times harder.

I grab my phone and request a therapy appointment, knowing I cannot keep this self-destructive pattern of working so hard I have no time to think. This is the first break I've allowed myself in two weeks and it has my body crashing.

I needed a night like tonight—just time spent with my best friends, my chosen family. It helps dull the pain I've been in over the past few weeks. The empty space is still there, all of us aware of who we're missing, but it's less than it has been lately. It's nice to have moments like these, where I don't feel like I might be crushed under the weight of the sadness of missing him.

"C'mon Ave, it's your turn. I've had enough of losing to Marcus for the night," Morgan says as she flings the remote in my lap. Her blonde curls bounce as she gets up and walks into her room.

Marcus laughs from his seat next to me, his big hand covering my knee and giving it a squeeze. The comfort of it makes my eyes get all watery. He looks at me with some sort of understanding. "Yeah Ave, let's go. I could use someone that offers some real competition."

A loud scoff follows from the area Morgan ran off to. A giggle slips out of my mouth at their antics.

From his spot on the floor, Grayson asks, "How is the shelter, Ave? Have you had any new dogs this week?" His demeanor is quiet and steady, helping to settle me. He's such a peaceful force to be around, always there as a shoulder to lean on.

Marcus started bringing Grayson around sophomore year, and he immediately blended into our little family. As the complete opposite to Marcus's chaos, he brings calm to this group. We haven't spent as much time together one-on-one as I have with the others, but I know that if I ever need anything, Grayson will be there without a moment of hesitation.

The week of the breakup, he alternated between sleeping on my couch and Kane's, in case either of us needed him.

"It's been good," I reply. "We've had several, unfortunately. This time of year is always hard, with people dropping off puppies they got as gifts without realizing they actually have to take care of them. We have one, Silver, who's about to have puppies, and she is just the sweetest thing. I wish so badly I could bring her home." I'm wistful as I think about Silver, something about her calls to me. Her eyes hold so much, the deep gray still filled with hope, even after everything she's been through. I'm in awe of how willingly she trusted me, especially knowing she's faced so much abuse and suffering throughout her life.

It never gets easier taking in a dog like Silver. You almost can't imagine giving them up again, but you know you have to because there are always more dogs to look after.

I wish my life wasn't such a mess right now so I could bring one home. It's always been my dream to have a lot of animals at home—Kane and a bunch of dogs were all I needed. But that's why it's called a dream.

I force myself out of that fairytale, focusing back on Grayson. He gives me a sad smile, like he knows exactly where my mind drifted.

"I would love to come by sometime," Grayson says. "I've actually been thinking about maybe adopting a dog. I've always wanted one, and it might be nice to have something to come home to." He scratches the back of his neck, a flush filling his cheeks as if he's embarrassed.

"Of course!" I reply excitedly. "You should come by tomorrow. I would love to show you around. We have a lot of animals right now. We're actually hosting a fundraiser in a month—Sharlene wants to go all out and do a fancy gala to try to bring in some extra funds. Dinner would be included in the ticket price, and we're hoping to get some physical donations from local businesses so we can have an auction."

A broad smile spreads across my face as I think of all the plans that have been slowly coming together. This gala is something we just came up with, and it's given me something fun to work on at the end of each day. The amount of support we already have from the community is astounding.

"Well, sign me up for a plate, Ave. I would love to come," Grayson replies.

Morgan walks back into the room, dramatically stomping her feet before stopping in front of me and bracing her hands on her hips. "Hey, what about me? I want to come too! Put my parents and me down, and I'll make sure their calendars are free that night." She squeezes in next to me on the couch, practically forcing me into both her and Marcus's laps.

"Why wasn't I invited?" Marcus pouts, getting up from the too-small sofa and moving to sit in the reading chair closer to the TV.

"It's a gala, Marcus," Morgan states, rolling her eyes. "You'd have to actually dress up and act like a man, which is impossible for you."

"Oh, I can show you just how much of a man I am, since you're still doubting me," Marcus quips with a wink, hands moving to his belt as he stands again.

"Dear god, Marcus, do not drop your pants right now!" Morgan shouts as she rises from her seat. Her arms are crossed over her chest, fire burning in her gaze as she stares at Marcus. Grayson and I share a look, both of us fighting back a laugh.

Marcus mirrors Morgan, his laugh cocky as he adds, "You keep testing me, sweetheart. Part of me is starting to think you actually want to see what I'm working with."

"Please," Morgan scoffs. "As if I want to catch any diseases you're carrying around. You should come with a warning label." She retakes her seat, turning to face the TV. Her stare remains furious, but the red flush in her cheeks suggests she's anything but.

"All right, children," I start. "Please, Marcus, sit down. No one here wants to see your dick. Can we please just play the game? I want to see how many races I have to win before Marcus starts to cry."

I lean down and grab the controller off the coffee table before I sit back on the couch and watch as we all play the game, letting the sounds of my friends bickering and bantering keep the sadness at bay for just a little bit longer.

"AND HOW DOES that make you feel?" Susan asks from her warm brown chair, writing something down in her notebook after the joke I just made. I hope she plans on using it later —I'm pulling out all my best material today.

"You know, if you don't start laughing at my jokes, I'm going to start taking it personally," I deflect, laughing. It was silly of me to think I could just drop the Kane bomb and move on without her questioning it. I twirl my fingers in my lap, my palms beginning to sweat as the itch I felt in my spine when I first walked in here returns.

I glance around Susan's office to the crisp beige walls, lightly decorated in a modern boho style, with warm browns and rustic orange accents. The carpet is plush under my feet, with a long coffee table separating me from Susan, where she sits in her preferred chair.

I grab the ruffled orange pillow from my side and place it on my lap, like a shield that can somehow block the emotions threatening to spill out of me.

When I look back up at Susan, her expression is unchanged as she waits for me to answer her question.

"Shitty, Susan. Really shitty," I finally admit, clearing my throat to prevent the tears that threaten. "I just wanted someone to fight for me for once, and he didn't."

"Have you two talked since the breakup?"

"No, and he hasn't tried," I reply.

"Have you?"

"No," I reply honestly, then add, "And why should I? Why does it have to be me? I asked him for weeks what was wrong, and he always said nothing. But I *know* him. I spent four years dealing with him pushing me away for days or weeks at a time, only to pull me close again right after. He'd insist everything was fine, that he didn't want to talk, and I'd give him his space until he was ready, and he always came back. But *I* needed him. I was already worried about our future, and I needed his reassurance that everything would be okay. That it would work out. But he couldn't give me that."

The words spill out of me before I can stop them, and so do a few stray tears. I brush them away quickly as Susan summarizes, "So you ran away before he could hurt you."

"Maybe," I admit, picking at the strings on the pillow. I feel vulnerable under Susan's watchful gaze, knowing she's waiting for me to say more. "I just want someone who will fight for *me*. To show me I'm worth it. All my life, I feel like I've had to beg to be seen, to be loved. I've been surrounded by people that can't bother to look away from themselves. And when I finally let myself be vulnerable with Kane, he shut me out."

"Which made you feel neglected and reaffirmed your core belief that you aren't good enough for anyone to stick around for," Susan says in her therapist talk.

I clear my throat again, trying to dislodge the lump. "Yes, I was scared. He was the only person who's ever made me feel like I deserve to be loved, but when I needed it most, he couldn't do it for me." I finally lift my gaze to meet Susan's. Her brown hair is thrown up in a bun, her hands in her lap. The pen in her hand rests above her notebook, but she doesn't write anything else down. She just lets me sit in these feelings.

For weeks, I have been shoving this all down, hoping that if I didn't let it show, it would go away on its own. But there's this ever-present feeling of never quite being good enough that stays in the back of my mind. That's what happens when you're raised by parents who are more interested in themselves than the daughter they obviously never wanted. I was never their priority when I was growing up, and I'm still not.

"I'm very proud of you for coming today, Avery, and for opening up about this. I know it's not easy for you, but it has clearly been weighing on you over the past month," Susan starts, shifting her legs with her pen in hand. "But, we've also talked about how not everyone is your parents. When you decided to go no contact with them, I was very proud of you for making that decision for yourself. To let yourself feel good enough for you and not worry about them anymore. But you need to extend that into other parts of your life too. So, this week, I want to focus on you. What do *you* want to do next? Do you *want* to continue to let what others do affect how you view yourself?"

Going no contact with my parents is something I've been working toward for the past two years I've been seeing Susan, the catalyst of which was that they have never shown up for a single event in my life. My constant panic attacks through college forced me to finally find a therapist to talk to so I didn't flunk out.

That's when I met Susan, and I have been seeing her regularly ever since. Together, we determined that my anxiety spiral in college was a result of unresolved issues from childhood. The feeling of never being good enough, of feeling like I had to act a certain way for people to care about me, of feeling like if I wasn't succeeding or being useful in some way, there was no reason to love me, all stemmed from having parents who didn't care about me. They were always gone, either off on a trip or checked out at home, never bothering to check up on me. As soon as I was old enough to stay home alone, they'd leave for weeks or sometimes months at a time, and even when they were home, I could never get their attention. I spent more time at Marcus's house than I ever did at my own, his mother becoming a maternal figure for me in a way mine never did.

I realized a year ago that I was never going to heal if I kept them in my life and let them hurt me time and time again. That I had to remove myself to be able to figure out who I was without their voices in my head. It's been a hard year without them, but there isn't much for me to miss in the first place. I've mostly just mourned who I wanted them to be, and the hope that maybe one day they would change and become the parents I needed. Some days I still miss them, or who I want them to be, but it's gotten easier. Especially with my friends and Kane always reminding me that I don't need that, of how good I am on my own. It's made losing Kane that much harder.

On that note, we end the session. I say goodbye to Susan then make my way to my car. By the time I reach it, my eyes have dried, but when I look in the rearview mirror, I notice they're still red and my face is slightly puffy. I pull down my visor to fix my makeup, finding the photo of Kane and me that I still haven't gotten rid of.

I steel myself, rubbing a finger under my eyes to wipe away the running mascara. Enough of my makeup survived that I can head straight to work, and I think I'll even treat myself to an iced coffee. One thing I've learned is that on the really hard days, I get to treat myself to something sweet —because I made it to therapy, and most days, just showing up is the hardest part.

On my drive to work, Susan's words replay in my mind, reminding me how, for my whole life, I've let other people's words and actions define who I am, instead of figuring it out for myself.

I don't want to be a person who doesn't do anything in life out of fear that I won't be enough. Life is about failure and about trying something without worrying about whether you'll succeed. But I've been too scared to do that, and I realize now just how little life I've lived because of it.

I no longer want that to stop me.

As I pull up to Second Chances, I spot Kane's big black truck in the parking lot with him loitering next to it, and my stomach sinks. My tongue gets stuck in my throat as I stare at the man who has haunted my dreams.

He has his phone up to his ear, frustration evident on his face. His dark hair gleams in the light of the fading sun, the gentle wind ruffling it the way my fingers used to. I can still feel the ghost of his hair in my hands, still picture the way his eyes would close as he'd lean into me. It fills me with a small sense of calm, the same way it used to, before a sharp pang stabs through me, remembering that I can't do that anymore.

My heart skips a beat as his gaze shoots my way. I duck down to hide from his view, despite my car being wedged between two larger vehicles. I hear a vehicle start, and when I look up and see his truck pull out of the lot, I let out the breath I hadn't even realized I'd been holding.

CHAPTER NINE

avery

Landslide – Fleetwood Mac

"Ave, I really hate to be the voice of reason, but are we sure this is worth a breaking and entering charge? I mean, I have bail money, but I did not wear the right outfit to wear for the clink," Morgan says from behind me as I press the unlock button on Kane's spare set of keys.

"We won't get arrested—I have a key. It wouldn't be breaking, just entering."

"A key that Kane doesn't even know you took! This feels like a bad episode of *Cops* waiting to happen," she mumbles. She's dressed in a *Charlie's Angels*-esque spandex suit that she, for some reason, already owned, with her hair pulled into a tight ponytail.

"That's beside the point. I had a key to get into the apartment to get the spare truck key. They don't need to know that I didn't ask for permission. And it's not like we're going to damage anything—I just need to jam his radio so it's stuck on one station." I pray to whoever is listening that I follow the tutorial correctly and don't accidentally blow the whole thing up. With my luck, I'll cross some random wires, and suddenly the truck will only go in reverse.

I laugh at that mental image while I jimmy the radio out. I thank the higher ups that Kane decided to get an older model truck after he sold the Audi his dad had bought him, which means this should be a fairly simple, yet hilarious, prank. Though, I don't think I have the ability to pick the station, so I hope the one it gets stuck on is worth it.

After completing all the steps from the video, I lower myself from the truck. Morgan is standing next to the truck scrolling on her phone.

"I thought you were supposed to be my lookout," I say while locking the doors.

"It's 2 p.m., in broad daylight. If someone was going to see it, I couldn't have stopped them." She slides her phone back in her pocket. "So, what now?" Morgan asks, wiggling her eyebrows at me. "Do you feel satisfied yet? Are you ready to be a mature adult and have a grown-up conversation with him?"

I turn, walking back to the townhouse to return his key before Dumb or Dumber get back. Marcus told me that he and Kane were going for an early lunch with Grayson before his game later, so I knew both the place and Kane's truck would be empty and available for me to pull off my second prank.

"I am being a perfectly reasonable adult and handling my problems as anyone in my situation would," I reply with my nose in the air, ignoring her suggestion to talk to him.

"I'm not sure I like this side of you. My Avery is kind and sweet and usually the one reining me in. I'm not meant to be the rational one," Morgan replies half-heartedly as we get back in her car after returning the key. It's a small, white car that cost more than our entire house probably does.

The McIntyres have more money than God, with Morgan's father owning several high-rises in the city. I grew up in an upper-middle-class family, but compared to the McIntyres, we were penniless. But Morgan sat down next to me in ninth grade English, and that was it. We've been partners in crime ever since.

She's the blonde sunshine to my dark and broody brunette. She balances me out perfectly with her extroverted ways, always convincing me to leave my shell and try new things. Morgan is always out and about, meeting new people, off on some adventure, which is something I've always envied about her.

But as her best friend, I also know her effortless air is mostly an act. She may not open up much, even with me, but I know she's been through more than she lets on.

My gaze lands on her as she drives down the expressway to drop me off at work. The wind blows through the windows, sending our hair flying, and we both laugh, singing along to Morgan's "party girl" playlist that I made for her last month, which is full of all her favorites. The sunglasses on her face were a Christmas gift from her family, some luxury brand I've never heard of. I let myself enjoy the moment, the music, the sun and the wind, all my problems disappearing for a little bit.

Work has been chaotic since I walked in. We had a meet-and-greet today in hopes that it would draw more people in and get more animals adopted, or at least just taken home for a night. Studies show that even one night out of the shelter, in a quiet environment, can do wonders for a dog's spirit. All the noises in the shelter can be overstimulating, which results in a lot of dogs being more withdrawn and scared, and therefore, it's harder to get them adopted.

We try to host these events often, and with the traction we've been gaining on social media, fifty-six dogs are out for the night. It makes for a lot of paperwork for me, but I'll gladly do it if it means even one of those dogs gets adopted.

I'm hours deep into paperwork before I finally take a break. I head to the back to make my rounds before heading home for the night, and that's when I hear it. A soft voice flows from the back, one I could recognize anywhere and listen to forever. It's deep and husky, rolling over me like black smoke as he sings. The soft song pulls me toward the kennels, until I reach Silver's.

Kane sits with a guitar in his lap, his back to me and his legs spread out in front of him. Silver's head rests on his knee, her eyes closed and her breathing steady, while her puppies sleep beside her—just a few days old and as cute as can be—as he strums the tune of "Landslide" by Fleetwood Mac. I take a moment to drink him in, admiring his long legs and toned arms holding the guitar. It's the same one he's always had, which means he must have replaced the string I took. His voice makes me melt instantly, sending a shiver down my spine and goosebumps breaking out over my arms.

I could listen to him play forever, something I didn't realize how much I missed until this moment, when I'm struck with an aching hollowness. As if something fundamental has been taken from me, a phantom limb or the oxygen I breathe. I lean against a post as he finishes the song, the words bringing tears to my eyes as I realize that this is another one he learned for me.

He would play it for me on my bad days—when the demons were too strong and getting out of bed seemed impossible. He would grab that guitar and sing to me, until I either cracked a smile and got up, or made room in my bed for him to hide away with me.

Silver cracks open her eyes as the song comes to an end, and that's when she spots me. She immediately gets up from his lap, moving toward me, her adorable tail wagging. Excited whimpers escape her as I make my way to her, and I hear a sharp intake of breath come from Kane when he realizes who she's giving this reaction to.

I keep my eyes locked on Silver as I unlatch the door and let her greet me. Trying to keep her from jumping or getting too excited, since it's only been a few days since she gave birth, I get down on one knee and let her kiss my face.

"I know, I know, Mama. You got your own little concert tonight," I say, scratching her face until she gently lays on her back, belly-up so I can rub her there too. A soft laugh leaves me, making me brave enough to look up at the man standing over us.

I suck in a breath as my eyes reach his face, his gaze on me and Silver. His expression is so soft, I almost want to burst into tears over how much I've missed him. His eyes meet mine, and I see it then—the dark circles beneath them, their sparkle dimmed, and the gaunt of his cheeks, sharper than it was a month ago. The changes would be subtle to anyone else, but I've spent the past four years studying every inch of this man, and I can tell he's not been as unaffected as I had previously thought.

The thought causes a flurry of sadness to erupt in my chest. The urge to hold him, even just for a moment, is so strong, I need to stop myself from jumping up and letting him catch me again.

For a moment, we're locked in each other's gaze. The

silence stretches, until Silver yips from the lack of attention she is getting from us.

I turn away from Kane to give her more pets, and he finally breaks the silence.

"Sorry, I didn't realize how late it had gotten." He scratches his head, his eyes on Silver now.

"It's okay. I was supposed to be gone hours ago, but..." I trail off. He already knows how easy I get lost in my work here. There were many dates and dinners waiting for me to pick up my phone and realize I was running late. But Kane never complained, always greeting me with a smile, no matter how much time got away from me.

He lets out a soft chuckle, a tiny smile gracing his face. His little dimple is barely visible, but still enough to send my heart tripping over itself.

I take in the rest of him while I pet Silver, lavishing her with the attention she craves. His big frame eats up the small kennel we're in, his black Henley stretched across his chest and arms, hiding his tattoos. I feel greedy as I admire the tightness of his shirt and the way his hands grip the guitar, sending a flush to my cheeks as a flash of other things he's gripped like that hits me.

I shake my head as I remember him and that blonde at The Grunge a week ago. The butterflies in my stomach vanish, my anger from that moment resurfacing.

"Ave—" he starts, uncertainty in his voice, but I cut him off.

"We really don't need to do this," I tell him, standing to face him. Seeming to notice the tension, Silver moves back to lie with her puppies. "We can coexist in the same space and just pretend the other person isn't there." I cross my arms over my chest, as if they can shield me from him as my frustration grows.

A look of confusion crosses his face, his brows dipping as the corners of his mouth turn down. I force my gaze away from them, not needing or wanting the reminder of how soft his lips always were.

"Is that really what you want?" he asks, putting his mask back in place. His expression shifts to one of indifference, as if we're discussing a grocery list. Though his knuckles wrapped around his guitar are nearly white, like it's his lifeline.

"Yeah, Kane. It is."

"Noted," he murmurs softly. "Excuse me."

He slides past me, walking back up the row of kennels. His long strides eat up the distance, not once looking back at me as he leaves.

Defeated, I slide down the chain-link fence, placing my head between my knees. I take deep breaths, willing the tears not to fall, but when the door from the kennels to the lobby slams shut, I stop fighting them. I let my tears consume me, until a wet nose hits my hand.

When I glance up, Silver sits in front of me, looking at me expectantly with her tongue hanging out. I brush her ears back, using her soft fur and gentle presence to ground myself, giving me some relief from the pain that makes me feel like I'm choking.

CHAPTER TEN

kane

when was it over? – Sasha Alex Sloan (ft. Sam Hunt)

Did I piss off some higher power and this is my punishment?

First, I wake up late for my shift, spill half my coffee on the way out to my truck, and then discover that the radio is jammed on the most irritating station. I mean, it must be a joke that someone who has dubbed himself *Alpha Adam* has a radio show where like-minded idiots call in to complain about why women don't deserve them and everything they bring to the table. I listened to his grating voice for a total of thirty-four minutes—*yes*, I counted—before determining that I'm officially living in my own personal version of hell and turn the radio off. I'm unable to drive in silence and risk my own suffocating thoughts, but I'm really not sure which is worse to face this morning.

It's only made my already foul mood—the one I've been sporting since running into Avery last night at Second Chances for the first time since the breakup—even worse, like a dark cloud hanging over me. I was up all night tossing and turning, replaying every moment of our conversation and trying to figure out why she switched up so quickly.

She had been smiling. *At me.* It felt like a good sign, like maybe after some time apart she was ready to talk. I was about to ask her if we could at least plan a time to have a conversation when she did a complete one-eighty, switching from joy to anger. I still haven't figured out why.

Now, the angel herself is walking into the bar on my first shift back after two weeks. Part of me wonders if she knows it's my first night back, but knowing Avery, she wouldn't have come if she did. She's avoided every place we might run into each other since the breakup—even going as far as to kick me off her music playlists, leading me to find her profile so I can keep up with all the new songs she's listening to and learn them on guitar.

How pathetic of me to resort to some light stalking just for more of her.

After what she said last night, I can't imagine she'd be here if she knew. But of course, here she is anyway, looking like my fucking wet dream in skintight pants and an intricate top that reveals a strip of her smooth stomach. A dream I've had every night since she left, slowly torturing me with the reminder of what I've lost.

I turn around, readjusting myself in my pants before someone notices and calls the cops for public indecency. Apparently, even seeing a glimpse of her stomach nowadays makes me hard, though I shouldn't be surprised given that just being around her left me constantly aching when we were together. It was a test of my willpower, trying to avoid locking her in the closest room and having my way with her constantly.

Ever since the first time I saw Avery senior year, I

haven't been able to look away. I don't see that changing now.

Her brown hair is impossibly long and straight, practically reaching her perfectly round, toned ass, and her makeup is slightly heavier than her usual everyday look, though she still wears her signature all-black outfit.

I watch out of the corner of my eye as Morgan and Avery take a seat near the dartboards and pool tables to the left side of the bar. Of course, every man in here has already spotted them, appearing to call dibs around their respective friend groups. My fists clench at my side.

Unable to look at Avery for a second longer without storming over there and demanding she talk to me, I pop my knuckles to release some of the tension, then turn to grab the Tito's, only to run into Lindsay.

"Geez, giganto. Just because you're three feet taller than the rest of us doesn't mean you can walk around without looking. You ought to look down occasionally to make sure you don't run over us bottom dwellers," she jokes.

I swear under my breath, hoping the commotion doesn't draw Avery's attention this way. I don't want to break my cover of getting to watch her without her knowing yet.

"Hey, Kane, what's wrong? Why do you seem broodier than usual?" Lindsay asks. "I didn't even think that was possible. You've definitely held the title of King Brood of all my friends thus far, but this seems abnormal for your normal..."

Lindsay follows my gaze toward Avery, who thankfully still seems unaware I'm here. When I look back down at her, an unnerving smirk spreads across Lindsay's face. I roll my eyes and pretend I didn't hear her comment. She needles me constantly and I pretend to hate it, but she's starting to feel like the sister I never got to have.

When I don't respond, she continues, "So that's the girlfriend, huh? Pretty. Too pretty for you, that's for sure."

"Ex," I mumble, turning back to my task at hand—a vodka soda and two vodka Red Bulls—before they're whisked away by one of our servers.

"Ex?" Lindsay scoffs. "With the way you're mooning over that girl, are you sure you know you're her ex?" She leans next to me on the bar, clearly loving the way my skin is crawling with this conversation. "Matter of fact, does she know she's yours? Because with the way she's been watching you every time you turn around, I can practically smell the angst from here."

My body stills. I guess Avery has spotted me, then.

Fuck.

"Yes, ex. It's recent," I clarify, not making eye contact. I continue filling orders as they come in, hoping she gets the hint that I don't want to talk about this anymore.

"Recent." She lets out a low a whistle. "So, you were checking your messages the other night and not secretly watching porn under the table? I will say, I'm very happy about this revelation. I was worried. My brother had a porn addiction, and it was scary. I mean, who wants to listen to moans over waffles?"

"Lindsay," I say, exasperated as I put the finishing touches on the drinks, adding a little bit of extra lemon to the Coke and vodka before getting Grayson's draft beer.

"Right, okay. So, she's your ex. Why'd you break up?" Lindsay prods.

"I don't know."

Lindsay narrows her eyes. "What do you mean you don't know? You have an ex that you're clearly obsessed with. But you don't know *why* she's your ex?"

"No," I grunt. She rubs two fingers against her temples,

as if I'm a child who won't listen the first time I'm asked to do something and she's already sick of me.

"This is why I'm a fucking lesbian," she mutters under her breath. "Okay, so here's what you're going to do. The blonde one ordered drinks. I think you should take them over there." Lindsay hands me a tray.

"I made their drinks before she even ordered," I mutter, placing the drinks on the tray. I hold it out to Lindsay, silently letting her know I'm not delivering them.

"Oh no, I'm not doing your dirty work," she says, waving me away.

I freeze, tray in hand, and ask, "What the fuck do you mean?"

"Put your big-boy pants on and go deliver drinks to your *ex* and your friends. Maybe by the time you get to their table, you'll learn what words are and how to fucking use them, dumbass." She moves toward the back of the bar, effectively stopping any rebuttal I might have had.

I guess I'm delivering these drinks.

To Avery.

CHAPTER ELEVEN

avery

right where you left me – Taylor Swift

Oh my god, he's coming over.

Of course.

As if today hasn't thrown enough in my path, apparently it decided that a night out for a little distraction would lead to yet another encounter with my past. Which also means I'll be drinking extra to forget the way I had to fight not to gasp the moment our eyes finally locked. I hadn't realized he would be working tonight, but after the heinous day at work, I needed a drink, desperately.

He looks good. I mean, he always did—*does*. His hair is messy in the way that suggests his fingers have been combing through it. His standard black T-shirt stretches tight across the chest I've slept on more times than my own pillow, putting the beautiful art covering his thick biceps and veiny forearms on full display. His dark jeans strain against his thighs as he eats up the distance between us way faster than I'm prepared for.

I smooth my hair away from my face, nervously twisting the strands.

After our encounter last night, I'm not sure how to act. I know I was harsh, but all I could see was him and that blonde, the way they looked together, and it hurt.

It *still* hurts.

I look down, taking a deep breath and readying myself as he approaches the table.

"Hey."

His smoky voice floats over to me, reminding me of the first time he spoke to me—as the kid who was dropped into our tiny town in his senior year of high school and sat behind me in English.

"Your drinks," he states, pulling me back to the present. He looks away as soon as my eyes meet his, setting the drinks on the table. He places the beer in front of Grayson before sliding mine across to me, already knowing which drink was mine given he made it for me every time we came to this exact place. Either while I watched him working or out with our friends when he'd come behind me wherever we sat, wrapping his arms around my shoulders and letting me use him as a backrest for however long I sat there.

"Kane!" Morgan shouts. "What a coincidence. We were just talking about you."

I shoot daggers at her, wondering what in the world she's talking about. I mean, we *were* just talking about him, but *he* did not need to know that.

Grayson looks at me with a faint guilty expression before his eyes drift over at one of the TV hosting some sports game.

I grab my drink, shoving the straw between my lips as I look up, finding Kane's eyes staring at my mouth. When he notices my gaze fixed on him, he quickly looks away, red rising to the apples of his cheeks.

"You were?" he asks, looking a little spooked.

"Yes, see Avery and I are swamped. I'm talking so busy, blah blah blah, and unfortunately today our dishwasher broke. I was going to call a plumber but then Avery remembered the last time you fixed it. And I was saying that a great way to save money would be to see if you could come look at it again." Morgan lays it on thick with Kane, refusing to look at me as she speaks.

A laugh comes from across the circle table before Grayson tries to cover it with a cough into his fist. I throw a scowl in his direction before placing my look back at Morgan.

I had no idea our dishwasher was broken, so this is news to me. Truthfully, I really would not put it past her to have broken it herself, just to shove Kane and me in a room together.

I kick her shin under the table to get her attention. I'm impressed when she barely flinches, still refusing to look at me.

"I, uh—" Kane stammers.

"Morgan, it's fine. We can just call someone. I'm sure—" I start, but Kane cuts me off.

"No."

I blink at him.

"I can come check it out tomorrow." His voice carries a nervous lilt as he looks at me like we're the only two people in the bar.

I know if I told him not to, he'd listen. He's always been so good at reading me, better than anyone else. I always said he was psychic, but he insisted he just paid attention and that all he had to do was look at me to know what I was feeling—claiming that he categorized all my facial expressions with how often he stared at me. If he sensed that I didn't want him there, he would make an excuse not to come.

But I *do* want him there.

Pain shoots up my leg as Morgan kicks me under the table. Another snicker slips out of Grayson before a sharp *ow* and a look to Morgan follows.

"Uh no, that would be great if you could, thanks," I stammer out, ignoring their antics around me.

Kane, coming over.

To our place.

After I just told him we should avoid each other.

Yeah, I'm totally going to throw up in the bathroom thinking about this later.

"Okay," he says, his face brightening for the first time since he walked over and warmth flickering back into his eyes twinkling under the warm bar lights. "Okay, cool. Well, I'll, uh, text you and see what the best time is?" he asks, still looking at me.

"Perfect, thanks Kane! Ugh, you're so sweet and such a lifesaver," Morgan replies as my brain scrambles for something to say.

"Okay, well I need to get back, our new hire is still being trained so..." he slowly trails off while starting to walk backwards, eyes lingering on me.

I nod, then with one last glance and soft smile my way, he turns and starts heading back toward the bar. I don't miss the way he looks back at me every so often though, almost as if what just happened was all just a dream.

When he's out of sight and occupied again, I turn sharply to Morgan as she sips on her drink, innocently scrolling on her phone.

"There's a fucking code, Morgan Belle McIntyre. What the fuck wrong with you?" I lean closer to her so we're not overheard.

"What? Our dishwasher is broken. I don't think I was supposed to put that much soap in this morning." A glint in her eye as she speaks.

"You're dead to me."

"I hate when mom and dad fight," Grayson chimes in, grabbing his beer and taking a big gulp as he looks at the dinner menu.

LATER, when Kane is no longer standing behind the bar, I brace myself to go order another drink. Morgan and Grayson are playing pool with a group of guys from North Chester University. They tried to get me to join, but the guy flirting with me finally got the hint that I'm not interested, giving me space to breathe.

Striding up to the counter, I take the first seat I can find. My feet ache, making me regret the choice to wear my new boots that I bought after a late-night doom scroll trying to ignore my feelings. They made the girl who posted them look so powerful, and I wanted to manifest some of that power for myself. The *you may see your ex but you have these killer boots and you're unaffected by his stupidly handsome face* power, that I'm not sure I'm channeling. Instead, I'm just giving *sad, grumpy girl in black checkered Doc Martens and skinny jeans*. Which, unfortunately, would not be wrong.

I sit on the stool and pick at a napkin in front of me, trying to release some of this anxious energy that has had its hold on me since I walked into The Grunge tonight. Soft music plays overhead since it's still early, and the dinner crowd hasn't quite left yet. I get lost in the melody of a man unable to move on from a lost love, feeling my heart tug a bit. I glance around at all the couples mingling in the back booths, noticing how half of them appear oblivious to the crowded bar around them—the same way I used to feel with Kane.

Before I can sink too far into that feeling, I face the bar again. "Hey there, can I get a Coke and vodka with lemon?" I ask the blonde bartender whose back is turned to me.

When she turns around, I suck in a sharp breath. It's the girl I saw Kane with.

Of course he'd be fucking someone from work. The bitterness that runs through me shakes me.

"Of course. Oh hey!" she exclaims. "You're Kane's *ex*, right? I'm Lindsay." She leans her elbow on the black bar top, making sure to put an extra emphasis on the word ex, which confuses me.

"Uh, yes. Why?" I reply hesitantly. The last thing I want is to be that ex who creates drama with the new girl, but I don't know how long I can pretend to be nice if this is some sort of *look what I have now*.

"Oh, you know, since Kane is so talkative he obviously told me all his deepest darkest secrets," she says, loaded with sarcasm, then adds, "Kidding. I saw him mooning over you and basically had to torture the truth out of him. You'd think I was trying to get nuclear codes out of him or something." She chuckles, and my confusion grows. She seems carefree for someone who caught her new guy staring at his ex.

"I'm surprised he said more than five words to you at once, he's not really much for talking," I reply, wondering if this new drink was worth it. She mixes the perfect amount of vodka to Coke, which is even more impressive considering she isn't even looking at the drink she's making.

She looks effortlessly chic in her deep maroon jumpsuit and platform Converses, because of course, she has that cool-girl vibe without even trying. Her bracelets jingle against the counter as she works.

I look down at myself, wondering why it doesn't feel so effortless for me, as she laughs like we're sharing an inside joke. She stirs the drink lightly and pours it into a glass, adding the squeeze of lemon before sliding it my way.

"Oh yeah, I couldn't get him to shut up," she replies with a wink.

My hackles rise with how she talks about him, jealousy settling low in my stomach as I take a sip of the perfectly made drink. Damn, I really wanted it to suck so I could have a valid reason to hate her, but I chastise myself with how unfair that would be of me—it isn't her fault.

"I remember telling my girlfriend that I was a little worried he couldn't speak at first. When he offered to show me where a good place to eat was, part of me thought he was going to lure me to his van." She chuckles as she leans onto the counter toward me. I startle in slight confusion.

My brow furrows, catching on to what she said at the beginning. *Girlfriend?*

She continues, "When we got to this little hole in the wall place, where different types of macaroni were the only thing to eat, he got quiet again. Naturally I filled the silence, and I think he wanted to crawl out of his skin." She laughs, and I feel a chuckle bubble up as I picture Kane sitting there eating their buffalo mac—because he's a creature of habit—playing with the end of his sleeve, like he does when he's out of his element.

"I—uh...yeah, that sounds exactly like Kane. Did you say girlfriend?" I question, trying not to make it obvious that she'll make or break me with her relationship status.

"Yes, Claire! She came to meet us at the bar afterward. We moved down here for Claire's new job, so finding this gig was a godsend for me. I worked at a bar back home while doing freelance during the day and I hoped to find something like that again." She busies herself with the few drink orders she's gotten while we've been talking.

Relief floods through me as I sip my drink, now more than half gone without me even thinking about it. I should really slow it down as I can already feel the world spinning a bit. The one thing I've always been made fun of in the group is how much of a lightweight I am.

She must see something on my face, because the next second she's putting down the shaker and staring directly at me. "Wait, don't tell me you thought Kane and I were together?" she inquires, leaving the question open.

"Well..." I start, unsure what to say next. "I saw you guys here and just...well, kind of"—I take a breath, placing my now-empty glass on the countertop between us, playing with the straw and ice—"assumed, I guess. I mean, I told you Kane isn't really a talker, even with some of our best friends. So, when I saw him with you, laughing, I guess my brain just jumped there."

She seems to sense the unease coming off of me as she slides a new drink in front of me and takes away the old one. "Oh my god, no. He feels like a little brother already. And truly, penises do not impress me. I tried once, obviously, just to make sure, but when he whipped it out, I screamed a little and called my mom to pick me up. Kind of solidified to me that I am purely a woman-only type of gay." She chuckles, as if she's remembering this exact memory in her mind.

"That is...good news. That is, wow," I ponder, feeling more drunk than I thought. I make a move for my wallet to pay for the drinks she gave me when she stops me.

"Oh no, don't worry about it." She waves my card away. "Kane said to put all your stuff under him. If I took money from you, I'd have to deal with even more of his brooding than usual." She grabs the dirty glasses and turns to take them to the back, but before she leaves, she adds, "It was great to meet you, Avery. I really hope this isn't the last time we see each other," Lindsay says, a soft look of sincerity on her face.

I smile, then stand from the lowered black stool I've been sitting on, ruminating on why Kane would still cover my drinks. I stumble a little bit as I head back to Morgan and Grayson, clearly not missing me as they're still talking to the same white-collar, clean-cut frat boys. Grayson is having some debate with one of them about our local baseball team and their newest pitcher. I never thought I had a type, but staring at these guys, I miss arms covered in ink and unruly hair that never seems to have one set style.

I slide back into my abandoned chair, noticing the world starts spinning a bit more. That doesn't stop me from taking one of the shots the boys put in front of us, though. I shoot one back, and before I know it, three are gone and all thoughts of Kane finally go quiet in my head, the feeling of warmth flooding my veins.

CHAPTER TWELVE

kane

FOUR YEARS AGO, HIGH SCHOOL

Tripping Over Air – Aiden Bissett

I pull up to the address Avery gave me and take a second to breathe, my hands still gripping the steering wheel. When it becomes clear my heart rate isn't settling down anytime soon, I wipe my sweaty palms on my jeans and turn to look at the wicker picnic basket in the back seat my mother foisted at me when I mentioned the date, full to the brim with snacks and sandwiches. I wasn't sure what Avery likes, so I basically just grabbed one of everything—some sweet, some spicy—and I worry I may have gone overboard. The lady at the grocery looked from me to my items before shaking her head and scanning them all.

That's when I realized I might be freaking out a bit. My mind is full of the curve of her smile when I reminded her our date was this weekend. I blacked out at the sight, and somehow, I ended up grabbing spray cheese for the strawberries and some black licorice instead of the red ones I've seen her munch on at lunches occasionally, not that I've been looking too hard.

Who am I kidding? My eyes are magnets finding her in any crowd so far, even a particularly fun time when she was bent over her desk and I had to avert my gaze before my dick got too excited.

I laugh to myself. My stomach feels like an explosion of butterflies went off, and my heart has been racing since I woke up this morning. This feeling is so unfamiliar that I googled the symptoms of a heart attack before I left, just to make sure.

Opting for the front door instead of texting Avery that I'm here, I take a deep breath, then haul myself out of my sleek black Audi. The car is so ostentatious, I wince a little at the thought of Avery seeing it. My dad got it for me the last time we moved, right before my sixteenth birthday. It was his way of keeping me quiet and compliant, and unfortunately, I needed a car. Which means I'm stuck playing nice until I can make my own money and free myself from his strings.

I push my fingers through my hair and smooth down my shirt as I walk up to the brown brick house. It's bigger than it appears from the drive up, with trimmed landscape and freshly cut grass. Rust-colored leaves fall on the sidewalk with the autumn breeze blowing in.

I make my way up the long walkway and the stairs that lead to the red front door. It feels huge, looming over me as I take another breath and knock. I fiddle with the bouquet of light pink flowers in my hands, now feeling a little ridiculous for grabbing them when I was shopping for food. The peonies—at least that's what the sign in the store said they were—instantly made me think of her. The beauty of them struck me in the same manner Avery's has. My heart rate accelerates with the sound of footsteps coming closer on the other side. My ears start pounding, and the back of my neck feels hot as I wait for the door to open.

When it finally does, I'm blinded by the sight of her.

Her long hair is pulled back away from her face in the front, long strands disappearing behind her shoulders down her back. I'm struck dumb by her blue eyes as they take me in. Her makeup seems heavier than usual, her pouty lips painted a deep red, and all I can think about is what they taste like. She's wearing blue skintight jeans with holes in the knees, showing off every inch and curve of her legs, with a red top to match her lips and a leather jacket thrown over top.

The groan that rises up in the back of my throat threatens to spill over as I stare at her, at a loss for words.

What does someone say when faced with their biggest fantasy, only to realize it's becoming their greatest weakness?

"For you," I say, thrusting the pink flowers at her awkwardly. The brightest smile lights up her face.

Fuck me. If that isn't the best thing I've seen in my eighteen years on Earth. This girl, smiling at me as if I just gave her the greatest gift she's ever received.

"Oh Kane, they're beautiful," she gasps, grabbing them from me and pulling my hand to drag me inside after her. My hand burns where she touches me, and I find myself never wanting to let go of this girl. I wrap my fingers through hers and let her take me wherever she wants to go.

I could be walking straight to my death, but as long as she's still holding my hand, I would go with a smile on my face.

I take in the interior of the house as we walk. The place is spotless. The furniture almost looks untouched—the couch and two twin chairs with perfectly plumped pillows, and the stark white rug suggesting that not many people sit here every day. She takes me into an equally spotless kitchen, the counters gleaming and all the stainless-steel appliances free from a single fingerprint. She reaches up high in a cabinet above the refrigerator, and I move behind her until her back is a breath away from my front. The heat of her sets me ablaze from my head to my toes.

I reach above her and grab a spare vase, her heavy breaths mingling with mine. The proximity seems to affect her just as much as me. I take a step back, lowering the vase to the counter as I watch her turn around. A pretty pink tint is evident on her cheeks, the flush rising up her neck as she looks at me with a soft smile on her face.

"Thank you. Just let me put these in there and then we can go. I'd hate for them to wilt too soon," she remarks bashfully.

"I'll just buy you more if they do," I reply with an air of nonchalance. If this girl wants flowers, I'll make sure she never goes without.

The blush in her cheeks brightens. I stare at her, unable to put together words to describe how Avery makes me feel. I may barely know her, but I can already tell that she's the kind of girl you do anything to keep right next to you.

Avery arranges the flowers in the vase after trimming the stems, discarding the extra leaves and wrapping in the trash—which is also empty. The house feels as if a model showroom was bought sight-unseen and they just moved in. Every room I have seen so far is decorated so precisely.

She turns to me. "All right, I'm ready. Where are we going?"

"Do you need to say bye to your parents?" I ask, curious that I haven't seen or heard another soul since we walked in. The stillness of the house almost has an eerie quality to it.

"No, they're gone," she waves me off nonchalantly, turning away from me to grab her purse, ducking her head a bit so I can't see her face well. I want to ask more, but I'm ready to get this date going. I reach out to take her hand again, my heart soaring as she grabs it with enthusiasm and I hustle her out of the house.

I wait for her to lock up then walk her back down the walkway and open the car door for her, helping her inside before closing it. A grin stretches across my face at the thought of the next couple hours alone with her, her citrus scent drowning me.

I make my way around to my side with a pep in my step and get inside. The silence is comforting as I start the car and hand her my phone.

"Music?" I ask her, as she grabs the phone from me and holds it delicately in hers.

She looks at my phone as if I asked her to name all the United States presidents.

"What's that look for?"

"You're giving me your phone? What if I go through it?" she asks, wringing her fingers together in her lap. The question is laughable, considering there isn't a thing I can think of that I wouldn't let this girl do.

I shrug. "Have at it, the password is zero-eight-one-nine."

A jolt rushes through me at the thought that she may know what those numbers mean.

The day I first saw her.

"I'm not talking to anyone else, if that's what you're worried about," I reassure her as she scrolls through the playlist I had queued up.

"It's okay if you are. I mean, we haven't really even hung out before." She tucks a lock of her long brown hair that escaped her clips behind her ear. I track the movement, wishing I could reach out and feel those strands between my fingers.

"No, I mean when I asked you out, I was hoping for exclusivity. I know we just met, but I know that I like you and I want to see where this goes," I remark lightly, speaking nothing but the truth, no matter how ridiculous I sound.

If I only have one shot, I would rather lay it all out there now.

There isn't a chance I'm missing out with Avery. The feeling in my stomach is taking on new levels, churning whenever she's near, and I feel as if I can breathe a bit easier when she stares at me. I have been waking up every morning so excited to just see her. Even if all I get is a small glance each day, it feels like enough just to know she's near.

I watch as the words hit her, surprise lining her features. Her lips form a small "O" shape, her hand going to her chest.

We make the short trek from the car to the place where I laid the blanket, the one I purchased just for this. I'm about to take back what I said when she finally speaks.

"I want that too," she answers in a small voice. Almost as if she hopes the words get taken by the slight autumn breeze rolling through the park. The leaves have already started to fall, a sea of orange and red blanketing the ground. The rustling of them fills the silence as I absorb her words.

I can't help the smile that breaks out on my face as I take a seat. My lips stretch wider than I've ever felt as a mirrored smile takes over her face. It transforms all of her features, leaving me awestruck as she stares down at me. I hold my hand out to her, and she slips hers in mine, letting me pull her down to the blanket next to me.

The vivid fall background turns blurry as her blue eyes fill my field of vision, capturing me in their waves, as I imagine a siren lures in men. If I'm caught in her spell, I hope to never come out of it.

Her smile is radiating, her full lips stretched wide over her teeth. The breeze blows her hair back in her face, and before I can talk myself out of it, I reach over and push it back behind her ear. My fingers graze the shell of her ear as it glides through the chocolate strands, and a shiver runs through her, her breath hitching.

I lean in just slightly, checking to see if this is what she really wants. If I'm what she really wants.

When she tilts her face toward me, I don't hesitate to capture her lips with mine. The kiss is featherlight at first, testing each other, until she presses into me a bit more. That's all it takes for me to meld our lips together completely, so we're unable to tell where I end and she begins.

My hand slips into her hair, flowing like silk through my fingers as I angle her head up to get better access. I slowly tease her lips with my tongue, until her mouth opens and her tongue meets mine. The fire that has been simmering in me starts raging like an inferno, and I match her stroke for stroke. I lose myself in her, in this feeling I never want to end.

Her hand grips my shirt, pulling me closer to her. The kiss is unrelenting, until I hear a bark in the distance, reminding me where we are. I pull back slightly, keeping my hand tangled in her hair.

When I take a look at her face, eyes cloudy and half lidded, lips red and slightly puffy, I can't help but lean in for one more kiss. A quick meeting of our lips, nothing but tenderness. So vastly different from the passion that ignited with our first kiss, but incredible all the same.

I don't want to stop, but I know I need to. She deserves a proper date, not me pulling her to the back seat of my car. So I pull back, resting my forehead against hers. My hand still holds the back of her head as we catch our breath. Her grip on my shirt loosens, but she doesn't pull back further. Our breathing mingles in the air around us, until a light laugh breaks out of me.

"Wow," is all I can say, still speechless as I stare at Avery. Her blue eyes shine, cheeks flushed red as she stares back at me. Her gaze roves over my face, as if she's trying to catalogue my features—like I am with her.

As we sit there in silence just staring at each other, I'm hit with the sensation that there isn't a thing this girl could ask for that I wouldn't give her.

More dates? She doesn't even have to ask.

Flowers every week? I'll have them on special order.

A kidney? I'll take mine out right now.

My heart? I think she already stole that.

Maybe it's always been hers.

CHAPTER THIRTEEN

kane

NOW

Caffeine – Max Drazen

I push my way through the door separating the back of the house from the bar, coming from the office where I've been helping with the payroll for the last couple of hours. The sounds that were muffled come at me in full force, a rowdy table of football-watching guys along the bar and '90s underground music playing softly over the game.

I nod to Seth, the bar's owner, stationed at his usual spot behind the packed bar. I start a mental tally of what might be needed in back stock, then turn toward the table that's been occupying all my thoughts—only to see Morgan quickly eating up the distance between us with a grim expression on her face. She ignores the lingering stares pinned to her ass in the cutoff denim shorts that I know are Avery's by the little sunflower detail on the front pocket. A small grin fills my face remembering how many times she pricked her finger trying to sew that thing on one night.

"Kane, I need your help," she rushes out when she gets close enough.

Alarms shoot through me, worried that something happened to Avery. I storm out from behind the counter without a second of hesitation, letting the bar top slam back down, causing the couple behind me to flinch.

I'm in too much of a panic to apologize, instead forcing my legs to take quicker steps as I ask, "What's wrong?"

Morgan matches my stride. "Okay, so, Avery is drunk. I mean, really drunk. I don't think I've seen her drink this much since spring break freshman year, when we got that all-inclusive drink package down in Mexico, and you had to hold her hair back for the next twelve hours."

The alarm bells in my head ring louder at that. Avery has always been one to know her limits most of the time, preferring to sip one drink throughout the night. One benefit of my height and *don't fuck with me* look is that people get out of my way quickly.

"Why did she drink so much?" I probe as I finally see her. Some boy leans into her while she laughs at something he says, almost falling off the chair. He reaches for her as she slides sideways, and I see red as thoughts of what I'm going to do to his hand if he *actually* touches her race through my mind.

I make it just in time to stop her from falling, knocking the guy's hands out of the way. I angle my body between them, glaring at the offender who tried to touch *my* girl.

"Okay, pretty girl, I think you've had enough," I whisper in her ear, pulling her off the chair and into my arms. She comes easily, as if she's been waiting to be in my arms all night.

Like she fucking belongs there.

I carry her bridal-style, her arm instantly wrapping around my neck, her fingers playing with the short curls at my nape.

Having her in my arms again after fifty-seven days really cements how much my heart aches for her. It feels as if I'm finally taking a breath of clean air after months of smoke filling my lungs.

I grab her bag and phone from the tabletop and I turn my body to move toward the exit. Her legs dangle over my arm, kicking slightly as she tangles her fingers further into my hair—nearly eliciting a soft moan from me.

"Kane!" she almost yells, and I stop immediately as she looks toward the other guy. "I was just telling...uhh..." she trails off, appearing to have forgotten his name.

"Brad," the guy finishes for her. I examine his too-gelled brown hair, almost a perfect mold on his head, not a single hair out of place. It reminds me of my unruly waves, the complete opposite of him.

Is this the type of guy she wants now?

He pushes up the sleeves of his sky-blue button-down shirt, showing off the silver Rolex. I scoff at the very unsubtle flex.

Who the fuck wears a button-down to a bar? I want to punch him in the face just for that.

"Yes, Chad," she slurs. My girl is *drunk*. I chuckle softly when I see the expression on his face dripping in anger. "We were just talking about you. Right, Chad?"

"Brad," he corrects, clearly annoyed that she's in my arms and that she keeps forgetting his name. It's funny that he thought he had a real chance at taking her home to begin with.

He crosses his arms, looking like someone just sideswiped the BMW his daddy bought him, as he glares at me like I'm beneath him—little does he know.

I let a lazy smirk tug at my mouth and subtly flex my

arms as I hold onto Avery, just to remind him what a real man looks like.

"Yeah, that's what I said." She has a look of utter confusion on her face, a cute wrinkle resting between her brows. "Well, he was saying he wanted a tattoo and I was telling him all about yours and... Hey Morgan! When did you get back?" she rambles, swinging her head around to look at her best friend. I glance around, just now realizing the whole bar is looking over at us. Avery kicks her legs in my arms some more, making me grip her thighs tighter to keep her from kicking some poor person squeezing by us on their way to the bar.

"Okay, that's enough. It's time to get you home." I stride away from the group without another look as Avery reaches around me waving and yelling bye with a huge smile on her face. I chuckle seeing her like this.

She rarely gets this drunk, but when she does, she's like the energizer bunny on an caffeine-fueled diet. This isn't the first time I've had to physically remove her before she insists on becoming friends with every single person at the bar.

I love seeing her being so open to people, something she's always been too self-conscious to do sober. I know she could easily take over the world, make everyone else putty in her hands if she chose to, but she never will. I used to stand guard behind her the whole night until she had her fill of whatever place we were at, just to be the one who got to take her home and make sure she got there safely.

I never cared how late we stayed out, even if there was a reason to be up the next day. I always just felt honored she felt safe enough to let go like that around me, knowing I would be there to take care of her.

I stride past the bar, dodging people left and right, not

giving a fuck who stares at us as I make my way over to Seth to tell him I'm heading out early. When I reach him, he takes one look at Avery almost asleep in my arms and nods his head in understanding. I take off toward the parking lot, pushing people out of my path as I head to the door.

Fortunately, I arrived a little early tonight, which means I got a closer parking spot than usual. Avery isn't heavy, but I'm hoping to get her home sooner rather than later, given that I have no idea how close she is to puking all that alcohol back up.

When I finally make it to my black pickup, I open the heavy passenger door and place Avery onto the seat, helping her buckle. She mumbles something that sounds awfully like "you overbearing brood" while swatting my hands away. I finish up the buckle and swipe some of her fallen hair back behind her ear, chuckling to myself at how cute she sounds when she's angry.

Her piercing blue eyes meet mine momentarily before I take a breath and step back. I shut the door, making sure nothing gets caught in the frame before rounding the back and hopping in. I turn the heat up higher since the cold returns when the sun sets and Avery is wearing an outfit designed to torture me—a cropped black corset top that she always told me she hated, her breasts almost spilling out the top, with ripped jeans and boots I don't remember her owning.

Are we finally in the place where I stop recognizing everything she has?

I force my gaze from her and shove the truck into reverse, throwing my hand on the passenger headrest. The warmth from her head is dangerously close to my hand as I back the truck out of the parking spot. A sigh escapes her when my hands drop back to the center console, and I think about turning on the radio to break this crushing silence until I remember that it's still stuck on that god-awful channel.

My hands dance on the steering wheel, counting the seconds we've been silent. It feels like torture.

It never used to be like this. Even in the silence, I found comfort. It used to feel safe, and now I find myself racking my brain for something I could possibly say to get her to talk to me. The neighborhoods and streetlights blur past us out the windows as the quiet seems to get louder the farther we drive.

"Why are you driving like an old man?" Avery finally breaks the silence to say, and a sigh of relief rushes out of me. She turns toward me, angling her body so she's facing me and not the windshield. Her arms are crossed over her legs as she sits with her feet up on the chair. The new Doc Martens gleam in the passing streetlights.

I shift my posture up, loosening my hands from the steering wheel. I drop my right forearm to the console again, not realizing just how hard I've been clutching the steering wheel. "What do you mean? There's a speed limit, Avery. A law to abide by," I answer sarcastically. She doesn't need to know that I'm going the speed limit now hoping to prolong the time we spend together.

She giggles, knowing full well that I've never followed the speed limit before, always the one to remind me to slow down and be careful. It warmed my heart, those words a reminder that someone out there actually cared about me and wanted me home at the end of the day.

I glance over at her, noticing the way her eyes drop to where my arm is resting between us. She swallows, my rings glinting in the passing lights as her gaze tracks over the snake tattoo running up my middle finger that Marcus talked me into. Her fingers twitch as if she wants to trace the lines like she used to when we'd drive. A way to calm her anxieties, she'd always say.

"Please, you have never seen a speed limit that you didn't take as a suggestion," she scoffs. "And why did you go all Tarzan and Jane and sweep me out of there? I was perfectly fine." She slurs a little on the word *fine,* but I don't call her out because I love seeing the twinkle in her eye and soft smirk on her lips when she's giving me shit.

I split my attention between her and the road, thankful for the lack of traffic this late at night so I can really take in her features as we pass the streetlights, lighting her up like the star she is.

Before I can stop her, she reaches over and turns the volume dial up where Alpha Adam seems to be dishing out advice about how a woman saying she doesn't want to go out with you is just incentive to try harder. Avery bursts out laughing and turns to me again.

"Oh my god, Kane. What are you listening to?" She's barely able to get the question out over her laughter, tears gathering in the corner of her eyes.

"Wait, no," I start, laughing at myself along with her. "The freaking radio is stuck!" I explain, trying to defend myself. I turn the dial back down, cursing myself for not making time to fix it before now.

She looks at me. "Oh sure, 'the radio is stuck,'" she replies with air quotes. Still laughing to herself, she reaches over and turns the dial up again. The irritating sound of Adam's theme song that he sings live every night fills the cabin. Another round of giggles hits Avery, making my smile grow too.

"No, I'm serious. Please, try to change it. I have been trying for days, and eventually just gave up and started driving in silence. Anything would be better than this," I reply, waiting for her to try to change the station. I look over at her while we approach the stop sign outside her neighborhood.

Only two streets from the townhouse Marcus and I rent, Avery and Morgan's little cottage comes into view, its white siding shining in the moonlight and greenery spilling along the front. Between Morgan's plants from a few years ago blossoming in the yard and the brown porch swing and decorative porch goose—the one Avery begged me for last Christmas, that she and Morgan now dress up for the holiday—it feels as though it's straight out of a storybook.

"Okay you're right, it's stuck," Avery says, twisting the dial slightly only for it to get stuck again.

"I know. I've been meaning to open it up and try to fix it, but I've been so swamped lately. I think right now is the first time I haven't been rushing off to get things done this week." I slow the truck and park in their driveway, right behind Avery's old Toyota Corolla.

Worry flows through me thinking of her driving that car.

When was the last time she got an oil change? I should really come by one night and check her tire pressure now that it's warming up again. She'll never remember to do it herself.

I shift the truck into park as Avery muses, "Well it won't take more than ten minutes."

"What?" I ask as a wrinkle forms on my brow, turning to stare at her more directly now that the truck isn't moving.

She startles a bit and looks over at me as she grasps the door handle. "I just mean it won't take *you* more than ten minutes. You were always very...handy," she replies, glancing down at my hands, and sending signals straight to my cock.

She looks back up at me with her doe eyes, not realizing how her little comment will spur tonight's fantasies further when I get home later.

I turn and jump out of the truck before she can see my reaction to her, hoping the cool air gives me a minute to calm down—a half hard-on is the last thing I need when we're having our first good conversation since the breakup. I round the cab just in time to see Avery jumping down from my lifted truck, wobbling a bit before grabbing my shirt to steady herself.

"I was coming to help," I grumble, miffed that she didn't wait for me. I never let her open her own door while we were together, why would I suddenly start now? I pick her up again, legs thrown over my left arm. I reach back for her things and shove the door closed with my right before heading up the three steps leading to her front door.

"I just...wasn't sure..." she says, burrowing into me like she's seeking my warmth, finally content after a restless night.

I give her a gentle jostle her awake. "Hey pretty girl, no sleeping yet. I need your keys," I whisper, uncertainty laced in my tone. I still have my key to her place, but I'm not sure I have the right to use it now.

Her only response is soft breathing, so I dig my set out of my pocket, taking a bit longer than necessary so I can keep her tucked up against me for as long as possible.

CHAPTER FOURTEEN

kane

Look After You – The Fray

I open the door and catch myself before I turn on the lights. Avery and Morgan's house is always softly lit by plug-ins and string lights because Avery refuses to use the big lights, while I usually turn on every light I pass. She used to laugh and then get annoyed, saying she could always tell where I'd been from the lights she had to turn off behind me.

My heart warms at the memory.

I bypass the mess Avery and Morgan made this week, throw Avery's bag on the growing pile covering the table, and head toward her room.

I push the door open, noticing a wrinkled old T-shirt of mine on the end of the bed. I don't know how many shirts I've had to replace over the past four years because they would mysteriously go missing, only for her to show up in them at random times. Always stolen from my truck, gym bags, or my closet back at home. And because I love the sight of her in my things, I never said anything, but she knew I knew by the way she'd smirk and come sit on my lap, letting me discover she had nothing underneath.

I lay her down on the light beige covers. She rouses a little, looking at me through sleepy eyes.

Fuck, the sight of those eyes sends me stumbling backwards, toward her ensuite bathroom. She turns on her side, sliding her hands under her face as she watches me.

I walk into her bathroom and find her makeup wipes, grabbing one out of the pack. I walk back to her bed and sit down next to her, gently wiping the makeup off her face since I know she'll regret leaving it on in the morning. She closes her eyes, her breathing evening out again as I carefully remove every trace of tonight from her face. I take in her long, thick lashes and the dots of freckles that have now come out with the washed away foundation.

The freckles lining her nose and cheeks, like a constellation I could use to find my way back home.

I used to count them when she slept, just to make sure I never missed a new one. There were nineteen when we first got together in high school, and I remember thinking how fitting that number was. The nineteenth of August was the first day we met, which is also the password to my phone to this day. When she asked about it, I told her it was the day my life changed. That still rings true today.

Last time I counted, there were twenty-seven freckles, the number growing just as my love for her has. I wish I could stop and count now, just to make sure I haven't missed any in the time we've been apart, but I don't. With an aching heart, I wipe the last bit of black from under her right eye, then turn to throw the makeup wipe away when I hear her mutter a small *thank you*, followed by a sniffle.

I turn back and sit next to her again, brushing the hair from her face and letting my gaze linger, drinking in her features. My hands linger in her long brown hair, feeling the silky strands glide through my fingers, the feel of them almost imprinted on my fingers after all these years.

"Do you need help getting changed?" I ask her softly. Her eyes are closed, enjoying the feel of my fingers against her scalp. "Or I can give you some privacy." I pull my hand back, getting ready to stand and let her change.

"No, stay," she says, her hand shooting out and grabbing my wrist. I reach over and grab my old T-shirt, then help her lift her arms and slide her top off. The corset she wears is tight, taking some strength from me to get it undone. I toss it into her overflowing basket in the corner before sliding my shirt over her head. I unhook her bra once she's covered so she can slide it out under the shirt, trying to be as respectful as I can since she really can't consent to me touching her in this state.

She shimmies out of her jeans, then pulls down the damn fishnets that peeked through the rips in her them. The scene is straight out of my favorite fantasy as my eyes get stuck at all the imprints left on her thighs, the skin so delectable that I glance away before I let my mind run with the memory of what it feels like under my tongue. I would trace every divot and groove up her leg until I got where I wanted to be—fully seated home.

I flex my hands as I force myself to look away, suddenly feeling empty without touching some part of her. The imprint of her skin is permanently etched into me. I shake them out slightly, hoping this feeling goes away.

She's always been so beautiful to me. The first time I saw her, it was as if I had been seeing the world in black and white, and suddenly the brightest colors exploded into my vision. She instantly had me wrapped around her finger, and there hasn't been a single place I'd rather be since.

I used to find new ways to get her attention, pretending to forget pencils and paper so she would have to talk to me. She would roll her eyes at me and chastise me for being unprepared, not knowing I would throw my pencils away before that class for an excuse to have her look at me at all. The first time she cracked a real smile at me, I felt my heart ache in my chest. Time stopped, and I knew then that I'd spend my life fighting to keep that smile on her face.

One smile, and I was gone.

She's fully changed when I turn back around, and she looks sad, a stark contrast to how I always remember her being in my presence.

Before I can ask, she races into the bathroom where I hear the consequences of tonight's decisions hit. I rush in to hold back her hair, brushing it all back and gathering it into the braid she taught me to do when she didn't feel like doing it herself.

I grab a hair tie from her bathroom floor, securing it just as she finishes up, and she sits back so her upper back rests against my chest, her breathing deep.

I lean back so my back rests against the cold wall next to her shower, taking her with me. I hold her against me gently, waiting for the moment she may need to lurch forward again. The silence becomes a warm and comforting presence, the stillness of the moment calming my racing heart.

I just sit there with her, letting her breathe, softly stroking my thumb across her stomach where it rests.

"I'm so sorry. I really did not mean to drink so much. I'm a mess," she groans, starting to get up. I stop her before she can make it far, lifting her with me as I stand.

I carry her back to bed, then go get a fresh bottle of water from the kitchen and coax a few sips into her before setting it on the nightstand. "You are not a mess. You forget to fold your clothes and then complain about the wrinkles later, and you make me do the dishes even if most of them are yours. You may be messy," I comfort, finally getting that smile back on her face, "but you're never a mess. You shine way too bright to ever be anything but perfect, especially to me." I hold eye contact with her so she knows how I feel, a raw moment of honesty between us. Her blue eyes dance with so much emotion that I look away before I force a conversation neither of us are ready to have, especially not while she's in this state. When we have that conversation, I need her to remember why I'm in her bed in the morning.

She lies back down, placing herself under the covers so just her head peeks out from her cave of blankets.

"Want me to sit with you while you fall asleep?" I ask, standing over her, unsure what to do next. All I want to do is lie down next to her, pulling her close so I can feel her breathing all night. But I don't want to push my luck—I'm grateful just being in the same room with her again.

She nods, and I look around at the floor, deciding that's where my bed will be tonight. I grab a spare blanket and pillow from her bed and throw some random things to the side, then take my spot, staring up at her ceiling.

A beat of silence passes, and just when I think she's fallen asleep again, her voice comes in a barely audible whisper as she says, "I thought she was your girlfriend and I got sad. Sorry I stole your string."

"What?" I sit up, spare blankets tangled around me. I wait for her to answer, but her breathing evens out again, and I know she really is asleep this time.

I lay back down on my makeshift bed for the night, my hand propped up under my head, while what she said swirls around my mind.

My string?

My guitar string?

That can't be what she means.

I asked Marcus and he said no one had been over, but as I think back, he did seem extra cagey that night. I thought I had just come home while he was watching porn again. It happened once, and I don't think our friendship has been the same. Not since I found him pant less in the kitchen, dick in hand, eating a cupcake.

I shake my head, forcing that image out before it can ruin my life all over again.

The night I asked him about the string comes back to me instead—his shifting eyes, his hand running through his hair nervously. I should've caught it, but I'm not always good at reading what people aren't saying, especially when I'm already stressed. I go quiet and shut down. It's something that always created so much space between me and Avery.

I study her sleeping silhouette, suddenly putting it all together.

She's been fucking pranking *me, hasn't she?*

One year Marcus filled Morgan's car up with balloons full of confetti and cling-wrapped the doors shut. It took her hours to unwrap it, and Morgan retaliated by somehow getting one hundred pounds of glitter in Marcus's room. Three years later, and half his clothes still have gold sparkles in them.

Confusion hits me as I stare at her ceiling fan rotating. Hands over my chest, I listen to her deep breaths.

She broke up with *me*, without much reason I could rationalize. She said she needed space, so that's what I've been doing—giving her space. I really had thought everything was fine.

I can't help but replay that night in my head, as I've done every night before bed, hoping something I missed before jumps out at me.

"Kane, we need to talk," Avery says, finally breaking the silence that has lingered long enough to watch three episodes of whatever show we put on—some new TV drama she demanded we start, and I agreed because I've never been able to say no to her. She queued it up while I cooked for us, but then I got lost in my thoughts, the message from my father burning a hole in my pocket as we watched, distracting me from both the show and her.

I turn to face her and see tears brimming in her eyes. Panic instantly shoots through my system, wondering what I could have missed over the past two hours while I was checked out.

I reach for her but pull back quickly when she flinches from my touch. Confusion races through me.

"What's going on?" I ask, my hands hanging awkwardly between us.

"Us. Kane. Or the lack of us, I guess," she says, wiping a rogue tear with the sleeve of the oversized black hoodie she's wearing—which she must have taken from my closet when I wasn't looking.

I stare at her, unsure where this is going, hoping she takes my silence as a cue to continue. The familiar grip of anxiety slowly worms itself into my chest, tightening as my breathing begins to come out unevenly and my hands begin to tingle. I drop them back into my lap.

"Do you have anything to say?" she asks, anger replacing

the sadness on her face. She rubs furiously at her cheeks as tears spill down them, turned just enough for me to see every inch of her beautiful face filling with more and more hurt.

"I mean, I'm not sure what's going on… I thought things were fine. It's just been a long week," I say, rubbing the fog from my eyes.

"And how would I know it's been a long week, Kane? We don't talk. You don't talk to me. And when we do talk, it's like you're so mentally checked out of me and our relationship, I'm not even sure why I'm here." She throws her hands up in anger as she stands, moving toward her bag and shoes by the front door. Frustration lines her tone as her steps quicken away from me.

I race after her, grabbing her wrist and spinning her around to look at me. "What are you talking about? We talk all the time," I implore, not understanding what's happening, but feeling the heaviness of panic flood my chest as I stare at her nonetheless. I grip my hair with my hands, pulling trying to loosen the anxiety that's holding tighter and tighter in my chest, shortening my breaths. I try to grab her hand again, a way to center myself for this conversation.

She rips her arm out of my grip and takes a step back from me, my feet stuck to the cold tile floor. "No, I talk to you, but you never talk to me anymore. And now you're not even noticing?" More tears spill over and fall down her cheeks. She can't wipe them away fast enough before the next ones come, and she eventually gives up, letting them drip to the floor. The tears hit the ground, and my hands itch to reach over and wipe them away for her, but it's clear from the way she pulled away that that is the last thing she wants.

"Wha—" I start but quickly cut myself off as I try to get my racing thoughts in order. The all-too-familiar edges of panic creep into the sides of my vision, rendering me speech-

less on what to say, how to fix this. My brain feels like it's scrambling, thoughts hitting me faster than I can keep up with.

You're not good enough for your dad and now you're not good enough for her.

See, you're too much for her.

Quit your crying, emotions are for girls.

Before I can find the right words to say, Avery picks up her bag and looks directly at me.

"I can't do this anymore, Kane. I can't feel like this anymore," she stresses, pointing at her chest as if it's causing her physical pain to be around me. Her lips are swollen from crying, her perfect nose dotted with the softest freckles reddened, and those beautiful blue eyes are a deeper blue as her tears continue to track down her face. The star of every dream I've ever had, the cure for every nightmare I've endured in my sleep.

Until the next words come out of her mouth. "I need to think. I need space. I think we should break up," she finishes, tears streaming down her beautiful face as my eyes track her every feature.

My ears ring. Break up?

She wants to break up.

I reach into my head for anything to say, for the panic that has taken over to let me out so I can stop the love of my life from walking out that door.

How can she think this is what's best for us?

"Ave—" I gasp out, my mouth feeling as if it's full of sand as she opens the door.

She turns back toward me, hand on the door handle and tears still filling her eyes. "I just...need space, Kane. And you need to let me go."

The door slams shut behind her.

I stare at the closed door, willing her to walk back through it. I slump down the wall next to the door until I hit the tile, then drop my head into my hands and let the tears roll down my face. My breaths come out in short pants, and, unable to stop myself from shaking, I finally let the panic take me.

My airway feels like it's closing, the walls around me squeezing tighter and tighter. My shirt is almost too tight on my skin and my thoughts are so clouded with black, I feel myself getting lightheaded.

How in the hell did we end up here?

I don't know how long I sit there before my thoughts start to clear and the brain fog starts to lift. The shaking has receded to small aftershocks, the tears lining my cheeks slowly dry up.

I get up and race across the foyer and into the living room for my phone. I try calling her and it immediately goes to voicemail. I throw my phone across the room and it shatters on impact. Knowing it's a lost cause until I can replace it tomorrow, I sit down where I'm standing and let it all out. The sobs wrack my body as the thoughts penetrate me from every direction.

You're not good enough for her.

You're not good enough for anyone.

Minutes or hours later, I finally peel myself up off the floor again. The TV returned to the streaming home screen, the fan the only noise in the house. I decide to pick up the pieces of my shattered heart.

I contemplate running after her, but she asked for space. If that's what she wants from me, I'll listen...and just hope that someday, she finds her way back to me.

I SNAP BACK to the present, racking my brain for something I could've missed that night. Avery was hurt, but *she* still left *me*. But if seeing me with another girl made her jealous enough to bring this old game back up, there must be more to it.

I finally pull out my phone to let the group know not to worry about her for the night, only to find a text from dear old dad waiting for me. I've turned alerts for his texts off, a part of what my therapist tells me is *setting healthy boundaries*.

Instead of getting upset the second I see his texts, I can look at them when I'm in a more clear headspace. Which means not now, given where I'm currently lying. But since I clearly haven't put myself through enough emotional damage tonight, I click on the message.

SPERM DONOR

If you insist on behaving in such a manner, I request your presence at dinner next Thursday night. You may bring the girl if it suits you.

I scoff then send back a quick *got it*.

The girl.

As if Avery hasn't been over countless times through the years. She's been at my side for every big function, acting as a buffer for me and my dad and letting me show her off to all his rich prick friends.

But I haven't told my parents we broke up. There's no point—I plan to get my girl back eventually. May as well save myself from my father offering me up as a marriage candidate for the daughters of all his high-society friends to broker a business deal.

I blow out a breath to try to calm the racing thoughts inside my head and turn on my side, gazing up at Avery. I reach up to feel her breathing, resting my hand on her stomach as I slowly doze off, feeling more at peace than I have in weeks.

I stare up at the spinning fan blades as my mind turns over itself. My chest is loose as I feel her breath but my mind spins faster than it's in weeks trying to piece together how we got here. The pranks, the breakup, my dad and his ultimatum swirl around me until finally my eyes can no longer stay open and I succumb to the sleep that takes me away.

CHAPTER FIFTEEN

avery

Dancing With Your Ghost – Sasha Alex Sloan

I wake with a start, my head pounding as I sit up and try to get my bearings.

The haze of last night still fogs my mind as I sit and stare at the crumpled blanket on the floor. A flash of Kane standing over me taking off my makeup makes me clutch my stomach, the mixture of butterflies and alcohol churning.

I glance over at my nightstand to check for my phone and spot a Gatorade bottle I don't remember grabbing, with a note tucked underneath. I reach for the ripped notebook paper, immediately recognizing the slanted handwriting that's almost too messy to read.

Good morning, pretty girl,
Drink this and take the medicine. I got you some breakfast and fixed the dishwasher, so I won't be coming by later. Feel better.

K

Something is scratched out, but I can't read it. My heart clenches as I read the messy *pretty girl*, that one simple phrase as familiar to me as the back of my hand. A small smile curls on my face. I read the note two more times before opening my top drawer, where a couple of other—recently reread—notes from Kane rest. I place it on top of the others and close the drawer.

I stare at the wall, trying to recall everything that happened last night. I remember going to The Grunge—after an hour of Morgan insisting and basically dragging me to the door, dressed or not—and Kane delivering drinks, and meeting the blonde who is *not* his girlfriend. Everything after that is blank.

Fuck, I drank way too much. I was tired of feeling, tired of pining and thinking, and I just wanted a break from the constant noise inside my head.

The thoughts all come at me way too fast. The doubt that's ever-present. I almost drown in self-pity of never feeling enough for anyone. How my parents have always put everything before me, the way being their child was never enough for them to slow down and really *see* me. How complicated and messy things are with Kane.

I shake my head, trying to clear the thoughts before they ruin my day before I even have a chance to get out of bed.

I take the drink and medicine Kane left for me on the bedside table, swallowing it down before slinking back under the covers.

He was sweet last night. But that has never been Kane's problem. He can also go quiet, retreating so deep in his head that I can't reach him. The weeks leading up to the breakup, I was lucky to get a few full sentences from him. He was always withdrawing from me or brushing me off.

I tried to reason with myself that he was just tired or

overworked, picking up random bar shifts when he could. We still had sex, he still cooked for me, still did the little things such as reach for me on nights out and during our shows together. But the physical connection could only sustain us so long, and I craved the emotional connection I always valued with him.

I felt that the more he pulled away, the more I latched on, fighting for the *us* that was still there.

Tears start to well in my eyes, and I furiously wipe them away, sitting up and choking them down before the grief decides to dig its claws into me again.

How could he let me walk out of his life without a fight, but come to me last night as my knight in shining armor, whisking me away with so much care?

For the first few weeks, I let the grief overtake me, finding a strange comfort in the numbness. I lost not only my boyfriend but my best friend, the person I spent the past four years intertwining my life with. The person I gave my heart to before I even realized I had one, that organ I kept tightly locked in my chest for so long. I willingly handed it over to him on a silver platter that autumn day when we were hidden among the leaves. With the kiss that changed my whole life and tilted my world on its axis.

I miss the soft smiles he would share with only me. The way he'd look at me first when he found something funny, or when something was happening that we knew we would debrief later. The way he would always look for me in a crowded room, and the way a smile would spread across his face when he finally spotted me—the one reserved just for me.

Kane has always been hard to the world, walking around with a tough exterior, but he would soften for me.

And I loved being the only one who could bring that out of him.

It was as if I gave him somewhere he was safe to be himself.

I miss his deep voice when he would whisper filthy things in my ear at the worst times and walk away with a chuckle, knowing he was leaving me flustered and thinking of him.

His actions the night we broke up don't make sense when I think about last night. He slept here all night just to make sure I didn't get sick again. He turned back into *my* Kane. The man I so desperately fell head over heels for, with no way of stopping myself. But where was he months before that and the months since?

It seemed so effortless for him to let me walk away. I can't conceptualize how we got here.

I startle slightly when I hear Morgan banging around on the other side of the wall our beds share. Which can be unfortunate at times, given that Morgan is a night owl and comes and goes at all hours of the night and day. But I appreciate the grounding feeling that hits my chest when I hear her, knowing I'm not alone if I don't want to be.

I know now I only have a few minutes of peace before she decides to check on me after the events of last night. I'm still a little upset with her that I ended up in Kane's arms, but also relieved by how right it felt to leave with him, knowing I was safe wrapped in the quiet comfort of his truck.

I blow out a big breath, then pull myself up and into the bathroom. Refusing to see what a mess I appear this morning, I adjust the dial to the shower, letting the mirror fog up and obscure me from view. I click on my more upbeat breakup playlist, sliding myself into the shower. The banging on my door begins just as I begin lathering my body, and before I have a chance to say anything, it crashes open. Why Morgan even bothers to knock when she never waits for a response, I will never know. The lack of boundaries between us could shock any normal person, but we're more like sisters than friends—there's very few things we don't share.

Besides the unfortunate events of my breakup.

A moment later, the shower curtain is yanked back, and Morgan is staring at me, hands on her hips.

"It's cold," I say, trying to grab the curtain to close it, but she holds on to with a death grip. I step back under the stream, rinsing off the soap and any lingering tears, then reach over and shut the water off before turning back to Morgan.

"Are you going to say whatever you came in here for, or are you just here for a show? Because the cover fee just went up to twenty dollars," I joke, grabbing a fluffy pink towel from the rod and drying myself off.

"Our dishwasher is fixed," she starts, looking at me as if I'm keeping some massive secret from her. She stands with her arms crossed over her chest as she waits for me to respond, but I ignore her, wrapping the towel around myself.

"Kane walked you out of the bar last night. Well, whisked you away, more like it. Your very own broody bodyguard. Feels familiar, doesn't it?" she muses, a slight tilt in her lips.

"I know, I was the one he whisked away, remember? Which now that I think about it, you're the one who got him involved in the first place, so what is this interrogation about?" I slowly begin getting dressed, trying to stop the spinning of my hangover from making me sick.

"Would you like to share with the class?" Morgan implores, leaning against the counter next to me as I do my skincare, trying to make myself look like I didn't drink my body weight in liquor last night.

I finish up, continuing to ignore Morgan and how annoyingly perky she seems this morning. She's dressed in an all-pink tracksuit, her face fresh and her blonde hair pulled back into an effortlessly perfect bun. Clearly, I was the only one who decided to test the limits last night.

I walk out of my room and into the kitchen, Morgan trailing behind me. I start to dig into our bare fridge, making a note to go to the grocery store at some point. I can't keep living on takeout and the granola bars I find in my purse.

I grab my leftover dinner from last night and go to put it in the microwave, only to notice the glass plate is missing. Confusion runs through me, and I turn to Morgan, who continues to wait for me to fill her in on what happened after the bar last night.

"Where the fuck is the plate?"

"What plate?" Her brows furrow as she moves to stand next to me. "Oh, the microwave plate?"

"No, Morgan. The other plate. Of course, that one." I place my bowl on the stovetop and glance in the sink, wondering if one of us put it there to be washed.

"Okay, check yourself, grouchy. Where else could it be?" She seems just as confused as me.

I open the dishwasher to see if it's inside, but it's not there either. "Well, it's not like a plate just gets up and walks away."

Was I so drunk last night I don't remember moving it?

Did I try to make something to eat?

I go back into my less-than-put-together room, checking the dresser and various piles of clothes on the floor for the plate—and deciding I really need to get my shit together before my shifts this weekend. I've let the laundry pile up, empty takeout containers and cups littering every surface, and I wince when I realize Kane saw all of it—how I've barely been surviving the past few weeks.

Still not finding the plate, I abandon my dirty room as my stomach growls again. Frustration works its way out of me in a low growl as I stalk back the short distance to the kitchen.

"Okay, I don't see it anywhere," I say to Morgan, sitting down at our light wood table with green chairs—chairs Morgan splurged on a week ago when she said the *feng shui* of the place wasn't vibing anymore. She told me my funk was stinking up the place, so she changed most of the shared furniture after forcing me up and down the aisles of Pottery Barn and Crate & Barrel, giving her credit card tied to her father's account a workout.

"Okay, well, if you don't have it, it seems to be officially MIA. Has anyone been over this week?" Morgan asks.

After what feels like minutes, an idea comes to me. It doesn't make any sense at first, but the longer I sit there, the more the idea starts to take shape in my mind.

"Do you think..." I start. "Do you think Kane might have taken it?" I look at Morgan to see if she thinks I'm as nuts as I feel.

Her face screws up like she can't tell if I'm joking or spiraling. "Why would he take the plate? That seems like something one of those jack-offs would have done during college."

"I think that's exactly what happened," I muse, sitting back and crossing my arms over my chest, letting my mind wander. "I think somehow that motherfucker figured out what we've been doing, and this is his retaliation." I stand up quickly, a light bulb dinging in my brain. I hurry to grab my phone and dial Marcus. I pace my room while it rings, waiting for this turncoat to answer his phone, only to get his obnoxious voicemail.

I toss my phone on my bed again with a huff.

I turn to Morgan, who stands in my doorway looking at me like I've lost my mind. "You call him. He always answers when you call."

She scoffs, crossing her arms at the mention of Marcus. "He's probably busy jacking himself off or something," she replies with an air of nonchalance. Her blonde ponytail bobs as she flounces around the room, avoiding my stare. I huff a laugh. We walk back to the kitchen to reconvene at the table.

"So if Kane knows, what next?" Morgan asks, grabbing the peanut butter and bread. She pulls out four slices and plates them. She smothers them with way too much peanut butter, then turns and hands one to me as she retakes her seat opposite me.

"What do you mean?" I reply around an oversized bite of sandwich. The peanut butter sticking to my mouth makes the words come out muffled.

"Cute," she teases at my full bite. "I mean, do we stop pranking him? Or do we get him back even harder?"

"Of course we get him back. That fucker doesn't get to win just when he started to play."

"Or you could talk to him, you know. *Have a conversation.* I know it sounds wild, but as a rational human, it should be considered," Morgan suggests, one perfectly manicured eyebrow raised at me.

"Look, just because he isn't actually dating someone else doesn't change why we broke up. He checked out, he gave up on me long before I broke things off. And bringing all that up again is painful. So, what happens if I do and nothing changes and he still doesn't want me? He let me walk out that door and didn't come after me. I waited up all night hoping for a knock on the door, or even a phone call, and got nothing." Tears fill my eyes because that's the part that hurts the most. The broken, abandoned part of me needed him to come after me and prove I was worth keeping. That I wasn't defective or unwanted, as my brain likes to remind me on the rough days—the days when losing my parents feels all consuming.

"Honey, there hasn't been a single second since that man met you that he hasn't wanted you. I saw the way he chased after you in high school and he hasn't stopped chasing you since. I don't know what happened, but I know whatever thoughts you have spinning in that beautiful head of yours are wrong. He is not your parents," she soothes, always able to read my mind and see the parts of me I work so hard to keep hidden.

She reaches across the table, grabbing my hands in hers. The feel of her soft palm gripping mine calms my racing brain and fills me with enough courage to keep speaking. The thoughts circle my brain, the pain from my parents an ever-present bruise that feels as if someone pressed on it. They abandoned me too—maybe not physically, but I can't recall a single second they fought for me to stay in their lives. When I told them I wanted to go no contact, they didn't even seem bothered. They acted as if my therapist was manipulating me into cutting them out of my life. Their inability to see me and the damage they did is something I've been trying to heal from since long before this all happened.

"I know, Mor," I rasp as my voice cracks. "I just don't know if I can handle it if this is it. If it's officially over.

These past few weeks, I've been walking around with the delusion that someday we will be us again. That I will wake up one day, and this nightmare will be over, and I won't be walking around with this gaping hole in my chest. I know that I wanted to break up, but I just needed him to fight for me, to see the cracks already forming in our relationship and work on repairing them." A sob wracks through me.

Morgan rushes to my side of the table and pulls me into her, cradling my head against her stomach. She strokes my hair as the tears continue to pour out of me. I grip onto her as I let all my emotions pour out of me.

When my breathing finally slows, Morgan brushes my hair from my damp face. "Okay," she says softly. "What's the next prank?"

The panic recedes, pulling a strangled laugh from my chest. Her laughter follows until we're both a mess, clutching onto each other.

CHAPTER SIXTEEN

kane

WYD Now – Sadie Jean

I whistle as I drive my truck back to my apartment. The glass microwave plate sits on the passenger seat, the sun hitting it now and then. I chuckle to myself, one hand on the steering wheel, wondering when Avery will notice it's missing. Probably soon, given the sad mix of old takeout boxes and microwave meals that filled her fridge. My gut clenched when I saw it, and coupled with the state of her room, it leads me to believe Avery's been struggling more than she'd ever admit to me.

Before I left, I placed a delivery order of fresh produce and simple ingredients Avery can use to cook for herself—and won't require the microwave, for obvious reasons. She's never been good at asking for help, which is why I made sure we ate together a couple of times a week, needing to know she was getting well-rounded meals. I used to make extras to pile in her fridge for lunches she could take to work, making sure she had something to eat on her busy days.

I don't even want to think about what she's been doing since the breakup. The thought sends another pang through my chest.

My phone buzzes in the cupholder as I pull up to the townhouse. I shift my truck into park in my spot, then grab it, expecting it to be a text from Avery about the missing plate. My excitement is immediately replaced with frustration when I find a text from my father instead—that somehow snuck past the Do Not Disturb setting I have our conversation on—reminding me of my required presence at the estate this Thursday for my mother's birthday.

I sit back and release a big breath, clearing my head before getting out of the truck, plate in hand. I close the door and walk up the steps, waving hello to my elderly neighbor who seems to enjoy the early morning hours as much as me.

When I walk inside, I drop my keys and the plate on the counter, ignoring everything else and heading to my room. I shut the door behind me before lying down on my bed. I slept like shit last night on Avery's floor, waking up with every little sound she made, worried she was getting sick in her sleep. I did help her puke three more times, holding her hair and singing to her softly.

As poorly as I slept, though, it also felt incredible being near her again. The unrelenting loneliness receded for just a few hours as I held my hand on her stomach. The gentle rise and fall of her breathing calmed me, feeling as if I was taking my first real breaths in weeks.

I glance over at the clock, noting that I have a couple of hours to get some sleep before my shift at the bar. The Sunday crowd starts mid-afternoon, which gives me time to get a few things done later.

I check my phone one more time, hoping for a message I'm not even sure is coming. When a blank screen stares back at me, I throw my phone next to me and roll over, letting sleep claim me before my racing thoughts threaten to bring me under.

"I'M TELLING YOU, she wanted me," Marcus argues, looking at Grayson, whose shit-eating grin slowly takes over his face the longer he riles Marcus up.

The two of them stumbled in a couple of minutes after my shift started this afternoon, meaning they tracked my location to come to bug me.

Marcus insisted on all of us sharing locations, claiming it's for safety reasons, but I think he just enjoys being a pest. The number of times I've gotten a text when I conveniently pull up somewhere for food asking me to grab him whatever he wants is astronomical at this point.

Although, I guess I should thank him for making us all share with each other because that means I can check up on Avery. Not in a stalker way, just to make sure her car isn't lying in a ditch anywhere. I have gotten better at not checking it, though. The first couple of days, when I felt out of my mind not talking to her, I checked frequently—so much so that Marcus locked my phone in his room...and then proceeded to lock himself *out* of the room. I knew I had a problem when he resorted to such extremes. Now I check a couple of times a day, the need to reassure myself she's okay sometimes the only way I can calm the rising panic that threatens to take root.

"She did not. She checked her phone at least ten times

while you were there. I just know she was calling in reinforcements," Grayson says, taking a swig of his drink.

Marcus snorts. "Oh yeah, you're so familiar with a girl needing a way out of talking to you, huh?" he goads.

With my own thoughts swirling in my head, I haven't offered much to this conversation—though I'm clearly not needed at this moment.

"Oh, so you're saying I can't get any girls?" Grayson flips his hat around to face backwards, revealing his fresh buzz cut. It's some weird baseball ritual—buzzed at the start of the season and not cutting it again until the season's over.

"I'm just saying, you seem mighty familiar with what rejection looks like, given how sure you are that's what it was."

"You're such a fuck. Of course I know what rejection looks like, I've had to watch you pining over Morgan for years. How is that going again?" Grayson teases on a drink, a smirk taking over his face when Marcus's smile drops. I chuckle at their idiocy.

"It's going wonderful, yeah just last week she let me sit next to her without gagging, so I would assume we're just about to send the invitations," Marcus replies sarcastically.

Marcus's pining over Morgan when she constantly gives him the cold shoulder has been a running joke between us for years. I always thought he liked the chase the best, but when Morgan had her first serious relationship in college, he barely ate for weeks. When they eventually broke up, Marcus insisted he was fine just being friends with her, even though he stayed in her orbit, constantly circling her as if he was the moon. The way he looks at her is the same way I look at Avery.

"How about you, Mr. Chuckles over there?" Marcus

turns his attention toward me. "How's your relationship going, huh? Any sage advice to give us?" Marcus sits back down on the bar stool in front of me where I'm cleaning glasses.

"Great, actually. Yeah, I only cry maybe once a day now. Thanks for asking," I reply, dry sarcasm rolling off me.

Grayson jumps in, shooting a sharp look at Marcus, who looks properly chastised for once in his life. "No, seriously. How's it going with Avery, Kane?"

"I don't know. Each time I think we might finally talk, she pulls away again. Last night when she was wasted, I took her home, and it was nice. It was like we were us again, but I ran away before she could wake up. I couldn't handle it if she woke up and decided to kick me out or told me last night changed nothing, you know?" I sigh, wringing the dish towel in my hands.

The rings on my fingers shine under the neon lights of the bar, my newest one staring up at me—a big *A* engraved into a leaf design I had made months ago. It just came last week. My heart pinched when I opened the package and realized what it was. I wanted to rush over and show her what I'd made.

When the memory of the breakup hit me, I had to close the box.

There were two rings in that order, but I've only been able to open this one, which hasn't come off my finger since. My ring finger on my left hand is the only one still bare.

I shake myself out of these thoughts and stare back at my friends, who wait for me to continue.

I still find it hard to be vulnerable with them. My parents have never been the sharing sort. The surface-level conversations go back as far as I can remember, every emotion being shoved down in favor of making it seem like they had the perfect kid, with the perfect family. The backhanded compliments slowly ate away at my self-worth like a fungus infecting my whole body, until I realized being silent was preferred. A different sort of silence to the one Avery grew up with, but the loneliness mirrors between us.

"My dad's throwing my mom this birthday party. I haven't told them what's happening and I'm dreading it. He's been on my ass more than usual since I got access to the trust fund my granddad left me. I think he knows he's losing his power over me and he's scrambling. If I show up without Avery, he'll pounce, and I'm not sure if I'll be able to get out of his web again," I rush out in one breath. The truth pours out of me, and sharing it lightens a little of the weight I've been carrying.

"My dad is...a tyrant, to say the least. He was always this huge, imposing man when I was younger, and even when I got physically larger than him, he somehow still made me feel small. Saying no to him isn't easy. It never has been, and I worry that I won't be able to this time. Usually I have Avery, and while they tolerate her presence at best, they leave me alone with her around." I brush my hair back from my eyes, then drop my arms, trying to shake out the tension trapped all over my body nowadays.

My friends both look at me solemnly, matching faces of understanding. I don't know if I have opened up to them like this before. Sure, I've told them pieces—they know the gist of my dysfunctional relationship with my parents. But they don't know the way I feel bled dry after a single encounter with them. The way I shut myself away until I am ready to face them again, all my problems shoved so far back in the recesses of my mind until I feel human again.

The way the broken side of me hides under a mask of indifference.

Marcus moves to speak, but before he gets a word out, I see the door open out of the corner of my eye. My head whips up in recognition as Morgan and Avery walk across the threshold.

I draw in a breath and almost choke on it. Avery's hair is loose around her shoulders, the light from the door behind her making her look like an angel walking toward me. Her ripped jeans and checkered print shoes, paired with the classic over-sized band tee falling off one shoulder, bring a smile to my face.

This is the look I remember on her most.

"Hey, Ave, Morgan!" Grayson calls out as Marcus stands up to greet them. He gives Avery a hug, which sends a pang through my heart at how much I miss the familiar touch of her. They whisper something to each other, and Avery looks pissed, but Marcus has a shit-eating grin stretched across his face. She slaps him in the stomach, making him fold over.

Grayson slides over and pulls another bar stool up until they're all gathered around in front of me.

It's been so long since the five of us have been like this. Fifty-eight days to be exact. I try not to stare at her too hard. She is clearly still suffering from her hangover, those effervescent blue eyes that always shine as brightly as the sun dimmed and slightly puffy. She sits on the stool, back straight and arms on the counter as she grabs Marcus's Coke and takes a heavy sip.

I set the one I started when I saw her walking in—with extra lemon—down in front of her. She rewards me with a small smile when she glances at it, her eyes turning slightly watery. She mouths a quick *thanks* and my heart skips a beat, unable to calm down when she's around. The irregular rhythm would be concerning if I wasn't staring at the whole reason it beats at all. An angel sent just for me, the penance for a shitty childhood, the gift I was given for still being here.

The urge to fix what's wrong between us is strong, so I make myself grab a new glass and dry it off before setting it with the back stock. Then I grab another and start making Morgan her drink to keep myself from launching over this countertop and demanding to know what happened and how to fix it.

"What have you guys been talking about?" Morgan asks as I slide over her drink. She beams at me and takes a drink, giving me a thumbs-up.

"Oh, Kane was just telling us—" Marcus starts. I whip a towel at his hands on the counter—a sign for him to keep his big mouth shut. He looks over at me with a quiet *ow* and a shake of his head. My glare is cutting enough that he mimes zipping his lips, mirth shining back at me.

"Kane was just telling us about dinner at his parents' house," Grayson finishes for him. I turn my glare on him, but he purposely looks away from me toward Avery, too cowardly to face me as he reveals my greatest secret at the moment—aside from being desperately and hopelessly in love with the goddess sitting across from me.

The faint whiff of her lemon perfume crosses the space between us and has a groan coming up to the seam of my lips, threatening to spill over. The scent triggers memories I have no business thinking about while clocked in at work.

"Your mom's birthday?" Avery asks me, causing my brain to short-circuit because she's talking directly to me, something I've missed so much over this past month and a half. Her eyes twinkle in the light—my North Star trying to guide me home. Her pouty lips glisten under the neon lights, a small frown in the corner of her mouth that I want to kiss away.

"Yeah, and Big K here hasn't told them you guys broke up," Marcus jumps in for me, my cheeks heating.

I groan. "Please do not try to make Big K a thing again."

"Agreed. That was terrible the first time, Marcus," Morgan says with a swing of her long blonde ponytail.

"Hey, Ave, why don't you go with him?" Grayson, my *former* best friend, says. I turn my head toward him so fast I'm not sure how I don't get whiplash. He better start running the second I can get out from behind this bar.

"I think that's a great idea!" Morgan chirps from her seat next to my other traitorous best friend. A bright smile spread across her face, full of mock innocence.

"Oh yeah, Morgan?" I say, my voice dripping in sarcasm. "You seem to be really agreeable tonight."

"I just know a good idea when I hear one. You need your parents to think you and Avery are still together, so why doesn't Avery just go with you? I mean, you two can handle being in the same room for a couple of hours, right?" She feigns innocence, slurping her drink as if nothing interesting has caught her attention, as she avoids Avery's gaze.

The group is quiet for a moment, a song by The 1975 blaring over the speakers and the soft murmuring of other conversations filling the silence between us.

"It's okay, guys. Really, I can handle—" I start to say before I'm cut off by a soft voice that will always stop me in my tracks.

"No, I'll go," Avery says, quiet but certain. Her shoulders are set defiantly, as if she's gearing up for me to fight her on this. The gleam in her eye tells me she's sure, a look of determination shining back at me.

The only reason I don't argue that I should go alone is because I *want* her to come with me. Not even to protect me against them—though she will save me from fielding the women my father will throw my way if I show up alone—but because it'll give me an excuse to be near her, to touch her like the breakup never happened. I want to feel her again, even if it'll be fake.

"You really want to go?" I look at her, knowing I can read the truth from her better than anyone else. Her baby blues suck me into their orbit, and I grip the counter for something to keep me afloat while we stay in this limbo.

"I do. It could be fun. Elena always has the best food anyway. Where else can I get a free Wagyu steak?" she says with a laugh—the best music my ears have heard since she kicked me off her playlist months ago. The past two months drowning in silence has been deafening when her laughter was my favorite music, the loss of it cutting me worse than any pain I've felt.

"Okay. Great. Yeah, that's great. Okay," I stammer, the words coming out faster than my mouth can keep up. The thought of spending time with her again in just a few short days has rewired my system.

"Smooth, buddy. You're doing great," Marcus whispers, finally piping up from his suspicious silence in the conversation. There's never been an opinion he hasn't shared, so I squint at him, trying to figure out what he's up to.

You would never guess that he has a genius-level IQ with his carefree playboy attitude. He graduated with a double major yet shrugs off any recognition. The dumb look of ignorance on his face is some sort of ploy, but I'm too tired to figure it out.

I stare at Avery, cataloging her features. The freckles dotting her cheeks are out today, free from any makeup, and my breathing quickens with the need to trace them with my fingers, drawing a map of my favorite place to be.

"Okay." I huff a nervous laugh. "I'll text you the details and I can come pick you up, or we can meet, whatever is easier... I mean, carpooling is better for the environment, you know. But we can totally meet there. It's Thursday." My words spill out in a ramble, trying to bridge the gap and keep her here, looking at me like she might still feel the pull I've always felt toward her.

"Was he always this fucking bad with women?" Marcus turns to Grayson, talking about me as if I'm not a couple of feet away.

"I think when you meet the love of your life at eighteen, it limits your capacity for flirting," Grayson replies, finishing his drink and standing up. "I need to run, you guys. We have weight training later and I need to catch a nap before." Grayson gives the girls another hug before making his way to the door.

"We have to go too," Morgan says, standing and pulling Avery toward the door from where we were stuck staring at each other.

"We do?" I hear Avery whisper to Morgan, a look of confusion crossing her features before she straightens. "Oh, yeah, we do."

We say goodbye and I watch as Morgan and Avery leave the bar, my eyes following her the entire way to the door. She turns around just slightly, giving me the most beautiful smile before heading out into the rapidly fading daylight. My eyes linger, hoping for just one more glimpse after being deprived for so long.

I finally pull my attention from the door, finding

Marcus smiling at me, his dimples shining and a goofy fucking grin stretched across his face.

"Well, don't you want to say thank you?" he teases. I throw the towel I used to dry the glasses at his face, his laughter filling the space around me as I turn around and head toward the back, leaving him out there alone.

CHAPTER SEVENTEEN

kane

Leaving – Zach Bryan

Monday morning comes far too quickly, but somehow I'm awake before my alarm. I even have time to go grab a coffee instead of drinking the shitty stuff in the teacher's lounge, the brown sludge that barely passes for coffee most days. I've started bringing in more high-quality stuff just to be able to make it through the day.

There's an extra pep in my step, courtesy of the little brunette I get to see again in just a few days. The prospect of spending some actual time together has done more for me than any type of caffeine ever could.

I spent the whole drive to work laughing my ass off, because somehow, over the span of the past twelve hours, all of the shoelaces in my apartment vanished. I spent a good chunk of time this morning looking at all my shoes and trying not to burst out laughing. I have no idea when she did it, but every one of my shoes was cleared of the laces, leaving me with one option this morning: the slip-on Vans Avery got us two years ago so we would match.

She must have come in when I was still at work last night, and the fact that the shoes I was wearing last night *also* vanished overnight tells me they got to Marcus before I could get him on my side. He always was the easiest to break.

I sit in my chair and boot up my computer, taking a long drink of my coffee. My gaze snags on the picture of me and Avery, and the grin that tugs at the corner of my mouth from looking at that alone tells me how much trouble I'm in.

I check my calendar for this morning, grateful to see that Trevor is coming in at ten. I haven't seen him since early last week, not even in the halls.

My schedule is booked today, but I still have some free time to get caught up on other work. My 2 p.m. therapy session stares back at me from its slot. It's only my fifth appointment, the second since we started me on a low-dose medication he referred me to someone else for so I could get some extra support—which has helped more than I could have hoped for.

My racing heart and sudden onset panic have lessened since starting, and my mind feels clearer, allowing me to take deeper breaths. My body feels as if it's coming down from a bender, the fog clearing significantly.

I don't think I ever realized how much anxiety was affecting my everyday life. Steve, my therapist, said I may have had it since childhood. A coping mechanism to protect myself from an unstable childhood, and eventually all those repressed emotions had to make their way to the surface and come out somehow. We're still working on getting me to identify my emotions, and letting myself feel them, since my first instinct is still to shove them down to where they can't be felt. Steve says that is the worst thing to do, and the only way to get better is to work through them.

Nothing has been harder work than therapy. The emotional bandwidth it takes from me, and the mental exhaustion that follows feels unreal some days. Having to relive some of the worst moments of my childhood is brutal, but after just a few weeks I feel lighter, knowing I no longer am forced to carry all of that around.

Some days are easier than others. The anger gets to me on the worst days. When I just feel so angry at everything they did, the unfairness of how they treated me, and now it's up to me to put in the work to undo all the damage they caused. Steve said that's normal, almost as if I'm going through the stages of grief. Mourning for my past self, the sadness, followed by anger, then finally giving way to some sort of acceptance.

I scoffed when he said that to me. Acceptance, as if I could ever accept what they did to me. As if someday I'll have to say, *"Oh, it's okay that you destroyed my entire childhood and still feel no remorse for all the things you've done."* But Steve is hopeful, and I'm trying to borrow some of that hope for myself.

We have obviously talked about Avery too. I don't think I'm capable of going too long without speaking about her. I told him everything—the panic attacks, the distance I unknowingly put between us, the breakup and the way I've felt since. I wasn't even sure the distance between us was there until Steve pointed out the times I may have made her feel that disconnect when I was too blinded battling my own brain.

It felt good to finally get it off my chest. To unload everything and talk it through. I know if I came to Marcus or Grayson and told them, they would be there for me and be nothing but supportive, but I still find it so hard to let myself be vulnerable in that way. To let someone see that side of me, the side I have been trying for so long to pretend doesn't exist. The weak version of me that feels too strongly, who has always felt more deeply than he was allowed to.

I'm still trying to find a way to let him exist peacefully with the other part of myself—the strong one who has endured more than he should have in the past twenty-three years.

I grew up with everything a kid could want—money, private chefs, every toy I could think of. But I was missing the things that really mattered. I never felt love, or acceptance for who I was; I was never held and told it would be okay when I tripped and fell; I was never told they were proud of me. No paintings hung up on the fridge, no ice cream when I got a report card. Instead, I was yelled at and berated for getting an eighty-five instead of one hundred. Belittled for crying when I scraped my knee and being told to be quiet and unseen on more nights than I can count when my parents were entertaining company.

None of this shit has been easy, but I have an end goal, and at the end of the day there's nothing stopping me from getting back what I lost. I've been my own worst enemy for too long, and it's time I face my demons and get my future back—because there isn't one without her. She's it, but she also needs me to heal. Or at least be on my way to it.

I've learned that I can't be good to her if I'm not good to myself. The work to get her back starts with me, and there's no mountain I wouldn't climb to reach her. No monster I wouldn't slay to be next to her every day going forward.

The high from the morning fades with every appointment I have. Three of my early appointments were with kids who have no interest in being here and are struggling to keep up with their classes. Many students I work with aren't headed down a path of continuing their education, instead choosing to start working immediately after graduation since the scholarships and funding are often too little for what they would need to even begin. Some already have part-time jobs they'd rather be at than a school that has shown little interest in them, with families that depend on their income.

I take a big breath and let my shoulders fall, letting some of the day drain from my body before Trevor comes in. I almost drove by his work to see if he was there since I haven't seen him in a while, but it's hard to know where the line of overstepping is.

There's so much that goes into being a good counselor, and the part that matters most days is showing up for the kids who need it. The kids who may not have anyone showing up for them anywhere else—Trevor being one of them.

This is only my first year here, and I may not make that much of a difference yet, but I plan to make an impact, no matter how small. If I can be a place for one person to feel better, feel supported in the way they need, that's enough for me.

The clock ticks as I sit here, welcoming the silence and letting myself take a breather. This job can be a heavy one. One I've had to learn to compartmentalize at the end of the day. Not every problem can be solved by me, as much as I wish it could.

My stomach grumbles, the early morning snack I ate doing very little to hold me over for the next two hours. I have some time after Trevor when I may be able to run to the cafeteria for a snack. I look at the clock and see the minutes counting down, and I wait with bated breath to see if he shows today.

My mind wanders to a certain someone, and my fingers itch with the need to text her. I stared at our old messages for hours last night, contemplating what to say as the last message between us haunted me.

I pull out my phone, unable to keep the need to say something at bay much longer. I finally have something to text her about, and I'm stalling.

What if she blocked my number?

What if she doesn't respond?

The thoughts swirl in my head. An edge like panic starts to close in, and I make myself take some deep breaths the way my therapist explained to me. In for four, out for four. I do this six times until breathing becomes easier again and the fog disappears from my brain.

I stare at my lock screen, at the picture of Avery in one of my sweatshirts—a Grateful Dead hoodie she always preferred—the size dwarfing her as she smiles up at me with a crinkle in her nose.

I made that my background just over a year ago. When I looked over at her and just couldn't help but think how fucking lucky I was. This girl stole my heart at eighteen and hasn't let it go since. I remember the bickering afterward, her wanting me to pick any other picture of her with her hair and makeup done, but I knew this was the best one I would ever take. Because that face she made was always just for me.

She tries to make herself less noticeable when she's around other people, but she gives me raw openness. She comes alive when she's with the people she loves most, and I love opening my phone to that face every day. The confidence and love that shine back at me make my cheeks widen further.

Like the first breath after being underwater too long, lungs burning, and finding the most beautiful sunset waiting over the ocean. That's what she was—and still is—to me.

It caused relentless teasing from Marcus when he first found out. But he would always get this wistful look on his face too, as if he could imagine the exact moment he also felt that way about someone.

I open our messages, the last texts we exchanged before I picked her up that night staring back at me.

ME

Be there in 5, love you

PRETTY GIRL

Love you!

It was a simple exchange, but one I took for granted. I always meant those words when I said them, but did I always make her feel them?

Did I always make sure she knew that she was the best thing in my life?

Any word can be said with the best of intentions, but when it's not backed up by actions, it becomes meaningless. And I'm starting to see how meaningless I may have made her feel. The problems in my head felt as if they eclipsed my whole world, like every day became just another day to get through.

I begin to type out some messages.

Hey, so I know you agreed but

I hit delete until I'm staring at the empty message bar again.

Did you block me?

I delete that too, shaking my head.

I drop my phone down, the unlocked screen staring up at me as I run my hands down my face. The button-down I'm wearing feels like it's choking me, so I pull the collar away to get more air, my chest tightens slightly before I remind myself to take some deep breaths. I pick my phone up again, thoughts swirling in my head. Maybe I'm making this harder than it needs to be.

ME

Hey

I hit send and immediately grapple to take it back.

ME

It's Kane by the way

I hit send on that too and laugh out loud at myself. I'm about to type out another message when one from her pops up on the screen, and I swear I feel my heart stop.

PRETTY GIRL

I know who it is lol

I chuckle with her. I agonized over this text for hours and ended up making a bigger idiot of myself than I did yesterday. It's as if she short-circuits my brain and I no longer know how to function when she's around. Everything between us just feels so precarious right now that I'm scared to do or say something that will damage us permanently, something we can't come back from.

ME

I just wanted to text you the details for Thursday night. It's at my parents' place at 6:30. Did you want me to pick you up? I'm out of school a bit earlier that day.

The longer the seconds tick by with the dots appearing at the bottom of the screen, the more my chest tightens.

I text a follow-up.

ME

Which you don't have to come to. If you don't want to. I can handle it

The need for her to know she's off the hook is so strong. I don't want her to come out of pity—I never want anyone's pity when it comes to my parents. I almost jump out of my chair when my phone vibrates with a message from her.

PRETTY GIRL

Shut up, I'm coming.

I need to be at the shelter until 6 so I'll just drive myself since it's out of your way to come pick me up.

ME

I don't mind. We can be a little late.

PRETTY GIRL

We both know if you're late Elena will never let you hear the end of it.

I laugh at the thought of us showing up late to my mother's party and the hell that would ensue.

ME

She'll forgive you for it at least

PRETTY GIRL

Well because I'm perfect in her eyes

ME

Not just hers

The bell rings and I swear under my breath, not wanting to walk away from this conversation. But there are very few moments until Trevor walks through that door, and I owe him my full attention.

ME

Okay so meet on Thursday at their house around 6:30. I'll let my mom know you're coming separately

PRETTY GIRL

6:30 it is. See you then

The disappointment that runs through me with the lack of *I love you* at the end makes it hard to breathe for a minute —fear that I really have lost her for good.

I shake my head to try to dislodge those thoughts before they can run wild, place my phone on my desk, and sit back. The sounds of students walking around and the chatter that follows them hits my ears, the warning music playing softly overhead to let students know they only have two minutes to get back to class.

I'm about to return to my paperwork when a mess of brown hair enters my office, head down and quick steps bringing Trevor barreling into my office and slumping into the chair in front of my desk with a huff. It takes my brain a second to process what I'm seeing. Trevor's arm, in a sling. The blue material covers over a heavily bandaged arm in black casing.

I see red when I get a good look at him. I know that look

on his face that he is about to try to feed me lies about what happened. Trevor is very good at wearing a mask if you don't know exactly what to look for. But it's hard to mask around someone who perfected that look years before he was born.

"What happened?" I ask, trying to keep my voice even and the anger shoved as far down as it will go.

"I fell at work," he replies, stone-faced, as if that's the least interesting thing he has heard all day.

"How?" I lean forward to rest my hands on my knees, remembering to keep my body language open and engaged with him. I'm hoping that extra prodding from me today doesn't send him shutting down and shutting me out.

He fucking shrugs at me.

"How did you fall and break your arm, Trevor?"

"I just fell at work, okay? Can you leave it alone?" he spits.

"I can't leave it alone, Trevor. Not when you come into my office with new bruises telling me you fell or slipped. I want to help you, and I cannot do that until you are honest with me," I try to reason, getting up from my chair and coming around to the other side of the desk and sitting in the one next to Trevor. I close the door from my chair and let the silence envelop us. "Tell me what's going on, and I will help you."

As the silence surrounds us, I can hear his breaths coming faster than before and notice the small fidgets of his fingers around his new cast. My eyes land on the cast, sending a bolt of fury through me.

"I'm fine." A small voice rips out of him, full of agony.

"I can help them too," I say softly referring to his sisters, letting him hear the truth to my words. I would help them all. I would report their father and work with social services to make sure they get removed. I would do all that I could to make sure this is the last time he shows up to my office battered and bruised.

"You can't promise that. You can't promise that me and my sisters will be sent to the same place, and I won't risk being away from them. They need me and I refuse to abandon them like our mother abandoned us," he replies, anger dripping from every word. "I don't care what happens to me."

He's despondent, as if he truly doesn't care how many times he's shown up in this state or been hurt by who I assume is his father.

"You should care, Trevor. You can't keep showing up here hurt and broken. And more than that, you shouldn't have to," I say, trying to reason with him. I could go behind his back and report my suspicions, but I know that if they do a welfare check on the house and Trevor doesn't admit to it, he could end up worse than he already is.

"But I don't," he replies brokenly, as if he has already given up on himself.

My heart shatters at the realization that he doesn't want better for himself. He has already been dealt such a hand in life that he just accepts the treatment he gets, almost as if he deserves it.

"I don't care, and I won't risk my sisters. I keep them safe. I do my best to make sure they have everything they need. We don't need more than this. I only have two more years until I'm free and I can take them away," he says, determination lining his features, his dark brown eyes hard as he stares at me.

I realize I've entered a losing fight and sigh. I let the silence welcome us back.

"Okay," I say on another sigh. "I won't push. But I need

you to know I am here for you. It doesn't matter when or where, okay? I want to give you my phone number just in case." I reach over for a sticky note and pen and scribble my number down before handing it to him. He takes it with his good hand and shoves it in his backpack.

I ignore the potential repercussions of giving a student my number. I know I would do anything to make sure this kid is safe, even if it means I lose my license. Some things are worth risking everything for, and I know that if I stood by and did nothing, I wouldn't be able to live with myself.

"Thanks, Mr. D. I... I'm okay, really. But thank you for being here. It means... Well, it means..." he stammers, suddenly unsure and hiding behind his mess of hair.

"I know, and that's what I'm here for. I'm on your side." I stand and move back to the other side of the desk to give him some space, knowing I need some space myself. I try to rein in the feelings today has brought. The high of my conversation with Avery to the low of this conversation and just how helpless I feel in all aspects of my life right now.

He stands, slinging his backpack over his shoulder. "I got to run. Katie is meeting me to go over the test so I can see what I missed. But I'll come by later this week?" he says, gathering his backpack and standing up.

"Yeah, Trevor, of course. You know my office is open for you anytime." I plaster a smile on my face despite my gut twisting inside. I take in his appearance one last time—there are no other bruises or cuts that I can see. The bags under his eyes are less severe than when I saw him last, telling me he at least has been able to get some sleep.

"I know." He slips out the door, leaving the silence heavier than it was before.

CHAPTER EIGHTEEN

avery

House With No Mirrors – Sasha Alex Sloan

"Hey, Mama, how are you doing today?" I say in the sweetest baby voice I can muster as I walk up to Silver's kennel. Her puppies are sleeping in the most adorable pile. They just turned three weeks old and are the cutest set of puppies to come through here—not that I'm biased because they're hers or anything.

She gets up and comes to the door, her whole body moving with her tail when she hears my voice. The brightest smile takes over my face when I see her. I check her log and note she already ate and had a walk today.

We had two new intakes that had to be isolated for potential parvo—the poor things were brought in yesterday after being found on the side of the road, and the vet assumes they're littermates. I had to take them to the emergency clinic because our on-call doctor couldn't get here today. The puppies are staying overnight and hopefully can be picked up in a few days to be introduced to some of the younger puppies once they're cleared.

"You got a walk today. Look at you. You're gaining so much weight, big girl," I praise her, giving her pets as she dances around me.

"Do I get that kind of greeting as well?" a male voice asks behind me.

I turn to see Grayson standing there, watching me with a soft smile on his face. He looks to Silver, and his eyes warm even further. Silver runs to the kennel door, eager to greet a new friend, her tail whipping against the chain fence.

"If you're as cute as her, sure," I tease, trying to clean up some of the bedding she destroyed as Grayson lets himself into the kennel. He volunteers here a couple times a month when his schedule isn't too packed and he has more free time. He's familiar here, and most of the workers know him.

"Well then, damn. There's no way I'm as cute as this one," he replies, sitting down and letting Silver attack him with kisses. The sight warms my heart at how easily she takes to him. Silver loves humans, but she's more wary of men, giving them a more tentative approach. Yet she so easily climbs into Grayson's lap.

"What's up, Gray?" I ask as I sit down across from him, next to the puppies and plop a couple in my lap, trying to get all the extra serotonin I can before tonight.

"I just wanted to come by and check on you. I know the party is tonight, and I wanted to see where your head was," he remarks, petting Silver and looking up at me to gauge my reaction. "And I also was thinking about maybe adopting a dog," he adds, as if it's an afterthought.

"Really?!" I wasn't sure if you still were since you never brought it up again," I exclaim, wanting to jump for joy but not willing to move the puppy pile that has gathered in my lap.

"Yeah, it's been a little too quiet over at my place. I think it could use some chaos." Bashfulness enters his voice as he continues to love on Silver.

"Did you want to take a look around? We can do meet-and-greets, and you can pick someone up today if you want. I don't need to do a home visit, obviously, and I know the kind of man you are."

"Actually, I think I want to take her." He looks down at Silver, my presence completely irrelevant as she moons over him. She alternates between being in his lap and attacking his face with kisses.

"She needs to stay here until the puppies are at least eight weeks old, so she has about five weeks left. Is that okay?" I ask as I lay the puppies back down and start to get up. The pile of paperwork on my desk is not getting any smaller the longer I sit here.

"Yeah, that's fine, as long as you wouldn't mind watching her when I have to leave for away games. I know this isn't an ideal time to get a dog, but I don't know... Feels right."

"Of course I will. She'll have sleepovers with Auntie Avery and Auntie Morgan, won't she?" I coo at her, giving her one last bit of love before locking the kennel and straightening up beside Grayson.

"Great. Then yeah, take me to the paperwork," he replies happily. "Now, don't think I didn't catch that you ignored my question about how you're doing."

He shoulder-bumps me as we walk side by side. The nudge trips me up a little, and I laugh.

"Ugh, you're annoyingly perceptive," I remark. "I'm okay. Nervous, mostly."

"You know you don't have to go. Kane would understand if it was too much for you," he answers softly. He grips my elbow and nudges me to face him, then lets go, and I let my arm hang limply by my side.

The hallway empties as we get closer to my desk. The kennels behind us are mostly silent as the two of us linger in it.

"I can't just not show up for him, Gray. I know he needs me."

I wring my hands together, the anxiety creeping up on me. The feelings rise all too fast at the sincerity in Grayson's gentle tone.

"Of course he needs you, Ave. He's been desperately in love with you since I've known you both. I don't think I've seen two people more right for each other than you two. I know you can get past what happened." His words are dangerously close to things I haven't let myself start to think about lately.

"I'm sure we could, but I'm not even sure he wants to," I rasp, my voice almost a whisper in the quiet. I'm too scared to talk any louder, as if the universe might hear me and try to keep me from what I want most.

"What do you mean?" Grayson asks, sheer confusion lining his features as he crosses his arms over his chest and peers at me.

"It's just that you didn't see him in the last few weeks. He wasn't him, and he wouldn't talk to me. I was invisible to him. He pulled away, and no matter how hard I tried to pull him back, he somehow got further from me until I felt like the rope tied itself around my neck and I couldn't breathe." I sniffle, my vision turning hazy with the unshed tears brimming in my eyes.

"I don't know why he did that, but I know it isn't because he doesn't love you anymore. You know Kane doesn't talk to anyone, but I think you should force him to talk you. Stop taking no for an answer and demand it," he challenges as he crosses his arms over his chest.

"I can't." Exhaustion clings to me as I wipe my eyes to clear the haze. "What if he doesn't want me to? What if he decided, just like them, that I'm not worth his time? I can't bear to lose him. Even if I already have in some way, if he says those words, it's final, and I have no idea how I would ever recover from that," I finish with a sob.

Grayson closes the distance and pulls me into a hug. I wrap my arms around him and let myself lose it. The tears come faster than my breath can until I'm sobbing into his shirt.

After a few moments, I finally calm myself down enough to pull away slightly and wince at the wet marks on his shirt.

"Sorry," I apologize as I wipe the evidence of my crying fit from my face.

"Don't apologize, Ave. That's what I'm here for. That's what we're all here for. We're your friends, and you need to let us be there for you," he remarks, clearing one more tear that escaped my eye.

"I'll work on it," I agree with a small smile.

"Good," he says. "And look. I know I haven't been friends with you guys as long as the others, but I would never doubt for a second that you're everything Kane could ever want."

"What makes you say that?" I muse, folding my arms across my chest and taking a few breaths to clear all the emotion from my voice.

"Because he looks at you as if the world begins and ends with you. From the day I met him, he hasn't looked at anyone or anything the way he does with you." He remarks softly, keeping eye contact with me and letting what he says sink in. "You guys will be okay. I know it. I'm more certain about you than I am about the sun rising tomorrow. You and Kane are inevitable."

The poetry comes out of him as if he's telling a tale of two stars on their path to each other.

"Thank you," I say as a small kernel of hope catches in my chest, a seed planted in the root of my heart, waiting to be watered by actions. "Come on, let's go finish up that paperwork and get you a dog." I smile and hold out my arm for him.

He ropes his arm through mine, and we walk off to my desk together, lighter about everything for the first time in weeks.

Everything that could go wrong has up to this point today. We've had an abnormally high number of intakes for this time of year, and our shelter cages are starting to overflow. On top of that, the number of volunteers getting everything done has diminished. So, I've been here late every night this week, which usually would be what exhausts me. Instead, a certain golden, brown-eyed man has been a near-constant ghost haunting my every thought.

I feel as if I've barely slept in the four days since the bar. The look of him—black shirt stretched taut over his biceps and the subtle flex of his arm every time he dried a damn cup—had me unable to focus on little else.

Until the bomb dropped about his parents' party and I saw the look on his face—the look of a little boy still wanting his parents. I knew then that I couldn't let him go by himself. Even if Grayson hadn't been the one to say it, I would have offered myself.

On top of stressing and trying to prepare myself for every outcome that may happen today, I raided Morgan's closet for something to wear. We did a whole fashion show last night since I knew I would have no time to stop home and get ready, settling on a long black dress, leaving my shoulders bare in an off-the-shoulder moment with my curves wrapped in velvet. Once I put it on, Morgan refused to allow me to try anything else because Kane will "eat his heart out when he sees you in that dress." And I had to admit, she was right. It made me feel confident in my skin, which is usually only achieved by a giant T-shirt.

My heart did a little flutter when I imagined what Kane might do when he saw me in it. I rarely dressed up when we were together, but when I did, he always made a point not to let me leave the house without at least one orgasm first.

I immediately put a stop to that train of thought. There will be none of that tonight. I'm just glad we can talk to each other again. Maybe that means we can at least be friends. The thought of not having him in my life is a kind of grief I can't even imagine. There's no universe in which he and I aren't intertwined. Even though the thought of him someday finding someone else shreds me to pieces more than anything my parents ever did, I would endure it for him. There's very little I wouldn't endure for that man.

He has had all my firsts: the first guy I had sex with, the first one I gave my heart to, the one I fell in love with so easily it scares me. The one who stood by me on some of the darkest days of my life. The one who ruined me for any man after.

I take my makeup bag and dress into the employee restroom, hoping it was cleaned before Keith left so I can just get ready and go. The night shift is here to sit with the dogs and rougher intakes overnight. Sharlene believes in never leaving the shelter completely empty after a particularly hard case was left alone all night and sadly didn't make it. I'm not sure she has ever forgiven herself for not being here.

As I start to apply my mascara, my phone buzzes somewhere on the counter. I dig under the pile of products I have yet to put away and find my phone shoved inside the makeup bag. The pink checkered print bag was way too expensive—a gift from Kane last Christmas that also came loaded with brand-new versions of all my everyday makeup products.

I free it from the mess's clutches to see Morgan calling. I blow out a breath, already knowing what she's calling for.

"Hello," I say, putting my phone down on speaker so I can finish up my mascara.

"Are you getting ready?" she implores, ignoring my greeting and going right for what she called for.

"Yes, Mom," I sigh.

"Just making sure you're not a chicken shit and somehow halfway to Canada to avoid your feelings," she says, smugness in her voice.

"I can still make it to Toronto in eighteen hours, and you would all be none the wiser," I tease.

"Please, as if Marcus wouldn't have clocked it and informed us all what freeway you were taking on your way out of here."

"He is nuts, isn't he?"

"Oh yeah. I stopped sharing a long time ago, when he started showing up on my dates because he said he didn't trust men," she scoffs.

"He just used my phone, you know. He didn't stop

tracking you," I confess, knowing Morgan is probably going to lose it on him the next time they're together. I welcome the chance to see it after they pushed me and Kane together.

"How dare you, Avery? That is against the best friend code," she says, faux anger lacing her tone.

"You're both my best friends, and you know what—you deserve it after being in cahoots with Marcus and Grayson to get me to go with Kane today," I mention as I finish with my lipstick and cap the tube—the blood red color making my eyes brighten further.

"I have no idea what you're talking about," she muses, pure innocence dripping from her words.

"I love you guys, but you're not exactly as subtle as you think you are. You practically dragged me to the bar, knowing Marcus was there, and were willing to miss the farmers market," I reply, unconvinced by her nonchalant attitude.

"Whatever. I did nothing but try to encourage my best friend to get out more. Sue me for caring, I can afford it," she says, and I laugh at her. She always has a way of making me feel lighter. "Go finish getting ready and send me pictures. I expect a full, detailed breakdown of the night when you get home."

We say bye, and I hang up.

I look at myself in the mirror to make sure there is nothing I missed. The smoky eye I decided on is deeper than what I usually do.

My eyes have always been my best feature. Combined with my pale skin and dark hair, I always knew how I looked to boys, then to men. I grew up with naturally blonde parents, so it was another way I never felt as if I fit in. Somehow, the dark hair skipped a generation and landed on me. I remember all our family photos as a kid and the stark contrast between them and me. My mother would note my hair and how dark it was, how her bouncy blonde was a gift from her own mother, and somehow make mine feel as if I was born cursed. She would talk about coloring it nearly constantly, and my grandfather was the only one willing to make her stop. He would always be the one to calm her down on my behalf.

He died when I was twelve, and it was unmanageable to be around my mother afterward. No one would stop her from criticizing me constantly, always comparing me to her. I started wearing bigger T-shirts to hide any weight I had gained, even though I was always thinner than most girls. There was always a way to be better in her eyes, something I have never achieved. Since going no-contact, I have started to appreciate myself more: my dark hair, always long and slightly wavy, the perfect beach wave.

I take in my red lips as they gleam under the bathroom lights. The lighting is less than flattering, but somehow, I don't look half bad. I take the velvet dress off the hanger and slide it onto my body. I decided against Spanx, not wanting to hate myself later for them. I have always been self-conscious about my weight. I went from a kid being bullied on the playground for being anorexic, to gaining a healthy amount of weight after I met Kane, to now learning to embrace the curves I've grown into as a woman.

It always helped that no matter what size I was, or how much weight I gained in college, Kane never looked at me any differently. He would trace my body with his eyes and hands, telling me how beautiful I was. He would only encourage me to work out if it was what I wanted. He would help me at the gym and always make sure I knew how much he desired me. Little by little, I started to fall back in love with myself. Now I can look at myself and really appreciate the way I look.

The velvet clings to my body like a second skin as I put on my heels and snap in my earrings. I stare at myself in the mirror and take a deep breath. This is the best I'm going to get. I spent a little more time than usual, knowing the type of crowd Elena surrounds herself with and the way they'll size me up next to Kane, measuring me against some standard they deem acceptable for their son.

I clean up my mess and take everything with me, waving goodbye to Sam, the night-shift full-timer, who's behind the desk when I pass.

The April night is thick, the days becoming warmer than usual in the south for this time of year. There's heaviness in the air, and the humidity clinging to my skin is a telltale sign of a good storm.

I get into my car and start it up, letting the cool AC blast through the vents and cool down my overheated skin. The thought of seeing Kane in just under thirty minutes has me working up a sweat. I take off, trying to let the words of the song playing on the radio give me strength to get through this night with at least a couple pieces of myself intact.

CHAPTER NINETEEN

kane

Lie – Sasha Alex Sloan

I roll my truck up to the ostentatious gate, the looming gold bars almost blinding me as the sun hits them, the whole thing attached to a beige brick fence that surrounds the property like an impenetrable force.

The manor sits in front of a backdrop of half-dead trees trying to break through with the warming Tennessee spring. Spring showers are finally bringing life back to the plants that lie dormant during the brutal winter months.

Subtlety was never Angelo D'Antonio's strong suit, especially when he bought a luxury estate nestled in one of Tennessee's smaller towns outside Nashville, located directly next to Cherry Hill.

I type in the code and watch as the gold bars open, reminding me of the gates you see when they let you enter the underworld, with demons waiting to strike.

I take my truck up the never-ending drive, the pit in my stomach getting heavier the farther I go.

It's another dinner for my father to talk about himself

with his disgustingly wealthy friends, who all hate each other and throw money around all night. The second you walk into one of these things, you can feel the air being sucked from the room by their overinflated egos. I'm not sure why I keep showing up. With my trust fund now mine, I have no reason to be here, but some part of me is still hoping my father or mother will recognize me as their son.

I tap my fingers on top of the steering wheel, the silver of my cuff links gleaming in the sun. The rings stacked on my fingers feel like armor. I rub the *A* ring to give myself some courage for the night.

I take in the scenery around me, the soft, fluffy clouds sparse against the vibrant blue sky, reminding me of Avery's eyes. The blue is so clear it feels as if you can see for miles above you. The air carries that ever-present scent of humidity, finally. My black truck is freshly washed ahead of tonight, not that he'll be checking. But with my anxiety reaching an all time high, I figured it was best to cover all bases.

I glance to the side where Avery should be sitting as panic starts to tighten further in my chest. It started this morning, dull but familiar, with small bouts of pressure I know too well. I thought of going to visit the rescue shelter as a way of taking my mind off of it and maybe catching a quick sight of Avery to help, but I was way too behind on my paperwork to go. I opted to get dressed early and swing by on my way here, just to see her car in the parking lot.

I saw Grayson's car too, and it brought a smile to my face knowing one of our friends was there with her, taking care of her like I hope to one day again. Grayson may be the newest addition to our group, but he has created such a soft spot in all of us. We opened up to each other in ways the others don't understand. We don't always need words to communicate, and he gets me sometimes in a way the others don't.

I'm grateful she agreed to this charade, but us not arriving together reminds me of the stark difference between now and the last time we came here.

It was my father's birthday, an over-the-top gold-on-gold party that we left laughing together, when Avery slipped an expensive bottle of champagne under her dress and ran out of the house after the first appetizers were served. The joy that radiated from her face as I peeled out of the driveway is something I'll remember my entire life. We made a run for it as if we were Bonnie and Clyde and the night was ours for the taking. The sight of her long blue dress on my bedroom floor was even better than it had been on her, though the way it hugged her curves had left me drooling after her. I spent my time thanking her. Properly.

I blink back to the present and park in front of the fifteen-car garage in my usual spot. My space in the garage was quickly filled with some sports car my father bought the moment I left for college, another excuse to show off his ever-growing wealth.

I put my truck in park and inhale a breath, letting the cool air from the vents blast me in the face. Slowly, it helps lower my heart rate. I count in for four and out for four, until I can feel the tips of my fingers come back to life.

I lean back against the leather seat and give myself a few minutes to get my guard up before facing what I'm sure will be a nonstop test of my sanity.

I take my phone out of the cup holder, my heart leaping at a new text from Avery shining on the home screen. I ignore every other message and unlock my screen as my background photo blares at me: a photo of Avery with my guitar across her legs, me behind her, helping her learn. I change it weekly to a new picture of her or us, another way to keep her close to me, even when the gap between us feels so vast.

Her long, thick hair is up in a messy bun, with a soft smile on her face and a wrinkled brow as she tries to understand the chord progression I'm explaining, mid-laugh behind her. I can remember the way her back molded so perfectly to me then, the guitar resting softly in her lap, my arms curled around hers as I helped her trace the patterns of the music. A record played softly in the background, a tune I was trying to have her follow.

Warmth floods my chest at the memory, calming the last of the panic along the recesses of my mind. I open her message.

PRETTY GIRL

I'm leaving now. The new intake took longer than I thought. I'm so sorry!

I grin down at the message, imagining her soft voice as if she were speaking the words directly to me. I know she probably saw a new dog ready to board and immediately lost track of time making it comfortable in its new cage. It was always her favorite part.

ME

No worries. I just got here, and I know my mom is staring out the window wondering why I'm taking so long. Don't text and drive.

PRETTY GIRL

stoplight 😬 go inside and get it over with, be there in 15!

ME

Drive safe, pretty girl

I watch as she reads the message, then lock my phone and slip it into the front pocket of my dress pants.

One more deep breath, and I run my now damp hands down my black dress pants. I open the door and peel myself out of the safety of my truck. I pull the sleeve of this ridiculous dress shirt down and straighten my tie. I grab my jacket from the passenger seat and shrug it on.

The thick air hits me immediately, and I wish the sun would set faster to break some of the heat. The black dress shirt has me baking under the full sun.

I hurry across the brick driveway, past the huge circle fountain in the middle and the big gold monstrosity behind it, an eagle or phoenix type of animal taking up much of the front of the house from my angle.

My all-black outfit contrasts with the subtle brick and light beige house, the multicolored stone lining the door to offset the rest of it. It's a look I know Avery prefers. Not that my ex-girlfriend's opinion should have been a factor, but knowing she would be here tonight, knowing how her eyes would heat up at what I chose...

Yeah, who am I kidding? It was the only factor.

I leisurely stroll up their seven-step staircase to the biggest door this side of the Mississippi has seen. The door begins to open before I can even reach it, someone in a suit hired for this event standing on the other side. He bows his head at me as I breeze by. A slight nod of my head makes me look like a dick as my nerves bounce in my stomach, but I'll never let my face show.

My mask is on and firmly in place, the role my father expects me to play as his only son. The heir.

As I stroll through the foyer, I take note of all the gleaming surfaces, not a single piece of dust to be found, not even a stray piece of mail lingering about.

The lightly painted walls are lined with various pieces of artwork my mother has collected over the years, following the grand staircase as it splits and rises to two separate wings of the house. The marble floors shine with a perfect polish, something I'm sure my mother had done this morning. I follow a path to the first living room on the main floor, where soft music is carried from the open back doors. Tonight, the party is an outdoor affair, the back glass walls of the house open completely so the patio looks like an extension of the living room.

The patio is done up with tables of flowers and drinks scattered about. People mill about, sipping champagne and dark-colored drinks from frosted tumblers. Most are dressed in full suits and soft cocktail dresses, more diamonds than I have ever seen shining off the women. An obnoxious rich man's laugh echoes from every corner. My left eye twitches at the sound, already grating on my nerves. I take in the "small" dinner party of at least fifty people and roll my eyes —though I'm thankful for all the fanfare, since hopefully the heat will be off me tonight. I hope to blend straight into the crowd and keep my father from spotting me too quickly.

I take in the various servers with trays of food, then snag a champagne off one tray for Avery and a whiskey neat for me. I'm not much for alcohol, especially around my father, but it gives me something to hold while I avoid the numerous handshakes and fake back pats of his friends as he shows off his heir. The good ol' boy routine I've come to expect.

I spot my mother somewhere on the back patio, near the long table used for hosting these events, as she laughs with a group of her country club friends. I head that way to get the hellos out of the way, hoping Avery can find me easily when she gets here.

"Mother," I say in greeting, leaning in to let her kiss my cheeks. She turns, and her face lights up at the sight of me.

"Finally, he comes home," she says, pinching my cheeks, which is hilarious at her five-foot-two height to my six-four, but I let her anyway. My height comes from my father's side. Her dark brown hair is up in some intricate twist, and her ears drip in diamonds—a new gift from my father, I assume. She's dressed in a deep green dress that shows off her olive skin. My heart warms at the sight of her smiling and having a good day. I let her give me one more hug.

"Kane, you remember the girls. Girls, my son, whom I must beg to visit home nowadays." She scolds me, pulling me slightly to the side, away from her group after a chorus of hellos.

"I've been busy, Mom." I exhale, knowing I won't be able to get away with that excuse for long.

It's not that I don't love my mother and wish I could see her more. Things have always been unpredictable with her. One day, she's a loving and involved mother, and the next she's defending and siding with my father. She would shield me from his worst moods, putting herself in the line of fire, but at the end of the day, she always stayed with him no matter what he put us through. My brain has a hard time reconciling both sides of her: the dutiful mother and his sidekick.

"You look handsome. And tired," she muses, placing her hand on my cheek, then my forehead, as if she's checking my temperature. "And where is Avery? It has been ages since we've seen her too."

"She's coming. She had to be at work late, so she

decided to just meet me here." My gaze moves toward the front of the living room inside to see if she's arrived yet. My heart falls a bit when I don't see her. The urge to check my phone in my pocket is strong.

"Oh, Mary, wait!" my mom says, abandoning our conversation as she hurries after her friend.

I let out a breath and take a drink of my whiskey as I pull out my phone, but there's nothing from Avery. Sighing, I lock my phone and slide it back into my pocket, then take another strong pull from my drink. The whiskey is smooth as it slides down, missing the burn I'm used to from the stuff at the bar.

I debate whether to call her when I glance up, and there she is. The world starts to fade a bit as I catch an eyeful of her.

Her long dark hair spills down and curls softly around her face. Light makeup highlights her features, and red lipstick draws attention to her delectable lips. I almost groan at the sight of them, the bold red against her pale skin. The stark contrast of colors makes her stand out in any room she's in. I take a minute to drink her in, unashamed since she hasn't seen me yet, as she talks to one of my mother's friends, whom I'm sure she's met dozens of times over the years at these things.

She wears a tight-fitted black dress that flows down to the floor, with a dangerous-looking slit coming up her left side that makes my heart stumble at the sight of her creamy pale thigh peeking through.

I want to follow that trail of freckles that goes up her inner thigh with my tongue.

There are thin straps across her shoulders, with her small but full breasts just peeking through the top, a sight I couldn't miss. She wears black heels that give her a couple more inches, and before I realize it, my legs are moving toward her.

I set my half-finished glass on a tray carried by a server quickly passing by and continue my stride until I reach her side. She tucks her long locks behind her ear with a radiant smile on her face as she listens to the group around her.

I almost trip at the sight of it. She's laughing at some joke from some golden-haired douche clearly attempting to move in on his next conquest.

I slide up to her, and my hand slips around her waist, pulling her against me. The feel of her plump ass sends haywire signals to my brain. I grip her body even tighter into mine until she's completely molded into me. I hear her sharp intake of breath, too small to be heard by anyone else. Wide eyes peer up at me before she hides her surprise with a quick smile. I dip down and lay a kiss on her forehead, not wanting to push things too fast, but loving the feel of her too much to let go.

"Avery," I greet.

The world fades away as I stare into those baby blue eyes, softly lined with black and framed by her long lashes.

"Kane." Her soft voice is husky as she peers at me over her shoulder, the top of her head coming up to my chin. Her heels give me a better view of her face.

"How was work?" I ask as I turn her around with my hands and settle both palms on her hips, effectively cutting us off from their conversation. She raises one eyebrow at me, asking without words why I'm behaving this way.

Her hands come up to rest on my chest and fiddle with my tie. It sends tingles up my spine as I feel the warmth of her fingers through my cotton shirt. The thin material is only a small barrier between me and her full warmth. She's playing along nicely with this narrative we created, that we're still together, a fact my brain seems to forget with the way my hands hold her with a bruising grip.

"It was long. We had four new intakes today. All dogs found abandoned close to the old roller rink. Clearly dumped! I mean, come on, you can't even drop them at a shelter? Those poor babies were skin and bones. Adorable little Lab mixes. I think they were all part of the same litter. We had a call earlier, and I raced in the truck to get them. I mean, it was only thirty degrees out this morning when the call came in! Someone had tried to stop, but they were so scared. I raced out of bed," she fumes, clearly still fired up about her day. Her face is so animated as she talks, her brows furrowing and her lips pursing with frustration.

Usually, I would have leaned down and kissed her just to make her relax a bit, watching those divots between her brows straighten out, but I keep my place on her hips. My fingers make slow circles on her back, feeling the velvety material beneath them. My heart stutters, knowing how lucky I am to get this contact with her. I have been starved for her touch. I think it would take a couple natural disasters to pull me away from her right now.

"So naturally, you did something unsafe by going to that part of town to get them. Did you go alone?" I quip, a constant argument between us about the situations she would put herself in for those dogs.

I love her passion and how much she cares for them, but sometimes I wish she cared enough about her own safety. I can remember the countless times she got a call early in the morning or late at night about a dog, and I forced her into my truck instead and drove with her. I knew while she was getting those animals to safety, I could focus on her safety. No matter how tired I was after. She would care for and look after the dog, and I would look after her. I would stay vigilant and alert, scanning the surroundings for anything off when she came running back with her prize.

"Before you start lecturing me, *Dad*," she quips as her black nail digs into my chest. "I did not. Keith went with me, thank you very much. He met me there with all the supplies from the truck." She tries to back out of my hold, and instead, I grab on tighter and bring my hands around her back, resting them just above her ass. The one that looks so appealing in this dress my hands are itching to slide down a little bit farther.

This back-and-forth is easy between us, a small break from the mounting tension that has filled the moments before this. It feels like a truce. It feels like a good reminder that the chemistry is still there between us, and that this is still just as it was meant to be. I stand here staring down at her, my eyes searching for those missing freckles, hoping she feels the same rightness I do.

She looks up at me, hands still playing with my tie, and her breath hitches. The moment seems to slow, and I wonder if she wants me to kiss her. I usually would have by now, and we're here to put on a show. People think we're still together. There is nothing to stop me from doing it.

Still, I hesitate. Would she even want that right now?

Would I be crossing some invisible line she drew when she said she needed space?

The longer I stare into her eyes, the more my gaze traces down to her soft, pillowy lips, begging to have that lipstick smeared by me. I slowly pull her in closer, giving her time to say no, but she comes willingly, her hands sliding up my shirt and linking around the back of my neck.

Seconds tick by as her body molds to mine, her front entirely flush against me. Every piece of her fits so perfectly against me, like our bodies remember exactly how to come together.

All the worries about my dad and this party fade away the longer we stay here, in the middle of the chaos, locked into each other. Her head slowly rests on my chest, and I feel some of the tension she held when she walked in fade away. My own body relaxes as I breathe in her familiar scent. The soft sounds of music and conversation surround us, the cool breeze from the finally set sun kicking up. Goosebumps trail up her arms, and I rub my hands up her back to warm her as I hear the faint hum of the outdoor heaters turning on.

"Kane!" a deep, foreboding voice yells. The tension of it goes through my body, making every muscle taut as I brace myself for an incoming fight.

Slowly, Avery picks her head up and sends me a *you ready?* look. I give her a small nod and reluctantly peel myself away from her. My right hand grabs hers before she can get too far, and I guide her in front of me. My left hand lands on the small of her back, the strands of her hair so long they brush against my hand as she walks. We shoulder our way over to where my father beckons us.

CHAPTER TWENTY

kane

Let You Down – NF

As we make our way through the small gathering, I quickly get my mask in place: the *fuck off* look I've perfected for every event like this—the look of the son worthy of Angelo D'Antonio.

My dad has taken up his throne for the night, his friends gathered around him and hanging onto every word as if he's a god. He looks imposing where he stands near the edge of the deck, overlooking the lights below the small hill the house sits on. The acres beneath us are also owned by my father, stretching all the way to the regal golf course on the other side. A barn sits somewhere in the distance, unused since we moved in.

The gold railing comes up to his hip as he rests one arm on it. His hands are clasped around a glass, the amber color telling me it's scotch. His suit is as pristine as his hair—the same color as mine, only perfectly styled. The contrast is stark against my messy curls, which I've left wild and slightly longer these past few months. The closer we get to him, the more my chest tightens.

The voices dim a bit as we get closer, the sound of the waterfalls out back growing more prominent with less music playing. The pool gleams in the moonlight beneath the balcony deck, bright lights hidden throughout the yard between trees and bushes, closer to my mother's prized garden.

As we approach, I see the tightening around his eyes, the disapproval evident on his face. As if I could know what caused it. There's little I do that he's proud of. Maybe he's assessing me and doesn't approve. Maybe my hair is too wild for his liking. Or maybe my socks are the wrong shade today.

My hand tightens a bit on Avery's back before she reaches around and links her fingers with mine. A reassuring squeeze follows, and she looks up at me softly as we approach the group. The five other men make room for us to join. My father dismisses them with a nod until it's just the three of us.

He takes a sip of his drink, preferring to draw out the dramatic pause. He's always looked younger than his fifty-five years. The gray in his hair is barely visible at his temples, the lines beside his eyes only just present. It makes it hard to look in the mirror some mornings and know exactly what my future will be. He was always so proud as I grew up, because I was a spitting image of him. He would gloat to all his friends about how blessed he was to have another version of himself. His rich friends would laugh along with him.

"Kane, how nice of you to come home. Your mother misses you. Have you seen her?" he provokes as he leans against the railing casually. A false front for the anger radiating from his eyes as he stares at my hand clasped with Avery's at her side.

My hand tightens on hers as I shift slightly in front of her, as if I can shield her from his words. Her other hand comes up to my bicep, anchoring me to her in this moment. The tension hitches my shoulders up slightly.

"I have. I've been busy. School started back after break, and the bar has been busy," I defend—my mask firmly in place, my voice indifferent toward him. I'm not willing to let him see any of the cracks in my exterior.

"Hmm, yes, the bar. How is the high school thing going?" The disdain is evident in his tone. The tension in the air is so thick I feel as if I can't take a full breath. The tightening in my chest worsens as I stroke my thumb over Avery's hand, more to calm myself than her.

The soft scent of lemons from her perfume distracts me, giving me a moment to take a deep breath, clearing some of the black that creeps at the edge of my vision, signaling a panic attack is near. I say nothing as I stare at my father. Knowing him, he doesn't want a response anyway, so I forgo my rebuttal.

"Avery," my father grunts, finally acknowledging her presence. He stares at her fully, ignoring me as if I'm not there. He straightens his stance as if to greet her, but one look at me keeps him where he is. My father is built and has always had broad shoulders, but somehow, I came out bigger.

I'm the tallest in my family so far, my shoulders and muscles haven't stopped growing since I learned my way around a weight room. I was proud of my body. I worked out hard, I played harder. I could have gone further in football and played in college, but every interested team was too far away. Avery's grades were average, and she needed a scholarship. I offered to pay, but she wouldn't even entertain the idea. Her parents refused to pay a dime, even though they had more than enough. They said if their daughter wanted something in life, it had to be earned, not given—as if she never earned their love either. So I declined every offer and followed wherever she went.

Football was never my dream anyway, at least not once I met her. Football was never going to give me the future I craved. The recognition, the money, the fame—none of it truly meant anything if I didn't have her to come home to at the end of the day. She wanted to try long distance, claiming she wanted me to follow my dream, but what she didn't get was that I did—by being with her. And I have never once regretted that decision. Even now, if this is all we ever have, it will always be enough for me. She will *always* be enough for me.

"Mr. D'Antonio, nice to see you again," Avery replies softly, so small as if she'd rather not be heard. "This is lovely. Elena has truly outdone herself with all of this."

Avery is not new to this level of wealth, having been here daily during senior year and many times since then, but she is still always in awe that this is someone's house—whereas this is all I've ever known.

"Yes, she did," my dad agrees, his expression slowly softening at the sound of my mother's name.

While I never knew if my father loved me, I did know he always loved her. He gave her whatever she wanted in life, except for fidelity. He showers her with the most lavish houses, vacations, every diamond and gift she could ask for. He gives her his full attention when he is home. A love story that could almost seem like a dream—yet in every city we've been to, it hasn't been enough. My mother has truly never been enough for him, and neither have I.

"Kane, we need to talk about what's next," my father declares as he takes a sip of his scotch, the glass nearing empty. His third or fourth, I can conclude by the faint smell when he talks. My father has never been one to stop at just one drink, overindulging in every aspect of his life.

"There is nothing left to discuss," I spit back, gripping Avery's hand harder. I get us ready to turn and leave if needed. A small look of confusion crosses her face at my father's words. "We talked. I said no. End of discussion."

"It is not the end of the discussion. You are a D'Antonio, and you will do as expected. This little rebellion you have going on: the school, your little job, her—"

"*Her* name is Avery," I cut in. "And like I said, it is not up for discussion. I would choose your next words very carefully, because if you speak one word against her, this will be the last time we speak at all."

Avery's hand tightens in mine. Her other hand grabs the back of my shirt to anchor me as I stare at my father, unflinching. Steam practically pours from his ears at the way I speak to him, especially with someone else present.

He speaks of her as if she's just some phase he's waiting for me to grow out of. The future—*hopefully*—mother of my children somehow reduced to a mere inconvenience in his mind. He's unhappy not getting what he wants. He demands I marry the daughter of some business partner of his choosing, training under him and following him around, ready to take the reins of the family business.

My wants and needs have always been ignored when it came down to business.

"Oh, there you two are!" I turn my head to see my mother striding over to us, ignoring the tension swirling in the air. My shoulders relax as a smile appears on my father's face, not quite reaching his eyes, as my mother sidles up to him, always trying to be the peacekeeper between us. "Dinner is about to be served. Are you ready?"

I turn with Avery's hand in mine and lead her away from them, no excuses given, as I head back toward the table. I try not to pull Avery behind me, so I slow my pace until she can catch up and walk side-by-side with me.

CHAPTER TWENTY-ONE

avery

Exile – Taylor Swift (ft. Bon Iver)

We're sitting at the table, the soft sounds of metal against glass filling the space around us as dinner is served. Elena opted for a shorter dinner this time, with just one main course. I try to eat my food slowly, but my hunger is obvious after the long day I've had. I forgot lunch when things got away from me.

I glance at Kane out of the corner of my eye, his food barely touched. He's pushed things around his plate with his fork, but it's a stark contrast to my already half-eaten meal. I take a sip of my water and set it down when I see Kane turn his body toward mine.

Since the showdown with his father by the gardens, Kane has been quiet. As usual, he's working some small problem out in his head instead of talking to me. I try to tamp down the hurt and understand how he might be feeling. I try to be grateful he wanted me here at all. I know I can't force him to talk to me, but I thought we were making some progress. Maybe not quite ready to fix our relationship, but maybe ready to be friends. A way to co-exist in the same space.

I was shocked when Kane agreed to this charade. He isn't all that close with his parents, but I thought it would be something he told them. So when he admitted what happened, my heart leaped. A small kindling of hope started in my chest and stayed there all week. It had me reaching for my phone so many times to ask him why he never told them.

That hope fades the longer we sit in this silence.

Kane turns toward me, and I arch a brow at him as I take another bite. The perfectly cooked, juicy chicken melts in my mouth, an embarrassing moan working its way up my throat. A small chuckle leaves Kane, making his whole body move as he reaches up and tucks my hair behind my ear, his hand lingering as his fingers glide through the strands.

"Did you eat today?" he asks, his smile soft, his body completely turned toward me and his knees wide enough to trap my entire chair between them. The warm light from the candles and the lamps outside illuminates the side of his face by the table. I shake my head as I finish my bite, and he lets out another chuckle. I'm sure that has him remembering all the times he's had to remind me.

A chill races up my spine as the temperature drops further in the night. The moon now crests in the sky while the last rays of the sun peek over the horizon. He looks at me and signals a waiter, asking them to bring one of the heaters closer. Warmth suddenly presses at my back as he runs his palm up and down my arm, which breaks out in goosebumps for an entirely different reason.

I'm hesitant to break the moment between us, but I clear my throat and implore, "Are you okay?"

He looks away into the darkness on the other side of the

house, his jaw tightening as his hands return to his lap. A sudden boyish expression moves across his face, his brown eyes sad as he shrugs at me.

"Just another family dinner," he replies, a mask of indifference on his face.

The sad eyes of a lonely boy stare back at me. His parents are down at the opposite side of the table, laughing along to something someone next to them said. An act of PDA is on full display as his father holds his mother's hand over their dishes. Kane looks at them and sighs before returning his gaze to me.

"You can talk to me. You don't have to pretend this doesn't bother you. I don't know what your dad meant, but —" I begin, hoping to get him to open up to me.

"No," he scoffs, cutting me off.

Hurt lashes across me at the dismissal.

"It doesn't matter." His jaw clenches and his fingers flex with tension. His silver rings gleam under the warm light as he twists one around his finger, the restlessness evident in his shaking foot.

I try to pry a little harder. I reach over and place my hand on his knee to still its movement, causing him to look up at me as I inquire softly, "It's clearly not nothing if you're upset."

"I said nothing is wrong, Avery," he says, effectively dismissing me again. I pull my hand back and place my napkin on the table, then stand and take off toward the house, the hurt of his denial to talk about it coursing through me.

Silly me. How could I forget that we aren't even together, and he no longer owes me to talk about his problems? Not that he ever did before this.

But there were moments today when I saw Kane. *My Kane.* The sweet boy I fell in love with.

My Kane, who talked, joked, and laughed with me.

That ember of hope is thoroughly crushed as I make my way through the living room, searching for the powder room in the hallway. I hear footsteps behind me, but I ignore them, uninterested in small talk. I almost reach the bathroom when I'm pulled back by my wrist and turn to face Kane. Shock courses through me at the sight of him, out of breath and standing behind me.

"Avery, stop," he begs. He lets my wrist go as he drags in a few deep breaths.

"What Kane? I need a minute. I'm not interested in what you had going on back there," I bark, crossing my arms over my chest.

"I know. I'm sorry. I'm—" He drags his hands roughly through his hair and pulls at the strands.

"You're what? Not going to talk about it? Yeah, I got that." I turn, attempting to make my way to the bathroom, but Kane takes my hand and pulls me after him. I follow begrudgingly to the end of the hallway and up a back staircase that opens right to his childhood bedroom.

The room I practically lived in during our high school days. My body sighs in defeat as I let him haul me through the doorway and close the door behind us.

A wave of nostalgia hits me with the force of all the memories spent inside this room. The nights we spent studying together, playing rounds of PlayStation, and the night he took my virginity. I take in the scene around me. Everything is perfectly in place, just as it was the last time we were here. His bed is made with a dark blue bedspread, and the photos above the desk across the room mark our final year. Marcus and Kane playing football in one photo, the championship trophy they won for our school in the next, and his old boutonniere, dried up from our prom together. A small smile touches my face as I stare.

"Avery, I do want to talk. I just... What am I supposed to say?" Kane says wearily, defeat written across his face as he leans back against the door. His head hits the wood, and his body sags against it.

I take a few steps and sit on the bed across from him, my heels out in front of me as I stare at them and wait for him to continue. He stands up straight and looks at me until I make eye contact again.

"I'm angry with them. I'm still fucking angry. It's been how many years, and nothing changes. It's party after party, them putting on a show for everyone they know, yet when do I hear from them? When do they show an interest in my life? I'm not doing what they want, so I'm iced out, banished to the end of the table. They've known you for how many years, and the way he dismisses you like that pisses me off."

He spits the words out, hands raking through his hair as he starts pacing back and forth in front of me. "And the constant talk of the 'family business.' It was never my dream. No matter what my father says. They want me to get married, did you know that? They want me to marry whoever my father thinks will benefit the family best while I learn to take over. But no, I go to a normal college, graduate, and take a job that fulfills me. I pick you, and it's still not good enough."

He all but yells the last part into the room. "The calls have gotten worse too. Calls to remind me what a disappointment I am, that I'm selfish and ungrateful, that everything I've been given and for what he claims. I'm wasting it away," he finishes coming to sit beside me on the bed, flinging himself back. He lies next to me, his arm over his eyes, trying to catch his breath.

Shock courses through me as his words repeat in my head. "I... I didn't know all of this had been going on. For how long?" I ask softly as I watch the rise and fall of his chest.

He peeks one eye out from under his arm, his gaze piercing me. "When hasn't it been going on?" He sits up and puts his back against the headboard. "The marriage stuff? Recently. It's why I never told them when we... when it happened. Me being a disappointment? I don't know. Since birth, maybe," he confesses.

"You're not a disappointment," I chastise as I turn my body to face him, the slit of my dress sliding dangerously high on my thigh. I watch his eyes track the movement and darken as they linger there.

"Should we go ask him?" Kane asks as he sits forward and makes his way to the side of the bed next to me. His shirt is wrinkled a bit, his suit jacket gone and still hanging on the back of his chair downstairs.

"I don't need to," I protest as Kane gets off the bed. My body turns to track his movements when he kneels in front of me, his big form folding so he's eye to eye with me.

His hands come up and rest on either side of the bed next to me, barricading me in. A darker expression streaks across his face as he snares me with his eyes before they dip to my lips and slowly make their way back up.

"You don't need to. Why is that?" he asks, his voice husky and dark.

The silence of the room makes our breathing loud. The only other sounds are the distant ticking of a clock somewhere in the distance, and the laughter outside, barely reaching us through the walls. I watch as he drags his thumb over his thick bottom lip, the slow perusal of his eyes. The heat gathering low in my belly deepens under his stare, and spreads to my other limbs with the itch to touch him. The urge to pull him over me, to feel his heavy form press me into the mattress until the heat of him consumes me completely, almost suffocating me, until he's all I can think and feel.

He brings his body closer, still caging me in place, and I reach out. I follow the same path his thumb took across his bottom lip, making his eyes go black with lust. The tip of his tongue touches my thumb, the act sends tingles straight to my core. I trace my hand up and over his cheek before sliding my fingers into his hair and pushing it off his face.

"You are good enough, Kane. Just as you are. Even if they can't see it. Even if they can't see you," I declare, staring straight into his eyes, not wanting to scare him with my words but needing him to hear them.

I watch the words wash over him. He closes his eyes for a moment and absorbs them as a shudder starts where my fingers stroke through his hair and rolls down his body. Some of the tension releases from his shoulders, causing them to drop from his ears. Just as I'm about to remove my hand from his hair, he opens his eyes and grabs my hips roughly in his hands.

The heat in my stomach becomes a full inferno under the way he looks at me, lids hooded as he stares at my lips. His hands trace from my hips down to the middle of my thighs.

My legs part without a thought as he reaches the hem of my dress, only to start sliding the material up my thighs. He looks up at me, testing to see what I'll do. I meet his stare and open my legs further, lifting my butt slightly to let him slide my dress up to my hips. His eyes fall to the small scrap of black lace covering me, panties so sheer he has to see exactly how badly he's affecting me.

He slowly licks his bottom lip, and a small "fuck" leaves his mouth. He bends his head and starts kissing up my legs, starting at my knees and slowly making his way up, switching sides until I drop my hands from his hair and lean back against the bed with both arms behind me. The sensation of his scruff dragging over the sensitive skin of my thighs, and the little swirl of his tongue with some of the kisses, sends shivers across my body. The way he keeps looking up at me as he makes his ascent sends shockwaves down to my core.

"You think I'm good enough, pretty girl?" he purrs, looking up at me. He yanks the tie loose around his neck and takes it off, wrapping it slowly around his hands. The image fills my fantasies, and I can feel my pussy pulsing the longer he stares at me, the tie taut between his hands.

"Yes, I do," I vow, my voice full of desire.

He has this way of making me tongue-tied the longer he stares. He lays his tie next to me, moving his hands to the waistline of my underwear. I lift a bit and let him slide them down my legs. Gone is his slow perusal as he yanks them off and spreads my legs far enough apart for his shoulders to nestle between them. He takes a long look before he uses his hand to stroke me, just once.

His thumb slides over my soaked core, the movement sending lightning through every nerve in my body.

"*Fuck*, baby. How good am I?" he begs with a sinful smirk. His face takes on a playful quality as he teasingly strokes me, never quite going where I need him most. The lack of touch to my clit makes me wetter with every stroke.

His left hand grips my thigh, the bruising force balancing the soft strokes that set my body ablaze. No other thoughts come to me in this moment, the party all but forgotten with the feel of him between my legs.

"So good. You're *so good*," I moan, my eyes closed as he finally swipes over that small bundle of nerves screaming for attention. My head falls back, exposing my throat as he starts making slow circles over me again. The pace is teasingly slow but firm as he remembers exactly how to draw this out. A moan rises up my throat as my hips try to move on their own, chasing pleasure that is just barely out of reach.

"Uh-uh, pretty girl. If I need to be good, so do you," he whimpers, pulling back and stopping my moving hips with his hands as they swallow my whole hip and stall any movement. Before I can respond, he lowers his head and takes a long lick from the bottom of my slit to the top.

"Mmm... what a *good* fucking girl," he growls into my pussy. "Fuck, if this isn't the best dessert I could have imagined."

I moan so loud that embarrassment heats my cheeks before I lean back farther to give him better access. The soft light of the moon shines through the blinds and illuminates him in the otherwise dark room.

His tongue laps at me, moving in circles around my clit. My stomach tightens as he goes over it again. My body begs for more as one of his hands drifts farther down my thigh until it disappears. Then I feel him pressing through my slit before he slides inside.

A cry rips out of me as Kane's pace quickens, then he adds another finger. I feel them curl up to that sweet spot that always makes me come. The pressure of his callused fingers rubbing my inner walls makes my breathing break into irregular pants. The edge of the cliff rapidly approaches.

He continues his assault on that spot he knows makes me see stars, stroking me deeper. His tongue continues to circle me, and when he sucks on my clit and lightly scrapes it with his teeth, my body coils on that bundle of nerves, and I break apart as my release finally spills over.

The feeling is never ending while his fingers continue to work me through it. The wet sounds should be embarrassing at how loud they are in the quiet room, but I'm too blissed out to care. When his fingers slowly slip out of me, aftershocks still course through my body, and I can only watch as he brings them to his mouth and cleans them off with his tongue, a cocky smirk on his face. The groan he rasps out is indecent as he stares at me over his fingers.

"So, pretty girl, was I good enough then?" he quips, wiping his lips with the back of his hand as some of me drips off them, making my face heat.

I finally get him to talk to me, and somehow, I end up without my underwear, coming down from the best orgasm I've had in months.

"Very," I blush, trying to get my bearings. I lower my dress so it covers me, suddenly shy. "Do you want me to, uh..." I trail off, my cheeks heating further.

He laughs and brings my face up to meet his before planting soft kisses on my lips. The tenderness he kisses me with feels too soft after the filthy way he just undid me, each lingering brush of his mouth making my heart break a little more.

The feel of his lips again after so long fills my soul in a way I can't even describe. The giant hole that has been my heart for months finally starts filling under his exploration. He comes back every time he breaks away, for just one more kiss. Heat returns to my belly, my body begging me to deepen it when he pulls back.

"No, pretty girl. I'm good. That was for you," he explains, his hand still holding my face as he looks at me, eyes bright and shining, the slight twinkle returning to them. He pulls me in for one more kiss, almost as if he can't help himself. A look passes over his face that I can't quite read. Could it be adoration?

"But I—" I grin, then look down and notice a slightly darker spot on his black pants. "Oh."

My cheeks flush red as I look back up at him. He came in his pants from just going down on me, which makes me giggle a little. Kane follows, the sound lightening the situation.

"This feels like high school all over again," Kane groans as his hands drop from my face and he stands. He straightens his shirt and pulls me up after him. He brings my dress down and smooths it out for me, then flattens my hair—which I'm sure will be impossible to brush through later—before reaching down to grab his tie from the bed. I peek around for my underwear but come up empty in my search. I rustle through the blankets on the bed, trying to ignore the giant elephant in the room.

"Avery?" Kane asks from where he's standing in front of me as I pretend to look for my missing thong in the now-messed-up bedcovers.

"Hmm," I reply, my search still fruitless, before I finally take a breath and steel myself as I turn to him.

"Thank you," he expresses softly, his hands in his pockets. A boyish quality takes over his features, showing a shyness I've so rarely seen in him.

"For what? Uh..." I gesture toward his pants, causing a laugh to burst out of him. He drops his head back and laughs with his whole body, infecting me until I join him.

"No, thank you for coming," he flirts, a smirk on his

face. "Okay, get your mind out of the gutter. I mean tonight. I know things have been different, but I really appreciate you coming with me anyway. For being there with me," he finishes. He runs his hands through his hair, one of his telltale signs that he's nervous.

"You're welcome," I start softly as I walk closer to him and bring my face up to meet his. I stare into his warm brown eyes, the gold flecks shining back at me with so much love that I have to clear my throat to dislodge it. "You are enough, Kane. I want you to know there has never been a time since I met you that I haven't noticed what a treasure you are. You're worth more than your weight in gold to me and to the people who care about you. Your heart is so big. Don't let them close that part of you off. Don't let them take it away from you, because your heart is my favorite thing about you. Your parents not seeing you says more about them than it does about you. They have all this money, all these things, and they're missing the most priceless thing of all: your love. I feel sorry for them," I whisper to him, his eyes slowly turning watery as I speak.

I trail my finger along a stray tear that leaks out, catching it before it can fall. "You were *always* enough for me," I finish softly, my heart heavy as I straighten and prepare to leave, wanting to run from this situation on a high note.

I give him one more look, waiting until he can see the truth in my soul, before I turn and walk away. I open the door and find my way down the stairs. The party is still in full swing outside, so I stay along the darker hallways and grab my bag from the guest closet as someone lets me out the front door. The air has turned cold, the wind whipping with the storm the forecasters broadcast earlier.

I let a tear of my own fall, finally. Not for myself, but for him. I let them fall for the Kane who has had to fight tooth and nail against the belief that he needs to be anything other than himself to be enough. I wish more than anything I could change the way he sees himself, that I could let him see himself through my eyes. That he could see the beautiful boy I met who turned into the devastating man he is now. Every part of him is so wonderfully made, so beautifully crafted to love every part of me. How could I not do the same?

I can't be what fixes him, I realize. Nor can I force him to confront all these parts of himself that make him feel unlovable. That's something he needs to do on his own now, and I wish like hell I could be the one by his side when he discovers just how wonderful he is.

I roll my car down the drive and let myself mourn for that lost boy. I let myself mourn what we had and what we could've been. I don't believe this is the end of our story, but how can I ask him to heal if I'm still holding on to past hurts?

CHAPTER TWENTY-TWO

kane

Trauma – NF

I sit here in my room until the music has long since faded away. I hear the doors closing outside and the engines starting, yet I sit here until there's nothing but silence to greet me.

The moon is bright in the sky, illuminating the dark room, the only light as I wallow within the darkness. It could have been hours or days that I've been sitting here with my back pressed against the wall, my arms thrown over my knees, reeling from tonight.

The images of tonight flash across my mind. Avery sitting on the bed, telling me I am enough, the way those words gripped my throat and made it hard to speak. Hearing those words fall from her lips left me unable to contain everything I feel for her. I had to watch her leave again. Avery in her black dress. The way her curves looked. The way her eyes lit up when she told me how much I mattered, that fierceness blazing back at me. That fire she doesn't let burn enough.

The way she looked walking away from me, hips swaying and my heart in her pocket. The room seemed to get dimmer when she left. All color seemed be to sucked out, painting it in shades of gray until they faded to black when the sun officially set and the storms rolled in. My mind wanders to her cries as she came for me, then drifts to the anger that hits when I realize my parents haven't even bothered to call. They haven't even noticed or cared about my absence, apparently. All the emotions from tonight leave me drained.

My mind lingers downstairs, and I hold on to that anger, refusing to push it down again. I let myself feel something for the first time with them, the mask firmly slipping away and leaving me raw. The pain is unable to hide anymore, not with the way my heart is battered and bruised after years of abuse.

My therapist said it doesn't benefit me to shove it down and pretend it doesn't exist because the body remembers. It reminds me in the panic attacks that hit me in my lonely hours, in the way I refuse to be vulnerable and open up to the people who matter most, convincing myself that once they see me, they'll hate it. All this stored-up trauma will come out in one way or another, whether I acknowledge it happened or not. Since exploring and talking about these experiences throughout my youth, I have noticed it is easier to manage my anxiety. Combined with medication, I can't remember the last time my brain felt so free from the fog that has plagued me most of my life.

My skin itches as too many emotions hit me. Once I get up from the floor, I go over to my old dresser and open the drawer to take out some old sweats and an old high school football T-shirt that I left here. I change out of these clothes and throw them away in the empty wastebasket next to it, not caring what happens to this suit.

Once I throw the shirt over my head, I grab my stuff, shove it into my pockets, and finally let myself out of this self-imposed prison cell. I stop to stare at the pictures that line the mirror, a picture of me and Avery from senior prom, the next one of her laughing in the bed of my truck, the time we had a food fight with Marcus and Morgan, and lastly, the one I didn't know was taken at the time. Her standing in front of me with my arms wrapped around her as she's looking up at me, laughing at something while my eyes are caught on her, the small smile on my face as I gaze at the center of my universe. I grab the photo and tuck it into my pants. I grasp the door handle and let myself out of the room as quietly as I can.

I hear soft voices that come from the living room and pray that I can sneak out without them acknowledging me—not that they have ever seen me before.

When I hit the landing, I hear, "Kane?" from my mother's soft voice. I let out a breath and debate going that way. "Are you still here? Your truck is outside."

I continue down the hallway until it opens to a cavernous space, where I find my mother on the couch sipping from a glass. Her hair is down from its updo earlier, with my father sitting opposite her, sans suit jacket, taking up space in the chair, his hand around yet another glass of scotch. The look of disdain is evident on his face.

"Yeah, just leaving," I sigh, ignoring the imploring looks from my father. His deep stare almost cuts into the side of my face. A mask of indifference slips onto mine. *My armor is ready for battle.*

"Oh honey, come sit. I feel like we haven't gotten to talk much tonight. I want to know how school is. And is Avery still here? What are you wearing?" my mother asks excitedly.

I linger in the doorway, playing with the rings on my fingers as the anger rises yet again. *As if it was my fault that we barely spoke tonight.* The party took all their attention and I was thrown to the side again. The hours I've been missing are empty from their minds, as if we spoke only minutes ago. The fact that they didn't call to check on me speaks volumes.

"I spilled on myself," I answer wearily, trying to keep the anger from my voice. The flames of frustration rise higher the longer I stand here opposite them. My parents are completely unaware of their actions, or how their lack of concern for my absence in the last few hours feels like a mirror for the last twenty-three years of my life. I let the angry little kid in me come forward as he begs his parents to see him, to give a fuck. That sad little boy with a crushing loneliness—his lifetime companion—who was abandoned by two people he saw every single day.

"Sit, Kane," my father demands with his low but powerful voice, the tone made to leave no room for argument as he commands me the way he does his boardroom.

"No," I say, my tone cutting. The anger seeps into my pores and takes over my body from the inside. The fire rages within me, ready to be released.

I study my father, or the person who claims to be one, because his actions have never shown him to be. This man who was supposed to play catch with me after work. The one who was supposed to be at my football games, cheering from the sidelines. The same man who was supposed to teach me about sex, the one I was supposed to run to with my first crush. The man I was supposed to be able to come to for advice on how to fix how badly I fucked up with the love of my life.

Instead, I got a man who was always disappointed, who showed no emotions unless he was berating me. The man who saw a seven-year-old cry about a bruised knee and told me if I was this pathetic, how was I ever supposed to make it in the world? The very same father who saw my tears as an inconvenience. The emotions of a fragile kid being too much to deal with.

I tug on my shirt and push my hair back. "I'm leaving."

My father slams his glass down on the table with force, some of it spilling over the side. "I said—"

My mother flinches with his tone.

"No!" I yell, my hands flying out in front of me, cutting my father off in a move I have never done before. "I'm done. I'm done with you two. I don't care anymore. Cut me off. I don't need your money anymore. I have my trust. Nothing is worth this anymore. So don't pretend to care now. Don't pretend that I owe you my time when I have been here all night, and this is the first time you can be bothered to talk to me about just me," I lash out, my chest rising and falling with pants.

The surprise at my abnormal outburst is clear across my parents' faces. I turn around, and my legs eat up the distance until I've reached the grand entrance. When I hear my mother's heels clicking against the marble floor, the sound gets louder as she hurries after me.

"Kane, wait, what? Where is all this coming from?" my mother begs to my back, stopping a few feet from me. The sound of my father's steps slow as well. Disbelief courses through me as they chase after me. I keep my back turned and let out a few breaths as I comb through my thoughts, letting the black edges of panic recede a bit from my vision.

I turn to the two people who were supposed to love me unconditionally yet only loved me when it was convenient for them, if their behavior is what can even be considered love. Parents who have never made me feel that just being me was enough. The two people who were supposed to accept *me*, not the mold they wanted me to fit.

My mother's appearance is frazzled for her, her hair pushed back a bit as if she ran her hands through it too many times, the edges sticking out in all directions. Even my father's normally stern features seem to soften slightly with confusion. Neither of them speaks as they stare at me.

I take a moment to take it all in. My eyes roam this house, the marble floors that lead up to the staircase to my room. The heavy feeling, still present, that I felt when we moved in. They trace over the opposite wings that made the distance between me and them almost poetic. Me on one side and them on the other—a metaphor for how our lives have been since I was born.

I steel my spine and look at them. "Am I ever going to be enough for you?" I whisper, my voice cracking on the last word. Devastation immediately washes over my mother's features. She takes a small step toward me, but my body instantly retreats a step back. She notices and stops her advance. Her hands come up to her face, but I don't let myself look at my father. I can't bear to see his reaction to me ripping my soul to shreds right in front of them.

"Of course you are. What makes you say that?" my mother worries.

I laugh sardonically, the sound ripping out of me. I glance at my father, the tightening of his eyes clear. Yet he hasn't spoken a word.

"Am I? Because every time I come back, I'm reminded that I am constantly a disappointment to him." I gesture to my father. "Nothing I do is enough because it's not what he wants. I'm finding who I am in this world without you both. I'm forging my own path, and that still isn't enough for you. Fuck the family business. I never wanted it. I appreciate everything it has given me, but that was never my dream," I pant, looking back to my mother. "There were so many things I wanted, but most of all, I wanted you both to give a shit. I wanted a mother who stood up for me instead of letting a little kid take the brunt of his anger. I wanted a mother who left the first time he cheated. I *needed* a mother to hold me when I cried at night because our driver was the only one who showed up to my flag football games, both of you off doing everything but being my fucking parents."

By the time I finish, tears stream down my face. I let them fall, not bothering to wipe them away. It's time I finally see what they've done to me.

I'm not some lost little kid anymore who is too scared to get smacked around. I'm someone who has been broken down by life, who has given everything for the people in front of me to really see me. To see me for who I am despite what they did to me.

Most people think abuse can only be seen from the outside, but the real damage happens on the inside. The way you're slowly infected with it until it invades every aspect of who you are. When you've been so emotionally neglected your whole life, you're not even sure what emotions you possess anymore.

Parents who made it so impossible for me to stop the one good thing I ever had from walking away from me. Those words she so desperately needed from me, I couldn't find them. The chaos in my head was always too much against the emotions battling me. They laid the foundation that has cracked. I'm just now going through and repairing all the gaps, watching as slowly each piece becomes whole in my mind.

"You wonder why you never see me, yet where are you? When do you text me just to ask how I am? Where are the phone calls? You ask where I am—where the fuck have you been my entire life?" I demand, slowly breaking apart, unable to hold back. "Where the fuck were you when my world was falling apart, losing the love of my life and I don't even know why? I've had to pull myself off the ground and fix myself. You want to point the finger at me for the state of our relationships when you should look into a fucking mirror. When you're both alone in the big fucking house surrounded by all this shit that was always more important to you than me and wondering where the fuck I am, it won't be anywhere near you." I stare at my father as I sneer this, a look of genuine hurt streaking across his face.

I push myself through the tears. "Thank you for showing me exactly what not to do when I have kids one day. Thank you for showing me what type of parent I don't want to be. My kids will never feel the way you two have made me feel. I had great memories of us, but they're so tainted by all the bad that it's as if they were never there. I'm done being a disappointment to you. I have someone I've never had to beg to love me. A person who has seen every version of me and still wants me. *Wanted* me. And I'm going to do what it takes to get her back, because when someone loves you in the way you've craved your entire life, you don't let that go. Fuck if I won't get on my hands and knees begging for a sliver of her attention again until I bleed," I profess to my father.

The house is silent, except for the faint sound of the large grandfather clock ticking in the background and our three breaths mingling. The anger slowly recedes until the numbness creeps in. I take another long look at my parents, feeling nothing as I stare back at the two people who have disappointed me more than I could ever have disappointed them, and turn to walk out. I let the words linger between us, feeling the finality in them.

I get into my truck and throw it into drive. The roads pass me by, but I'm not really seeing them, driving on autopilot.

The truck is silent, my thoughts empty as I continue on. When I stop, I'm not shocked to find myself parked outside a familiar white cottage. The lights are on outside, with her car parked in the driveway. The red time on the dash states it's 11:23 p.m. I throw my truck into park and rest my head against the steering wheel, finally letting the tears fall.

CHAPTER TWENTY-THREE

avery

Silver Spoon – Erin LeCount

Time blurs as I sit on the edge of my bed, countless thoughts swimming through everything that happened. My black dress is still on my body, though my heels are long since kicked off.

Nothing went the way I expected. I didn't anticipate tonight, but I can't find it in myself to regret it. Of all the ways I had built the night up in my head, it wasn't Kane and me alone in his room with his head between my thighs.

Things between Kane and me were always amazing when we were together, but we never dug deep. I knew he loved me. I felt it down to my marrow, in the way he'd stitched himself into my soul. But with both of us coming from such complex childhoods, neither of us ever really learned how to process what we were feeling. I think that's where the problem started—the lack of knowledge about what the other person was feeling and the inability to talk about it. It was easier for us to ignore the distance growing between us than to confront what might be wrong in our relationship. We had the naivety to believe being together could solve all our issues.

Except when the complex stuff arose, I couldn't articulate how I was feeling before starting therapy. It made me realize what a gap we had in our relationship. I knew Kane. I could map out his body in the dark, pinpoint every divot and crevice with my eyes closed. But what we lacked was the capacity to open ourselves up to the core and pull out the hard stuff, refusing to let the other see us completely bare.

I shake the thoughts away and stand to get out of this dress, tossing it into my overflowing laundry basket before stretching out the stiffness from sitting in such an uncomfortable position.

I grab the closest shirt to me, which happens to be a favorite of mine—one of Kane's old band T-shirts from when we went to see The Lumineers. The concert was after the start of our first semester. I remember the hours we drove to get there, and the way Kane surprised me with the tickets as we pulled into Nashville. I remember the way we screamed the songs along with hundreds of other people but somehow felt lost only in each other.

The shirt always brings me back to the way Kane and I felt infinite. Us lost in each other and the black sky on the way home, hand in hand, driving into the night with an endless number of possibilities on the horizon.

I shake myself out of the past as I make my way to the kitchen, the dim glow of the string lights hung around the house illuminating my path. The quiet of the night follows alongside me.

I take a deep breath and grab a bottle of water from the fridge. When I close the door, I glance out the front window over the sink. The large window facing the road reveals a black truck parked along the curb. The familiar sight sends a jolt through my system, my heart pounding. I look further into the dark. The lack of streetlights on our road makes the figure almost invisible as it sits on the front stoop, head bent forward.

My heart rate accelerates as I grab my jacket from the kitchen table, open the door slowly, and shrug it over my shoulders. Silence greets me as I close the door behind me and take a seat on the top step next to him. The cold of the concrete immediately seeps through my shorts, sending chills through my body.

The air is cool now, with the lingering scent of rain from the storms that swept through earlier. Spring in Middle Tennessee is constant whiplash, storms raging through to clean the slate of the rising humidity. The crickets are out in full force tonight, creating a symphony in the background as I glance at Kane's profile. The clench of his jaw is prominent as we sit here, his deep breaths almost perfectly in sync with mine.

I'm not sure how long we sit here, the silence enveloping us as we exist in the same space. Kane's head turns to me slowly, and I look over at him from the spot my eyes have been tracing along the cracks in the concrete. Red rims his eyes, a sheen that makes my heart ache to smooth it over coating them. His hair is sticking up in every direction, the telltale sign of his hands constantly dragging through it. He's changed out of the suit he wore earlier, now in an old T-shirt and sweats I recognize from our high school days, the Cherry Hill High logo staring back at me. His tattoos that snake along his arms catch my eye, the familiar *A* inked on the inside of his bicep, following a snake that wraps around his forearm, the look of dripping ink coming off it.

My hands make their way out of my sleeves as I rest one

between us, my palm meeting the cold concrete before I feel his pinky finger slide into mine. His grip is loose but solid, our pinkies intertwined as we sit there. I study the contrast of his larger, tanned hand next to my smaller, very pale one in the moonlight.

I turn and take Kane in, noticing his jaw loosen and his shoulders lower. I can see the anger slowly melting from his body as he sits here. His breaths even out, and when he turns to me, those stark golden-brown eyes snare me with the pain reflected back in them.

My heart breaks at the sight of him showing me his most vulnerable state. I can't remember the last time I saw him this way, if ever. All his walls are completely lowered, and every single thought seems to stare right back at me. I'm not sure how long we stay locked in one another, one moment bleeding into the next, stripped completely raw for the first time in years. Of every moment we have shared together, this one right here—just me and him, lost in each other—is what I crave most. We are two hearts that have been crushed and disappointed by life, finding solace in one another. When the world seems too loud, too much, we can just exist in this moment. Two people who could have been anywhere else but somehow found each other despite every circumstance, every choice that might have led us away from this, only for it to inevitably bring us here, his hand in mine.

Kane peers out at the darkness and clears his throat while he confesses, "I told them." The emotion is thick in his throat as I stay quiet and wait for him to continue, acknowledging that he needs this moment. "I told them how I feel. Not in the best way, but I said it all."

He doesn't look at me, still lost in the darkness around

us. His pinky stays locked with mine, the grip tightening as he speaks, as if he needs an anchor for this moment.

I take a few seconds to think about what to say next. "And how did they take it?" I implore quietly, not wanting to spook him. He scoffs while shaking his head but keeps our fingers intact. He pulls my hand into his lap and covers mine with both of his, warming my hand from the slight chill it's taken on since we've been out here. I relish the feel of his hand stroking the back of mine while I wait for him to continue.

"I don't know. One moment I was trying to leave unseen, and then I was exploding. All the years of hurt and resentment just boiled out of me before I could stop it," he sighs, fully interlocking our fingers together, the feel of his calluses sending goosebumps up my arms. He takes a deep breath. "But it felt good. Is that weird to say?" he asks with a slight laugh. "It felt needed. I feel freer, or less burdened, I should say. Now I'm not the only one carrying all this weight. They can carry some of it now." His voice gains strength the longer he talks.

I give him a moment to sit in that feeling before I speak softly. "I'm glad, Kane. You deserve that. You deserve to speak your truth, even if they're not willing to change. At least you said it."

Those sad but striking eyes make their way back to me from where they were lost in the night. Those soft irises roam over my face, tracing a path down to my lips and lingering a moment before slowly rising to meet my gaze, which hasn't strayed from his face while he spoke.

I catalog every moment, every shift in his expression to file away for later. On days when we may not talk as much, I can remember how it looked when Kane took his power back. The moment he finally released some of the burden on his shoulders and the way his eyes brightened just slightly for the first time. I note the tension leaving his brows, softening his whole face, and the peace that crosses his features all at once.

"Thank you," he whispers.

His eyes lock with mine again while his thumb continues moving in circles, the feel of him warming me from my fingertips down to my toes. The chill is long forgotten with the way his presence heats me up.

"I think it helped. Losing you," he clarifies just as gently, the words sending my heart plummeting.

My hand immediately starts to pull away from him, but he holds on, keeping me from running.

"Hold on. Listen," he continues gently. "It helped losing the one person who never made me feel like I was anything less than perfect. Who saw me. I needed to know there wasn't something wrong with me, that they're the ones with the issue. It took losing you to show me just how much I don't need their approval. Maybe I never needed it. All I needed was you, and then I needed to really find myself. I know what true pain feels like now, Ave. I knew it the second you walked away."

My heart pounds and my thoughts swirl as I try to piece together Kane's meaning.

"It's not over, Ave," he vows. "You and I are inevitable. I'll be here when you're ready to talk, because we both know this isn't the end for us. So go do what you need to do. Find yourself, if that's what this is. But I know in this life and the next, it ends with us. There's no other way for it to end but with you coming home to me every night."

He turns to face me on the steps, his eyes imploring me to believe him. My traitorous heart yearns to reach out for him before the stark reminder hits me that he let me go. He watched me walk out that door when I laid my heart bare, ripping myself apart for him to communicate with me. The hurt rises in me, whether from now or years past, until it all blurs together in the moment.

There are layers of hurt here. Months of begging to be seen. To be enough for someone to stick around. To be someone worth chasing after. I can't breathe as I look at the one person who has had my heart since I learned his name. There's an ache in me from years spent as a forgotten kid with parents who never wanted her. The lines blur between him and them.

Why can't anyone see me for what I am before they lose me?

Why do I have to walk away for someone to realize my worth?

My thoughts jumble, and the words I need are nowhere to be found.

He stares at me, softness in his features, understanding gleaming in his eyes. His hand comes up to cradle my cheek. My face falls into his hold as tears I didn't notice escape are wiped away by his thumb. My heart aches with so many unsaid things laid out between us.

He closes the distance between us, and his lips land on my forehead, soft and barely touching my skin, causing my eyes to close in the moment. Our breathing fills the space between us. When he pulls back, he takes one last look at me, then gets up.

He walks down the last couple of steps before his stride eats up the pavement. The flowers lining the driveway seem to wilt as he walks by and takes my heart with him. I haven't moved, haven't breathed, since he got up and walked away from me. I wish I could conjure up any words to speak in this moment, but my mind empties the longer I sit here.

When he reaches his truck, he turns back—his stare holding me in the night—before rounding the cab to his door. The moonlight bounces off his face, those severe features eating me up.

The moment lingers with a small shake of his head, and then he gets in. The truck starts with a roar in the night before he takes off, the lights fading into the distance.

I'm not sure how long I sit there, but the chill seems to seep into my bones. The shorts I have on do nothing to protect me from the cold taking over. The thoughts are still jumbled in my head, the past and present becoming one until I peel myself off the step, the feeling of his lips on my forehead following me inside.

I stumble my way to my bed as I reconcile how much Kane seems to have found himself in these past few weeks apart, less burdened by the demons that have constantly plagued his mind. He confided in me, and I feel as if I caught a glimpse of the man who was always hiding beneath that masked exterior. The man I only ever caught glimpses of before in flashes, small moments when he allowed himself to be raw with me.

But the hurt from the last couple of months doesn't just go away after one moment of vulnerability. It rips open old wounds I have been working to fix. Those old feelings of abandonment don't get erased with a few months of therapy and self-reflection. It's a permanent scar that stains your heart.

Nothing in life has ever lit up my soul the way Kane has. It's as if he is the sun, and I could never help but be drawn into his atmosphere for warmth and safety. I have been learning how to live without the sun for weeks now, and I haven't crumbled the way I thought I would without him. I have persevered in a way I needed to know I could. I can stand on my own two feet without him there holding me up. As much as my soul craves his, I'm not sure where to go from here.

I feel the tears dry against my cheeks—nothing left in me to expel. I turn on my playlist, listening to the sounds of a poetic song about losing the love of your life, wondering if that's how our story ends.

CHAPTER TWENTY-FOUR

kane

If You Love Her – Forest Blakk

With the start of a new week, I took over the weekend shifts at The Grunge for an employee who had a family emergency, and I'm feeling it this morning. I had to drag myself out of bed, snoozing my alarms numerous times until I realized I'd never beat the morning traffic down Main to get to the high school. Since South Hill sits on the outskirts of town, bordering the next one over on its way to Nashville, the morning commute can be brutal if I leave late enough.

I was grateful for the extra shifts, though, since they left me little time to fixate on Thursday night. The highs and lows of that day seem to be unshakable. I feel good about where I left things with Avery. It was a step in the right direction. I know she can't be enough to fix me, but she gives me a clear goal in mind of what a healthy, healing Kane could look like with her by my side.

I roll into school a bit later than usual, the first bell ringing and all the kids out and about on campus. The chaos of the morning soothes me, and the routine of seeing some of my favorite students today has me hustling across campus to make it before someone is there waiting for me.

I spot a mess of brown hair hurrying through the crowd and away from where everyone else seems to be going. His head is down, but the blue sling tells me exactly who he is.

I try to walk a bit faster and catch up with him as he breaks through the crowd. I gain on him and yell, "Trevor!"

His body tenses and he stops walking, but he doesn't turn to look at me.

"Hey, where are you going?"

"I gotta go, Mr. D," Trevor mutters, his back still turned to me.

"Trevor, please look at me and tell me what has you rushing away from school before the day has even started." I reach out softly with my voice. He turns to me fully, and I finally see what he was hiding—the entire area around his eye is *black*, swollen nearly shut.

I attempt to mask my surprise, but some of it slips through my features, causing him to step back farther, his guard coming up.

"Don't, Mr. D. I'm fine." He snaps the words out.

"You're clearly not fine, Trevor. You have a black eye. Have you gone to the doctor?" I ask.

"No, and I don't need to. This isn't the first black eye I've gotten. I'll be fine in a week or two," he huffs with a self-deprecating laugh.

"Trevor, you can't keep showing up with bruises all over and expect me to do nothing. Not if someone is hurting you. I can help you. Please let me," I stress, hoping he hears the seriousness in my tone.

I won't keep dropping this for much longer.

I've had my suspicions for a while that he's being

abused at home. He has all the classic signs, on top of taking care of his two youngest sisters. He's a *boy* carrying the weight of the world on his shoulders, stuck between a rock and a hard place.

"I need to go. Sara called me, and she won't stop throwing up. I'm the only one who can go get her." His body angles like he's ready to bolt at any minute.

"Fine, but you need to come into my office tomorrow to talk about this. I'm making a call. This isn't going to keep happening to you." The finality in my tone leaves no room for argument.

The courtyard has long since emptied out, the students all in class. The silence stretches between us. The labored breathing of the boy across from me wrecks my heart.

Who has been looking out for *him*?

How long has he had to take care of his sisters when he should be a kid?

He should be enjoying high school, playing a sport or thriving in academics. Maybe he'd be in theater or band. Instead, he's barely making ends meet with his part-time mechanic job and flunking out, all to keep his sisters afloat.

"You don't have to keep shouldering this alone, Trevor. Let me have your back. Let me stand with you while we get you help—for you and your sisters," I reason, hoping he hears me. I don't want to just help him. I want to help *all* of them. "I'll come with you if you want. I'll make sure they can put you somewhere together." I coax the promise out as gently as I can.

"You can't promise that, and you know it. We'll get lost in a system that doesn't really care about us. I was in it before, and I refuse to put my sisters through that," he spits, then takes off toward the parking lot.

My feet move forward, if only to run after him, even

knowing it's futile. I need him to admit something is happening, but who's to say calling CPS won't just make things worse for him at home? If he won't tell me, he's not going to open up to a random social worker.

But I'm left with no choice, the signs can't be brushed off any longer.

I sigh and run my hands through my hair, feeling my rings scrape my scalp as I pull in frustration before spinning around and marching back to my office. I throw my bag down on the ground next to my desk and heave myself into my chair. I blow out a breath and try to focus my racing thoughts—the panic swirling in my brain about what could be happening to these kids. My mind wars with making a call or waiting just one more day.

Am I damaging these kids further by doing nothing but respecting Trevor's wishes? I want to do right by him. That's how I've gotten him to trust me so far, but I feel that trust fraying each time I push him. If I call, will I be pushing him over the edge? Will I irrevocably ruin that trust and lose any chance of helping him at all?

The conflicting thoughts whirl in my brain until my office phone rings and I'm thrown back into the now. I stare at the ringing phone for a moment before answering. Dawn tells me my appointment is waiting. I hang up, straighten my shirt, and take out the paperwork I brought home last night, trying to gain some sort of balance within myself before welcoming the student in and getting on with the day.

And before I leave for the day, I make the call.

CHAPTER TWENTY-FIVE

avery

Don't Let Me Go – Cigarettes After Sex

"What the fuck?"

I have been sifting through my whole sock drawer to find a pair before I head off to work, and every single sock I pick up does not match. How is that possible?

It would be reasonable to assume that I would just wear mismatched socks, but I hate the feeling of different toe seams on my feet. So, as I scatter all the contents of my drawer on the floor, frustration rises inside me, and I let out a loud groan the longer it takes to search and come up with nothing.

Morgan sticks her head in my room and sees me on the ground as I scavenge through the contents on the floor.

"Uh, Ave, did you finally have that mental slip from sanity we've all been worried about? Or is there a reasonable explanation for why you're on all fours throwing socks around the room?" Morgan muses, coming to lean against the door frame, her laughter audible even as she tries to muffle it behind coughs.

"Definitely the sanity one," I confirm and sit back.

"It was really only a matter of time," she jokes, coming to sit on the floor across from me with her back leaned against my bed. "But really, what's going on?"

"I feel like I'm losing it. I did laundry yesterday while you were out, and somehow I'm missing the match to every pair of socks. I can only find one of each kind." I explain, picking up random socks and showing her.

"What the fuck?" she mirrors my sentiment from earlier.

"I took a nap, and when I went to fold my clothes from the dryer, I didn't really check. Now they're missing."

"Did you check the dryer?" she asks.

"No, Morgan, I just decided to throw out my entire drawer and didn't check the dryer where I got them from," I reply sarcastically, rolling my eyes and flinging myself back to starfish on my bedroom floor in the destruction of socks I've created.

Suddenly, Morgan breaks out in laughter, and I crack one eye open to stare at her.

"What's so funny about this situation?" I ask, frustration finally taking over.

"Those losers took them!" she bursts out, bending over with laughter as tears gather in her eyes. "You took his shoelaces, and he took your socks, knowing you can't not match them!"

Her head is thrown back in laughter, and a chuckle slips out of me. It is actually a good one.

"You know how we should get them back?" she muses, looking at me with a mischievous glint in her eye.

"How?" I ask with one eye closed and my hand thrown dramatically over my head, not ready to let go of the pity party I'm throwing myself.

"We go on a double date," she suggests, smiling wide at me with a manic look in her eye.

"No," I answer, leaving no room for argument. From what I know of Morgan, no isn't an answer she accepts easily. She's always had a knack for getting me to do things outside my comfort zone.

"Come on, what else do you have to do besides sulk in the house for another weekend?" she prods, hitting my foot with her hand to get me to open my eyes and look at her.

"I'm not sulking," I groan.

"I'm sorry, I meant pouting," she snickers and hits my foot again.

"I'm not pouting either."

"Okay, and what would you call staying inside all weekend and watching back-to-back rom-coms on the couch?"

"Taking care of my mental health, obviously."

"What would be good for your mental health is getting out and meeting people. Not sitting at home all alone because your ex—maybe not ex-boyfriend—hasn't reached out since he ate you out like a Thanksgiving meal in his childhood bedroom and told you he was still in love with you."

"He did not say he was still in love with me."

"Sure, Jan," she replies, making a *Brady Bunch* reference and getting a laugh out of me. It's something we binge-watched together in high school after diving into older sitcoms.

"I don't know Morgan, I don't think I'm ready."

"You never know if you don't try, and you can't not live because you're scared," she reasons.

I know she's right. I can feel the truth in her words and

how worried she is about me. The indecision swirls in my head as I sit here.

"I'm just not sure about a date. I don't think I'm ready to meet someone else." I hesitate while picking up some socks in front of me and tossing them softly back in the drawer.

"Then just come out, no expectations. Meet him, and if you like him, maybe go out with him again. Or don't. I just want you to get out. I hate seeing you sitting here just waiting around for him to be ready," she states, grabbing my hands and looking into my eyes—her brown ones on my blue. The socks are scattered around us, but with my best friend in front of me, I feel okay for the first time in days.

"Okay, I'll go, with no expectations. But I will only meet at The Grunge if Kane isn't working," I relent as the brightest smile appears back on her face.

"Yay!" she yells. "OMG, this is going to be so much fun! And the guy I'm meeting with is yummy. I met him at a LANY concert last week in Nashville, and they're willing to drive out here just to take us out." She bounces up and down, her blonde ponytail swinging with the movement.

"But just drinks at the bar," I warn, wagging my finger at her before she gets too excited.

"Just drinks, I promise," she agrees while making a cross-my-heart sign.

I chuckle at her excitement, and she laughs with me. Small seeds of unease slide into my stomach at the thought of meeting someone who isn't Kane for drinks, but it's harmless, *right?*

"Okay, now take some of my socks and go to work! Bring that leather mini skirt and tights with you to change into before The Grunge. You'll make every man's pants a little too tight once they see you," she jokes, wagging her eyebrows at me.

I laugh. "Ew, you pervert. Okay, I'm going. I'll see you tonight," I respond, grabbing the clothes and socks. With a wave, I run out the door to Second Chances.

Changing in the staff bathroom should be an Olympic sport for me at this point. I take myself in and am amazed at the way I'm able to make myself look this good in such a small space. Except the fluorescent lights are harsh on my skin, highlighting the dark circles under my eyes that even my highest-coverage concealer cannot seem to cover.

I slip into my leather mini skirt and admire how it grips my ass and immediately makes me feel more confident with it on my body. Morgan and I found it last year while shopping in Aspen while her family went skiing. I put it on and completely fell in love with it. Of course, I couldn't afford a thing in that store, so Morgan secretly took a picture after I refused to let her buy it for me, and somehow Kane had it waiting for me back home by the time we got back.

I finish the look with my signature ripped fishnets and my Doc Martens, which pull the look together with a low-cut maroon crop top. The weather is finally hot enough at night to ditch the long sleeves. My lips are wine red, and with one last swipe of gloss, I feel much better. Not that I'm really trying to impress the guys Morgan has us meeting, but it feels nice to get dressed up and leave the house.

I refuse to tell Morgan that.

The uneasy feeling from this morning is back in full force, turning my stomach into a pile of knots as I close up and get the rest of my stuff from the staff back room. My stomach rolls as I think of any guy who isn't Kane sitting across from me. What will we even talk about? Am I supposed to ask his favorite color?

What if he thinks this is a date?

I'm aware that I'm spiraling, but as I get closer to The Grunge, traffic after seven is a mere whisper compared to what it was earlier in the afternoon. I try to play some of my favorite songs to psych myself up for this, but even my kick-ass girl-power songs can't seem to shake the unease I'm carrying. It feels wrong. I know I agreed I would go out and experience things, but what if this is the rest of my life—going on date after date, searching for someone who makes me feel even a sliver of what Kane does?

He stole my heart when I was young, and I have yet to get it back. It feels as if I walk around with half a heart most days, that missing spot impossibly large.

I try to banish these feelings from my brain, chalking it up to nerves at meeting new people. My brain short-circuits whenever someone new is around and I have to make small talk. My skin begins to itch, and I tend to overshare. After every encounter, I go through the entire conversation in my head, imagining the worst—they must think I'm annoying, or they hate me. What if I talked about myself too much? It's a self-deprecating spiral that unravels inside me long after the encounter ends.

I pull into the parking lot way too soon. The bar appears crowded for a Monday night, and I shift my car into park. I take a few deep breaths to try to force this foreboding feeling out of my chest. The night is still and humid, the birds at the nearby park chirping, with numerous sounds coming from the bar as the door opens and some patrons exit. They hold the door for me, and I whisper a quick *thanks*.

The neon lights shine bright on the walls, and the music

is some sort of pop-punk track my brain tries to focus on as I search for Morgan. She texted me not that long ago that they were here and getting a table. I glance around for that blonde hair when I finally spot her facing me in the back with two heads sitting across from her—one with slightly longer hair pulled into a man bun next to a taller man with shorter black hair. My heart jolts for a moment, thinking it could be Kane, until he turns and I'm able to take in his profile.

Definitely not Kane.

He's cute in a boyish way, with an average-sized nose and lips that lean on the smaller side. He sports no scruff on his face and no visible tattoos. I expect my heart to calm down, but it beats harder the closer I get. The sounds in the bar send my already overwhelmed system into overdrive until Morgan stands up and gives me a hug.

"You're okay. I've got you," she whispers into my hair and smooths a hand down my back, sensing the unease running through me.

"Guys, this is Avery, my bestie I've been telling you about. Avery, this is John." She gestures to the man with a man bun and an impressive beard. He has Clark Kent glasses and perfectly straight teeth. I wish I could say he's not Morgan's type, but she's never had one. She always says she enjoys the male species in all forms, whereas my taste has always firmly been *Kane.*

I'd never given much thought to boys before Kane. Sure, I had some crushes the way young kids do before they fully meet the boy and realize how gross and immature they are, but once Kane walked into Cherry Hill High, I realized my type was tall, stacked, dark-haired, and blessed with beautiful hazel eyes.

"And that's Jordan," she finishes as she gestures to the

other guy at the table and sits down. I smile and give a tiny wave to the boys before sitting down across from Jordan.

He is cuter up close—next-door look to him. He appears to work a blue-collar job, judging by his callused hands, and I can appreciate a man who works with his hands. There is something so inherently male about watching them build something with their bare hands.

There's a Coke and vodka sitting in front of me with a slice of lemon on the rim, and my heart trips as I glance at the bar to make sure Kane isn't here. When my quick search comes up fruitless, I turn back to Jordan and smile again, hoping to defuse some of the awkward tension I can feel rising.

"Hey, Avery, you were the drag-along too, huh?" he muses on a laugh, flashing me a crooked smile that is oddly charming.

"Yes," I huff a laugh. "Does he do it a lot?" I ask while taking a sip of the drink and groaning as the perfect ratio hits my tongue. I love the way the lemon breaks up the bite of alcohol and the sugar in the Coke gives me a buzz.

"Uh...I feel like if I say yes, I'm calling him a player, but if I say no, maybe that makes me lame," he teases.

"No wrong answers here. Morgan is for sure a player, and she drags me to things all the time," I reply, and he laughs at me. I watch his eyes track down to my very generous cleavage in this top before flicking back up to me. His ears redden at the tips when he sees me catch him, and I smirk.

The two next to us have not stopped talking since I sat down. Morgan pats my leg and smiles at me every now and then to check on me. That's one of the reasons I always agree to be Morgan's plus-one. She constantly checks on me, and I know if she noticed I was uncomfortable, she would leave, no excuses or explanations.

"So, Avery, what do you do?" Jordan inquires as he takes a drink from the darker-looking beer that has been in front of him since I walked up.

After talking with Jordan a bit, I realize he's funny. I have been laughing so much the past few minutes, I must be halfway to a full six-pack. He also just broke up with an ex, so it was nice to lay that out there and have him feel the same way. He was just in the middle of telling me about a hike he and John went on that ended with them getting airlifted off the mountain after a mountain lion chased them a good couple miles through the Arizona forests until they got lost. I'm laughing so hard I spill my drink everywhere. Jordan jumps up to help me start wiping it up, and he grabs my hand to ask if I'm okay when I feel it.

The change in the air around me. I turn to look around and am transfixed by a dark force clad in black, headed this way with a furious expression on his face. He eats up the distance between us quickly, his strides impossibly long, as if some force is pulling him over here.

When he approaches us, he pulls my hand out of Jordan's grasp and puts himself slightly in front of me before he speaks darkly.

"How about you take your fucking hands off my girl before I remove them from your body."

CHAPTER TWENTY-SIX

kane

Work Song – Hozier

What a fucking Monday. The day has gotten progressively worse from where it started. I'm here for yet another extra shift to help Seth, exhaustion hitting down to the very bone at this point, but it was either this or sit at home all night and contemplate my CPS call and what the fallout could be. My mind has whirled since my interaction with Trevor this morning. The very last thing I want to do is serve drinks on a Monday night to people who can barely utter the word please.

Thoughts of quitting have been hitting me more and more now that I have access to my trust. I wanted to leave it untouched as long as possible, but constantly being here night after night is starting to wear on me. I feel as if these past few months I have been stuck buffering in life, unsure where my path should take me next.

I had been thinking about going back to school—maybe to get my master's and become a therapist. I'd always thought I'd like to be someone who works with foster kids or kids from abused homes, but I don't know. This is usually something I would run by Avery, making my already jumbled thoughts worse with the growing urge to text her. All I thought of all weekend was what I should say next. I told her she could take some time to figure out what she wanted because I knew what I wanted, but then I worried that maybe I wasn't clear enough when I said I wanted her.

I need her, in whatever capacity I can have her. I'm ready to let her in fully.

Steve and I talked about it during my last lunch session with him, about letting myself be my most honest self around her and trusting that she will keep that part of me safe. It's been nice to talk to Steve and have him help me discover new parts of myself I haven't appreciated before—how strong I am for getting on the right medication and letting someone help me sort through the mess my childhood left me with.

He helped me talk through the explosion with my parents and how finally letting them know how I felt frees me from the weight that has been on my shoulders. It was a good step in my healing, finally feeling safe enough within myself to tell them how I feel without knowing how they would react.

After spending the weekend ruminating on ideas of what to say to her, I feel ready to lay it all out there—even if she just wants to fight with me. I will let her rage at me all night if it means I get to be in her space again. These past few months have been some of the hardest in my life, harder in a way my childhood never was. I know that because I would relive that repeatedly if it meant I ended up meeting her every single time. Those years feel inconsequential compared to the way the past few months have felt without her.

The noise in the bar snaps me back to focus as I notice Lindsay at the other end—the little five-foot spitfire putting a man more than twice her size in his place. I give her a few moments before stepping in, but once I see she has the situation handled, I turn my focus to the couple in front of me.

I take their order and start on their drinks. The gleaming back wall of bottles looms over me—all two hundred and eighty-three bottles that decorate the back wall are stored with the more frequently used ones at the bottom and the more expensive bottles lining the top shelves. The count varies by season. The crowds seem to be bigger in the winter and spring months, leaving people to find things to do indoors to avoid the cold that moves in.

The hours behind the bar fly by, along with even a short stint in the kitchen when they need extra hands. Our usual line cooks have been taken down one by one with this virus going around, leaving the bar short-staffed. I spend the last hour in the back before I finally get to take a breather and cross the threshold that separates the back of the bar from the front. The crowd has grown since I went back there, so I survey the bar to see where I might be most useful until I hear it: that laugh. Something I could recognize long after every breath leaves my body.

I look around for the source of my every fantasy until I see her next to Morgan. Her long brown hair drapes over her shoulders—the maroon top she is wearing shows off her ample cleavage, and I feel the fire start to spread through my veins. The bright smile on her face blinds me for a moment, the radiance of it catching my breath.

My vision turns red as I glance over to see the cause of that look. A brown-haired douche sits way too close to my girl and makes her fucking *laugh*.

As if anything that pretty boy can say would be funny.

I huff out a breath through my nose and try to quiet the raging I feel inside my chest. My vision is hazy with one clear focus as I watch her lean over and touch the side of his arm while she laughs, the action causing her drink to spill all over the table. I don't realize I've started moving until I see the distance between us getting shorter. I make it to the table just as he reaches over and grabs my girl's hand.

I black out as I rip his hand from hers and shove it away. I take a small step in front of her as if I can shield her from him.

"How about you take your fucking hands off my girl before I remove them from your body," I threaten darkly, leaving no room for argument.

He takes a step back and raises his hands. "Hey, man, there's no need for that. I was just checking that she was okay."

"Well, next time don't touch someone without their permission," I spit as I cross my arms.

"Kane, stop it." I feel small hands pull at my elbow, my gaze unmoving from this jackoff. My blood is still pumping, rage still simmering low throughout my body.

"We were just talking, man," the fucker reasons as he looks at Avery behind me, as if he has a right to her.

"Well don't," I command.

"Kane," I hear again as the hands grab onto my elbow and plead with me to look at her. Yet I remain unmoving.

"Hey, she can talk to whoever she wants," the fucker has the nerve to say to me.

"Of course she can do whatever she wants, but you have no chance with her. She's too good for someone like you," I scoff as the hands let go of my elbow with a huff.

His eyes narrow as he sizes me up. The fucker has the

nerve to smirk at me. I take a step forward, and a look of fear crosses his face.

"Kane, enough!" a small voice yells behind me firmly, causing me to look at the little hell cat glaring at me, arms crossed.

"Look, man, I think some wires got crossed—" he starts, but I turn and glare at him, effectively cutting him off before turning back to face Avery.

"Really, pretty girl? Trying to date at *my* fucking bar?" I ask, tilting my head, regarding her. Fire burns in my veins as my eyes rove all over her face at the way she's done herself up for him. The jealousy eats me alive because he gets to see her like this. Her eyes are black with liner, and her lashes are impossibly long with mascara. I trail my eyes to her deep red lips and feel the need to bite down on my fist with how fucking irresistible they look.

"This isn't your bar, Kane, and you lost the right to tell me what to do months ago," she spits back, a haughty look on her face.

"I don't think anyone is brave enough to tell you what to do."

"You're interrupting something, Kane. Leave," she snarls.

"No," I fire back with an air of nonchalance.

"Yes. This doesn't concern you," she argues with a jut of her hip and mirth in her eyes.

"Anything having to do with you concerns me, baby, don't you know that by now?"

Shock lines her features at my words. The statement freezes her where she stands. Then she turns and takes off toward the restroom. I hesitate for a moment before I take off after her like a bullet, refusing to let her out of my sight again tonight.

CHAPTER TWENTY-SEVEN

avery

Worst Way – Riley Green

I slam into the bathroom, fuming with the shock of how Kane thinks he has the right to crash my night. He has the audacity to get mad at me for trying to live again—to feel something again instead of this numbness that has seemed to burrow itself into my very bones.

I lean over the counter and brace myself over the marble counter and the pristine white sinks you'd be shocked to find in this bar, trying to catch my breath before I go back out there. I turn the water on cold and put some on my cheeks to cool the redness from the anger of our heated conversation on the bar floor.

The door slams open behind me. I jump and turn to see Kane burst through the doorway after me.

We stare at each other, neither of us moving as the bathroom fills with the sounds of us breathing heavily. My chest rises and falls at a rapid pace. The bathroom seems to shrink with him filling the space before me.

"You think that's what you want?" he barks, pointing

back toward the bar. He turns and locks the door before taking a few steps toward me as I place my back against the sink counter.

This back-and-forth we've had going on has drained me. The endless months of missing him mixed with the small moments of hope, only to be crushed when we take steps back.

"Maybe that's exactly what I want, Kane," I taunt, a smirk forming on my lips as I see his eyes darken further. I cross my arms beneath my chest, pushing my tits up in my top, making them practically spill out with the movement. I watch him track it with his eyes, the flex of his hand at his side egging me on further.

"No, it's not. You think a man like that is enough for you?" he challenges as he eyes me like I'm his prey.

His hands brace at his sides, breaths coming in hard pants as I watch him fight to keep his control. His hazel eyes are wild as they take me in.

"And how do you know what's enough for me?" I reply with my arms crossed, wanting some barrier between myself and the man who seems to haunt all my waking moments. My heart rate spikes as he takes one step across the gray floor toward me. He stops, one side of those full lips quirking up in a taunting smirk.

"I know because I'm it, pretty girl," he challenges. "You don't want a man whose ego you have to stroke. You want someone who comes *undone* with just the thought of you. You want a man who would fall to his *knees* after one taste. Someone willing to worship the ground you walk on just for a sliver of your attention."

He advances toward me, shoes squeaking across the glossed cement floor until we're inches apart. Black Converse shoes fill my vision as I lower my eyes.

We feel miles apart still. My hackles are raised with the way this conversation has turned in his favor. I feel the heat bloom across my cheeks, thinking of all the ways Kane is very capable at handling me.

"You forget that I know every inch of you better than I know myself," he taunts, that smirk deepening on his face, eyes dark as he drinks me in.

His darker side comes out to play when it's just the two of us—the one that demands I submit to him. I can let all my fears and worries fade away in those moments, trusting him fully with my pleasure. I willingly give over the control of my mind and body to this man, submitting to whatever he wants in a way only he has been able to do.

"And yet you let me go. So you don't get to tell me anything anymore," I fume with my chin held high under his imploring stare. My voice breaks toward the end, and I hope he didn't notice.

I want to keep the higher ground, so I stand up straighter, wanting to feel more of an even match for his hulking size that fills up this dim two-stall bathroom. His presence used to take up my entire vision when we were together.

"Let's get one thing straight, Avery. I have *never*, not for one second, let you go."

Before I can get a rebuttal out, he is on me, consuming all the surrounding space, until the air is filled with the smell of him—leather, sandalwood, and everything that makes him inherently him. The faint smell of alcohol clings to his skin from the drinks he has been serving tonight.

He invades my whole vision until all I can see is him. Those thick brows are bunched together, his dark eyes fixed on me as his tongue trails over his teeth. He drags his thumb against my bottom lip, slick with gloss. He takes that thumb and licks it off.

The next second, rough hands grab the back of my neck and bury themselves in my hair, pulling me into a bruising kiss. One large hand skims my waist, the pressure almost painful as if it's keeping me from running again while his hot mouth devours me as if I'm the last meal he'll ever get, his tongue dueling with mine.

I feel those calluses on the edge of his fingers from the countless hours of playing guitar dig into my scalp with a small bite of pain. The pull takes me higher as my breath comes out in pants between kisses.

His big hands release me to grab me by the thighs and hoist me up to the counter with such force, the mirror rattles. He captures the nape of my neck, angling my head back to kiss me deeper.

The heat rises in my belly until my whole body feels too sensitive as Kane looms over me. At this height I'm closer to his face, giving me easier access. His tongue slides inside my mouth with little resistance from me—unable to keep that part of me locked away from him—after just one kiss, I'm liquid in his hands.

We barely take time to rest in between strokes, my head going light with the lack of oxygen. The burning in my stomach goes higher, making me drunk on the feeling of him. The cocktail I drank at the bar doesn't even touch the way he makes me feel—weightless.

His stark black hair and all-black clothes make him seem like the devil incarnate here to take my soul, and if that's what he wants, I will *gladly* let him have it in this moment.

Everything else around us ceases to exist as he continues his assault on my mouth. His tongue swirls around mine with expertise we've perfected over the years, our bodies remembering how perfectly they fit together, as he's locked between my thighs.

I let my hands roam up his back to his neck before I dig my fingers in his silky strands, appreciating the feel of them running through my fingers again. I pull gently at the strands until a groan leaves his throat, coiling the heat in my belly further, making me flush with a burning need.

His tongue dives in and out, until I'm left panting and pulling back to get air, only for him to dive back onto my lips in seconds, as if that's all the time he can handle being separated from them.

All I can think is how much I want this man—past and present be damned. I need him in a way that feels wrong to have ever denied myself. I was naïve to think there would ever be a time when my body would stop craving him, *wanting* him, *needing* him and only him. I was foolish thinking I could simply move on from someone like Kane—who has changed the very makeup of who I am. Someone who has woven himself so tightly around me that some days I struggle to find where one of us ends and the other begins.

When I saw him storm over to me, eating up the floor—all brooding confidence and thick muscles, the flex of his arms like he was ready to fight the world to get to me—I never thought his single-minded mission would lead here.

I feel his hands drop from my hair and skim up my legs as he continues to kiss me as if he can make up for the kisses we've missed over the past few months. He makes his way under my skirt to grab the very tops of my thighs, so close to where I've been aching since Kane stared at me as if I was an angel who fell from heaven. The leather of my skirt shifts easily, bunching around my waist.

His hand strokes me over my thong, and the gasp that

leaves me only spurs him on, making him press harder over the soft material. The silky black lace is impossibly wet and I find myself desperate for him to slide them to the side and put me out of my misery. The urgency to have him touch me where I ache for him and only him is overwhelming. I should be embarrassed by how wet I am, by how much he can feel how desperately I want him—need him—to touch me.

"Kane, more!" I cry out, coming up for air while he dives into my neck and kisses me in places he knows will unravel me. He pulls back to stare at me while his fingers continue their torturous motions on my clit, slow and unhurried.

"You want more, huh? You want to feel my fingers push this sexy fucking thong to the side and feel how wet you are for me?" Kane groans. His lips are just a breath away from mine but not close enough to touch. "You're dripping so beautifully for me, baby—making a fucking mess of these scraps separating me from your *perfect* fucking pussy," he rasps, a knowing glint in his eye that confirms he's torturing me, as my breaths grow heavier and faster.

My orgasm builds rapidly but is still just out of reach. The fire is so hot within me, and my body begs to eradicate anything that stands between us. My clothes feel too much on my overly sensitive skin, and I want to scream for him to replace them with his warm body flush with mine.

"Did you wear these for him?" he demands, holding my eyes and slowing his fingers over my bud, making a frustrated scream come out of me. "Did you wear them in hopes someone would take them off later?" he continues, as he pulls back and tilts my face up with his other hand until I'm nose-to-nose with him, so he can read any lies I may try to feed him. My chin stays locked in his grasp, his pleading stare has me snared in his clutches.

"No, I—" I start, cut off with the force of Kane's next assault on my lips, kissing me so hard I can't think of anything else but him.

He pulls back. "Don't lie to me," he growls while his right hand bruises my hip, the bit of pain taking me further. He's holding onto me as if I'm the last shred of his sanity keeping him tethered to Earth. He makes thinking in this moment, let alone *speaking,* impossible.

I sit up straighter and face him head-on, staring into those hazel eyes. "I'm not. I wore them thinking of you," I confess, breathing heavily and panting with his slow movement and the pinch he delivers to my clit, causing a gasp to leave my lips. "Because...even though you broke my heart, all I can ever think of is you. I go to bed thinking of you. I wake up *drowning* in dreams of you. You torture my mind every day," I moan, pent-up lust mixing with anger at the audacity of him questioning me about other men when *he* let *me* go.

He doesn't offer a response before he's back on me, kissing me, his hands diving into the side of my panties, finally pushing them aside and sliding over my wet heat.

I should be ashamed that arguing with Kane turns me on, but I can barely think as he starts to circle that small bundle of nerves. The heat in my stomach pulls tighter, and I start to move against his hand to encourage him to move faster. He slips just one finger inside and feels how drenched I am for him.

"If this is all I get from you for now, I want to take my time. But feeling you again, I can't wait any longer," he rasps as he pulls back and lifts me slightly off the counter and rips my panties down my leg. He shoves them into his front pocket and stares down at me as if he can't imagine a better sight than my hair mussed, lips swollen and dripping for him. "Fuck, Avery, do you know what you're doing to me? You make me fucking crazy, out of my mind with jealousy, batting those pretty eyelashes at some other man—who is lucky to still be breathing. Touching you as if you're his to touch," he rushes out between breaths, hair messy and hands flexing as if he wants to go out there. "As if he has the right to think of you at all."

Unable to wait any longer, I rip at his pants, undo his button and slide his zipper down, pulling him free. Just the sight of him hard for me—thick and heavy in my hand—has me on the verge of combusting. I pump him up and down and watch his eyes roll back into his head with a soft *fuck me* falling from his lips.

We stare at each other, panting, and the look in his eye tells me he's giving me the chance to say no and walk away. I know that no matter what, he would respect my choice and let me go...*again*. He would take every hit I give him, just to come back for more.

"Did your pretty cunt miss me?" He strokes my swollen lips with his thumb—the movement so similar to how he stroked my clit. The smell of me on him makes the pressure low in my stomach riot. "I bet she did. She's dripping just for me. I can't tell you how hungry I am after last time. There's nothing I want more than to get another taste, but if I'm not inside you in the next two seconds, I think I might die."

He moves his hand up and down on mine, his cock hardening further in my hands. The tip is leaking, and my mouth waters as I imagine bending down and licking it up.

"And she's going to take everything I give her, isn't she?

She's going to take my cock like the good *fucking* girl she is," he bites out as I pump his length up and down.

I watch as more pre-cum wets the tip and he rubs it over himself before putting that finger to my mouth. His eyes blow wide as I wrap my lips around it as if it were his cock.

"As much as I would love to see you on your knees for me, pretty girl, I can't go one more second without feeling you squeeze the life out of my cock."

I nod my head, unable to find the words for just how much I want this. I pump my hand a few more times before I see the last of his resolve finally snap and he pulls my hair at the nape of my neck.

He forces my gaze up directly into his as he steps into me, and my hand drops as he spits on himself. With his other hand, he reaches up and gently grabs my face, forcing my mouth open before he leans down and spits in my mouth. His hand on my neck forces my head down, and I immediately obey his silent command. I spit on his dick, watching as a mix of us drips off him, glistening under the low lights as he lines himself up to my opening.

I brace myself against the counter and stare into his eyes as he slides into me. His hand comes to my throat, grip tight but soft enough to feel my heart crack at the tenderness he holds me with. A smirk forms on his face as he stares at his big, tattooed hand wrapped around my throat—the words *pretty girl* inked between his thumb and forefinger that wrap around me like a collar.

I'm so wet, it doesn't take much before he's fully seated inside me. My eyes fall closed and a groan makes its way out of my throat. It feels like coming home and I almost cry at how right this feels. As if Kane was made to be mine, our bodies molding together perfectly.

"Look at me," Kane demands, husky as he slowly starts to move inside me.

He stares at me as he slowly brings his hands up my waist, pulling my top with them until my breasts pop out from under my shirt and he can grab fistfuls of them, groaning at the sight. I'm braless under my crop top—the bra felt too restrictive earlier—and I silently thank past me for forgoing it while he stares at me. He's still inside me as the heat in my stomach becomes unbearable. My hips try to move on their own, desperate for some sort of friction.

I look up to see Kane staring at me as if I'm the very reason he exists. His hazel eyes are blown wide with a look of awe on his face. I can feel his eyes drag down the side of my neck to the small butterfly tattoo I got last year with him —a symbol for the freedom I felt in that moment breaking free from the chains my parents shackled me to. His gaze makes its way to my bare breasts, then down my stomach until he finally gets to where he's fully seated inside me.

"You're so beautiful, baby," he whimpers softly, making my heart clench. "Now hold on while I fuck every thought of any other man out of you."

He pulls all the way out then slams into me. A cry leaves my lips as he moves at a punishing pace.

The bathroom fills with the sounds of us coming together—slapping skin, moans, and those beautiful soft grunts he lets out. I wish I could bottle these sounds and take them with me. I could live my whole life knowing I found true happiness once upon a time and be okay. I feel selfish for not bothering to quiet the sounds I'm making, hoping the whole bar hears us.

"Look at us. Look behind you and see how thoroughly I wreck you. You think anyone else on this earth can give you exactly what you need? That we weren't made for each other? Do you think that anyone else could ever be enough?" he grunts as I turn my head and watch as he slams into me repeatedly.

I pull myself back to face Kane and grab his hair, bringing his lips to mine. I feel my orgasm start to crest.

"No one will fuck you like I do. No one else knows exactly how to make those pretty legs shake the way I do. And when you start moaning deep, I know this pretty pussy is about to come for me," he rasps against my lips, slamming into me relentlessly while he caresses the back of my head.

Tension coils tighter in my belly, and Kane notices how close I am as he removes one hand from my waist and starts to circle my clit, giving me that extra bit of stimulation I need. His other hand drops to my back to keep me in place as he continues his assault.

I can feel him inside me—a perfect fit, long and thick—as the tip of him rubs my upper walls, just as he promised, causing my legs to shake.

"Come for me, baby. Show me how much you love me fucking this cunt. Show me what only I can do to you," he demands, pulling me in for a kiss. His tongue dives into my mouth, mimicking the circles he makes with his fingers. "Let everyone hear what a good fucking girl you are for me. My dirty fucking girl, getting fucked in the bathroom while her date is waiting for her."

His hand goes back to my throat as I try to hold myself up. I come suddenly, and the whole bathroom disappears as stars explode behind my eyes. The shockwaves of my orgasm go on forever, the feeling I'd been missing the last time Kane and I were together.

Slowly, I feel my body come back down from the high and notice Kane is staring at me with so much tenderness I feel like I need to look away, but I'm snared in his gaze.

With three final pumps, Kane comes on a groan that fills the bathroom. He stills inside me and grabs my face on both sides before he brings his lips to mine. He kisses me so gently my heart cracks in the middle.

After a few slow kisses, he pulls out of me completely and a hiss leaves my lips, the feeling of emptiness returning with the loss of him. He grabs a few paper towels and wets them before he cleans me up. When his cum begins leaking back out of me, he takes two fingers and pushes it back in. A moan makes its way up my throat and out of my mouth at the unexpected intrusion. He looks up at me—no shame on his face and fucking smirks while he throws the paper towel in the trash next to me.

He tucks himself back into his pants as I duck my chin. Confusion whirls in me at how in one moment he's fucking me without abandon and then cleaning me up as if I'm the most precious thing he's ever seen.

We stare at each other as if any words would break this fragile moment between us. He helps me pull my top up and right my skirt. We stay locked in each other's gaze until three sharp bangs against the bathroom door jerk me back to the present.

Oh my god, I just fucked Kane—*my ex-boyfriend*—in the bathroom of the bar where he works. I duck my head and go to rush past Kane, but he grabs my wrist and spins me to face him.

"Ave... I..." he begins, an unreadable look on his face that has replaced any tenderness I thought I saw.

Unable to bear hearing him say it was a mistake, I slide my hand into his, squeeze once, then drop his hand and steel my spine.

"It's okay, it was the heat of the moment. It meant nothing," I mutter as I take a step toward the door. I watch as his face crumbles and he grabs the back of his neck with one hand.

"But what if it meant *everything*?" he whispers, and my chest cracks wide open. The fissure that has been there for months is a full cavern now.

The banging on the door gets louder, so I turn to unlock it. The door flies open, and some girl gives me a dirty look before running into one of the two stalls, not bothering to look at Kane.

I refuse to turn around for fear I'll never walk away if I do.

"This isn't over, Avery. We're not over," I hear behind me, his voice low, absolution taking over his tone. The words cause me to pause before I take a breath and walk out.

I grab my purse from the table and ignore the imploring look Morgan throws my way as I head outside to feel the cool breeze blow against my sweat-soaked skin. A shiver works its way up my spine as I hurry toward my car.

Grateful I had the foresight to drive myself here in case I needed a quick escape from my date, I throw my door open and cast a glance back at the bar, hoping that I'll spot a broad-shouldered man with black hair following me out—*needing* to see him come after me.

When I realize no one is coming, a familiar ache rips through my chest. On a shaky breath, I get in the car as tears well up in my eyes. I take a few breaths to center myself before I throw the car in reverse and head for home, my mind and the radio silent as the neighborhoods blur by.

CHAPTER TWENTY-EIGHT

kane

If I Ever Saw Heaven – Roan Ash

"Fuck!" I yell as I burst through the kitchen back room and slide down the wall that houses our supply lists before I hang my head in my hands.

I fucked up.

I know I fucked up. I just couldn't see clearly—all I saw was red. My vision tunneled as his hands touched her as if he had some right to, as if he had some claim to be touching *my* girl.

In that moment, all I could think was that I had to get his hands off her so I could breathe again, until I looked down and saw the look on her face—she was pissed. So I reacted the way any rational man would and followed her. I didn't mean to invade her space, but I can't go on much longer without talking.

This permanent ache has filled my chest these past weeks, growing with all the small moments we've had together—the pranks, my parents' party, the picture I stole and taped to my bathroom mirror, where it taunts me every morning, reminding me exactly what I'm fighting for every day.

I gave her space for weeks. I *kept* giving her space, but that's no longer going to work for me. So I followed her, and I was going to demand she finally talk to me—to clear the air after my parents' house, and the kisses we shared in between, and then her being on that goddamn date.

We were at a crossroads, and I saw her standing there, a fucking goddess burning me with her gaze, so I snapped. I touched her, and my hands still feel the ghost of her skin under them. It felt like fucking heaven. The moans she made, the fiery look in her eye, the way pushing into her felt like coming home after years away.

It had always been explosive when we were together. Sometimes our sex life took a back seat to life and circumstances, but that never dulled how fucking perfect we were together. The second I was inside her, every thought vanished, and she consumed me from the inside out. I could live inside her and never tire of the way she feels.

Fuck, I feel myself hardening and the shame of the night eats at me all over again.

I'm still lost in my haze when the back door I just stormed through bursts open and shoes appear in my sight. A pair of shoes I could recognize anywhere, with the black heart on the toe, fill my vision. I brace myself for what he's about to say.

"You can't be back here," I mutter dejectedly to the shoes, hoping I see them walk right back out. I'm in no mood to explain.

"You really got yourself into it, didn't you?"

I pick my head up and look at Marcus. "Over four years ago, or just now?"

"Well, I would say about three months ago when you let

that girl walk out of the house, then refused to tell anyone what happened, but sure, I'll let you live in your delusions for a couple more seconds and say now," he quips while sitting on the floor next to me. I rest my forearms on my knees and let my head fall back onto the wall, staring at the square tile ceiling.

"I just saw some other guy with my girl, and I lost it," I sigh, hoping that sums up every emotion that has flitted through my body since.

"Okay, so you let your anger talk for you, and she's not your girl. If I remember correctly." Marcus mirrors my stance and turns his head toward me. I quickly look at him with murder in my eyes, jaw clenched as I try not to hit my best friend as he chuckles and continues, "All right, so if she's your girl...what have you been waiting for?"

"*Her*. She wanted space." I falter, the anger fading.

"Fuck that, Kane. I know you're not that dumb. I've never been in a relationship—*not for lack of trying*. But even I know when a woman asks for space you better get as close to them as possible and find out what's wrong. Jesus, don't make me call my mother and have her explain this to you. I remember I was twelve and had just stumbled inside from the yard, a warm spring day and finally headed to grab my afternoon Capri-Sun. I had just reached in the fridge when I heard a sniffle—my sister had run upstairs from the front door while yelling down at my mom about needing space. So she sat me down, and she said 'Marcus, my son, my favorite child—'"

"Has anyone told you to get to the point sooner?" I interject, the urge to punch my best friend strong.

"As I was saying, my mom told me that a woman never truly wants space. She said when a woman says she wants space, it's a way to tell us that we need to fix it. So quit being a fucking dumbass and make her talk to you. It's been almost three months since the breakup, and you two are still dancing around each other like children. You're being pathetic right now," Marcus huffs, raising his brow at me.

My anger rises, not at him but at myself. I've let these months pass me by, almost letting her slip through my fingers forever. I listen to the tinkering in the kitchen—the cooks preparing the last of the dishes before it becomes alcohol only for the night, the dishwasher finishing its last cycle—and stare at the rings on my finger, methodically twisting my favorite one as I attempt to gather my scattered thoughts.

I mumble sarcastically, "Tell me how you really feel."

"Okay, I will. You're being a little bitch. You let the love of your life go, for what? A miscommunication? A fight you two couldn't control? I wouldn't know because neither of you two idiots have spoken much about it. Maybe we're bad friends and didn't push as much as we should have, but this is enough. Man up, figure your shit out, and get your girl back. Before it's too late and you're actually stuck watching her date other guys—hell, maybe even marry one."

His words hit me like a final blow to the chest.

I picture what it would be like someday—having to watch Avery with someone else, holding their hand in the parking lot and buckling her into their car drunk, waking up on lazy Sundays and staying in bed together the whole day instead of getting up. The haze of the past few weeks starts to clear from my mind.

I've been walking around these past months in a fog, letting my anxiety and baggage cloud up my feelings. I've never stopped loving her. I don't think I could, even if my heart was ripped out of my chest. My soul is hers. It has been since she smiled at me—hook, line and sinker. I think it has been hers longer than it was ever my own. The girl who found this broken boy and gave him purpose, a home for the first time in his life.

I've never given much thought to what comes next—heaven or hell. If some divine god judges us based on the lives we've lived and determines where we go next. But I do know I'll go wherever she goes—gods be damned. In this life and whatever comes next, she's it for me. I'd strike whatever deal, make any bargain to go with her.

I've let her think she's less than that, and today is the last day she doesn't know my world begins and ends with her.

I've never put much faith in divinity, but I would give my life to worship the ground she walked on if she gave me another chance to get this right.

I stand quickly, wiping my hands on my jeans, my palms sweating as the anxiety spirals during this conversation. Marcus follows suit, and I turn to him, trying to gather all the thoughts jumping out to me at once.

"Look, there's a lot I haven't told you guys, even Avery. But I think I owe it to her to tell her first. I would really like to come talk to you later on," I say, reaching back to the table where we keep our possessions during shifts for my keys. The cold metal hitting my palm fuels me further.

Marcus slaps my shoulder and grips it, looking right at me, acknowledging that a light bulb has finally gone off in my head.

"We all know you have been going through something, even before this. We got your back. Go get your girl. We will talk later." He stares into my eyes, imploring me to hear him. I nod and hold eye contact for a moment before I break off, heading to the door.

My steps pick up the closer I get to my truck. I throw

the door open and jump inside. The sleek black interior is swallowed up by the night, with soft music filling the cab after I finally got it fixed last night.

The sky pounds with relentless rain, thick sheets blocking my windshield. I drive slower than I want to through the streets between Avery and me. I let my mind try to focus on what I need to say to her, what I *need* her to hear. The outside blurs in time with my thoughts, making the drive feel quicker than it is.

When I finally pull up to her curb, I turn the car off and sit back to take a few breaths. I tell the panic to subside and do my breathing technique—I look around for five things I can see, remind myself of four things I can smell, let myself feel three things I can touch, and ground myself in the moment.

I steel my spine as I jump out of the car, quickly slam the door behind me, and rush to the house. The floodgates opened up earlier, and it seems someone upstairs is hell-bent on punishing me for these last few months.

I welcome the rain, the bite of the cold against my cheeks, as I stare at her front door. The rain soaks through my clothes, chilling me to the bone when I bang on her door. The strands of my hair are already soaked and dripping down my face as I wait for her to answer. Seconds tick by and I feel my confidence weaken.

What if she no longer wants anything to do with me? What if I really fucked it all up by crossing the line tonight?

I pound on the door a second time, my rings clanking against the wood. Just as I'm about to give up and head back to my truck to regroup, the door opens.

A small crack in the door, and there she is—hair wet from the rain or shower, my old high school shirt and those tiny fucking shorts on her. Her face is in shock, either because I'm standing here, because of the state I'm in, or because I'm soaked and dripping on her porch late at night. Her arms cross over her chest as I watch her build up her defenses like she tried to do tonight in the bathroom.

I push my hair back and out of my face so I can see her past the rain. Her beauty pins me to the gray night.

CHAPTER TWENTY-NINE

kane

So In Love – Icarus Account

"We need to talk, Ave," I start, looking at her as I let the rain continue to beat down on me, if that's what she needs to see that I'm not leaving this time.

"I think we talked enough for one night, don't you, Kane? Or at least your dick talked. We had a good conversation, I must say," she snarks with a smile that doesn't reach her eyes.

She stands in the doorway, arms crossed and hip jutted out, with a look on her face warning me to back away slowly. Still, I step closer and steel my spine.

Get the girl, Kane.

"No, we didn't, and I think that's our problem. We haven't talked. *Not really*. Not in a while, and I know it's my fault. I put space between us. I pushed you out, and it was never my intention to do so, Ave. None of this was," I acknowledge, hoping she hears the pleading in my voice, the desperation bleeding into every word.

I wring my fingers together as my anxiety spirals. I watch her eyes track their movements, her head tilting at the new ring on my middle finger.

Avery regards me for a minute, her eyes trailing from my eyes down to my lips before she moves to the side and motions for me to come in. I brush past her, trying to stay far enough away that I don't soak her too. My clothes drip on the pink welcome mat as I cross the threshold into her home. The smell of lemon hits my nostrils—the feeling of rightness bleeding through my chest. My anxiety lessens with a few inhales of that soft scent.

It smells like home.

"Do you want...some clothes?" I hear hesitantly from behind me, that soft voice echoing in the living room of her cottage. The lights are all dim. I assume Avery was in bed when I knocked. I turn to her, the floor already soaked as the water drips off me. "I have some of yours still..." She trails off as she stands two feet from me and crosses her arms again, refusing to make eye contact with me.

"No, thank you. I need..." I pause, raking my hands through my sopping wet hair, trying to compose all the thoughts jumbled in my mind. "There are things I need to say, and I need to get them out," I strangle out, staring at her.

She looks back at me, her lips pursed, and that adorable fucking wrinkle in her brow staring back at me. Neither of us move as the water makes a bigger puddle around me.

"I'm sorry," I say simply.

She gives me a look as if to say *go on,* raising her brows and loosening her arms across her chest just slightly.

"For tonight. I'm sorry, I never should have crashed your date. I just..." I grab a towel from the back of the couch and run it over my hair and face. I give myself a second to clear some of the water from dripping into my vision. "I just saw red. There you were at our place with someone else and I lost it. And I know I shouldn't have, I have no right."

"You're right. You have no fucking right. And yet you did. You humiliated me. *You* broke up with *me*." She stabs each word at me, dropping her hands to her sides, fisting them like she's holding back from hitting me. The anger is clear on her face, her skin clear of makeup, showing every line and feature. The freckles like a beacon on her face, welcoming me home.

Confusion lines my face as I hold the towel in both hands to stop myself from reaching for her. "I did not break up with you. *You* said you wanted a break and that you needed space." I explain and watch as she scoffs and shakes her head. "And I'm seeing now that's not actually what you wanted. You wanted *me* to keep trying, and I am sorry. I should not have left that conversation the way we did, but I..."

She stares at me, emotions blank, and I feel my chest get tight, but I push out the next words while feeling the anxiety rear its head at me.

"I have been struggling with anxiety—panic attacks. My therapist says that's what it is anyway. I've felt it on and off throughout my life. After my childhood, there would be times when I felt so suffocated I didn't know how to talk to you. I could feel myself pull away from you, and it was as if I couldn't help it. My body was trying to protect itself from an unknown enemy, and I couldn't distinguish in my head what that was," I finish on a sigh, like it's some sort of cosmic joke—my body wanted to hide from the one person who has ever seen who I really am.

"Kane..." Her eyes soften as she drops her arms by her sides. "I didn't know," she croaks out, holding her hands in front of her—a move she's always done when nervous.

"I know you didn't. Why would you? I didn't talk about it. We *didn't* talk, and I know most of it's on me. You asked so many times, and I promise I wanted to tell you. But every time I opened my mouth, it was like my throat closed and my brain wouldn't give me the words I needed. How was I supposed to explain something that I had no idea how to explain to myself? It wasn't even until I forced myself to see someone that I realized what it was and that I wasn't okay." I brace my arms on the back of the couch and lean against it for extra support. I look back up at her and notice her bright blue eyes, wet and staring back at me.

"I should've—"

"No, you shouldn't have pushed me," I say, cutting her off. "I think I would have just pushed you further. I didn't even want to admit something was wrong until the night... you walked out, and I felt like I couldn't breathe. I was suffocating right there on the floor when all I wanted to do was storm out that door and pull you back. I wanted to spin you around and tell you how much I loved you. *Still* fucking love you, and that there's not a damn thing in this whole world that could ever make me stop. How since the day I somehow fell into your orbit, I've never wanted to escape. The day I met you, my dark, lonely world turned into the most colorful existence. Knowing you, *loving* you is the single greatest pleasure I will ever experience in this life or the next," I finish, letting the tears spill down my cheeks.

Some of the fog clears from my mind, and I see an angel standing right in front of me, lightly brushing the tears off my cheeks with her fingers. My chest warms and sends the panic receding back. She lights up my world with her touch, bright enough for when the darkness tries creeping its way back in.

She goes to speak when I reach down and grab both of her hands in mine, using her warmth to give me courage. I stand so close to her, allowing her warmth to encourage me to finish it.

"I should have chased you down until I erased every doubt, worry and fear from your mind. I fucked up. Then I continued to fuck up. I told myself I was respecting what you wanted, yet I was stealing pieces of you where I could. The pranks and having you come with me to my parents—where you still looked at me with so much love I know I didn't deserve. But I was scared. No, I was fucking *terrified.* What if I showed you this and you didn't want it? What if I showed you this side of me and decided I wasn't worth it anymore?" I choke out as the tears roll down her cheeks, and I wonder how one person can be so beautiful when they look so sad.

She lets go of one hand and wipes at her eyes with the back of her hand. I rub the back of her other hand softly in mine. I let this contact be enough when all I want is to kiss every drop that spills over her beautiful cheeks, erasing their mark on her skin.

"Kane, I..." she starts, taking a breath, her hand finding its way to my chest as it lightly brushes over my soaked shirt where my heart would be—as if she wants to reach in and hold it. I almost wish she could see it's been empty since she left, that she is my heart. "I will always want you. There's not a thing you could show me that I do not want from you."

"I—" I start.

"No," she cuts me off, some of her fire coming back into her voice. "Let me finish, please."

I nod and stroke the back of her hand, my backside leaning on the back of the couch as I take in every inch of her. My feet are apart to let her come in closer. I watch her take one more step, so we're almost chest-to-chest, but with some space left for her to peer her eyes up at me.

Fuck, are they hypnotic, pulling me in and luring me closer.

"There will never, ever be a time when I do not want you. I want complicated Kane. I want sad Kane. I want happy Kane. I want all sides of you that you show the world and the sides of you that are only mine. There's not a single part of me that is not completely and utterly yours, in the way every part of you is mine," she finishes.

"I know I should have told you. I didn't even know what I was feeling until I started therapy and he explained it to me in a way that made sense in my own head—that you won't reject me just because that's what I'm used to. I didn't take the past four years into consideration or give you the benefit of the doubt. It all just felt so overwhelming—so *suffocating*—I didn't know how to handle it." I stroke her palm and pull my other hand up to trail along her drying hair, rubbing it between my fingers. The feel of her so close has me able to push the lingering anxiety out of my chest.

"And how do you feel now?" she asks carefully.

"Better, or I will be. I feel more centered now that I know what is happening. When I feel the panic, I can help it go away a bit or take myself out of a situation until I feel more level enough to handle it," I explain, hands slowly going to the back of her neck, testing the waters, hoping she doesn't pull away.

I cup her neck and turn her face up to mine so I can really look at her. I trace her jaw lightly with my thumb as my other fingers lay under her hair, pulling her the last inch so she's flush against me, her front plastered to my drying shirt. The water is forgotten as I stare at her. Her hands loop loosely around my back, rubbing up and down slowly.

"We started me on meds, and I feel better. A lot better. My thoughts are less jumbled, things don't seem to trigger me as much," I add, still stroking her chin with my thumb, watching her lips part when I drag my thumb along her neck. The feel of her pulse matches my erratic heartbeat at her proximity. "But it's not an excuse for what happened. I saw you leaving and the panic just took over. I couldn't think of anything to say. All I know is I saw my whole world leaving me behind and I couldn't even chase her. Then for the next three months, I acted like a fucking idiot, because there you were and I couldn't figure my own shit out."

She rips herself out of my grasp and takes a step away from me. "You hurt me, Kane," she lashes out, pain evident in her voice.

"I know, baby, and I'm so sorry," I croak, my voice breaking. I stand up straight and struggle to hold myself back from grabbing onto her again. I watch as her brain wars with her heart. Her hands twitch to touch me, but the hurt stays unchanged on her face.

"I tried. I asked for *months*. I was so patient, and then when I wanted to talk, you said nothing. And I get it now. I do, and I wish I had known so I could have fixed it. I could have—"

I cut her off with a hard tone. "No, it wasn't your job to fix. I am not a project for you to fix. I need to fix myself. You don't deserve another person's problem on your plate."

"That's not what I meant, Kane. I could have been there for you. I could have gotten you help. I could've been by your side, and it hurts that you were going through all of that and we couldn't just talk about it. That's on both of us.

We didn't talk about the hard stuff. I let you get away with not talking about your dad, what was going on at work. I waited, but I should have pushed. I should've spoken too, about the way I felt earlier," she replies, sniffling softly. She wipes more tears that have escaped down her cheeks.

I drop the towel that I used to wipe my face and pull her into her bedroom, needing to be dry for this conversation as the cold has seeped into my bones, leaving my fingers unable to feel her like I want to.

I search my drawer in her dresser—the one where I always kept my things—to find it washed and folded. I grab the first shirt I see and rip the wet one off my body, tossing it into the bathroom before throwing the new one over my head.

I look up and see Avery standing in the doorway, frozen and staring at my chest. Realization strikes me that she hasn't seen it. I lift up my shirt and show off the part of my chest—I've always kept blank right over my heart. It was now full with her—her name, in script and a beautiful pink peony weaved throughout, her favorite flower. I always planned to get her tattooed on me more. I have little ones here and there, her favorite snack on my inner arm, her birthday in roman numerals down my spine, a small script of *pretty girl* etched on the back of my hand—on the skin between my pointer finger and thumb, curved just perfectly, like a collar that sits so snug on her neck. The sight of it for the first time kept us in her room for the night, using her new necklace until we were both spent, wrapped in each other.

I lower my shirt and walk toward her, those eyes not leaving my chest as if she can see through the black shirt. I take it off so she can look at it better, throwing the shirt somewhere toward the bed as her eyes heat with desire. I flex a bit and watch as her eyes drag back to that spot again. I take her chin in my hand and stand with my toes up to her bare ones.

"Eyes up here, honey," I say with a smirk as I close her mouth with my finger under her chin. She blinks a few times, speechless over what she just saw.

"When did you get that?" she asks, her voice cracking as she finally moves her eyes up to my brown ones.

"Shortly after everything. Maybe that's not fair of me to do. I had always planned on getting you there, but nothing ever clicked. I think because together, it didn't matter what was inked over my heart. You were my heart. You *are* my heart—ink or no ink, you were there. And when we broke up, I was a mess," I explain with a small chuckle, not out of humor but because of how hopeless it felt.

I release her chin only to move her hair back over her shoulders, clearing the view of her face, and smooth it against her back.

"Marcus had been asking for days what happened between us and I couldn't find the words. How was I supposed to tell him my whole heart had been ripped out of my chest? When I finally just told him I felt empty, he grabbed his keys and drove me to Johnny's tattoo shop and he told me 'then fill it.' So, this is where I filled the physical emptiness first. After that, I started working on fixing the emptiness inside."

She grabs my hand and starts stroking her hands up the back of my arms, slowly sliding closer to me until her hands finally reach my neck, where they wrap around me. I grab her hip, dig in my fingers when that soft lemon scent hits my senses, and slowly pull her back into me.

She hits my chest, causing my dick to perk up as her soft breasts press against me. I imagine the soft threadbare shirt peeling off her. Her arms drop down, skim my chest, and rest above where the art is. Her fingers lightly trace the words and lines.

My skin breaks out in goosebumps at her touch—too much across my sensitive skin.

CHAPTER THIRTY

avery

Until I Found You – Stephen Sanchez

I look up at this man as my fingers find their way back up his broad chest. My touch leaves goosebumps on his skin in its wake. I feel his thick fingers digging into my hips and his hardening cock against my stomach as we stand here in this position. I take in his fully tattooed arms around me, his forearm muscles flexing. Slowly, he releases his grip and slides his hands along my lower back as my hands settle around his neck.

I take in this man who looks at me with such devotion in his eyes. Those soft brown irises keep me captivated.

"I love you, Avery Jane. So much that my heart physically hurts when you're not here. It's been yours since you looked up at me in Mr. Adams' class. All doe-eyed, lips wrapped around that pencil. I remember thinking what I would give to be that. I was jealous it got your attention. And I never looked away. You became my sole focus. Football, my parents, the looming family business—none of it mattered anymore. I found what I was always supposed to be doing—loving you."

Instead of answering, I kiss him. I throw myself into him, knowing he would never let me fall, and suddenly the world falls away.

The earth shifts, the stars stop shining, and the sounds outside quiet as I feel his soft lips against mine. His hands tighten dangerously on my waist, gripping me hard enough to leave bruises and pulling us together so tightly I feel like I'm suffocating in him.

His lips move over mine as we tangle in an all-too-familiar dance. His tongue slowly traces my lips and my mouth parts, giving him full access. A soft moan escapes me when I get the first taste of him. My hands shoot up to his hair at the back of his neck, gripping the strands and pulling him farther down to me. He picks me up and I wrap my legs around his waist. My core settles right over that impressive bulge in his pants.

He slams the door closed and pushes my back up against it as he rips his mouth from my lips and slowly kisses down my neck. The heat in my belly burns hot as I feel his lips trail up and down my neck, softly sucking and kissing as my breaths come in pants. I slowly rub myself against him, my core on fire. The sexiest groan rumbles from his throat, making my hips move faster against him. He pulls his head back, a seductive grin on his face.

"Eager, are we, pretty girl?" he taunts with a chuckle, coming in for another kiss, this time slower, as if he's savoring the feel of our lips sliding over each other.

"Kane..." I moan out between kisses, panting with the need for him to touch me, for *more*.

One moment we're against the door, the next he turns us and sits on the bed. My core rests right up against him as

I straddle him. His hands are on my waist, then trail up, stopping just short of my breasts that tingle in anticipation.

"I know, baby. I know," he moans as he keeps trailing his hands up and down my waist, staring at me in reverence. "I know what you want." His hands drag slowly over my waist, stopping just shy of where I need them most. "But I think we should slow down."

I sit back with a pout.

He leans in and catches my bottom lip between his teeth, smirking when my breath hitches. "Don't pout at me. I'm trying to be smart about this."

His fingers flex against my waist, and the look in his eyes says smart is the last thing he wants to be.

"I don't see how sex is a bad idea. Even when we couldn't talk, we were great at it," I coax, brushing my hand over his dick and giving it a small squeeze. A groan follows as he closes his eyes. I stroke it one more time before he takes my hand in his and holds it behind my back.

"Please, baby. I'm trying to think, and I can't do that when you're making the blood go elsewhere," he groans, barely able to take a breath as a grin breaks across my face. I always loved how easily he responded to me. I felt powerful knowing how little it took to bring this man to his knees for me, and he looks *really* fucking good on his knees.

After a few more breaths, he opens his eyes and smiles at me. "Okay, here's what's going to happen. We're not having sex. And don't pout at me."

I laugh when he catches my bottom lip between his fingers as I jut it out, kissing it before letting me go and gripping my hips again.

"We're not having sex because I think we should go slowly. Talk to each other and learn to trust each other again," he finishes as I slump a bit on top of him.

The fire goes out of me as I realize he makes sense. While I think sex with Kane could never be a bad idea, I can see it means a lot to him, so instead of pushing my luck, I start to get up. Only his hands keep me in place on top of him.

"No, don't get up, I just got you back." He grins, his fingers digging into me and causing me to chuckle and wrap my arms around him.

I sigh contentedly as I rest my head in the space between his neck and shoulders. I inhale deeply, loving the smell of him mixed with the smell of fresh rain. Sandalwood and rain make my heartbeat calm and my hands twirl in his hair, feeling how the strands have grown in our time apart.

"I missed you," I profess softly into his chest, not wanting to break the moment but needing to say it—to get it off my chest that *every* moment apart was painful.

I dreamed of this moment and the times when he would wrap me up so tight in his arms nothing else mattered. The outside world couldn't reach me here—where it was safe and comforting and home.

I feel a featherlight kiss against my hair, and he rests his lips against my head, squeezing me tighter for a moment.

"I missed you too, pretty girl. Every fucking second," he confesses just as softly, and I let my eyes shut and let myself hold on to this moment, hold on to him.

We stay like this for minutes—maybe hours—until my bladder finally refuses to be ignored, like it always does when I cry hard. I peel myself away from him and stare into his eyes, seeing a lightness I can't remember the last time I saw.

"I have to go," I say with a smile, and he laughs as he releases me enough to get off him, his hands skimming my waist as I pull away.

I turn and make my way to the bathroom, catching a glimpse of myself in the mirror: the red, bloodshot eyes, the freckles on my face that somehow stand out more against my chronically pale skin to the the red marks on my neck from his long scruff and a small hickey that makes me laugh.

That territorial man.

When I'm washing my hands, I feel him come up behind me. I slowly lean back and let my ass graze him.

"Just ignore him. He's always excited when you're involved," he chuckles as he slowly kisses my neck.

I turn in his arms. "Or you could let me help with that?" I suggest, waggling my eyebrows suggestively.

A painful groan comes out of him before he finally looks up from my neck, a glare painted on his face. "You're evil." He pouts, taking a slow step back and finally letting me follow him out of the room. "As much as I want that, baby girl, tonight has been a lot for both of us. So we are going to sleep together."

I raise my eyebrows at him.

"Just sleep, get your head out of the gutter." He laughs, rolling his eyes, and peels back the covers, holding them up and turning to me. "Get in."

I slide in as I feel a quick smack on the ass. I turn back to him with a faux glare, only to see the most beautiful playful smile on his face.

He drops his pants and I watch as he switches to a dry pair of boxers from the dresser. My heart warms at the scene. I snuggle down under the blanket and watch him slide in after me, clicking off the lamp and encasing us in darkness.

The faint light from the window shines through, just barely making out his face next to me. His strong features glimmer in moonlight, from the thick black brows, those striking cheekbones, and impossibly angular jaw covered in a light scruff that makes him all the more striking.

I'm constantly in awe that this beautiful, hot-as-sin man is in my bed, looking at me with such softness in his eyes. His body turns toward me, a couple inches between us, and we stay locked on each other, savoring a moment neither of us can quite believe. He lifts his hand and drags it softly down my cheek, brushing my hair behind me as he continues trailing his hand down my neck to my arm, then back up.

"You're so fucking beautiful, pretty girl," he starts on a whisper, slightly hoarse as if it's been overused, "And I'm too damn selfish to spend another night away from you. I used to wake up every night and reach over, my brain not yet catching up that you weren't there. I would graze the cool sheets that used to be tangled up in you. I told myself when I got you back—not if, you were never an *if* in my mind—that I would never ever let you go again. I wouldn't take this moment right here for granted again. The good, the bad, the painful—I'll be here. I'll slay every man, every demon that comes your way, because you're mine, baby. Heaven, hell, and even purgatory can't keep me from you. I'm sorry it took me so long to get back to you," he rasps out and pulls me flush against him.

Every inch of him is surrounding me, from my pink pastel toes peeking beneath the blanket to the skin of my stomach that peeks out from my shirt, glued to his bare torso. The feel of his skin against mine makes my heart soar.

He kisses me so softly I feel tears well up in my eyes at how this man loves me. I know in every word, every touch, every kiss he's telling me in the best way he can.

"I love you, Kane, and not a single thing in this world could tear us apart this time," I vow as my eyes get heavy from sleep or emotions. I feel two soft kisses on my forehead right before sleep threatens to take me.

We are wrapped impossibly tight when I hear a faint, "I love you, Avery. More than this world can imagine."

Sleep quickly claims me after, easier than it has in months.

CHAPTER THIRTY-ONE

kane

Novocaine – The Band CAMINO

The first thing to wake me is a warm body plastered to the front of me. The smooth skin of her legs is thrown over mine, her head resting against my chest. I give myself a second to stare at her face and count the freckles. Relief flows through me when the same number I counted last night stares back at me.

I take in the softness of her features, the lashes fanned across her cheeks, and the small nose above her plump, thick lips.

"I can feel you staring, you know," she says with a smile, not opening her eyes before she buries her face deeper into my chest. I pull her closer, hoping to meld our bodies together so she can never leave me again, when I feel her fingernails trail down my stomach. The path her fingers take tickles before she slips her hand down the front of my boxers, gripping my already throbbing cock.

"Pretty girl..." I warn as she starts stroking me, a slight

tease to her movements, her hold lazy and exploring. I look at her face to see her staring up at me with innocent eyes.

"What?" she asks, faux innocence plastered on her face.

"You know what," I hiss as she grips me harder and starts pumping.

"Do you want me to stop?" she asks, suddenly serious, stilling her movements. "I know you wanted to go slow, but I want you, Kane. No, I need you. Waking up to you again is every dream I have had these past ninety-six days come true. I need to know you're really mine." She leans up and looks into my eyes as hers fill with tears.

Her hand slips out of my boxers as I flip over and cage her between my arms, staring down into those gorgeous blue eyes.

"Pretty girl, don't you know by now there's not a single thing I won't give you? If you want me right now, I'm yours, irrevocably," I reply. I brush a feather-light kiss over her lips before kissing her harder, the feel of her mouth against mine making me groan. The softness of her is a dream.

"I want to taste you," she groans against my mouth. "I'm so fucking hungry, Kane. Let me."

My blood heats with her words as I sit up and pull her with me. I lie down and let her climb over me. She straddles me and kisses me, my tongue immediately diving into her mouth. The sweep of her tongue undoes me, my cock so hard it's almost painful.

I dive my hands into her hair and pull her flush against me, kissing without stopping until I can no longer breathe. The outside world is all but forgotten as I swallow all the moans that make their way up her throat.

She pulls back and smirks at me as she makes her way down my body, leaving kisses in her wake. Her tongue drives me crazy as it trails down my neck to my abs, almost too much on my overheated skin.

She makes it to my boxers, hooking both fingers in the band and dragging them down as I lift up to help her. She takes off her shirt, letting her breasts hang down in front of her, and I attempt to sit up, my mouth watering at the sight, but she pushes me back down. I obey, willingly her prisoner in this moment. She grips my thick cock with one hand and strokes me up and down while holding eye contact with me.

The most erotic fantasy from my dreams stares back at me as she lowers her head and takes me in as deep as she can.

My vision blacks out when I hit the back of her throat, and I throw myself back onto the bed, trying to keep from blowing in her mouth at the first feel of her wet fucking mouth wrapped around me after so long.

"Fuck, pretty girl, are you trying to kill me?" I groan as I grasp her hair in one hand and pull it slightly, the tension giving me something to hold on to so I don't embarrass myself.

She groans around my dick as she sucks, her cheeks hollowing. I see stars, so close to combusting I feel it radiating up my spine, her wicked mouth doing too much to my brain after so long. She sucks like she was born to do it, all wet lips and tight grip sending me into another orbit.

She pulls back and smirks as if she knows how quickly she's undoing me. I sit up so fast and haul her back with me, flipping us over and pinning her underneath me before she knows what happened. I steal her next words with a bruising kiss, the taste of me on her driving me further as I slide her underwear down.

I find the bundle of nerves in front of her slit and circle it, her pussy impossibly wet as I stroke her and slide two fingers in. She clamps down on me, the feeling going straight to my cock. I chase her tongue with my own, unable to stop, knowing I need her lips more than my next breath.

I reluctantly pull apart as I continue to plunge my fingers in and out of her. I sit up and stare at her as she closes her eyes, the tension coiling tighter across her features. The only sounds in the room come from her dripping pussy as she takes my fingers like she was made for it.

"Uh-uh, pretty girl, I want you to look at me while you come so you know you belong to me. All of your orgasms are mine, do you hear me?" I rasp, and she opens her eyes again on a gasp, her orgasm so close as I curl my fingers up and rub that spot inside her.

I watch as her eyes roll back and a scream works its way up her throat. I lean over and swallow it up, continuing my assault as she comes down from her orgasm.

I slowly remove my fingers, now covered in her release, and lick them clean while staring straight into her eyes.

"Fuck," she rasps, breathless.

"Mmm," I moan, pull ingmy fingers free and giving myself a few strokes. "I'm not even close to being done with you."

"How do you want me?" she asks as she stares at my dick like it's a four-course meal.

"Fuck, baby, I can't tell you all the ways I want you, but right now I want you just like this. Eyes locked on me as I watch you come for me again. This time around my cock," I demand. I line myself up with her entrance, dragging the tip up and down along her slit, pushing in just slightly and pulling back out, teasing us both.

"Fuck me, Kane. Please. I need to feel you. I need you to fill me up," she begs.

"Condom?" I ask, then curse under my breath. "I

should've asked yesterday. Fuck, I'm such an idiot." Shame washes through me at how careless I was.

"Do we need a condom?" she asks, unsure. "I'm still on birth control, and I haven't been with anyone since..." She trails off, a look of unease on her face.

"Fuck, pretty girl, I haven't even thought of anyone but you since I was eighteen years old. There's not a single other woman who has touched me since," I answer her unspoken question.

"Then fuck me raw, Kane. Please. I need to feel you." She grabs my dick and places it at her entrance. "I want all of you."

I answer her as I slam home. The feeling of her tight heat sends shivers up my spine. I stay still, letting her adjust around me. Even after having sex last night at the bar, I know I'm big. I savor the feel of her wrapped around me. Her pussy grips me impossibly tight, like a vise. Her wet walls cling to me, making me want nothing more than to come right here and now and fill her up.

"Move, Kane, please," she whines, so I give it to her.

I pull out slowly at first, then slam home again, my pace punishing as I fuck her. I feel her pussy clamp down on me, squeezing me to death every time I hit that spot inside her. I grip her throat with my hand and fuck her with abandon.

The only sounds filling the room are the headboard slamming into the wall in a rhythmic pattern and her wet fucking pussy as it takes every single thing I give it.

"Kane," she whines as she grabs on to me, her nails clawing into my back, the marks feeling as if I earned a prize.

"That's it, baby. I feel you tightening around my cock. You're going to come for me, aren't you?" I ask just as she shatters around me, the tightness almost making me spill inside her. I hold myself back—just barely—wanting to stay inside of her longer, unwilling to let her go yet.

I release her neck and kiss her through it, letting her use me to draw out her orgasm impossibly further.

"Fuck, I love you," I profess into her mouth. "I love you so much."

I pull back and fuck her in earnest, unleashing it all onto her. The sound of slapping skin fills the room, mingling with our moans. I feel her pussy tighten again.

"Again already, pretty girl?"

She nods and opens her mouth in a silent scream, coming again around my cock, and this time I let myself come with her, unable to stop it as she tightens around me and milks every single drop from me.

As I finish, I fall on top of her and rest my forehead against hers, our heavy breathing mixing. I kiss her once, then twice, unable to let her go even as I soften inside her. I kiss her one more time, then pull out.

I stare down at her as she remains unmoving with her eyes closed and fumble my way to the bathroom, dawn just breaking through the curtains and brightening the room a bit more than when we woke up. I wet a washcloth and come back to her, cleaning both of our releases from her.

Once I finish, I lie down next to her and bring her to me again. The feel of her in my arms almost undoes me more than the sex has. Her back is plastered to my front, locked into me like two puzzle pieces.

"I love you too," she says softly, kissing my chest. "Sorry about breaking your slow rule," she finishes on a chuckle.

I laugh along with her. "Eh, it was a stupid rule anyway."

The alarm next to her blares, bringing me back to the

moment, and I realize I have to leave soon if I want to make it to school on time this morning.

She groans and rolls over to silence it, swinging her legs around and sitting up so they dangle over the side of the bed. I get up and rest my head in my hand as I watch her. Still naked, I drink in the sight of her back, all those curves begging for me to reach out and grip them again.

"I guess we should get ready," she suggests, getting up and walking to the bathroom.

"Or we could play hooky, stay in bed all day?" I half joke with her.

She comes around the corner with her toothbrush in her mouth and one eyebrow raised. "And here I thought you wanted to go slow?"

"I did, I just..." I trail off, getting up and standing in front of her. I take her face in my hands and kiss her forehead before she turns and spits out her toothpaste.

I open my drawer and grab some new boxers and put them on.

"I just want to get it right this time," I finish as I watch her get dressed, leaning in the doorway and taking her in. The sight of just being in her presence, no matter what she's doing, warms my chest.

"We will," she reassures me, stepping into me and giving me a soft kiss. Both of us seem unable to part longer than a few seconds now. "We just need to talk about everything. The hard stuff, the good stuff, the in-between. We need to make sure nothing is kept from the other and try to find who we are together again." She places her hands against my chest.

"Okay," I agree, bringing her hand up and kissing her palm. "I can do that."

"How are you feeling right now?" she asks, looking into my eyes.

"I feel good. Really good. I didn't let myself imagine this too much, but now that you're here right in front of me again, I won't lose this second chance you've given me," I answer.

"I know you won't," she reassures me with a soft smile, the look of adoration in her eyes aimed at me almost taking my breath away.

"I do need to go, as much as I hate it," I start. "I don't have any work clothes here, and since I have to stop at home, I'm going to be late if I don't leave now," I finish on a kiss and let her go, putting on my now-dry clothes from yesterday, then watch as she finishes getting dressed in her Second Chances T-shirt and skintight jeans—ones all I can imagine is peeling back off of her.

"Don't look at me like that, or neither of us will be leaving this room anytime soon," she warns, wagging her finger at me.

I chuckle when a muffled voice yells from the next room, "For the love of God, please don't start back up again. My vibrator is dead, and I really don't need live-action porn at 6:45 in the morning."

I laugh, and Avery's face goes red as she whips open her bedroom door to reveal Morgan standing there, her hip cocked and a bright smile on her face as she stares back at the two of us.

"As happy as I am about this reunion—and trust me, I'm thrilled—can we please be PG until after 8 in the morning?" she muses.

"Sorry, Morgan," Avery says, giggling.

I move up behind her, wrapping my arms around her waist and drawing her back to me until her back is flush to my chest. Morgan tracks the movement, her eyes getting bigger and her smile getting impossibly wider.

"So you're back together? Thank goodness. I was getting exhausted trying to throw the two of you together," Morgan comments.

"What do you mean?" Avery responds accusingly. I imagine her eyebrow is raised as she stares down her best friend, who apparently moonlights as a secret agent trying to push us together and into the same place over the past couple months. Several moments pop into my head that must have been orchestrated by Morgan, my head dipping in thanks to her for butting into our relationship.

"Yes, we are back together," I answer, ignoring Avery's question to Morgan.

Avery's head whips back to me, an imploring look on her face as she stares at me.

"I'm going to go so you guys can talk about this, okay, love you, bye," Morgan mutters quickly, then dashes off to her room and closes the door.

"What do you mean?" Avery asks as she turns in my arms to look at me. I hold her to me, unable to let her go.

"I mean that we're together again. I'm yours and you're mine. I'm not letting you go again, Avery. Don't ask me to," I respond, tucking a strand of hair behind her ear and cupping her cheek.

"So boyfriend and girlfriend?" she muses, those big baby blues staring up at me.

"You have always been my girlfriend, pretty girl. Even when we were apart," I answer her.

"Okay," she whispers, her voice small as I lean down and take her lips with mine.

"I really, really need to go. Can I see you later? I'll cook you dinner?" I ask, our lips just a breath away from each other as I rub my hands up and down her back.

"Okay, yes, I would love to," she answers with a smile. I pull her to me and kiss her one more time before getting lost in her and our tongues dancing together.

"Good God, please don't make me get the squirt bottle and hose you two off," Morgan says.

We pull back and laugh. I reluctantly let her go.

I grab my stuff and pull her back in for one more imploring kiss as Morgan throws a dish towel at my back from somewhere in the kitchen.

"I'll be seeing you, pretty girl," I add with a grin before I rush out the door and into my truck.

CHAPTER THIRTY-TWO

kane

Seventeen Going Under – Sam Fender

I walk into work with a lightness I haven't felt in months. This morning has been rolling around my head on a nonstop loop. It's not even the sex I can't stop thinking about—although that was a surprise I wasn't expecting—but being able to wake up with her in my arms again. The smell of her lemon shampoo fanned across my chest and face, the feel of her heartbeat steady within my reach, the beats melding with mine until they fell into sync.

I wave to Dawn on my way to the office, a couple minutes later than usual, but the extra minutes were worth it. I sit down in my office chair and boot up my computer, ready to get started for the day. With graduation in just a few short weeks, I've had a busier-than-normal calendar, with the anxieties of the future looming over the seniors' heads. The busier schedule has been nice to fill up my days when all I needed was a distraction from my life, but today, the busy day makes it hard to focus. I pull up my schedule and see that Trevor's appointment was marked with a cancellation request and a message to see Dawn.

I slide back my chair, take one last swig of my coffee, and toss it in the trash on my way out the door. The office is already abuzz, most people get here an hour early before the students to finish up last-minute tasks. The sound of ringing phones and typing keys is a welcome sound this Tuesday morning. I go round to the front of the office and wait while Dawn finishes a call. Parents line the corridor with children, signing them in for the day as the bell rings, marking them late.

I wait until I catch Dawn's eye, and she tilts her head, signaling me to follow her. The tightness in my chest hits immediately with the foreboding in her expression. I follow her with haste in every step until we make it to the teacher's lounge on this side of the campus. Dawn turns to me with her brows lowered, her eyes scanning from left to right to make sure the coast is clear.

"What's going on?" I ask slowly, the feeling of unease thick in the air.

"Trevor," she answers ominously, gauging my reaction.

"What about him? I saw his canceled appointment, but the notes were empty."

"There's been an accident." She hesitates, holding up her hands to put quotation marks around the word accident.

"What do you mean?" I press, hoping for a straight answer before the relentless what-ifs invading my brain take me somewhere bad.

"Trevor was admitted to the hospital. His father brought him in, saying he had tripped and fallen. But there were signs of intense bruising on his body that couldn't be accounted for with a fall. He was unconscious for a few hours, and CPS was called once he woke up. Unfortunately, Trevor corroborated his father's story, and there was nothing CPS could do. His father took him out of the hospital against medical advice a few hours later. Because they couldn't get Trevor to say there was any abuse occurring, children's services moved on. You know how short-staffed they've been in Williamson County lately," Dawn explains, setting a hand on my forearm before walking away and leaving me enveloped in the silence of the room. The only other sound is the low hum of the refrigerator as I try to let my thoughts catch up with one another.

I walk in a trance back to my desk as all the thoughts hit me at once.

Unaccounted-for bruising all over.

He fell and was unconscious for hours.

His father took him out of the hospital AMA.

My thoughts swarm me from all sides as my breathing quickens and I clutch my chest. I take gasping breaths as I double over in the middle of the hallway. I grab at my chest as it tightens, constricting my throat. My vision blackens and next thing I know is the floor meets my face. After some time when my breathes come easier and the trembling in my hands stops, I drag myself off the floor in a daze. The guilt is heavy in my stomach.

What have I done? Was it because I called? Did I do this?

I reach my office without knowing how I got there, walking on autopilot. I grab my keys and phone from my desktop before storming out. I hurry by Dawn's desk without a word. I hear someone call after me, but I can't hear them through the red-hot rage filling my mind.

The thought of Trevor being so unsafe he broke his arm and was knocked unconscious within the span of a few weeks—no one is that clumsy. All those marks and bruises were my fault. I saw what was happening to him, and I didn't call sooner.

What if something worse had happened to him?

What if he never woke up from his "fall"?

I can no longer stand by and do nothing. I understand CPS has more than enough cases to deal with, but a boy was brought in with clear signs of abuse, and no one can do a thing?

His father gets to take him home and walk away scot-free, no repercussions for beating the shit out of his fifteen-year-old son. The son who takes care of his sisters, who works a full-time job after school—I assume to help make ends meet for them.

I get into my truck, slam it into reverse, and peel out of the parking lot. Trevor's address has been memorized in my mind for a few weeks now. The first time he showed up with a couple bruises, I flagged his profile, noting the trailer park on the outskirts of Cherry Hill, bordering the Nashville city limits. A place known for kids falling through the cracks between counties.

I don't think. I just drive, needing more than anything to see with my own two eyes that he is okay.

The streets blur as I drive, the clock on the dash staring back at me: 8:56 a.m. Just two hours after I left Avery's bed, and fuck, how I wish I could turn back the clock and be there again, cocooned in her. As I get closer, my body starts radiating with energy. I keep shifting in my seat, trying to expel some of the pent-up rage coursing through me.

I pull into the trailer park and see two extremes: some trailers well kept and beautifully maintained, with blossoming flower beds and meticulous grass, and others that have seen better days, peeling paint on the siding, cars parked every direction out front, and piles of trash littering some of the stoops.

I stop in front of a dilapidated trailer with a sagging porch and little shoes lining the outside. Before I can stop myself, I dash out of the truck with it still running and bang on the door. My fists pound hard enough to make the whole front of the trailer shake.

I stand back and wait, the silence inside sending me reeling. Just as I raise my fist to knock again, it swings open to reveal a graying and balding man, at least five inches shorter than me, staring back. The clear evidence of a hangover sits on his face, the stench coming off him making me want to gag.

"Who the fuck are ya?" he bellows as I stand there, towering over him.

"Where's Trevor?" I ask through my barely concealed rage.

"Out, what's it to ya?" he counters, his country accent thicker than any I've heard in a while.

"I'm his counselor at school, and he didn't show up today. Where is he?" I ask, crossing my arms and sizing him up.

"Fuck should I know? The lil cunt does what he wants." He starts to close the door, but I slam my hand against it, forcing him to open it all the way.

The smell of rotten food and whiskey hits me, making my eyes water. The sight sends another punch to my gut, thinking of three children having to live in such conditions. The couch is brown and peeling in every visible place, the tables lined with ashtrays and empty bottles. Clutter lines the floors in all corners, creating piles of shit stacked at least three feet high in some places.

I see red, and suddenly my fist slams into the man in

front of me. A scream follows the crunch of bone, and I watch as he flies backward onto the floor.

The hangover clears from his face as rage replaces it, blood pouring out of his nose and quickly soaking his threadbare shirt.

"How do you like getting hit, huh?" I ask as I tower over him while he clutches his nose. "How does it feel to be the one getting smacked around by someone so much bigger than you, huh?"

I wait for this pathetic excuse of a man to answer before I flatten him to the floor and make him regret he was ever born.

"Ya broke my fuckin' nose!" he whines from his position on the floor, clutching his mangled nose.

"And I'll break a lot more if I ever see Trevor come back to school with so much as a paper cut on him. Do you hear me?"

"Who the fuck are ya to tell me what to do with my own fuckin' kid?" he seethes.

"I'm your worst fucking nightmare. You think you can go around and abuse your kids and no one will do a thing about it? Think again. If I see one more bruise, I will rain hell down on your life. I will take everything from you."

"You think ya so much better than me," he spits from his position on the floor.

"I *am* fucking better than you. Because I can tell the difference between right and wrong, and you're so drunk you use your own kids as punching bags. But I will be back. One cut, one scratch, and I will make your life a living hell. If that's even possible. You're a pathetic excuse for a man."

He crawls toward the stained couch, liquor bottles rattling across what I assume was once a coffee table.

"Do you understand?" I challenge, my temper a live

wire. I watch the flash of fear that goes through his eyes as he stares at me.

Good. He should be fucking terrified. If CPS won't listen, I'll make them. This is the last time this kid gets hurt when I can do something to stop it. I don't care what it takes. These kids are my responsibility.

I take a step toward him and watch him cower backward.

"Fuck, fine, I understand," he cries out.

"This is the only warning you get," I threaten before stalking out of the house.

I slam the door behind me, rattling the frame on the way out, and get into my truck. I take a few deep breaths after I shut the door and stare up at the trailer, vowing to myself that I will get Trevor out of this situation, whatever it takes. I have money, and I'm not afraid to use it to help him get out and get safe. I'll sink the whole trust fund if it means those kids have a safe place to lay their heads every night.

I stare at my hand, the knuckles raw and bloodied from his nose. The sound of his nose crunching is a beautiful melody replaying in my head. I never liked talking with my fists—knowing I tower over most people by height and weight has always helped keep me from needing them.

I drive the side streets back to school, needing more time to calm down than the highway would have left me. The morning traffic has finally died down, with most people already at work, giving me time to center myself.

I pull up to school when a text from Avery flashes on my phone in the cup holder.

PRETTY GIRL

I miss you

It's amazing that after what just happened, I'm able to

get a smile on my face, but Avery has always been that for me. She centers me. No matter what is going on in life, she is always able to make everything else feel inconsequential. I let the rage flow out of me as I stare at her name on my screen. I know I need to tell her what happened. We agreed on no more secrets, but how do I even explain what I've done?

ME

I miss you. How is work, pretty girl?

I see the bubbles immediately and sit back in my truck while I wait for her response. I already know I have a lot of explaining to do once I get inside, and I'm hoping to drag that out a little bit.

PRETTY GIRL

Ugh, busy already. But I will be at your place by 5:30 😘 How's work for you?

I chuckle and feel the ghost of her lips with the kiss she sends at the end.

ME

I'll explain later. Can't wait to see you.

I slip my phone in my pocket and head into the school, trepidation in every step.

CHAPTER THIRTY-THREE

avery

When Did You Stop Loving Me? – LANY

I don't think as I launch myself out of my car. I slam the door shut and sprint toward those big arms opening for me. Kane stands in front of the door in a blue T-shirt and sweats, and the second I reach him, I launch myself into his arms. He catches me easily, wrapping those big, strong arms around me so tightly it feels like he's holding on to me as if I'm his lifeline.

Today felt like an eternity had passed, even though I woke up in his arms this morning. I had rolled toward him as the sun barely peeked through the curtains, illuminating the room just enough for me to study the outline of his face.

I know we have a lot to talk about and even more to figure out, but standing here with his arms around me, my heart calms for the first time all day. Last night felt so much like a dream that I almost convinced myself it was one. I thought I was hallucinating when I opened my door and saw him standing there, drenched from the rain, looking at me with so much sorrow in his eyes. Everything after that felt like a fever dream, like I was finally hearing every word I had wanted to hear for the past three months.

We stand there wrapped in each other for a couple of minutes, both of us savoring how it feels to be like this again. The days we lost and the words we forgot fall away as we hold on to each other, breathing in sync.

I pull back just as he does, his hand coming up to brush my hair away from my face while the other stays firm on my back, keeping me plastered to his front.

He looks at me with a soft expression, a smile so small someone else might miss it. But there is little I miss when it comes to Kane.

"How was your day, pretty girl?" He places a soft kiss on my lips, and I close my eyes, savoring the feel of them on mine.

When he pulls back, I say, "Too long. How was yours?"

"Why don't we go inside?" He lets me go only long enough to grab my hand and pull me in after him. My hackles rise at his ominous answer.

"What aren't you telling me?" I follow him inside, the scent of something hearty hitting my nose and making my stomach growl. Kane glances back at me with a smirk as we cross the threshold into the living room. The open concept leads straight into the kitchen, with a small table to the left for keys and mail. The living room stretches ahead, and the bedrooms sit down the dark, quiet hallway to the left, letting me know Marcus must be out.

"Did you forget to eat again?" He pulls me over to the island, then goes back to prepping a salad he must have started before I arrived.

"Maybe," I answer slowly.

He laughs, and the sound warms my chest for a second.

I glance down as he chops cucumber for the salad and notice his right hand, gripping the knife, is red and cracked.

"Oh my god, what happened?" I grab his hand, forcing him to drop the knife onto the cutting board.

"Okay, don't freak out..." He cups my hands over his to stop my inspection.

"You know saying that actually does not stop anyone from freaking out." I shoot him a *please be serious* look. "Did you get into a fight? With who?"

He sighs and abandons the salad. After checking the oven, which still has twenty-three minutes left, he brings me over to the couch. He sits, angling his body toward me, while I sit crisscross, waiting for him to tell me what's going on before the chaos in my stomach gets worse. He places his hand on my knee and draws small circles with his thumb, as if he's grounding himself. I cover his cracked, clearly bloodied hand with mine.

"Do you remember that boy Trevor I told you about last semester?"

"Yeah, why? Did you fight him?" I joke.

"No, of course not." He scoffs, tucking a stray piece of hair that escaped back behind my ear and lingers a bit with his fingers brushing the strands. "I had been noticing things." He starts the circles on my knee again. "Bruises. A black eye a couple of times. Random scratches. A split brow. I thought maybe he had been getting into fights at school, but I asked around—other kids, teachers—and no one could account for where they came from. I know he has a full-time job at the mechanic shop on Bleaker in South Wind. I mean, Christ, he's only fifteen."

The room is quiet except for him, and I keep my eyes on his face so he knows I'm listening.

"So, I started asking him to come in increasingly, just to

see. Then one day, he comes in with a broken arm and this whole story about how he tripped and fell. But it was all too much to explain away by accident. He made some offhand comments about his dad..." he trails off, raking his hands through his hair, the distress clear on his face.

"Oh, god." My hands fly to my mouth as I realize what he's telling me. "His dad is abusing him?" I implore gently, taking Kane's hands from where he's anxiously twisting his rings and holding on to them.

"I'm pretty sure. He has never outright told me. But today when I got back to school, there was a note about him. He was in the hospital over the weekend. They brought him in unconscious and covered in bruises, most of which couldn't be explained by a "fall." CPS tried to get involved, but he wouldn't spill. His fucking asshole of a father pulled him out of the hospital."

"CPS couldn't do anything?"

"Not if Trevor won't admit to abuse. He stuck to the story they had already told. The kid is so scared of being separated from his sisters that he refuses to help himself," Kane rasps, broken and on the edge of despair. I can tell how deeply this situation is affecting him. There's a sheen of water over his eyes, his leg is bouncing under our joined hands, and I know he's itching to get up and move. The only reason he is still sitting here is because I have him in a death grip.

"So how did your hand end up like this?" I ask, unsure I want the answer.

He huffs out a breath, guilt and apology written all over his face.

"I lost it when I heard he was in the hospital, so I went to his house to check on him. I just needed to see he was okay. Except he wasn't there, and his sorry excuse for a father answered the door. He reeked of alcohol and bad decisions. So, I may have hit him."

I gasp. "Kane!"

"I know. I know I fucked up. I also threatened him. I just could not see that kid walk into school with one more bruise on him," he chokes out.

"Are you in trouble with the school?"

"They don't know. Dawn saw me leave, but she figured I just needed some air."

"You could lose your job, Kane." I grab his face and stroke his cheek, trying to quiet the anxiety I can now see taking over his body.

I don't know how I never noticed before. The way he pulled his hair, twisted his rings, paced for no reason. I wish I had paid better attention. I wish I had opened my eyes sooner. Tears well at the thought of him battling all this while I was too blind to see it.

"Don't cry, pretty girl. Please. I can't bear to see it anymore." He wipes away my tears.

"I'm sorry I couldn't see how badly you were struggling. I feel so stupid and so blind." The tears rack my body harder, and suddenly I'm lifted from my spot and settled in a warm lap. The feeling of safety blossoms through my chest.

"This isn't your fault, baby." He strokes my hair and kisses the side of my head repeatedly, trying to calm me down.

"I know, but I should've seen it." My argument is weak, but I can't seem to shake this immense feeling of guilt that we could have avoided these past couple months apart if I had just looked harder.

"No. It was my job to recognize something was wrong and that I needed help. You are not to blame for what happened." He rocks us until my sobs ebb into small hiccups. "I don't want us to keep dwelling in the past. It happened, and it was hard, but I think now we're better off for it. Now we know better. We know to talk, to trust each other in the silence, and to come to each other at the first sign of unease."

"How do you do that?" I ask softly into his neck, letting the scent of him fuel me, making me never want to move from this position again.

"Do what?"

"Make everything feel okay again."

"I just love you, and no matter what, we'll make it together." He lifts my face from his neck with a finger under my chin and kisses me.

The feel of his lips on mine instantly hits my core, and suddenly I don't want to talk anymore. I move to straddle him and deepen the kiss. Just as he slips his tongue into my mouth, the timer blares from the oven, scaring me enough to jolt backward.

He chuckles, his soft eyes and easy smile making me want to drag his mouth back to mine and forget about dinner. Then my stomach growls even louder than before, and he stands with me in his arms before placing me gently on the couch.

The heavy conversation fades as we eat and talk about the past few months we missed. Between his work and mine, we spend hours on his beige couch, the soft sounds of a LANY vinyl playing from the record player. The perfectly baked lasagna is long gone, our plates cleared. Hours pass as we sit there, reminding me of the years we've spent on this exact couch and how normal all of this feels, as if no time has passed at all.

A FEW HOURS LATER, we finally make our way to the bedroom. I brought an overnight bag just in case because, as much as I know we should ease back into things, I couldn't make myself want to be apart from him for another night. For months, I dreamed of this—going to bed wrapped in his arms again and waking up with him.

I pull out my pajamas and lay my clothes out for tomorrow so they don't get overly wrinkled in my bag. Morgan's socks, which she gave to me on loan, stare back at me, and I turn to Kane, one hand on my hip and my brow raised.

"Am I ever going to get my socks back?"

He smirks and looks me up and down, heat in his eyes. "Am I going to get my shoelaces back?" He leans his arms on top of the bathroom door frame, and my eyes on his biceps.

It really is unfair how fucking *hot* this man is, and somehow, he is all mine.

I turn around and dig into my bag until I pull out the wad of shoelaces, then throw them at him. Both of us laugh at the ridiculous way the pranks have unfolded. Kane drops the shoelaces on his dresser and opens the top drawer, revealing the mountain of socks he stole from me. I go over to search through them when an envelope catches my eye, my name written across the front.

"What's this?" I hold it up, watching his face go blank.

"Uh..." He scratches the back of his neck and avoids eye contact.

I look deeper and find a few more envelopes with my name on them. I pull them out and count twelve in total.

I lift them toward him and wait for an answer.

"I wrote them...for you," he says slowly. "Well, I wrote them to you. When we were apart. I wasn't sure how to talk about how I was feeling, so I thought maybe I could write it down. Just small things. Things I wanted to tell you over the past twelve weeks. Things I wish I had said and didn't."

Vulnerability is etched across his face, reminding me of the times he talks about his parents, as if he's waiting for disappointment to follow. I can see the anxiety in every twirl of his rings. The silver engraved A he showed me earlier catches my eye again.

"Oh, Kane." My eyes fill with tears. I clutch the letters to my chest in a death grip, unwilling to let him take them back from me. "Can I read them?"

"You want to read them?"

"Of course I do. This is..." I search for the right words. "This is beautiful, Kane. I want nothing more than to read your words."

"Okay, yeah..." Unease lingers in his features. I cross the room and take his face in my hand, his cheek leaning into my palm while I hold his letters to my heart. "Can I be in the shower while you read them?" he asks.

I nod, and he gives me a small kiss before he goes. He pauses in the bathroom doorway, one last glance at me, then back down to the envelopes clutched against my chest.

I hear the shower turn on and sit at the end of his bed, the sound of running water soothing the storm that erupts in my stomach at the sight of his script spelling out my name on the envelope.

I crack the first one open and marvel at a full page of his handwriting. He always had such beautiful handwriting for a boy, the small script a little messy but lined up perfectly. He has a habit of writing mostly in all caps, and I always found it so endearing.

Dear Avery,

You walked out of my house twelve hours ago, and I haven't been able to see the sun since. The world seems to be cast in an ever-present gray. My vision—my entire world—lost all color that seemed to have followed you when you walked out.

And I don't think I blame it. I don't blame my world for losing color when I lost the one person who ever made me see the bright side.

When you walked into my world four years ago, suddenly every color had more vibrancy than ever before. Blues sparkled like the sun hitting a wave just right, the hue of your eyes haunting my every dream. They shine so full of life that my heart stops whenever those baby blues are on me. Greens were crisp, emeralds shining like wet grass in the morning dew. And yellow—well, yellow became my favorite color, because when you smile at me, I swear that is my sun. The star I constantly study in the sky. You became the center of my universe, and I will never forgive myself for not chasing after you. For letting the demons inside my head try to keep me from you. For letting them win, even for a few hours.

I hate that I am at the mercy of my fucked-up

brain and the lies it tells me. The lies that I'm no good for you. The lies that you would be better off without me. Because how could that be true when you have become my reason for breathing each morning?

One day, I will win. I will slay these demons and come for you. Our story isn't over. Far from it. It almost feels as though it has only just begun. We have only written the prologue together, the before, and I promise when I get you back, chapter 1 starts and it doesn't end without a happily ever after.

Kane xx

I put the letter down, my eyes so full of tears I can barely see the words in front of me. I read it three more times and hold it to my chest. The words are so beautiful I almost can't breathe through the pain pouring off the page.

I drop the rest of the letters and take off toward the sound of the shower. I shed my clothes along the way, leaving a trail to the bathroom. When I open the door and step inside, a gloriously wet and naked Kane turns to me, surprise on his face. His black hair falls over his forehead, his chiseled jaw and light scruff lining his face making me weak in the knees. Every inch of him looks carved from stone, his muscles on full display, and his pert ass so bitable I have to force myself to focus.

"You read them all already?" He grabs my hips and pulls me under the wonderfully hot spray.

"Just one." I wrap my arms around his neck and pull

him flush with my body, feeling a very impressive appendage against my stomach, hard as a rock.

"Ignore him. You're naked. He gets excited," he jokes as I laugh and shake my head, stroking the back of his neck.

"What you wrote, Kane..."

"Sappy, right?"

I give him a look, and he mimes zipping his lips.

"It was the most beautiful thing I have ever read."

"It's just how I feel."

Kane continues as he strokes his hands up and down my naked back.

"I'm so sorry we lost all that time together. All that hurt and resentment for nothing. I think we needed it. I hated it too, but it forced me to confront what was happening. It forced me to get help and finally face things I have been avoiding for years."

The water beats down over us, fogging up the bathroom while we're too lost in each other to care where we are.

I open my mouth to argue, but he dips his head and captures my words with his mouth. The kiss turns searing immediately. We kiss until the water starts to grow cold, then hurry to wash off. Kane steps out first and hands me a towel before grabbing one for himself. After we get ready for bed side by side, the domestic feel of it all brings a smile to my face.

I have missed these small moments between us more than anything. Everything has always felt so effortless with him, even the mundane never felt quite mundane when we were doing it together.

I grab the letters off the bed after I get dressed and place them on the dresser, not ready to read more yet. I want to savor the first letter he wrote and the feeling of us being back together again.

He comes up behind me and wraps his arms around my waist, his mouth brushing the shell of my ear.

"You're wearing too many clothes, baby," he whispers, slowly pulling the shirt up and over my head, then throws it behind him.

He turns me around and backs me toward the bed until the backs of my knees hit it and I sit down. He follows me, strips off the underwear I just put on, and nudges my chest until I lean back. His hand grazes my breast before squeezing, and my core throbs at the move.

"We have lots of lost time to make up for, and I intend to not waste a second of it," he groans then suddenly his mouth is on me. The slow whirl of his tongue on my clit instantly makes stars burst behind my eyes.

He eats me like a man starved, watching me the whole time, gauging my reactions to what feels best until I can feel all the muscles in my stomach tighten and my legs start to close around his head as my climax nears.

"That's right, pretty girl. Crush me with your thighs. If that's how I have to go, I'll die a happy man."

I come—hot and fast—my vision going dark for a minute. He continues slow circles on my clit as I come down, and I collapse onto my back. He comes over me a moment later, placing a kiss to my lips.

"Did you think we were finished just yet? Oh, baby. I'm nowhere near done with you."

Then he makes good on his promise.

CHAPTER THIRTY-FOUR

avery

Prettiest Thing I've Ever Seen – LANY

"You're just the sweetest little thing, aren't you?" I say in the tiniest baby voice I can while this Australian Shepherd mix goes crazy on my lap. He licks my face, and I can't help the smile that breaks free.

The shelter has had fewer intakes this week, and I am grateful for the reprieve—it means I get to spend more time with each animal, giving them some interaction, and less time at my desk sifting through mountains of paperwork. Though Sharlene has been coming in less, giving me more responsibility than usual. I can't complain. I wake up every morning so excited to come here, and it fills me in a way I'm not sure I can describe.

I finish up with Roo, who has only been here a little over two weeks. His last family said he was too high energy and they didn't have time for him. My heart breaks at the thought of him being just eight months old and dropped off somewhere unfamiliar until someone decides they want to take him home. I get a few action shots of him and his adorable face to post to our socials and hope that by the end of the week he's adopted.

Keith has been called for a pickup for a stray found off I-40, which is a less-than-stellar dumping ground. He forced me to stay, even though I prefer to be there for most captures. I know Kane would be upset, so instead of fighting it, I let him go and get my puppy cuddles in. That freeway off-ramp is notorious for drop-offs and shady activities since it backs up to miles of forest and is not patrolled by any local PD, despite my numerous calls.

I lock Roo's kennel and make my way down the aisles. Every other kennel is empty, and I'm so happy to see the shelter clearing out a bit. Our volunteers have been so great about rotating the dogs for walks and social interaction. Some even rotate who goes home with them for the night, giving some of the more high-strung dogs the opportunity to relax in a way they can't in an environment like this.

I walk past Silver, who's asleep, her puppies just hitting seven weeks and so close to being ready for adoption. Grayson has been by every other day to meet with Silver and walk her. My heart is so full knowing she gets to go to one of the best homes I could have picked for her after the life she's lived. I round the corner to start back up the kennels and head to the cat room when a tall, hulking figure dressed in black lurks right behind me.

I let out a scream, my hand flying to my heart when the figure starts laughing. That husky laugh, wrapped in smoke, goes around me and invades all my senses.

"What are you doing here?" I ask, pulling him to me and wrapping my arms around him. Those big arms encase me, and the scent of him calms my system.

"The school had a half day due to state testing, and I

figured I haven't been by enough to volunteer." He leaves a kiss on the side of my head as he wraps his big hand around it, pulling me further into his chest. "And I may have missed you," he finishes, pulling back to stare down at me. He places a gentle kiss on my lips and tucks my hair behind my ear.

"You saw me this morning," I muse, pulling away to grab his hand and lead him over to Roo.

"Doesn't matter. I missed you the second I left your bed."

I unlock the kennel and let him in as Roo goes crazy. He jumps onto Kane and dances on his back two legs, trying to somehow reach Kane's face from the floor.

"This is Roo. He's just the sweetest boy." I look up at Kane with wide eyes.

"He is adorable. What kind is he?" Kane says.

"Some Australian Shepherd mix. We don't know for sure, but he's just perfect. Potty-trained, listens perfectly, nonreactive. And he was dumped just for having energy. How could someone do that?" I look down at him, wanting nothing more than to pick him up and take him home with me.

"We should adopt him," Kane says, mirroring my thoughts.

"What?" I ask making sure I heard him right.

"We should adopt him. Or someone else, if you want. I think it's time we bring a couple of these babies home to make a family of our own." He looks up at me, the softness in his features making my heart crack.

He looks good today. I told him so before he left this morning. His button-down is rolled up to show off those impressive forearms, the snake tattoo wrapped around his right arm on display. His hair is neatly styled, a difference from his usual mess of waves on top with the sides tapered down.

"What? But where would he stay? Do we just bring him back and forth between houses?"

"I guess we should move in together then, don't you?" He looks up at me from his puppy assault on the floor. I stand frozen over him, the comment he seems to have made offhand rendering me speechless.

"Wh-what?" I sputter, unsure if I heard him correctly.

He stands while Roo scampers off to his bed, seeming to notice the shift in conversation. His tongue hangs out of his mouth as he stares up at us. My eyes finally lift to the man standing in front of me, and he tucks his finger under my chin, forcing me to meet his gaze.

"We should move in together. We spend every night together anyway. I can't imagine anything better than waking up to you every morning in our bed, surrounded by our things. Your toothbrush next to mine, all the records we've collected together alphabetized on one shelf," he finishes on a kiss.

"Don't you think it's too soon?" I protest softly, my brain trying to catch up with my heart. Worry threads through me, of course. We still have so much to talk about—to figure out together.

"I don't think it's soon enough. It's something I've wanted to ask for years. Since we graduated high school. But you and Morgan were so excited to live together, and I didn't want to take that experience away from you. There has never been a day where I didn't wish we were in our own home, together. I think it's time," he continues gently, his other hand coming to wrap around my waist.

He's always touching me in some way when we're together, whether it's a hand on my knee when he's driving or the way his hands seem to search out some part of me before they settle something inside him.

"Don't you think we have more to figure out together?" I ask, wanting so badly to say yes, my heart screaming at me to jump this man and never let him go.

"All I need to know is that I love you, and I can't imagine spending another day without you. We agreed to talk and be open with one another, and I think we're both in a good place to talk first and worry second."

"Okay," I answer, staring up at this man. Love is shining so clearly in his eyes, pouring out of him and flowing into me.

A bright smile takes over his face, pure joy pouring off of him.

"Really?"

"Yes, really. But we need to promise to talk, to be open about everything and anything. If you're anxious or I'm feeling distant—" I barely get the words out before I'm silenced by a bruising kiss.

His lips capture mine, stealing the very breath from my lungs.

Suddenly, I feel little paws trying to climb up my leg. I break away and look down as Roo goes wild between us. Kane leans down and picks him up, making Roo look even smaller in those big arms of his.

"I promise. So should we adopt him?" he begs, petting him all over while Roo covers his face in kisses.

"Let's fill out the paperwork, and when we pick where, we'll take him home for our first night together." I beam, my face almost hurting with how happy I am.

"HEY, babe. Have you finally come up for air from your Kane bubble?" Morgan asks as I walk into the kitchen that night to see what she's making.

"Ha-ha, very funny." I roll my eyes and prop my hip against the counter to face her. I've been dreading this conversation since Kane and I decided yesterday that we're moving in together. Unsure where we are even going to live, I know I need to talk to Morgan first.

"Look, babe, I'm happy for you. It was about time you two got your heads out of your asses and figured your shit out. I, for one, am so glad it finally happened and you can stop moving around here like a corpse." She smirks at me as she stirs a delicious-smelling sauce.

"I should be thanking you for all your meddling."

"You should, yes. I accept flowers or chocolates as a thank you. Maybe make Kane buy me a new car with his fancy trust fund?"

"Don't you also have your own trust fund?"

"Pssh, beside the point." She shrugs, grabbing two plates and plating her famous spaghetti for us. Her Nonna made the recipe and handed it down through generations, and I still have not had such an aroma-rich sauce. The garlic-to-spice ratio is perfect.

We sit down at the table in our respective places, across from each other so we can have maximum yapping between us.

"So why are you here instead of sucking face with your super-hot boyfriend?"

"Uh, I live here?" I moan as the flavor hits my tongue.

Morgan was always the cook between the two of us, learning young from her father's mother.

She looks at me and rolls her eyes, her eyebrow raised as if she's waiting for me to keep going. I take a few moments and eat a few more bites, trying to get up the courage to tell her.

"But," I start, placing my fork down and putting my feet up on the chair. "Kane did ask me to move in with him."

"About time," is all she says, then goes back to eating, dipping her garlic bread in the leftover sauce on her plate.

"That's it?" I falter.

"Well, yeah. It's about time you two do it. I'm shocked it didn't happen years ago."

"You're not upset with me?" I ask softly, ducking my head a bit, not wanting to see the anger she probably has on her face. She reaches over and places her hand on top of mine, her perfectly manicured pink nails staring back at me, a stark contrast to my unpainted ones—desperately in need of some TLC.

"Babe." A soft smile graces her face. "Why would I be mad? You're in love, and you want to spend every day together. I'm happy for you. No, I'm thrilled for you. You two are meant to be together, and who am I to be mad that you're trying to follow your heart? After everything you two have been through these past couple months, you deserve this."

"But that means we won't live together anymore?" It comes out more like a question than a statement.

"Well, good luck getting rid of me even if we are apart. I know your parents left you, but you're stuck with me, babe. For life. We're still going to talk every single day. I will sleep over here and kick Kane to the couch, and you'll come stay with me. This doesn't change anything, just addresses." She squeezes my hand as tears well in my eyes.

Morgan has always seen me more than anyone else. The second we met freshman year of high school, she got me. We have been each other's person since, and the thought of being so far away from her is hard to comprehend.

But the thought of moving in with Kane of sharing our life together—I want it so much.

"Thank you for being supportive of this. It's a big step, and, well...I'm scared. After the past few months, what if we don't make it work?" I grasp her hand back, resting it between us on the table, food long forgotten.

"I think it's normal to be scared, but it also means you're doing the right thing. Change is scary, but change can also be exactly what you need. You two are meant to be together. You talk, communicate, and if he closes himself off again, well, I took karate in sixth grade, and I think I could take him," she proposes while coming around to hug me while I bury my head in her chest. Her ample cleavage almost suffocates me as I let her hold me. She pulls back and stares at me.

"Thank you for being here. For being my best friend," I blubber as my face is smushed between her boobs once again.

"Ditto, babe." She strokes my hair.

"So what do we do next? Kane and I need to start looking for what's available to rent in the area." I watch her walk around and grab her dish along with mine, then put them in the sink.

She comes and sits down across from me. "Why doesn't he just move in here?"

"Morgan, I'm not kicking you out of your own house," I reply astonished.

"You're not kicking me out. Besides, this house just suits you two. The built-in bookcases, the original 1930s build. It was practically made for you."

"But what about you? Where will you go?" I pick at my fingers as I think of displacing her from her own house.

"I want to look around and be sure. Maybe I'll move into Kane's room in the meantime while I look." She throws it out like it's nothing.

I freeze at the mention of her being willing to move in with Marcus.

"You want to move in with Marcus?" I hesitate.

"I mean, not particularly. Do I want to potentially catch whatever he's caught? No. But it's cheap, and I really don't want to keep relying on my father. I want to try to make it on my own. There's this cute storefront on Main that I have been eyeing. Maybe it's finally time I open the bookstore."

Morgan has always dreamed of being surrounded by books. She and I bonded over our love of romance and someday meeting our Prince Charming. We always have Tuesday night book club, just the two of us, which is just us discussing the books we read that week and laughing.

"Morgan, you should! You've been saying for years you want to, and your trust is enough to get it off the ground," I squeal, excitement coursing through me at the idea of my best friend getting to live out her dream.

"Maybe. It's a lot to think about. And with Queen Olivia getting married, it might be nice to have somewhere familiar to stay."

Queen Olivia is the nickname we gave her older sister Olivia—the golden child of the family who can do no wrong. Morgan, meanwhile, has been labeled the black sheep for wanting out of her family dynamic.

"Are you sure? We don't have to rush anything. You can

stay here until you're ready." I search my best friend's face, hoping she's being honest. The thought of finally getting to live with Kane has butterflies erupting in my stomach.

"I'm more than sure. I'm excited for you. And I can survive Marcus for a few months. Plus, it might be fun to move in just to fuck with him a bit. Cock-block him constantly or something." She smirks as she says it.

I laugh at her and Marcus's nonstop antics. I can't wait until she finally admits she has feelings for him. Those two have been dancing around each other for years, the push and pull tension so evident even someone with vision impairment would be able to notice.

"How do you feel?" she asks, thinking I won't notice her change in subject from herself.

"I'm excited," I beam. "I think this is everything I have ever wanted. I can't imagine waking up with him every morning, knowing he's mine and that this is the life I get to live. It feels bigger, moving in together, even though we usually don't spend a night apart. We're going to adopt a dog too. Did I tell you about Roo?" I ask, taking out my phone and going to my ever-growing album of shelter dogs. The forty photos I took of Roo today fill my screen, and one of him attacking Kane quickly became my new background photo. This tall, tattooed man being taken down by the cutest puppy is almost too much for my heart to handle.

"Shut up! Roo is the cutest puppy I have seen in such a long time. I'm so happy for you. You deserve this, you know. You deserve to hold onto this happiness and ride it out. You've found someone who is obsessed with you, who would do anything for you," she finishes wistfully.

"I'm going to miss you, though. We had some amazing years in this house." I reach over and grab her hands.

"We did, and this isn't over. We have so many more

memories to make together," she says back to me, both of us misty eyes.

We both laugh and get up from the table. I send a quick text to Kane that I'm going to stay here and spend time with Morgan tonight. We sit on the couch and turn on our favorite reality show at the moment, the ridiculousness of the plot making our stomachs hurt with how hard we're laughing, filling the room between us and reminding me just how full my life is with all the family I have been able to surround myself with.

CHAPTER THIRTY-FIVE

kane

Robbers – The 1975

"Thanks, Mr. D," Sam says, sitting across from me.

"I know how it is, trust me. When you live in a functional dynamic with an absentee father and an emotionally immature mother, it puts a lot of pressure on you to be the caretaker of the house. The one who must be responsible for everyone else's emotions, walking on eggshells to avoid a blowup of any kind. You make yourself so hyperaware of every shifting emotion that you try to predict what could happen next. But you deserve to go to the school of your dreams and live the life you want. You do not owe your parents your future just because they may need you." I rest my elbows on the desk, watching her carefully to make sure she hears me.

Sam is a strong student, and she was able to secure a full scholarship to an out-of-state college on the West Coast—in English lit—and has been in my office for days ruminating over her acceptance and how her parents have handled it. It's been jarring to have a mirror reflection of my own parents staring back at me, but it gives me the right background to guide her moving forward. To remind her that she still has time to heal, to move beyond them, to find herself and be her own person.

I'm grateful she showed up at my door a few days ago to talk about this. When she leaves at the bell, I sit back in my chair and blow out a breath.

The day has had an easy start. I've been riding the high of Avery agreeing to move in all morning. I haven't gotten to see her yet, but the smile has been permanently fixed on my face since. After my talk with Sam, I feel more conflicted.

One half of me is so happy with the way my life is shaping up. The girl of my dreams back in my life, the career I have worked so hard for, the acceptance to my own master's program hitting my inbox just this morning. But the thought of my parents brings me down a few levels.

My phone has been dry from them since the fallout, which is to be expected. But the first few days I had hope. Maybe just a text message that they'd heard me. I must have checked my phone a thousand times to see if I missed anything. I went most of my life avoiding their texts and calls, mostly from my mother, to now hoping for something.

It's been weeks, and I think I have finally given up on them, or at least accepted that this is the way things will have to be. I don't need to be good enough for them, because really, they are not good enough for me.

Steve and I have really been digging into how much they have impacted me and the core beliefs I have about myself, and I feel lighter. I feel less weighed down by all they have done—and didn't do—in my life. I haven't forgiven them. I'm not sure if I ever will, but I'm ready to move forward. I'm ready for my future to be my focus and my past to be just that, my past. My hands itch to check my phone, like maybe there's something I could have missed from them, but I know all that waits for me is crushing disappointment.

I turn back to my computer and browse the emails I missed during my last appointment. Nothing is urgent enough to require an immediate response, so I push back away from my desk. I reach up and stretch out my back from the position I've been in for the past few hours when my office phone rings. The sound is sharp and piercing in the once silent office, the red light blinking to show me it's an interoffice call.

"Hello?" I answer, the corded phone pulled tight as I stand behind my chair, ready to eat lunch.

"There's someone at the front for you, with food," Dawn greets and then hangs up.

Confusion wars through me because I don't remember ordering any food. I hang up the phone and grab mine, slipping it into my back pocket on the way. I head out of my office and hang right toward the front, and as the hallway comes to an end, I see her.

An angel wearing jeans and a Second Chances T-shirt, holding a bag of food with the brightest smile on her face. Warmth fills me up as I stare at her, my biggest dream brought to life before me. Her brown hair is down and hanging to her waist, thick and slightly waved, begging for me to tug on it. The light makeup she wears for work makes her eyes pop even more. I stare at her as I come closer.

"Hey, I brought—" she starts as I grasp her face and kiss her—maybe a bit more than I should at my place of work, but I can't help it when she stands there looking like that. As if my heart is walking around outside my body.

"You're here." I smile in reverence pulling back, my hands still on both of her cheeks as I take her in again.

"Well, you came to visit me the other day, so I thought..." she trails off as she holds up the food. The spicy aroma hits my nostrils, making my stomach grumble and a moan come up my throat. The name of our local Mexican place is printed on the bag—the one we always use to gorge ourselves.

"You're perfect." I smile, an awestruck as I stare down at her, wondering what I could have done to have this girl in my arms again. Her lemon scent hits my nostrils, and I feel greedy as I drink her in, letting myself melt into her presence.

I pull away to grab the food when something at the door catches my eye: a figure shadowed by the light behind him. He walks through the door, the shape of him sparking recognition in my brain.

Before I can place it, he's inside and staring right at me. I look down and see a glint of something in his hand as his eyes search around. When they land on me, a menacing look takes over his face as he sways slightly on his feet.

"Aye, we have some talkin' to do," Trevor's dad slurs, raising the gun in his hand and pointing it in our direction. I hear a gasp from Avery as I shove her behind me, dwarfing her with my large frame.

"You need to leave, right now," I demand as my vision snaps into focus, everything hazy except the man standing in front of us with a gun. The black metal gleams when the light from outside hits it, making it more menacing.

"You don't get to tell me what to do," he booms his accent thick, slurring slightly on a few words, waving the gun around. Gasps come from the front desk and to the right, but my stare stays locked on him.

I raise my hand toward him, trying to somehow defuse this situation. I feel a small hand grip the back of my shirt holding me, her forehead resting on my back as I take easy breaths, trying to keep the rising panic at bay until I can figure out how to get her out of this.

"You think ya so much better than me," he slurs, waving the gun and stepping closer. I take a step back to match his step, trying to keep enough distance between us.

"Mr. Wilde, let's put the gun down so we can talk about this," I try to reason. He looks drunk as he sways on his feet. His stained shirt and ripped pants hang off his frame, his hair beyond disheveled, the strands stringy and limp around him. He looks unkempt and unbathed. He looks older than his years, the alcohol clearly taking a toll on him as his body fights to stay upright, his finger on the trigger. My body tenses every time he moves.

"You want a threat, I'll give ya a threat!" he says, swinging the gun around, making the gasps rise around us. I take a step forward, hoping to reason with him.

"Give me the gun, and let's talk about it. No more threats. I just want to do what's best for Trevor," I caution, hands up as I take another step forward, trying to do anything to defuse this situation. Unable to look around, I don't know how many people are here. All I can focus on is keeping his attention on me and off Avery.

He looks around me, and his eyes change when he spots Avery.

"Who's the cunt ya have there?" he says with a gleam in his eye as he focuses on her. I see red and take another step forward, trying to block her from his sight, hoping he loses interest and focuses back on me.

"Don't fucking look at her. Your problem is with me, so point that gun at me, you abusive piece of shit," I taunt, wanting him to forget her.

"You think ya can talk to me like that, like ya the fuckin' king of the world," he slurs further, swaying on his feet,

"I can do what I want with ma own fuckin' blood, ya hear?" he screams, his face turning red as he waves the gun around. I must keep my own face firmly in place to keep myself from flinching at the move.

"Mr. Wilde, put the gun down and we can talk. We can work this situation out. No one needs to get hurt," I plead with him, hoping there is some way I can break through his alcohol-induced rage.

I hear a faint sound of sirens in the distance, my heart leaping at the hope that this will be over soon. Trevor's dad must hear it too because he whips his head toward the front door, trying to see behind the bright glare of the sun shining in. So far, the coast is clear, but the seconds are dwindling as the sirens get louder.

"Who tha fuck are ya to call the police? Ya think they gonna save ya?" He screams, the gun raised at me, the barrel in my focus.

I see my life flash before my eyes, the day I met Avery the first thing in my mind, her lips wrapped around the pen, our first date in the park, the leaves all around us creating a beautiful backdrop. I think of our dance at prom and the first time she told me she loved me. The smell of lemons every time I sink my face into her hair, when I wake up and we are wrapped in each other, unable to tell where she ends and I begin. I feel her curves and the way those baby blues shine when I play her a new song, letting her feel the chords and how desperately I feel the lyrics in my voice.

I take a step forward as a loud bang goes off, the gun smoking and kicking back hard enough to knock him off balance. He drops to the ground, and for one impossible second, I wait for the pain to hit. I stand still and feel around my body, expecting blood to be somewhere. Then I hear a gasp and something drops behind me.

I whip around and watch Avery crumple to the ground, the food scattered around her. The sirens outside pierce the air as they get louder, the sound setting every nerve on fire as I rush over to her and drop to my knees, the force of my fall sending sharp pains up my legs.

I reach over and grab her face in my hands, pain spread all over her face.

"Baby, baby, look at me. *Look at me.* What is it?"

I panic as I search her face for answers, then tear my eyes from hers and roam her body, searching for what happened, until I see a red splotch start to bloom on the right side of her upper chest.

"Oh my god!" I yell, pressing my hands to the wound.

The move makes her scream out, her eyes glassy and welling with tears.

"It's okay, baby, it's okay. I have to put pressure on it," I tell her, my brain working on overdrive as I try to rationalize what happened. How the bullet somehow hit her.

"I-it hu-rts," she gasps out, one hand coming up to clutch my shirt, her knuckles white as she grips me like I'm her lifeline.

"It's okay, baby. It's okay. Help is almost here," I stress. "Keep your eyes open for me, pretty girl. Keep those beautiful baby blues on me. You're going to be okay, do you hear me?"

The sirens are deafening, the sounds of chaos starting up around me, rustling filling my ears.

"Sir, I'm going to need you to step back," a voice says over me, grasping my shoulder to pull me away.

"No!" I yell, ripping out of their grasp and grabbing

Avery's face with both hands, keeping my eyes on hers, not wanting to look away for even a second.

"Sir, we need to help her, so we need you to step back and let us," the voice says again.

I'm unable to tear my gaze away from hers. My vision blurs as I try to focus on her, wetness tracking down my cheeks as her eyes start to flutter.

"I can't leave her," I say, desperate and hoping they hear me.

"We need to help her, and we can't do that if you won't let us." The person speaks softer now, holding onto my shoulder with one hand, grounding me to the moment.

I feel hands gripping me and pulling me away from her as I fight to get back to her side. The EMTs swarm her and start to work on her. I hear something about her blood pressure and a gunshot wound to the chest, a flurry of activity surrounding me. In the reception area, surrounded by cops, I see three officers haul Mr. Wilde out, him screaming unintelligibly at the top of his lungs, the gash the gun left dripping down his face as he's hauled outside. The screaming stops at the close of the doors at his back.

Two officers hold me back as Avery is lifted onto a stretcher, and I fight against them to rush to her. I need to see that she is okay.

"Sir, you need to calm down so they can help her, and we need to get a statement," one officer says as he grips my shoulders and forces me to stare at him.

"I'm going with her. I'm not leaving her alone," I plead with the officer, unable to let her out of my sight for a second.

"Let him go," another officer interrupts, releasing the first officer's hands from me. I rush over to where they are wheeling her off into the ambulance parked across the front entryway. I look around at the dozen cop cars and the flashing lights. Mr. Wilde is being hauled into the back of a car, shoved inside, the door slammed on him as he screams. They lift the stretcher into the back and look at me, waiting for me to climb in, seeming to accept she isn't going anywhere without me.

The back of the ambulance is a flurry, the EMTs checking her pulse and trying to keep her awake. Her eyes open and close, but no words make their way out.

"Is she okay?" I ask one of the EMTs, a young guy who looks no older than twenty-five, with deep brown hair and light stubble on his cheeks.

He looks at me, his eyes wary. "She's stable. She's mostly out from the pain, but we got to her in time," he says, leveling with me. "We called ahead, and they're ready for her. She'll most likely go right to the OR when we get there. The bullet is still lodged somewhere in her," he adds, and my stomach bottoms out, the fluorescent lights of the cab harsh on the gleaming surfaces. I grasp her hand tighter and try to keep her anchored to me.

Her hand is small in mine, still warm as I hold her, hoping that the tighter I grip her, the more I can keep her here with me.

After what feels like an eternity, the ambulance stops, the sirens still blaring, the sounds finally coming back to me as the doors are wrenched open and the space is filled with people. They're lowering the bed with my life on it, nurses rushing to her and talking at once, all the medical jargon going right over my head.

I jump down and go after her before I'm stopped with a hand on my chest, a male nurse standing in front of me as we enter the emergency room bay.

"Sir, you can't go with her. You can wait here, and I will

have someone come out and talk to you when we can," he says, trying to reason with me. "Are you family?"

"She's my wife..." I say, broken, knowing that if she comes out of this, I'm never letting her go again. "Please help her..."

"She's in good hands, sir. Let us do our jobs," he says. "Let me show you the waiting area."

He pulls me through a couple hallways until we enter a big room with a couple dozen chairs, a few TVs hanging on the walls. There are only three other people here, all seemingly lost in their own worlds. The only sound is the TV's low volume.

"There's a bathroom through there to wash up, and I will have someone come update you as soon as we can," he says, then turns to walk out, his steps eating up the distance between us.

I stare down at my hands, stained red from the blood I didn't even notice was on them. My silver rings covered in her.

I walk myself to the bathroom and watch as the red washes down the drain, the mixture of soap and blood swirling like my thoughts. The anxiety makes me spiral as I imagine every bad thing that could be happening right now. The urge to throw every door open until I can lay my eyes on her is strong.

I stumble out of the bathroom, my thoughts jumbled and my heart shredded in two as I reach for my phone and call Marcus, the tears streaming down my face as I tell him where I am, that Avery was hurt.

"On my way," he replies without hesitation and hangs up.

I sit down and place my head in my hands, trying to calm my breathing. In for four and out for four. The rising panic inside me threatens to drown me, the pain in my chest constricting. My breathing comes out strangled while I fight for every next breath.

I'm not sure how long I sit there before suddenly I'm surrounded by arms—six to be exact. Morgan, Marcus, and Grayson surround me as I break down, the tears streaming down my face and the breaths not coming in fast enough. Panic drowns me as I think of Avery, so far away from me. The look on her face when I turned around and she was there, on the ground. The way I was unable to protect her. The guilt is drowning me until I can no longer see through the tears pouring from my eyes.

When I finally pull back and stare at my family, matching tears shine in all our eyes, no words exchanged as we sit there together.

After several hours, some stilted conversation, and a few more tears, the same nurse walks through the door and I stand up before his eyes meet mine.

"She's out of surgery," he announces, instant relief going through my body at those words.

"Can I see her?" I ask.

"She's still asleep from the anesthesia. The surgery went well, and the bullet was removed without any permanent damage," he explains, the words soothing me. He looks at me and takes in my disheveled state. He places a hand on my forearm and squeezes, seeming to convey so much with no words.

I let out a breath I didn't realize I was holding.

"Only one person at a time for now," he says, looking at our makeshift family, taking in our tear-stained faces.

I look at our friends and over to Morgan. "Go, go see your girl," she says with a small smile on her face, eyes full of fresh tears. Her face is free of makeup and her eyes puffy, a mirror of my own. She's wearing two mismatched shoes, and her shirt is zipped and crooked.

I nod at her and my brothers and take off after the nurse, trepidation coursing through me with every hallway we turn down as the hospital bustles around me. The nonstop beeping of machines follows me around every corner, the med-surge floor gleaming at me. He brings me to a closed door, number three hundred and twenty-nine staring back at me, and opens it slowly, letting the harshness of the machines sink into my system. The beeping of the heart monitor is music to my ears because she's okay.

She's breathing.

CHAPTER THIRTY-SIX

kane

Waiting Room – Phoebe Bridgers

It's been thirty-two hours since we were rushed to the hospital, and I don't think I have been able to take a full breath since. I stare down at her, her face serene, clear of any makeup she may have had. She looks as if she's just asleep. They're not sure why she hasn't woken up yet, maybe from the blood loss. Nurses and doctors have been in and out over the past couple hours, but I've been here, unmoved from her bedside.

Morgan and Marcus stopped by trading in and out with Grayson, trying to get me to leave and eat, but I refuse to leave her side. It's my fault she's here. If I hadn't been so reckless threatening him, he never would have shown up.

The cops came by early this morning to let me know he is going to be charged with aggravated assault and a slew of other charges since he showed up at a high school with a gun. Apparently, he says he never meant to shoot it, that he just wanted to scare us, and the cops believe him, so he isn't being charged with attempted murder.

Regardless, I am willing to testify if it means that piece of shit is behind bars and Avery is safe.

The firm and steady beeping of the machines is the only reason I haven't completely lost it. My vision is blurry from lack of sleep, but my eyes refuse to close. My hair is disheveled and sticking up in all directions from the number of times I've run my fingers through it. The nurses have all stared at me as if I have lost my mind, but I can't handle not being here for every second. Thinking about leaving her side is a pain I can't even fathom.

Every minute that goes by without her opening her eyes, I die a little more inside. They explained the surgery to me, how the bullet nicked her lung, causing a tension pneumothorax and making the surgery a bit more critical than first anticipated. But the good news is she started breathing on her own immediately, keeping her out of the ICU and on the regular med-surge recovery floor, with a little extra monitoring.

"Come on, baby, I need you to open those blue eyes. I need you to open them and look at me again. I need you to drown me in your light because I can't be left in the dark again. I'm scared of the dark without you," I rasp out, my voice dry with disuse, her small hand encased in mine as I bring it up to my forehead and rest it against me. "I need you to wake up, pretty girl, because I can't—"

I choke on a sob, the tears welling up in my eyes threatening to spill over. "I can't do this without you. I don't want to do this without you. We have so much life left to live together. We need to move in together and pick up Roo. I need to give you the ring I've had stashed in my drawer for months. I need to stand across from you in front of all our friends and pledge my life to yours. Because it's already yours. All that I am belongs to you. So I need... I need you, pretty girl." I kiss the back of her hand, savoring the feel of it in mine. Savoring the warmth of it between my hands and letting some of my energy somehow flow into her and make her wake up.

I reach over and stroke her hair away from her face, letting my fingers trail down her cheek, the softness of her skin a stark contrast to the calluses on my fingers from my guitar. Her dark brown hair spills across the white sheets, making her stand out.

I hear the clicking of heels approach behind me. I don't turn around, thinking a nurse has come by to check on her, until they stop right next to my chair and a soft hand rests on my shoulder. I turn slowly, and shock courses through me at the sight of my mother standing next to me. Her perfectly done-up hair and pantsuit are unfitting against the dreary hospital walls and harsh lights. She looks at me, pain in her eyes and a soft smile on her face.

"Hi, baby," she says softly, her hand still on my shoulder as I am rendered speechless.

"Wh-what are you doing here?" I ask.

"I heard what happened. It's all over the news. It took me a bit to figure out what hospital she was at, but I rushed over as soon as I could," she responds, squeezing my shoulder once and letting go. Her ringless hand peers back at me, leaving me rendered speechless.

"But what are you doing here?" I ask still confused and unsure if my sleep deprived hallucinations are making me imagine this.

"I... I know this isn't the time or the place, but I wanted to be there for you. To show up for you in a way I should have your whole life. And I hope it's not too late for me to," she says softly, a little unsure. She holds her purse in front of her with both hands, fiddling with the strap as if this is harder for her than she thought.

I gape at her, unable to think of any words to say, my mind blanking.

"I don't expect you to say anything. I know I don't deserve it, but I have left your father. I moved out and have started the divorce process. I wanted you to know that I heard what you said that night, and I was heartbroken to know how much we have affected you. I failed as a mother, and I knew before I could contact you again, I had to get my life together so that I could put you first in a way I should have from the very beginning. I'm so sorry, Kane."

"It's okay, Mom. I shouldn't have blown up on you like that."

"Yes, you should have. I'm so sorry it had to even get to that point. I should have paid better attention, I should have noticed, and I should take full accountability for everything."

"Thank you," I say, clearing my throat against all the emotions that have started to climb up.

"Do you think... Do you think that someday you could forgive me?" she asks me, her features filled with remorse and a slight hint of complete devastation as her gaze drops to my hand clutching Avery's. The whites of my fingers show how hard my grip is, forcing me to relax a bit so I don't hurt her further.

"I'd like to...someday, but right now..." I trail off as my gaze goes back to my whole world lying in a hospital bed.

My mother shifts on her feet.

"Have you eaten?" she asks, changing the subject, making me so thankful to no longer have to deal with such heaviness while my mind is somewhere else. Lost to the universe, searching for Avery to come back to me.

"No," I reply, staring at Avery. I watch her chest rise and fall under the blankets, the sight soothing my inner chaos.

"Okay, well, I'm going to run down to the cafeteria and get you something. Marcus is going back to get you a change of clothes. You need to at least eat something. You can't end up in a hospital bed when she wakes up looking for you," she says, squeezing my shoulder again before she takes off out the doors, the heels clacking on the linoleum on the way out.

My gaze never leaves Avery, my mind begging hers to wake up. I trace her face with my eyes, drinking in the sight of her, counting the freckles on the bridge of her nose, breathing along to keep the anxiety at bay.

Finally, the exhaustion takes over me, and I rest my head on top of our clasped hands, just to rest my eyes for a minute. They're burning with exhaustion, but I refuse to give in to sleep, so worried that the second I do, I'll lose her somehow.

"That sounded like a hard conversation," I hear a small voice come from next to me. My head shoots up, my eyes opening as I stare at Avery's blue eyes, finally peering up at me once more. My heart leaps in my chest, pounding so hard I feel that it might burst.

"Oh my god," I gasp out as I take her head between my hands and kiss her, the kiss featherlight as I drink her in.

She reaches up and cups my cheek with her own hand, the feeling unlike anything I have ever experienced before.

"Are you okay? Are you in pain? Do I need to call a nurse?" I ask rapid-fire, not taking breaths between questions.

A soft chuckle leaves her lips. "I'm okay," she rasps out. "I was just taking a nap."

A small smile on her face, her eyes closing again as I lean my forehead against hers and drink her in. I don't know how long we stay there like that, just breathing each other in. My mind circles with things to say, but I don't know how to even start to apologize for how I was at fault for her ending up here, or if she could ever forgive me.

I pull back and sit down in the chair I have been sitting in for the last day and a half. I grasp her hand in both of mine and bring it to my lips, leaving one more soft kiss before I pull back and look into those eyes.

"I'm so sorry, Ave. I—"

She takes her hand and places it against my mouth, effectively cutting me off.

"Don't you dare apologize to me, Kane August D'Antonio," she says firmly, indignation written on her face as she peers back up at me.

"But this is my fault," I rasp out, my eyes welling with tears again thinking about how my reckless actions landed her here, fighting for her life, in surgery for hours.

"This is *not* your fault, and you better stop beating yourself up for it," she says with a no-nonsense tone.

"But—" I start before I'm cut off with a withering look from her, threatening me not to push her.

"These are the actions of an absolute madman who has been abusing his children and getting away with it. You did what was right and stood up to him because you saw an injustice and couldn't stand by. And I am so proud of you for standing up for that kid. I do not blame you for even a second. The *only* person to blame is him, do you hear me?" she says.

I hang my head and look at our joined hands. My tan, callused ones dwarf her pale, small one. The complete opposite of mine, but somehow fitting perfectly in mine. A hand that I never want to let go of as long as I live.

"Look at me," she whispers softly.

I bring my head up and look at those freckles, my very own constellation guiding me home. Those eyes on me like I had been begging anyone who would listen for hours.

"I love you," she states, knowing I need to hear the words more than ever. I reach over to stroke her cheek with one of my hands, the rings gleaming in the overhead lights. She moves her head further into my hand as if she is trying to burrow into its warmth.

"I love you so much. Thank you for coming back to me," I rasp with another kiss on her hand, unable to keep my hands or lips off her for even a second. An angel encased in white, a vision I never want to see again. These past few hours have taken years off my life, the rotation of nurses and doctors spiking my anxiety at every *hm* and new medical term they threw my way.

"There's nothing that will keep me from you again, not even a lunatic with a gun," she jokes. "Too soon?"

"Maybe a bit. I just got you back," I laugh, my own smile making an appearance at the one she has shining at me, impossible to resist. My heart flutters with the thought of that smile peering at me again, the hours of hopelessness draining the longer she looks at me.

Soon we're ambushed by a flurry of activity when the nurse pops in and sees she's awake. They check all her vitals and ask her about a thousand questions while I refuse to let her go even when asked. She rolls her eyes at that but I'm not willing to let her go for even a second again. The nurses are used to my behavior, working around me, knowing how immovable I am when it comes to her.

At one point, the nurses clear out and my mother pops

in. A small gasp leaves her lips as she rounds the bed to Avery's other side and grabs her face between her hands.

"Oh, my girl, how are you feeling? I'm so glad to see you're awake," she coos toward my girlfriend, my heart warming at the look of adoration lining my mother's face.

"I'm okay. It's good to see you, Mrs. D," Avery replies, smiling back up at my mother.

"Elena, please, darling. I won't take up too much of your time. I brought some food, so please eat," she fusses, making a pointed look at me, then at the pile of food that could feed an army of ten. The thought of her stacking the tray warms my heart at the effort. "I'll come back to check on you a little later," she finishes and kisses Avery on the cheek.

She rounds the bed, places a kiss on mine, and leaves the room with her heels clacking after her, her perfume lingering in the air even after she's gone.

"How are you?" Avery coaxes, looking at me, imploring me, and nodding her head at where my mother just vacated.

"I should be asking you that, pretty girl," I say, rubbing circles on the back of her hand, letting the feeling of her awake and talking fuel me. I take some bites of the food, bland and tasteless, but not wanting to collapse now that she's made her way back to me.

"She apologized," I start, my voice trailing off. "She left my father. She wants to be in my life."

"And how does that make you feel? That's good, right?" Avery asks, a hesitant look on her face. My heart aches at the reason it's there, needing to let her in more than anything right now.

"I don't know. It's what I wanted, but I'm not sure if I can trust it," I answer on a sigh, scratching the stubble that has grown back over the past two days.

"I think you should give her a chance, babe. If my

mother came back telling me she was willing to try, I would jump at the chance. Even if it doesn't work out, at least you know you tried," she reasons, bringing her hand up to cup my cheek, stroking my cheek and calming my heart rate.

Just as I open my mouth to respond, the door opens in a flourish, and chaos soon sweeps into the room in the form of a five-foot-four bubbly blonde who yells, "Oh my god! You're awake!" as she rushes to Avery's side and wraps her in a hug.

Avery lets out a huff.

"Sorry, sorry I got too excited," Morgan apologizes, stroking Avery's hair and staring at her best friend as if she's a mirage.

"It's okay," Avery replies with a laugh, as Morgan leans down and hugs her again. A warm hand clasps my shoulder, I look over to see Marcus and Grayson behind me, staring at Avery in awe.

"Move over, Viper, it's my turn," Marcus says, hip checking Morgan and diving in for a hug, trying to stay away from her right side.

"Hey, dummy, have you been terrorizing the nurses?" Avery asks, petting Marcus's floppy hair.

"Me? Of course I have," Marcus replies, a goofy grin on his face as he stares at his best friend. Marcus and I will always be close, but I know the bond between Avery and him is one that will forever be unshakable.

"Hey, Ave," Grayson greets as he moves Marcus out of the way and hugs her, my grip never letting go of her right hand. "How are you feeling, little fighter?"

"Good. I missed you guys," she replies, taking in our friends, the family we have somehow acquired when ours have always let us down. The room is filled with so much laughter and chatter in the next few hours, the nurses finally have to kick them out when visiting hours are done, almost having to shove the three of them out as they promise to visit first thing tomorrow.

The doctors come and look Avery over, giving her one more day before she can head home, just to make sure the wound is closing and she gets a few more hours of fluids after the blood loss.

Avery

It's later that night, hours after our friends have left. The hospital is quiet now, and the overhead lights are off as I try to sleep. The meds have started to wear off, and pain shoots through my body. I jerk with it, and Kane's head shoots up, taking in my face before he hits the nurse call light.

"I'm okay," I reassure him. He's still sitting in the chair next to my bed, my hand clutched in his. He refused to move even when the nurses offered to bring in a bed for him to sleep in. He wouldn't even entertain the idea of being too far from me. The bags under his eyes are so deep and purple my heart breaks a little to know what was going through his head in the hours after it happened.

The events are all a blur for me. All I really remember is showing up to bring Kane lunch and the smile that took over his face when he saw me. I remember arguing and Kane standing in front of me until pain overtook my body and the ground came up to meet my head. The rest is a blur of lights and words that felt all jumbled in my mind.

"You need to take the bed and get some sleep," I whisper to Kane.

"I'm okay here," he says, his voice gruff and his eyes red.

"Kane, you need to sleep. I'm okay, I promise," I plead with him.

He looks at me, firm in his stance of not leaving. I move over to the right a bit more and pat the left side of the bed, raising my eyebrows to tell him to get in.

"Avery, I don't want to hurt you," he says.

"Get in," I demand, leaving no room for argument in my tone.

He huffs and comes over to the other side of the bed. He slides in, then puts his arm behind my head as I roll over to my left side, wincing a bit at the pull but settling comfortably into his side. I let myself breathe him in, the smell of him calming me and making me drowsy.

He always had this effect on me, as if my body always knew how safe I was the minute I was in his arms. My brain would turn off, and sometimes I would relax for the first time all day when he was finally home and I was wrapped up in him. I always felt incredibly lucky to feel that safe with him, to know whatever I said or did, he would still be there. I had always wanted a place that felt like home, my childhood home never feeling like a safe place to land. Then I met Kane and realized that home was never a building but a person who made you feel as if you could never be anywhere safer.

"I thought I almost lost you," Kane croaks, so quiet I almost think I imagined it.

"It's going to take more than that to take me away from you again," I soothe, taking my head out of his neck and looking at him, those hazel eyes shining back at me. The love in them is so strong my throat clogs up with how perfect this man is.

"I felt like I couldn't breathe. For hours, I just sat here trying to fill my lungs, and it's as if my body forgot how to exist without you."

My heart breaks at the pain radiating from his voice. All I want to do is reach into his chest and soothe his broken heart, putting it next to mine for safekeeping.

"I'm sorry, baby. I'm sorry I couldn't come back to you sooner," I say, pulling his face to mine and leaving a soft kiss on his lips, the feel of them plush and warm against mine, filling the space in my heart that has felt empty without him.

"No more time apart. I'm all in. I want to spend every day waking up with you. I want to come home and make us dinner. I want to sing to you and listen to our favorite records. I want to marry you someday, hopefully soon, and I want us to be happy." He grabs my chin and places another kiss on my lips, this one more bruising than the last but with a gentleness to it still, as if he wants to make sure he can't hurt me.

"Does that mean we have to raise the white flags with the pranks?" I jab, trying to lighten the mood and get that smile back on his face. The idea of spending forever with this man and someday being his makes an impossibly large smile take over my face as I stare at the man who holds my future in his hands.

"All's fair in love and pranks, pretty girl," he says, finishing on a kiss. Sleep soon takes over both of us, the feeling of us bundled together the last thing on my mind as I drift to a dreamless sleep.

CHAPTER THIRTY-SEVEN

kane

TWO WEEKS LATER

Why – LANY

It's been two weeks since the shooting, and life is just now starting to get back to normal. The nightmares that have plagued me since that night have been dwindling. I've bumped up my sessions with Steve to twice a week and made sure Avery attends all her appointments. Her stitches have mostly healed, and she's gotten the all-clear to go back to work, but she still has to avoid any heavy lifting until her final checkup next month.

We haven't spent a night apart since she came home from the hospital. I have been slowly moving into her room one bag at a time. She thinks I haven't noticed her clearing space out and getting rid of half her closet to fit me in. What she doesn't know is I've taken all the bags she tried to donate and kept them for when Morgan moves out so I can make her a second closet in the other room. Along with all her crafts, she can have a getaway room all to herself whenever she wants it.

Morgan has been slowly packing up as well, not

wanting to be too far from Avery any more than I do. Marcus and Grayson have been by every day, all of us taking turns cooking and cleaning for Avery so she could really take these two weeks to heal.

The physical healing has been a lot faster than the mental and emotional healing. I know Avery has been having trouble sleeping, even though she's tried to hide it from me, which led to a big discussion one night about how this time, we have to talk to each other even when it's hard. There's no more hiding how we're feeling and letting miscommunication tear us apart.

Today is my first day back to work. The school gave me these past few weeks off as they processed the scene and resumed classes as normal. I'm not exactly thrilled about going back, not knowing what could await me. I know I messed up when I went to confront Trevor's dad without thinking about the repercussions.

My job aside, I don't regret sticking up for Trevor. I *do* regret how my actions harmed Avery and potentially could've harmed so many others, though.

Steve has me working on letting go of the guilt, reminding me that I'm not to blame—Mr. Wilde is. He's remained in jail and, in addition to the charges for harming Avery, he is also being charged with child abuse and domestic violence. The attorney my mother hired assured us he will be in prison for a very long time.

Trevor heard what happened before he arrived at school that day and finally decided to tell the truth. The state assumed custody and found his mother's grandparents, whom his father had told him were dead, robbing them of years together. I've been calling the social worker every day to see how they're settling in. She only tells me the bare minimum, but it's enough to keep me calm and glad that Trevor and his sisters get to stay together.

"Hey, what do you think you're doing?" I question as I see Avery fully dressed in her Second Chances T-shirt and skintight jeans. A mouthwatering sight that leaves me struck dumb for a moment. Her long brown hair is down and wavy, trailing down her back while tucked behind her ears. She's put makeup on for the first time since the hospital, and she takes my breath away every time I look at her.

"Going to work. Isn't it obvious?" she quips as she points to the name on her shirt, sitting down on the bed and attempting to put her shoes on.

A slight wince crosses her face, stopping my walk away. I rush over and take the shoe from her, opening the top and guiding her foot inside before tying it.

"You know I can do it myself now, the doctor gave me the all clear to resume light activities," she huffs, crossing her arms over her chest like a petulant child.

"Yes, light activities. He didn't say you had to return to work. Sharlene said to take all the time you need. Maybe you should take another week," I plead, putting her other shoe on and tying that lace too. I pat her knees and pull her up to stand with me.

I tuck a piece of hair that has fallen forward behind her ear and cup her cheek, forcing those brilliant blue eyes to look at mine.

"I'm okay, Kane. I want to go back to work, I can't just keep sitting here being waited on hand and foot."

"You can, but you're stubborn," I chastise her.

"Plus, what am I supposed to do all day while you go to work? I'll worry myself to death and put a hole in the floor from pacing. At least at work I can be distracted. I'm sure there's tons of paperwork to do. I promise I won't try to take any of the dogs out myself." She gives me the sweetest puppy-dog eyes, and I immediately cave, unable to say no to her when she looks at me like that.

"Fine, but I'm going to be okay, babe. He's in jail and he's not getting out. You heard the lawyer," I say, placing a soft kiss onto her pouty pink lips. I'll never get over the feel of her lips meeting mine, and I'll never again take for granted how it feels to hold her in my arms.

I wrap my arms around her waist, pulling her flush to me, unable to think about being away from her even for just a few hours, even though I know I need to. It's time to face the music, even if that means I lose my job. While I love my job and the kids I've met, I'll be okay.

I told Avery about the acceptance letter for a local master's program I had applied to and how much I wanted it, and all she did was scream and jump into my arms, telling me how proud she was of me.

"I know, I just..." she starts, smoothing her hands up and down my back. The feeling sends shivers down my spine.

"I know, pretty girl. Me too. But I love you, and I'll see you tonight, okay?" I promise with another kiss to her lips, still unable to detangle myself from this girl—I never want to.

"Okay, okay, go. But call me at lunch, okay? Or when you have any downtime. Maybe just call me a couple times?" she asks with a laugh, knowing how ridiculous she is being, but I'll do it anyway. No matter what it is, I'll make sure she knows I'm okay. "I love you too," she finishes, kissing me one more time on the lips before releasing her hold on me.

I reluctantly let her go and take a step back. She searches for her purse, somehow lost in a pile of clothes that have accumulated on top of the dresser—a reminder to clean up a bit more when I get home. With one more quick kiss, she takes off out of the bedroom. I hear her say bye to Morgan, a cheek kiss from both, and the front door slamming on her way out, my heart taking off with her.

I APPROACH the school with trepidation, the gleaming words of South Hill High staring back at me as I ascend the steps to the front entrance, forcing my spine tall and my steps not to falter. If I close my eyes, all I see is Avery crumbling on the ground, the red spreading over her chest as I try to find the source.

Panic hits my chest, my breath labored as I fight to keep the black from edging into my vision. The panic attack threatens to take me under, my forehead sweating and my pulse racing as I climb the last two steps before the doors are in front of me.

They've never looked this large and imposing before, as if they're dwarfing even my overly tall frame for once. I stare at the door, willing my hand to move and open it.

My phone dings in my back pocket, a distraction that has me blowing out a breath and shaking my hands out in front of me, hoping to release some of the tension that has been building.

I reach into my back pocket and pull it out. The picture of Avery and me calms my heart rate just a bit, reminding me that she's here, she's alive, and she's fine. Not even death can tear us apart now.

PRETTY GIRL

I'm so proud of you! Go in today and kick ass, can't wait to see you at home 🩶

My heart fills with the warmth I so desperately needed, the panic starting to recede as I give myself time to breathe deeply, not letting my fear control me anymore.

ME

See you at OUR home. I love you

I put my phone in my pocket and shake out any remaining tension. I flex my hands, grip the door frame, and wrench the door open before I lose the nerve.

I step through the threshold and am momentarily blinded by the harsh sun before my eyes adjust to the dimmer lights used throughout the school.

Dawn is the first person I see. She races up out of her chair and around the desk before flying into my arms for a hug. I grab hold of her and let her gush over me. She checks me over like a mother would, her tiny five-foot frame somehow making me feel eye to eye with her. When she sees I'm whole and here, she swats my chest.

"This has been the scariest two weeks of my life! The least you could've done is call! How is that angel of yours?" she asks in rapid fire. Her glasses are perched on her head, pushing her graying hair back so her face is clear.

"She's okay. She's back at work today too. And we got your fruit basket. Avery sends her thanks." I soothe her with a warm smile.

"Good. I'm glad to hear it. That one is a fighter, you know."

"She is. I don't know how I got so lucky," I reply, smiling at the talk of my favorite person. The brief distraction eases the tension building inside me. The area is surprisingly empty, as if Dawn knew I was coming and didn't want me to be overwhelmed. The carpet seems to be new, the smell clinging to the air, and my gaze drops right about where Avery fell.

I look around expecting a stain, and the relief that hits me when I realize it's gone nearly makes me stumble.

"Oh, Kane, maybe it's too soon. You should go sit down," Dawn says, fussing over me.

"I'm okay. It's just a lot to take in at once. Is Principal Danner in already? He wanted me to see him first," I say, worry lacing my tone.

"He is, but you can wait. Get settled in first. I'll hold him off," she tries to reassure me.

I want to rip the Band-Aid off and talk to him. I need to know whether or not I still have a job after this—I'm not ready to leave this place or these kids.

"No, that's okay. I'd rather get it over with," I say, giving her one last hug and then heading to the front of the building, the hallway leading to the receptionists in front of the principal and each year's vice principal.

I knock on the door and hear a gruff *come in*. When I turn the handle and push the heavy brown door open, Principal Danner is sitting behind his desk, glasses on the bridge of his nose and a mountain of paperwork in front of him.

He's in his late forties, the gray peppering his temples and mixing in with his light brown hair. He has youthful skin and an athletic build, and he also helps coach the boys' football team here.

"Kane! Good to see you. Come in and have a seat." His overly loud voice fills the room. I enter and close the door behind me, then make my way to one of the brown leather chairs in front of his desk and sit.

"It's good to see you, Principal Danner," I say, nodding my head at him.

"No need for all that. Call me Eric. How are you doing? How is that girlfriend of yours healing?" he asks, sitting back and crossing his arms over his chest.

"Good. We're good. Her doctor gave her the all-clear to resume light activities, so she went back to work already. We are both just trying to get back to normal," I reply, my hands fiddling in my lap, the anxiety threatening to creep up on me again.

"Good, good. I'm glad to hear it. I brought you in after going over your statement with the cops. They informed me about your previous encounter with Mr. Wilde and the events that may have led him to come here as he did," he starts, my head hanging in shame at the way my wrong actions somehow brought this down on the school.

"I'm so sorry, Eric. I really am. I don't know what I was thinking except I put everyone here in danger," I acknowledge, shame coating my every word.

"Yes, well, I don't blame you." My head snaps up to look at him, shock coursing through me.

"Wh-what?" I stutter out.

"I said I don't blame you. We all missed it, and we all failed the kid except for you. As teachers, it is our duty to notice these things, and no other teacher has done what you did to keep that kid safe. This is my fault as a principal, and I have failed the people trusted in my care. Going forward, all doors will be locked as soon as school starts. Access will only be granted through the front office, and an officer will now be posted there during school hours and for the hours after to protect my staff. You will be on probation for your actions, but as long as there are no more fistfights, you will continue to work here and advocate for these kids," he says with a no-nonsense tone, his eyebrow raising.

"Yes, sir," I agree.

"I would like weekly reports after meeting with these kids. Any single kid showing the slightest signs of abuse will come to me immediately, and I will make sure it goes through the proper channels. But other than that, the work you've done is invaluable. I have had students drop by my office all week to talk about you and the way you've helped them. None of them wanted to see you leave. And I know how to appreciate when I have someone valuable on my staff, but I also need someone here who is not a loose cannon."

"I agree, sir. I do. And I really hope that going forward, you can see something like this will not happen again," I say, nodding my head at him.

He reaches across the desk and shakes my hand, his grip firm but not bruising.

"Get back to work, and you come to me the second you need something. I mean it. My door is open, always."

I stand up and thank him, turning and heading toward the door.

"Wait, Kane. Trevor's grandmother dropped off this for you. It's a letter," he says, reaching into a drawer and pulling out a white envelope with a scrawled *Mr. D* on top of it. "Spitfire of a woman, that one. Wouldn't take no for an answer until I promised to hand-deliver this to you, with a promise that if I fire you, she'll make sure I lose my job right after." He chuckles, a smile on his face as if remembering the moment.

"Thank you," I falter as I reach over and grab the letter, my hands shaking slightly.

I take the letter and make my way out of his office in a

daze. I head to my office in the back, hoping to avoid everyone. As much as I appreciate the well wishes, I already feel exhausted from repeating the same things. I just want everything to go back to normal.

When I get to my desk, I throw my backpack on top and drop into my chair, my hands raking through my hair. I glance at the letter. There's nothing significant about the envelope it's encased in, but with the way I'm scared to touch it, you would think it was infected by some sort of virus.

Finally, after what feels like hours of staring at it, I reach over and open the top, careful as if I could somehow disturb the contents inside. Inside is a sheet of lined paper, some words visible through the back. I pull it out carefully and open it, my eyes immediately filling with tears at the contents.

Mr. D,

I stopped by to see you today, a couple days after the incident, and they said you would be off for a while. My grandmother (can you believe I actually have one?) told me that your girlfriend was hurt by my dad when you were just trying to protect me. I can't believe you would do something like that. I've never had someone who was on my side before.

I learned how to tell lies before I knew how to spell my first name, and I'm sorry I never gave you the truth. You deserved that much after everything you did for me.

I was ready to call it quits before you called me into your office and refused to give up on me. It was all too much. The beatings, the arguments, waking up every single day knowing two little girls counted on me to keep them fed and safe. That became my only purpose. School, friends and sports no longer had any meaning, because I was so close to death, I didn't want all those things to miss when I couldn't hack it anymore.

But you showed up again and again, even when I was a fucking prick (sorry, language, I know), and you kept showing me you cared. You got me help with school. You gave me Katie, someone who made it easier to just breathe and get through the days.

I wanted to thank you for all you did. I want to thank you for sticking up for me when no one cared enough to see me slipping through the cracks. If you ever need an oil change or any work on your car, you know where to find me, and I'd really like to thank you in person someday.

My sisters and I are safe. We're happy. I've never seen two little girls get so spoiled. And I owe every day of this to you, Mr. D. Good look watching out. I'll see you soon.

- Trevor Wilde

I put the note down after my third reread, the tears fill my eyes and threatening to spill over. The day hits me like a ton of bricks, and the exhaustion settles all the way down to my bones. Knowing he is safe and his sisters are cared for fills me up in a way I've never experienced before. I regret my actions and what the dominoes of that event caused, but I could never regret the end result: Trevor getting out of that situation and going somewhere better.

I pull a tack from my board and stick the note front and center, around all the pictures and other notes I've gotten in my career. When I look up at the board, I know this is what I'm meant to do with my life.

CHAPTER THIRTY-EIGHT

avery

ONE MONTH LATER

Iris – Goo Goo Dolls

The next four weeks pass in a blur. This morning, I got the all-clear from my doctor. She checked that my wound was fully healed and cleared me from needing any more physical therapy, and I'm so ready to move forward with my life.

Kane and I have scaled our therapy sessions back to once a week again while we continue to process what happened and work on our relationship. Since that day, we haven't spent a night apart.

Tomorrow is officially move-in day, and I couldn't be more excited, but a part of me is mourning living with my best friend and all the good times we had. I know this won't change our relationship, but any sort of change has never been easy on me.

Kane has slowly been moving in over the past six weeks, all of his stuff causing my room to basically explode before he brings over his bigger things tomorrow. I'm so ready to have us living together, to get to spend forever with someone and have him love me back just as much. It's more than I ever could have dreamed for myself as a little girl.

When my parents ignored me or left me alone yet again, I would sit in my room surrounded by books, dreaming of my own happily ever after with someone who would always choose me. Someone who would be my family not because blood deemed it so, but because they chose me. I never imagined I would meet my forever in high school and still be sitting against him with all my other chosen family beside me. And as I look around our table at The Grunge, I notice my family is all here.

Kane worked his last shift ever last night, and now we're all here celebrating at our favorite place. It's open-mic night, and after years of begging, Kane is finally going to perform. It may have taken some persuading—or a couple blow jobs—before I finally got what I wanted. I know Kane never plans to sing professionally, but he deserves to share his talent sometimes. Besides, I think this will be good for him. He got accepted into an early master's program that starts this summer semester, so we only have a few months to let loose again before the chaos takes over. But this time, I know whatever we encounter, we will do it together.

"Where did your head go, pretty girl?" a voice whispers in my ear as his arms come around me.

"Nowhere. I'm just really happy," I beam as I turn my face and take him in. His stubble has grown a bit, casting that beautiful shadow over his jaw. His lips look as delectable as ever, and those piercing hazel eyes drink me in, darkening slightly at whatever he sees on my face.

"You know, we could get out of here if someone hadn't talked me into performing," he muses, capturing my lips with his, taking a long, slow drink from me.

"We are here to celebrate you. We can't leave early," I jab back.

"I could think of better ways to celebrate, preferably with you on all fours and your perfect ass in the—" he says before I cut him off with my hand on his mouth.

"Don't you dare, Kane. We are behaving tonight and spending time with our friends," I laugh.

I pull my hand away as he tries to bite it and a mock pout takes over his face.

He opens his mouth to say something when his name is called from the stage and the crowd cheers, ready to see one of their own take the stage. He saunters up with his acoustic guitar in hand and settles onto the chair on stage. The black shirt is stretched taut over his biceps and chest, making my mouth water, and the lights gleam off his black hair. All those tattoos on his arms make it impossible to tear my gaze away from him. His hazel eyes spark as they stare across the space at me. The crowd roars as he takes center stage. Some girls a few tables over catcall him, causing a laugh to bubble out of me. He adjusts the mic.

"Hey, everybody, I'm Kane, and I'm only up here because my girlfriend promised me sex," he jokes into the mic, staring right at me with a small smirk on his face.

I gape at him as my face turns red and the rest of the bar hoots and hollers. He gives me a wink from his perch on stage, the single spotlight illuminating him.

"This is for her," he croons softly into the mic, staring right at me, the flush going all the way through me.

The opening chords of "Iris" fill the air, and the crowd goes wild, instantly knowing the popular beat. My smile breaks through at him playing our song, here in front of everyone. The biggest *I love you* he could ever say to me.

I watch him own the stage, the rasp of his voice making

me shiver and setting my body on fire. The crowd softly sings along as he hits the chorus, his beautiful features illuminated by the bright lights. I see women all over the bar fawn over him and catcall for his attention, yet his eyes never waver from mine. He sings to me as if we're the only two people in this room. Those hazel eyes have me snared in his trap, never wanting to escape.

I think back to the first time I saw him here after our breakup, lost and confused at how he moved on so quickly. My childish antics somehow brought us together, but I never would have pictured us where we are now, stronger than ever.

Morgan leans into me as a tear slips down my cheek. She slings her arm around me and drags me to her side as we sway to the song. Marcus comes up to my other side and wraps his arm around both of us. Then I feel Grayson come up behind us and engulf us all in a hug until we're singing and laughing along. Being here and surrounded by my family is everything little Avery could have imagined someday, and every day I thank my lucky stars that these are my people, and I get to wake up each day knowing that they chose me.

Kane's song ends, and the crowd loses it, people jumping up from their chairs to clap for him, our group included. I watch as he bashfully accepts handshakes and pats on the back while he beelines for me. He eats up the distance in long strides against the gleaming black floors. He gets to me and picks me up, crushing me to him as he continues walking, somehow navigating us through the crowd.

We shove past bodies and a few *whoops* follow us as Kane bursts through the bathroom door. I hear the click, and soon after, his lips dive into mine. His tongue sweeps into my mouth like an animal starving. My ass hits the counter as he places me on top and throws my skirt up so I'm sitting in just my soaked thong. My favorite leather skirt, worn just to make him crazy, is paired with a plaid lace corset top that accentuates every curve, and I've loved the appreciative glances Kane has given me all night. I feel his hard length pressing into me, the friction sending sparks down to my toes.

"Fuck, baby, do you know what you do to me?" he asks, voice ragged between kisses, barely taking any time to come up for air. "Fuck, I can't wait until we get home. I need you now," he groans as he rips my thong and the cold air hits my overheated core.

"Yes, please take me," I moan on a gasp as his finger enters me in one thrust.

"Fuck, baby, you're so wet. Did it turn you on to see me up there?" he breathes, his fingers hitting that spot inside of me that makes me pant into his mouth. Needing air, I rip my mouth away just for him to dive to my neck and kiss his way down until he gets to my chest.

"So much," I pant, my vision turning black with my impending orgasm. I come all over his fingers, and he continues to pump in and out as I come down. When I finally get my breathing under control, I open my eyes to see him take his fingers out and put them in his mouth. He licks me off him, his eyes rolling back into his head.

"Fuck, I could come from your taste alone," he groans into my mouth.

I can taste myself on my tongue as I reach down and undo his button, dragging down his zipper, reaching in, and freeing him. He's hard and heavy in my hand.

"Do you know how much I love you?" he asks on a

groan as I stroke him up and down, taking a bit of pre-cum from the tip and spreading it over him.

I shake my head until he wrenches my face up so I'm level with him.

"Tell me," he demands, his grip firm but not hurting me.

"I know, and I love you that much too," I promise.

"Good, because I'm about to fuck you like I don't. Hold on, pretty girl," he demands, bringing me down from the counter and flipping me around until I see us in the mirror. Him behind me all dressed in black as if he's a demon coming to take my soul to hell, and me in a black leather miniskirt and plaid lace corset top, the angel who can't resist his wicked ways.

A sharp smack hits my ass as a groan works its way out of my throat.

"Fuck, baby, you should see my view. There's nothing better," he purrs as he looks down at my naked pussy. Another slap echoes as he thrusts inside, all the way to the hilt.

The position is almost too much as I'm unbearably full of him, but also needing so much more. He stays inside me, not moving as he massages my ass, taking in the view.

"Kane," I whine. "Move, please. I need—"

"I know what you need, pretty girl," he assures me as he drags his cock all the way out and slams home. He does that repeatedly until it feels as if the counter is leaving bruises on my hips, the pain so pleasant when followed by such pleasure.

His pace is punishing as I feel my orgasm rise again, the tightening in my stomach and my breaths coming in shorter and shorter until I explode around his cock. My orgasm triggers him as I milk his cock, until we are both spent. He leans over and puts his forehead between my shoulder blades as we come down together. The sounds outside finally register in my ears, loud music and cheers filling the silence. Kane massages my ass where he slapped and kisses my back, a pleased moan escaping me. I hiss as he withdraws, the sense of loss filling me.

"Did I hurt you?" he asks as he pulls me up and turns me around. He lowers my skirt for me and smooths my shirt down. He runs his fingers through my hair and tucks a strand behind my ear, leaning in and leaving a gentle kiss on my forehead.

"Never." I smile as he places a gentle kiss on my lips next, lingering for a minute. I savor the feeling of him. I always love how he can fuck me so roughly, then turn around and take care of me so tenderly. It's like he knows exactly what I need.

Banging starts on the door, and we both laugh.

"What is with us and bar bathrooms?" I giggle into him as he pulls me up after him. He unlocks the door, and it flies open as two girls rush to the stalls.

"Have you seen you? I can barely wait until we get home normally, but today, I couldn't wait another second," he purrs, then pulls me into the crowd after him.

We settle back in at our table, and Morgan gives me a knowing smirk as she pushes a fresh drink in front of me. I take the chair next to her, seeing that our group has grown with Lindsay, the bartender who worked with Kane, and her girlfriend, Claire. Kane seems to really enjoy spending time with them, and they flow so seamlessly into our group. Kane takes up residence behind me as he usually does, wrapping his arms around my chest as he settles into an easy conversation with the guys.

Morgan takes my hand and squeezes, and I sit here and take everything in. My family. Grayson with his backward cap and soft smile as Marcus and his wild mess of brown curls make some wild hand gestures to the boys. Morgan with her blonde curls pulled back tight and knee-high boots as she shows me her newest match on the dating site she decided to join.

The night seems endless until the first yawn slips through my mouth and Kane announces it's time for us to go. Morgan agrees and decides to ride back with us since she had a few drinks, Marcus saying he'll bring the car tomorrow for move-in day.

We all head out into the early May night, the bugs out in full swing, their symphony carrying us to our car, and the slight crispness in the air cooling my overheated skin.

Kane comes around to help me into the passenger side, kissing my forehead before rounding the black cab and hauling himself inside. The car is quiet as we make our way back to the house. I must have dozed off because the next thing I know, I'm being lifted and carried, my eyes barely opening as he carries me into our room.

Kane places me on the bed and comes back with a big T-shirt, helping me get undressed. Moments later, I feel a warm body dip into the bed and pull me close. A gentle kiss is placed in my hair, and I'm surrounded by the leather and sandalwood smell I can never get enough of.

kane

THREE MONTHS LATER

Sound of Rain – LANY

I'm having the best dream: my girlfriend is on her hands and knees, her mouth wrapped around my cock. The slurping sounds and enthusiasm have me about to blow when I open my eyes and see that it is not a dream, and my girlfriend is, in fact, wrapped around my cock. The beautiful moans she makes as she fingers herself make my dick weep.

I come with a yell as she gasps around my dick, drinking everything down as she comes on her own fingers. The dream I had already had me ready to come at any moment, and seeing the love of my life dripping for me with her pouty lips around my cock, I'm a goner.

"Fuck, baby, what did I do to deserve that?" I ask, grabbing her hair and holding it back as she sits up. Her brown hair falls around her shoulders like a curtain, her full breasts on display, and my dick perks right back up like I didn't just come.

She says nothing as she smiles coyly and straddles me,

her soaking wet entrance hovering over the top of my cock, which is straining to get to her.

"I missed you," she groans as she lowers herself onto me. The vision of her taking all of me in one try has my vision hazy on the edges, my breath quickening with the need to come inside her. Her warm, wet pussy chokes my cock. The feeling of her bare never gets old.

It's been months of bliss. Early mornings and late nights enjoying each other. All the long talks we have now, no stone left unturned. We do weekly check-ins with each other, gauging where we are. My mental health has never felt better. I'm still on my medication and seeing Steve once a month to keep regular maintenance and try to go over all my fucked-up childhood trauma.

Avery is doing better too, both of us finally sleeping soundly after the shooting.

I pound into her, needing her to come before I can. I feel her walls tightening impossibly further, trying to milk every last drop from me as she comes, and I follow after her. Then she bends over, my cock still inside her, and kisses me. Her tongue mixes with mine, my hands running up and down her spine, causing goosebumps to appear on her skin.

"Morning," she says with a smile on her lips as she pulls back, that brown hair tickling me as it drags across my chest.

"Morning, pretty girl." I mirror her smile.

The sound of Roo scratching only gets louder, and I assume Avery kicked him out this morning before her ambush. She goes to get off me, my now-softened cock slipping out of her.

"Wait," I say, grabbing her wrist and halting her movements. I sit up so my back hits the headboard and pull her to me until she is straddling me again. The green headboard rattles against the wall with the movement. I put both hands on her hips, my grip tightening as the nerves threaten to choke me up. "I love you," I breathe, staring into those baby blues and the future they hold.

"I love you too," she beams.

She climbs off me and walks to the dresser, putting on one of my shirts and a loose pair of shorts. The summer heat is finally upon us, the AC working overtime to cut through the humidity plaguing us outside. I follow her up and slip my shorts on, mentally planning what to make for breakfast. We finally have a rare day off together, and the butterflies fill my stomach at the thought. I eye the bedside drawer and flick my gaze back up to her, tracing the lines of her neck with my eyes.

I steel my spine and walk over to the nightstand drawer next to me, where I've kept the box I have had stashed since we broke up months ago, knowing I couldn't go a single second longer without asking her.

I pull the box out and close the drawer. I turn and face her as she walks out of the bathroom and pauses in front of me. She gasps as her hands fly to cover her mouth.

"Kane..." she says, shaky.

I clear my throat a couple times, hoping I don't fuck up what I need to do.

"Avery..." I start, and see tears shining in her eyes, those crystal-clear blues holding so much love as they stare at me. I get down on one knee in front of her, my hands trembling, hoping the box doesn't slip out of my unsteady grip. "Avery, when I met you five years ago, I knew my life would never be the same. There was a before you, but I knew there would never be an after you. You are it for me," I choke out, my own tears swimming in my eyes, the emotions clogging my throat.

"My soulmate, my best friend, my home. You are everything in the world to me, and I can't wait a single second longer for you to be my wife. I want my ring on your finger. I want our house full of all the dogs you bring home. I want our kids someday, running around, all of them some perfect mix of you and me. My life started on August nineteenth, that autumn afternoon in the Tennessee fall, and now I want to start our forever together," I profess as I reach up and clear the tears streaming down her face. With my own tears dripping down mine, I choke out, "Avery, will you marry me?"

She nods her head feverishly, a barely audible *hell yes* coming out before she launches herself at me, her hands wrapping around my neck as she captures my lips with hers.

I laugh into her mouth as I get lost in her.

I pull back. "Wait, wait, put it on," I say as I open the box to show a solitaire emerald-cut diamond, three carats on a gold band, shining back at her. I saw it and immediately knew it was meant for her. It was the most stunning ring in the shop, the perfect mix of elegant and radiant as it shone underneath the glass, and all I could see was it on Avery's finger for the rest of our lives.

"Oh my god," she breathes out as I slide the ring on her finger. She covers her mouth to bite back a sob.

"I can't believe you asked right now, before I could even get properly dressed for today," she jabs playfully.

She slaps my chest, then stares at her ring like she can't believe it happened, like it could disappear at any moment.

"I'm sorry. I just couldn't wait anymore. I had this whole elaborate thing planned out, but being here in our home just felt more right than anything else could be. Did I do the right thing?" I ask hesitantly, wondering if maybe I should have waited.

"Yes, it was perfect," she says, taking my face in her hands and kissing me.

The door bursts open, Roo finally hitting the handle just right. Angry that he was left outside by himself that long, he lunges onto the bed and starts trying to get to us where we're standing beside it, until we collapse on top of the mattress with him, laughing. Unable to contain his excitement that both of us are awake, he can't decide who he wants more attention from.

I couldn't dream up a more perfect life: the one girl who has always had my heart, my ring finally on her finger, and our dog snuggled up between us as we soak each other in.

Life's a gamble. You win some and you lose some, but I'll never regret the decision to take a gamble on love.

On *us*.

THE END

acknowledgments

Writing this story was not something I ever could have anticipated, but when I sat down to write this story, I ended up finding myself within these pages. Kane and Avery's story was an important part of my journey into finding myself. I poured so much love and care into these two and I could not be more grateful to every single person who has picked up this story. So many people supported me along the way I'm not sure I can ever properly thank them for that.

To my beta readers for reading this draft at its worst and loving it anyways. Monica, Haley, Gabby, Sarah: thank you for reading these two and guiding me into turning this story into what it is now. I don't know what I would do without you.

To my editor Jenny Ayers, thank you for checking my atrocious grammar and your feedback helping me polish this story. Your guidance was invaluable.

To Alex, what in the world would I have done without you? Just over a year and half ago, I came to you with this plot wishing someone could write this story and you said to me, "why don't you?" I can't tell you how those words have changed my life. You supported me through the whole process, from the unlimited voice notes to encouraging me to keep going, letting me ask endless questions, and simply just being my friend. I'm so grateful to you and I hope one day I can return the favor.

To Sarah. Your support for this story has helped me beyond measure, from encouragement to sitting and helping with graphics when I drowning to reading this story and loving them. You have saved me and I hope you know how valuable your friendship is to me.

To Lauren, thank you for always reminding me that I can do this. Your friendship has been a light over the past year.

To Sharon, my main girl. I love you and I love that this was your first romance novel.

To Mason, I could write an endless amount of words about you. You are my best friend, my safe haven, and the person who none of this would be possible without. No one has ever believed in me the way that you do. You encouraged me on my worst days, pulled me out of the drowning my anxiety left me in and held my hand through this. You are my own personal book boyfriend come to life and there aren't words that exist to tell you how much I love you. Every word in this story is dedicated to you.

coming soon

More pranks with your soon-to-be favorite roommates, Morgan and Marcus, coming early 2027!

Follow me on Instagram or check out my website for updates.

about the author

Natalie Marie lives in West Tennessee with her husband, one child and three fur children. After spending her childhood tucked inside the pages of a book, she knew that stories were where she wanted to make her home. Now, she still loves getting lost in the world of romance, from romantasy to contemporary, whether from reading books or writing her own. She writes contemporary romance and hope to dabble in other romance subgenres someday. *All's Fair* is her debut novel.

www.ingramcontent.com/pod-product-compliance
Lightning Source LLC
LaVergne TN
LVHW091248150826
845673LV00006B/1358